SHIELDING EMBER

Delta Team Two, Book 7

SUSAN STOKER

Thank you to LaTonja King and Renita McKinney for making sure I made no missteps with Ember's character. Your reassurances and comments were invaluable.

CHAPTER ONE

Craig "Doc" Wagner sat at a cafeteria table in the dorm they'd been assigned to in the Olympic Village. The guys on the team had been looking forward to this assignment for months. Delta Force teams were brought in for the Olympics to supplement the local security forces. Their job was to protect not only the US athletes, but everyone who lived and worked at the venue for the month or so that the Olympics were going on.

This year the Summer Games were in Seoul, South Korea, and the Deltas were on high alert because of the proximity to North Korea. Intelligence reports indicated the leader of the communist country was desperate to show the world he was a force to be reckoned with. And what better way to do that than to make a move on the Olympics? Everyone's eyes were on Seoul and a terrorist attack would be huge news.

"You look tense," Trigger said to Doc as they ate their lunch.

Doc shrugged. "Conditions aren't ideal to keep everyone safe," he told his team leader.

"The athlete village has some of the highest security on

the complex," Lefty said. "No one is allowed inside the buildings without proper credentials. No parents, no reporters... only the athletes and trainers are allowed."

"Right, and no one has ever forged credentials before," Doc said sarcastically.

The dorm they'd been assigned to was basically a large luxury hotel. There were several located in the Olympic Village, built to hold the thousands of athletes who'd converged on the city to compete. The South Korean government had outdone themselves in building the living quarters. There were thirty floors in each building, with countries and teams divided by floor. It wouldn't be a good thing to put two highly competitive teams near each other, so the assignments were well thought out in advance.

Doc and his team had been assigned rooms on the twentieth floor of their building, along with the US water polo and modern pentathlon teams. Including the Deltas, that was around twenty-six people, and most had checked in already.

Trigger had gone around to each room, introducing himself and informing the athletes the team was there for their safety, requesting if they saw anything suspicious to please report it immediately. They hadn't advertised the fact they were Delta, just said they were in the US Army, brought in to help out with security.

"Anyone seen Ember Maxwell yet?" Lucky asked.

"No. Is she even staying here?" Grover asked. "I just assumed she and her entourage would be bunking in one of the five-star hotels in the city."

"She's listed as a resident on the paperwork I was given," Trigger said.

"Hard to believe she'll be *here*. On the same floor as us," Lefty said, the excitement easy to hear in his voice.

"Who's Ember Maxwell?" Doc asked.

Five pairs of eyes turned to him in shock and surprise.

"You seriously don't know?" Trigger asked.

Doc shook his head. "I wouldn't have asked if I did."

"She's only the most popular social media influencer out there. Word has it that if you can get her to post something on her Instagram account, whatever you're selling immediately goes up about four hundred percent. Her brand is that powerful," Brain said.

"How the hell do you know anything about how social media works?" Doc asked. "We aren't even allowed to have accounts."

"How the hell do *you* not have a clue who Ember Maxwell is?" Lucky fired back dryly.

"Because I don't give a shit about that kind of thing. I'm not trolling Instagram or any other social media site. They're a waste of time, and I prefer to *talk* to my friends to find out what's going on with them, not see what they've posted on the damn computer," Doc grumbled.

"You have friends? I mean, other than us?" Lefty teased.

"Fuck off," Doc said, balling up a napkin and throwing it at his teammate.

The truth was, he *didn't* have much of a life outside his Delta Force team. But that was fine with him. He loved these men like brothers, and now that most were married and starting families, he was content to have expanded his circle with their wives and girlfriends.

"Seriously, Ember Maxwell is like royalty," Trigger said. "Everyone wants to be noticed and mentioned by her, and she's beautiful to boot. Not only that, but she's an amazing athlete. Only two women and two men make the Olympic team for modern pentathlon, and she's one of them."

"Some people say she bought her way onto the team," Brain stated.

Doc didn't hear any censure in his friend's tone. "Did she?" he asked curiously.

"I don't think so," Lucky interjected. "I've seen her compete. Fencing isn't her strongest sport, but she's a decent swimmer and okay at riding, and her running and shooting are almost always excellent. The modern pentathlon is interesting *because* an athlete can be weak in one area, but still come out on top since everything is based on a point system."

Doc had never taken much notice of the lesser-known Olympic sports. He was more of a baseball, basketball, and football kind of guy.

"Anyway, she's supposed to be staying here," Trigger said. "Because there are only four members on the pentathlon team, they each get their own room. She's the only one of the four who didn't participate in the opening ceremonies the other day, and the only one who isn't here yet."

Doc nodded absently. It didn't matter to him where the pampered athletes stayed. He was here to make sure no crazy terrorists infiltrated the village to cause mass mayhem.

"Can you believe how crazy this place is?" Grover asked, changing the subject with a shake of his head. "It's like a sexual free-for-all."

"Right? There are bowls of condoms everywhere. In every common room, right inside the entrance of the building, and I even saw a bag attached to the railing inside the elevator," Lefty said.

"It's pretty insane. I mean, I would've thought everyone would be more concerned about getting quality sleep and preparing to compete...not getting their rocks off," Brain commented.

"Some people use sex as a coping mechanism," Trigger said with a shrug. "It gives them an outlet for their stress and nervous energy."

"And after they finish competing, all bets are off," Lefty added.

Doc tuned his friends out—he honestly didn't care if the

athletes had sex or not—and concentrated on his lunch. One thing he had to say for this mission, the food was much better than their usual fare. No MREs for them in Seoul. They could choose just about any kind of meal they wanted. High carbohydrate, high protein, gluten-free. And from a wide array of cuisines, including Asian food of course. In the evenings, there was even a McDonald's that set up in one corner of the cafeteria.

The building they were assigned to held the American, Canadian, and British athletes, so it was fairly homogeneous. Athletes were constantly coming and going, based on their competition schedule. From a security standpoint, the village itself should've been a nightmare, but the South Korean police and military did a good job of making sure no one got into the dorms who didn't belong. There were several check-points where credentials were confirmed and reconfirmed.

Tomorrow, Doc and the rest of the team would tour the sports venues they were assigned to, and hopefully the security would be just as strict. He knew there was always a chance someone would be able to infiltrate off-limits areas, or slip explosives or weapons past security in the venues where spectators were allowed, but hopefully that wouldn't be an issue this year.

"Anyone have any idea how we're going to find Shin-Soo Choo for Logan?" Lucky asked.

Everyone shook their heads.

"The baseball players have space in this dorm, but none are staying here," Trigger said. "They're all in a hotel nearby."

"Shit," Grover swore. "That's gonna make it almost impossible."

"We'll get it," Brain said. "We promised both Oz and Logan that we wouldn't leave Korea until we had it."

Oz, the seventh member of their team, had been allowed to remain stateside with his very pregnant wife, who was due

5

any day now. Logan was his nephew, and Shin-Soo Choo was the boy's idol. When Choo made the US Olympic baseball team, Logan had begged the guys to find him and get an autograph while they were over here. But even though the Deltas were part of the security force, they didn't have carte blanche to go wherever they wanted at the Olympic venue. It was going to take some creative thinking to figure out how to get anywhere near the extremely popular baseball players.

Just then, there was a slight commotion in the cafeteria. Doc looked toward the door and saw a woman had entered—and literally *everyone* was staring at her. But it didn't look as if she noticed. She went to the beginning of the buffet and grabbed a tray and began to work her way down the line.

Doc shifted in his seat. He had no idea who the woman was, but just looking at her made him uncomfortable.

First off, she was beautiful. Her brown skin with warm orange-red undertones reminded him of the penny collection he used to have when he was a kid. He'd loved running his hands over all that copper...and it was surprising that he felt an urge to do the same with *her*. The woman's black kinky curls were pulled back in a low bun at the nape of her neck, exposing the muscles in her shoulders and back, further highlighted by the tank top she wore. Her jeans hugged her muscular thighs and her curvy backside.

Everything about her looks appealed to Doc.

Despite that, the attention she was getting—while not even trying—made his lips draw down in a scowl.

He'd spent his entire life trying to fly under the radar, starting from a young age. He'd been the object of too many people's curious and downright offensive stares while growing up. He stuck out like a sore thumb in his family, and even now, he preferred to fade into the background. His job as a special forces soldier catered to his need to go unnoticed. Get in, get the job done, and get out. That was what he lived and breathed.

But this woman would never be someone who faded into the woodwork. She seemed to light up a room simply by entering. She drew everyone's gaze without trying. Just imagining that kind of attention made Doc uncomfortable as hell.

Grover whistled under his breath. "She's even more beautiful in person than in her pictures, if that's possible."

"For the record, Doc, *that's* Ember Maxwell," Lucky said with a smile, nudging his friend with his elbow.

Doc studied her, curious about the woman who everyone but him seemed to know. He'd expected her to be pretty, and she was. He'd expected her to be in shape, and her strength was obvious. And admittedly, he'd expected the woman to revel in the spotlight her social media fame had garnered.

But instead of finding someone thrilled to be the center of attention, Doc noticed her eyes were firmly glued to the floor...as if that would help her pretend everyone wasn't staring.

The more he watched, the more curious Doc became. He recognized some of the mannerisms in Ember Maxwell that he himself had adopted when he was younger to avoid being noticed. She didn't make eye contact with *anyone*, even the servers. When someone in line spoke to her, Ember ducked her head further and simply shrugged. She wasn't acting like Doc had expected she would—which surprised him.

When a man at the table next to theirs took out his cell phone, called her name, and took a picture when she turned around, Doc saw her shoulders hunch inward as she quickly looked away.

This wasn't a woman who reveled in the spotlight.

When she'd made it through the line and turned again to face the cafeteria, biting her lip and looking extremely uncomfortable as she studied the room, Doc was sliding his chair back and moving before he even thought about what he was doing.

This was extremely out of character for him, but he didn't think twice about it.

Doc walked up to Ember and, without a word, took her tray from her hands. She looked at him in surprise.

"You can sit with us," he said quietly, before gesturing toward his table with his head.

"Um...okay," Ember said.

The warm honey of her voice didn't do anything to make Doc more comfortable in her presence. Everything about this woman unsettled him, but it was too late to turn around and pretend he hadn't intercepted her. He turned without another word and led the way back to the table where his friends sat.

The friends currently staring at him in shock, probably wondering what in the world had gotten into him.

Not only that, but every other eye in the cafeteria was on them as well.

Internally squirming and berating himself for doing exactly what he hated most—putting himself in the limelight —Doc was even more brusque than normal as he turned to Ember.

"You can sit here," he told her, putting her tray down between Trigger and Brain.

"Um, okay, thanks," she muttered.

Doc turned to see *all* the men at the next table now had their phones out. He stalked toward them and leaned over the table, speaking in a low, menacing tone. "If you don't put down those fucking cameras, you're gonna regret it."

As far as threats go, it was kind of weak, but Doc wouldn't actually hurt the men anyway—even if he wanted to.

The three guys immediately lowered their phones.

"Thank you," he bit out. "It looks like you're done eating, so I suggest you be on your way."

Without a word, the men gathered up their trays and headed for the tray-drop and the exit.

Doc should've felt better, but he could still see the majority of people in the cafeteria looking in his direction. He turned toward the table where he'd deposited Ember and saw her staring at him with huge brown eyes. She looked nervous and confused.

He knew he wouldn't be able to sit at the table with her and have a normal conversation. Not with everyone in the room staring at them. It made his stomach churn to even think about finishing his lunch.

Without a word, he stalked over to his place at the table, grabbed his tray and headed for the exit.

CHAPTER TWO

Ember stared at the stranger's back as he left the cafeteria as abruptly as he'd deposited her at his table. She wasn't an idiot, she knew looks weren't everything...but it had been a very long time since she'd been dismissed so completely out of hand. She couldn't help but feel a little offended. And confused.

One of the men at the table cleared his throat. Ember turned her attention from the gruff man who'd just left and glanced at the guy next to her.

"I'm Trigger," he said, holding out his hand.

Ember shook it. "Ember."

"I know," he said with a small smile. It wasn't condescending or leering. It was...gentle. If a smile could be gentle.

"And I'm Brain," the man on her other side said. "That's Lefty, Lucky, and Grover," he went on, indicating the others at the table.

"And the grumpy asshole who just left was Doc," Trigger said.

"Wow, I thought *my* name was unusual," Ember murmured.

Everyone chuckled.

"They're nicknames," Lucky said. "We're part of the security force hired to keep everyone safe."

Ember nodded. That made sense. "I'm guessing you're in the military," she said.

"Why do you say that?" Grover asked.

He was a large man. Both tall and muscular. Ember might've been intimidated, but her parents had hired many bodyguards for her over the years, so she'd gotten used to muscular men. "Your nicknames. The way you all carry yourselves. It's just kind of...everything."

Everyone laughed again.

"So much for flying under the radar," Lefty said. "We could be wrestlers," he said with a lift of an eyebrow.

Ember wasn't sure why these guys didn't make her feel uncomfortable, like just about everyone else...but they didn't. Maybe it was the rings most wore on their left hands, indicating they were married. Maybe it was because they didn't look starstruck. Maybe it was the way they looked her in the eye when they spoke to her. Whatever it was, she felt her muscles relaxing.

She'd put her foot down with her parents and insisted on staying in the athlete village instead of the suite they'd rented in a nearby hotel. She needed some space from them. Her parents meant well, but over the years, they'd completely taken over her life. Taken away any decisions she might've made on her own. Never asking her what *she* wanted to do, always assuming they knew best.

They were smart, had built her online persona from nothing, hired the best coaches to help her become an Olympian, and made so much money with her name, it was almost obscene. But none of it had been her choice. She'd just gone along with their decisions.

Until now.

They'd ranted and raved, but nothing had changed her mind. She'd wanted to feel normal for once. Wanted to be just another athlete.

She should've known that wasn't actually going to happen.

She'd felt good as she'd checked into the dorm. She'd gone to her room and put away some of her things before taking a break to get something to eat. The second she walked into the cafeteria, she remembered who she was. She wasn't Ember Maxwell the Pentathlete. She was Ember Maxwell, social media star. Someone to be gawked at. To be scrutinized.

She lived in a fishbowl, and she'd forgotten for a split second.

When the man had approached her while she'd been trying to figure out where to sit to eat her lunch, she'd been taken aback. Had been ready to fend him off. But he hadn't looked as if he was infatuated with her. Hadn't been excited to meet *the* Ember Maxwell. He'd seemed almost...irritated. Not with her, but just in general.

She hadn't missed his threat to the men sitting at the table next to theirs.

She would have told Doc that she didn't even notice when people filmed her anymore. That it was simply a part of her life. She didn't like it, but she'd learned to live with it when she went out in public. But she didn't even get a chance to thank him. As soon as the men at the other table had left, he had too.

"Ember?" Lucky asked. "Are you all right?"

She mentally took a breath. She'd spaced out, gone into her head, which she knew she did all too often. Rather surprisingly, since she was constantly surrounded by people. But none of them really cared to get to know her. "I'm good. Thanks."

They all nodded, then began to talk amongst themselves as if she wasn't there.

No, that wasn't fair. They included her in their casual conversation. She just wasn't the center of their attention. It was...

Awesome.

"How's Chance?" Lucky asked Brain.

The man sat up in his chair. "He's great. I talked to Aspen last night. He slept a whole five hours straight and she was so happy. Apparently that's not normal for a newborn, but we'll take it."

"That's awesome. Anyone hear from Oz?" Lefty asked.

"He texted me last night," Grover replied. "Said Riley's doing great. He thinks she's gonna have their kid before we get back, so it's a good thing he didn't come with us."

The conversation continued, and Ember listened as she ate, enjoying how they spoke openly about their significant others. She'd tried to get to know a few of the men who'd been assigned to guard her when she left the house, but none seemed all that interested in chatting. The dichotomy between these men—who sounded completely devoted to their women, but looked as if they could crush someone with one blow—was intriguing. She wasn't intimidated by them. On the contrary, Ember had always been attracted to rough-looking men. Maybe it was because the guys she'd grown up with in Beverly Hills were more concerned about looking pretty than getting their hands dirty.

"So what's your story?" Lucky asked.

Ember swallowed the food she'd just taken a bite of and wiped her lips with a napkin before asking, "What do you mean?"

"Where are you from, how'd you get into competing in modern pentathlon, how old are you, what's your favorite thing to do on your time off, how in the world do you deal with every single person in the world knowing who you are... you know, that sort of thing," he clarified with a large, open smile.

Ember knew she should put up the shield she usually employed when people asked questions that her parents deemed too personal. She should giggle and deflect...but she felt comfortable around these guys. And her parents weren't here, watching her every move. "Beverly Hills. I was a decent swimmer and runner but would never be gold-medal material, so my parents decided the pentathlon was perfect, since I could be average in an individual sport, but still come out on top. I'm twenty-five. I *have* no time off, and I honestly try not to think about everyone knowing everything about me."

"I'm not sure there's anything average about you," Grover countered.

Ember turned to look at him. He wasn't leering or smirking. It seemed as if he was just making a general observation.

"Thanks, but trust me, I'm honestly pretty boring. Social media can make *anyone* look like the most fascinating person alive."

Grover didn't laugh. Neither did anyone else. Instead, his gaze bored into hers. Finally, he said, "You've got a pretty thick shield around you, keeping everyone out. It's not surprising, with twenty-five million followers on Instagram and your life in pictures, plastered out there for everyone to see. You remind me of Doc."

Ember was surprised at his insight. But she was more curious about their friend. "What's his deal? Does he not like Black people or what?"

Silence met her question—and Ember felt uncomfortable for the first time.

She knew many people in the world were still racist. Still

judged people by the color of their skin. She might've grown up in Beverly Hills, with wealthy parents who could provide her with everything her heart desired, but that didn't erase the hate and disgust in some people's eyes and hearts when they looked at her. They didn't care if she was a good person. An accomplished athlete. An Olympian. They would still cross the street so they didn't have to be near her, as if they were afraid she was going to rob them if they got too close. Then there were those who thought she was either too white to belong to the Black community, or too Black to belong to the white community.

Trigger pushed his tray aside and leaned his elbows on the table in front of him. He studied Ember with a look she couldn't decipher. Then he said, "Doc's the absolute last person who would judge you for the color of your skin. You two have more in common than you'd think."

Ember snorted. "Right. He's what, a decade older than me? And white. And in the military. What could we possibly have in common?"

When no one answered right away, Ember had a feeling she should've kept her mouth shut.

She'd gotten complacent. Had felt comfortable with these men. She'd forgotten that everyone wanted something from her. An autograph. A mention on social media. A picture. A blow job. It was always *something*.

Now she wondered what *these* men wanted. Doc had been the one to lead her to the table, but maybe that was part of a practiced shtick. Maybe they'd been lying about their wives and children.

As if they all realized at once how unnerved she was getting, the five men casually leaned back in their chairs, as though attempting to give her space.

"Do *not* be afraid of us," Grover said in a quiet tone. "Out of everyone in this damn place, you're safest with us. Physically, and with the real you. To answer your question, Doc is thirty-four. He's the oldest on our team. He's had a hard life. Yeah, he's white and you're Black, but that literally means nothing to him."

Ember wasn't so sure about that. People said they didn't see color when they looked at others, but she knew firsthand that wasn't always true.

"You'll see," Brain said.

He sounded so confident, Ember became even more curious about Doc's story. But she didn't get a chance to ask anything before Lucky began speaking.

"You've got a room on the same floor as us. You been up there yet?"

Ember nodded. "I dropped off my stuff and came straight here."

"Leila, Nick, and Aiden headed out on a tour of the city this morning, said they'd be back after lunch," Lucky said.

Ember nodded. Leila Mason was the other woman who'd made the modern pentathlon team. She knew her fairly well from the competitions they'd been in together. Aiden Covington and Nick Hodge made up the men's team.

"The water polo team has been here since before the opening ceremonies, and from what I understand, their competitions don't start for another week," Lefty said. "When do you compete?"

"The pentathlon is a two-day event," she told the group. "The first day is the first round of fencing. We fence in thirty-five rounds, going one-on-one with every contestant in a one-touch bout. We get ranked on how many victories we have."

"Holy crap, that's a lot of matches!" Trigger exclaimed.

"Yeah. It takes most of the day. The second day, we go through the second round of fencing. The two lowest-ranking competitors go first. Whoever wins that round moves on to face the third-lowest-ranking person. And so on up the line until everyone's competed again."

"How does the swimming portion work? Are you ranked by who gets the fastest time?" Grover asked.

Ember was pleased that they seemed to be genuinely interested. "No. It's not like the regular swimming events. We don't have a finals and we aren't technically competing against each other. We swim two hundred meters and get a score based on time. A time of two minutes and forty seconds earns two hundred and fifty points. Every tenth of a second above or below that benchmark is equal to plus or minus one point. So obviously the faster you swim, the more points you get, which is what we want."

"Interesting. I never thought about how it works. I guess I'd just assumed it was whoever won that portion got more points," Brain said.

"Well, that's kind of true," Ember said. "Because the more points we earn in fencing, swimming, and show jumping, the bigger head start we get for the combined shooting and running event at the end. Once the run starts, the winner is the one who crosses the finish line first, so it's really important to get as big a head start as possible."

"So you could be in last place, but still manage to win," Brain said.

"Technically, yes. But speaking from experience, it's very hard to do. You'd have to hit every one of your shots in the shooting portion without missing to have a chance," Ember told them.

"What's your best event?" Grover asked.

Ember loved this. Loved educating people about the pentathlon. Loved not talking about other influencers, or branding, or any of the other crap her parents loved and she couldn't care less about. "Shooting," she said without hesitation.

The men all grinned.

"What?" she asked.

"Too bad we don't have a shooting range here, I'd love to ask you to join us," Trigger said.

"I wouldn't want to embarrass you," Ember teased.

They all chuckled, and she had a feeling they were humoring her.

"Using a laser gun like you do in competition isn't anything like shooting with real bullets," Lefty said.

"I know," Ember agreed. "Although, I can hold my own."

"I have a feeling you can," Trigger said. "You have plans for dinner?"

Ember blinked. Was he hitting on her?

"Not because I'm trying to get in your pants. I love my wife more than life itself and would never cheat on her," Trigger explained, reading her mind. "I just thought that if you were interested in eating somewhere other than the cafeteria, we've got tonight off—it's the only night we *all* have off —and I thought you might like to join us."

"Oh, that's really sweet. But I don't want to leave the Olympic Village. And I have to get up early to get some practice in tomorrow. But thank you. Seriously." And she meant it. She liked these guys. They were down-to-earth and funny, and they made her feel...normal. To them, she could tell she wasn't Ember Maxwell, social media darling. She was Ember the athlete...which she liked.

"All right, but if you change your mind, just let us know. Our rooms are scattered throughout the floor you're staying on. Since you've been up there, you've probably seen that we have an S on our doors for 'security.' Just knock, or slip a note under one of our doors and we'll grab you before we head out."

"I will, thanks."

"Anytime."

"And...Trigger?"

"Yeah?"

"Will you thank Doc for me?"

"For what?"

"For bringing me to your table to eat. I wasn't sure where to sit, and as high-handed as it might've seemed, taking the decision out of my hands was a relief."

"Of course. And for the record, you're totally out of Doc's comfort zone," Trigger told her.

"What do you mean?"

"Just that. Doc *hates* attention. Marching up to you, *the* Ember Maxwell, in a crowded room, bringing you to our table was totally out of character for him."

"Oh, well...I appreciate it. That, and for making those guys stop recording me or whatever they were doing."

"That happen a lot?" Brain asked.

Ember shrugged, trying to downplay it. "Often enough."

"Right. So it happens all the time," Brain muttered.

"I kind of gave up my right to privacy once I gained so many followers," Ember explained.

"Wrong," Grover told her. "You shouldn't have to worry about someone filming you while you're eating. Or doing anything privately. You're at the fucking Olympics. Other athletes should have your back, not add to your stress."

His words felt good.

"For what it's worth...Doc's a good man," Trigger told her. "He can be pretty intense, but he's also one of the most loyal men I've ever met. He can be hard to get to know, but once he decides you're worthy of his friendship, there's nothing he wouldn't do for you."

"Um...okay," she said after a long pause.

Ember appreciated his reassurance, but wasn't sure why

Trigger was telling *her*. It was obvious the man hadn't been all that impressed by her, if his hasty retreat was anything to go by. His friends might say he wasn't turned off by the color of her skin, but his reaction to her was all too familiar. She'd seen it time and time again in the white world of Beverly Hills she'd grown up in. Her parents had gotten very good at ignoring the racism, but she couldn't be as blasé about it.

She liked these guys, and appreciated their offer of friendship, but her time in Korea was short. Best not to get too close. In just days, she'd go back to her life in the States. She wasn't sure how *much* of a life it was, working out fourteen hours a day, but it was all she'd ever known. Her parents had pulled her out of the local high school, in favor of an online school, so she'd have more time to train. College had been out of the question, as it would've taken way too much attention away from her training. She'd just missed qualifying for the last Olympic Games, so it had been their dream that she make this one.

"We've learned the hard way never to judge someone by how they look," Trigger continued quietly. "The cutest kid could be a decoy so his father can detonate an IED near where we're patrolling. The prettiest woman in the room could be the most deadly person there. Brown skin, black, white, yellow...we see color, of course, but it means nothing to us. We read people in other, deeper ways. Obviously, Doc read your discomfort and felt a need to help, despite his need to avoid attention. That's not something we see him do often."

"Why does it matter?" Ember asked. "You're here for security, and I'm here to compete. When I'm done, I'll go back to California, back to my life, and you'll go back to... wherever you came from."

"Texas," Lucky said helpfully. "Fort Hood, to be exact. Near Killeen."

"Right, you'll go back to Texas and I'll go back to my life."

Trigger stared at her for a long moment, and Ember had no idea what was going on behind his guarded expression.

Finally, he said, "All I'm trying to say is that even though Doc doesn't like to be the center of attention, he won't let your fame stop him from protecting you...or anyone else here at the Games. Same for all of us."

His words reassured Ember.

Trigger stood, not giving her a chance to comment, as did the others. Ember did the same, not wanting to be left sitting at the table by herself. "Come on, we'll walk you back up to our floor. Make sure you know where our rooms are. Then we'll leave you to unpack and do whatever it is elite athletes do before they compete in the freaking Olympics."

Ember followed the group to the bins to drop off their trays. They all got into the large elevator together and rode up to their floor. The men said their goodbyes and told her how good it was to meet her, before they disappeared into their own rooms.

Trigger hung back. "We've got the rest of the day off. We'll all probably call our wives; the time difference is a bitch, so any chance we have to talk to our women while we're gone, we take it," he said. "Then we'll all go to dinner together later, like I said."

"You all seem very close," Ember commented.

"We are. There's nothing I wouldn't do for those guys. Or their families."

Ember didn't understand that kind of friendship, simply because she'd never had it for herself.

"Here's my room," he pointed out as they passed his door, continuing to hers. "If you change your mind about tonight, just let me know," he told her.

"I wish I could." And she meant it. Hanging out with

these men seemed much more appealing than staying in her room, hiding from the public...and her family.

"If I don't see you before you compete...good luck."

"Thanks."

Trigger nodded at her respectfully before heading back to his own room. Ember closed her door behind her and leaned against the heavy wood as she shut her eyes, exhausted.

She should have been bouncing off the walls. Excited to compete and hopefully win a medal. Everyone was waiting to see if she could pull it off. Could be an Olympic medalist. And she *did* want to do well, because she was a naturally competitive person. And she had fans who genuinely wanted the best for her.

She also had those who wanted to see her fail.

Her parents had hired people to manage her social media, so she didn't often see the comments people left on the staged pictures posted to her accounts...but she couldn't always quell her curiosity and sometimes had to log in to see for herself what people were saying.

She almost always regretted it. People could be incredibly cruel. They disparaged her because she was pretty. Or because of the connections she had with other very well-known celebrities and athletes. Or because she was wealthy. She understood that many of the mean comments were a result of jealousy over what they perceived she had and they wanted. But the comments that hurt most were the ones about the color of her skin.

Some said she did the Black community a disservice by acting too white and not acknowledging her heritage. Others flat-out threatened her life, saying all Black people should die. Many thought she shouldn't be at the Olympics in the first place, that there was no way a Black person could've made the modern pentathlon team without having bribed some-one. They spouted shit about how Blacks couldn't swim, though they weren't surprised she could shoot so well. As if the color of her skin had anything to do with either of those things.

There were also supportive fans, of course. Those who seemed to really want her to succeed. Who always posted positive messages. Ember's mom had given her a few letters when they'd landed from fans who wished her well. Beth had told her she was the prettiest woman in the Olympics. Thomas had written that he was praying for her to do well. Christine had written her a very sweet poem about being confident in her abilities. Alex had sent a two-page hand-written letter, detailing why he admired her and had faith that she'd be a gold medalist.

The last one had been the cutest. A little girl had drawn a picture of Ember on top of the medal podium, smiling huge.

She wandered over to her bed and sat, staring at her bags on the floor. She needed to finish unpacking, but her mind was whirling.

Ember was at a crossroads. Her choice to stay in the athlete village had pissed off her parents, but she'd needed the break. They loved her, but they were smothering her. They ran every aspect of her life. Both had quit their jobs to manage her. Training, public appearances, photo shoots, marketing...you name it, they'd taken over. She hadn't wanted to do that stupid reality TV show a few years ago, but they'd somehow talked her into it, against her better judgement. She'd been miserable, hated having cameras in her face all the time, but the show had skyrocketed her popularity and upped her overall wealth by eight figures.

And it was all bullshit. Deep down inside, Ember wanted more. Or rather...*different*. But she had no idea what.

Meanwhile, her mom and dad were already talking about the next Olympics in four years.

Ember didn't want to spend four more years training all

day, every day. She wanted to live. To travel. To fall in love. To have a family.

And she didn't want to be in the spotlight. If she could delete her Instagram account today, along with all twenty-five million followers, she would. Her parents would have a heart attack; it was her biggest social media platform. But she was quickly getting to the point where she didn't care.

She was twenty-five and still lived at home. She didn't grocery shop for herself, she didn't cook, she didn't have to lift a finger to clean. Her room back home was as big as some people's entire houses. She knew that wasn't normal—and Ember desperately wanted normal.

As long as she lived under her parents' roof and allowed them to run her life, she'd never get that.

She'd never lived anywhere but California. She'd traveled for competitions, but rarely went much beyond the hotels and the venues. She yearned for adventure. To get it, she'd have to disappoint her parents—and endure the mother of all guilt trips.

And not just disappoint her parents, but her coaches. Sergei, Helen, and Lonnie were amazing. Hard when they needed to be but also encouraging. And then there were the athletes she trained with. And her fans and followers.

Suddenly, it felt as if the weight of the world was on her shoulders. Everyone wanted her to win more than Ember did, herself. That was crazy. Insane.

What was she doing? And how could she break free?

No answers came to mind as she sat in the middle of the sparse room in the athlete dorm. She heard several people talking out in the hall and figured it was members of the water polo team returning from practice. They sounded happy and keyed up. And why wouldn't they be? They were at the freaking Olympics.

Ember sighed and stood to continue putting her things

away. There was a state-of-the-art workout facility in the basement of the building. She'd head down there in a while and jog on the treadmill. That would help clear her head and get herself back in the right frame of mind to compete. She loved to run. She would put her headphones on and lose herself in her music.

CHAPTER THREE

Doc glanced at his watch. Ten past eleven. He and the rest of the team had returned to the village about an hour ago, after going to a local restaurant for dinner, away from the Olympic Village. They'd stayed out longer than usual, since it was their only night off together for a while. Their time would be spent surveilling crowds, patrolling the grounds, and making sure the athletes that had traveled to South Korea were safe as they competed to be the best of the best in their respective sports.

Trigger and the others had talked about Ember Maxwell throughout most of dinner. Relaying what she'd told them about herself and her sport—and giving him shit for bailing on lunch.

Doc couldn't explain why she disturbed him so much. It wasn't just that she was pretty and obviously always the center of attention. It was...something else. Something deeper.

She definitely seemed to need a friend. When he'd seen her hesitating after getting her food, looking around the room for a place to sit, he'd recognized the signs of someone who was uncomfortable. He didn't know *why* Ember was uncomfortable; he guessed she was probably surrounded by people most of the time. But her expression and body language were dead giveaways, so he'd immediately moved to help her out.

He'd been in her shoes. Felt out of place and out of his element. No matter how well known she was, or how popular, her sense of uneasiness struck something deep inside Doc. And he'd acted on it.

Then he'd been irritated with himself afterward for caring about those assholes with the cameras, and confused about why he gave a shit about a woman who obviously had everything her heart desired and more.

Feeling restless after dinner, and not wanting to sit in his room and risk obsessing about his actions at lunch, Doc had decided to take a walk around the dorm, just to make sure things were secure. He'd checked every floor and found nothing out of the ordinary, and was now heading back to his room. He'd heard more than a few loud parties in the rooms while on his rounds, which just made Doc shake his head in amazement. Things here sounded much crazier than at the previous Olympics he and the team had worked. How anyone could prepare for the competition of their lives while partying was beyond him.

Stepping off on his floor, Doc was grateful the athletes on twenty seemed to be asleep. Or at least they weren't partying. He walked past the common room on the way to his door—and stopped in his tracks.

He backed up a step and stared.

Ember Maxwell was sitting in a chair she'd pulled as close to the tiny window in the corner as she could. The window was no more than a long slit, and there was no way she could actually see much out of it. But she wasn't looking down at the world going by. She was looking up.

"Ember?" Her name popped out before he could think better of it. He should leave her alone, but he hated seeing her look so...lonely. She had her feet up on the bottom cushion of the chair and her arms around her knees. Her shoulders were hunched slightly, even as her chin was craned upward.

Upon hearing her name, she whipped her head around and stared at him for a moment before saying, "I'm sorry. Am I bothering you?"

For some reason, that irritated Doc. "Of course not. You're quiet as a mouse, which is more than I can say for a lot of the people in this dorm. Are you all right?"

She blinked. Then nodded and said, "No."

Doc couldn't help but snort. "Which is it? Okay or not?"

Ember sighed and rested her cheek on her knee and stared out the window, effectively shutting him out. "I'm fine," she said softly.

Doc knew he should leave. Go to his room and get some sleep before his shift in the morning. But everything his friends had told him at dinner echoed in his head.

They'd specifically mentioned how Ember had looked lost. That she should be thrilled to be at the Olympics, but instead it seemed as if she was just going through the motions.

Brain had also pulled up her Instagram account on his phone, showing Doc some of the pictures. In most, she was laughing and seemed to be having the time of her life. There were inspirational quotes on pictures of her working out, pictures of her posing with various products—obviously paid promotional shots—and in every one, she looked as if she'd just stepped out of the salon. Her hair was perfect. Her teeth shining brightly. Her earrings cute and dangly. Her skin and makeup flawless.

But *this* Ember was much more attractive to him. She was

real. Not a caricature on social media. Her hair was messy, the sweatpants she had on were obviously old, and her T-shirt had a rip in the sleeve. She was approachable—and not someone the world got to see.

Doc looked up and down the hall and saw it was empty. He could still faintly hear a get-together from the floor above, but at the moment, it was just the two of them.

"I'm sorry I left so abruptly earlier," he told her.

"It's okay," Ember said without looking up.

"It was rude," Doc insisted.

"Seriously, it's fine," she assured, still staring out the window. "You weren't the first person not to like me at first glance, and you won't be the last."

Doc frowned. "It's not that I don't like you. I don't *know* you. How can I not like you?"

Ember lifted her head at that and pinned him with a look so intense, Doc had to force himself to stand his ground. "There are plenty of people who don't like me based on what they see and read online."

Doc didn't flinch. "Then they're ignorant assholes."

Ember stared at him for another beat. "You really mean that, don't you?"

"Yes. Look, I know I didn't make the best impression earlier, but if I dislike someone, it's not going to be because of what I read about them online. It's going to be because they're rude. Or discriminatory. Or because they smack their lips when they eat."

She gave him a tiny smile, then asked, "So why'd you leave then?"

Doc considered lying to her. Telling her he wasn't hungry, or that he'd had a phone call to make. But he couldn't do it. Something about the sadness in her eyes spoke to him. Drew him in like a moth to a flame. He knew she could possibly pierce the armor he kept around him at all times, but he couldn't resist her. "Because you make me uncomfortable."

Her brows furrowed. "I do?"

"Yeah."

"I'm sorry."

Doc shrugged. "Don't be. It's really me, not you."

She gave him another small smile. "That sounds like a line," she informed him.

"It's not. You make me...feel things I don't want to. I'm uncomfortable with the attention you garner. I'm used to hiding in the shadows, and you're like a bright, shiny light. And anyone who gets near you is engulfed in that light."

His words seemed to make her even sadder, which hadn't been his intention.

"Yeah, that's true. And since we're being honest, I'd give anything to turn that light off. Just once. To hide in those shadows with you."

They shared a long intimate gaze. He realized that she was being sincere.

He never would've guessed after seeing her Instagram page that Ember Maxwell was uncomfortable being in the spotlight, but he should've known. Social media was all bullshit. People said things to try to fit in, to seem more popular and interesting than they actually were. They claimed to be one kind of person, but in real life were completely different. And Ember was living proof of that...just not in the way he'd expected.

"What are you doing in here?" he asked.

She shrugged. "Trying to see the stars."

That wasn't the answer he'd expected. "Pardon?"

"The stars. Every night before I go to sleep, I sit in my window and look up. The world is such a huge place, and seeing the stars twinkling reminds me that there's so much more out there than my narrow little life. But I can't see them from my room. There's another dorm right outside my window and the lights from it make it impossible to see anything. So I came down here. But the view's not much better."

"I can see them from my room," Doc blurted.

She stared at him again.

"Look...you don't know me, but I swear on my honor as a US Army soldier that you're safe with me. If you want to come to my room for a while, to look at the stars, I'd be okay with that." Doc knew that sounded like the worst pick-up line ever, but he didn't regret the offer.

"My room must be on the other side of the hall from yours," he went on. "I face the stadium and the track. When a game or match is going on, you can't see anything because of the lights, but tonight it's quiet and there aren't any clouds, so you should be able to see the stars."

"Why?"

He wasn't surprised she was skeptical of his offer. "Because regardless of my actions earlier, I usually don't shy away from things that make me uncomfortable. Hell, my entire life has been uncomfortable. Letting you sit in my room for a while isn't that big a deal in the grand scheme of things. And if it'll help you be able to sleep, so you can be on top of your game when you compete, all the better. I'll even stay in here if you want, so you'll feel more comfortable."

Ember wrinkled her nose, and Doc couldn't help but think it was adorable.

"I'm not kicking you out of your room. People might think I'm a diva, but I'm not."

Doc took a deep breath and stepped toward her, holding out his hand in invitation. "Then let's do this, so you can get some sleep. I'd never forgive myself if you lost out on a medal because you were exhausted from staying up too late."

She gave him a shy smile. "Trust me, I've gone plenty of

nights with not enough sleep. Especially before a competition. That won't be the reason I don't medal."

Doc stayed where he was, with his arm outstretched, practically holding his breath as she came toward him. He had a sudden feeling that the second she touched him, his life was going to change forever.

For good or bad? That was the question.

Their fingers touched, then she was gripping his hand tightly.

As Doc turned and headed for his room, Ember's hand tucked in his, he knew he was right. Knew his life had taken a turn.

It was ridiculous. He didn't know Ember, and she didn't know him. Her life was everything he didn't want—fame and fortune and the limelight. But he could've no sooner walked away from her in this moment than he could turn his back on his family.

He'd caught a glimpse of the real Ember Maxwell hidden below the glitz and glamour she showed the world. And he was intrigued. Wanted to know more about her. Wanted to know *everything* about her.

It made no sense...but then, being with her right now made more sense than just about anything he'd done in his life.

He kept hold of her hand and led her into his room, only reluctantly letting go to push the one chair in the room over to the window. He walked to the bathroom and flicked on the light, then turned off the lamp on his bedside table. It would be easier to see the stars in a completely dark room, but he figured she'd be more comfortable alone with him if the room wasn't pitch black. Finally he headed back to the window, pulled up the blinds and took a step back, gesturing to the chair as he did. "Your throne, my lady."

Ember rolled her eyes but walked toward the chair and

sat. She looked up, and Doc heard her sigh in appreciation. "Oh, yeah. This is what I needed." She leaned forward, as if that would get her closer to the stars she was admiring.

Doc took a step back. Neither said a word for several long moments. Ember was soaking in whatever it was the stars did for her, and Doc soaked in the view of the beautiful woman sitting in his room.

Objectively, he could appreciate her looks. She had an athletic body that was strong and in peak condition. But that wasn't what attracted him to her. It was the little things he doubted anyone else noticed. The way she nibbled on her lower lip as she stared up into the sky. The way some part of her body was constantly in motion, as if she had so much stored-up energy she had to move to keep it from exploding out of her. The toes on one foot tapped against the floor. Then her fingers drummed on her thigh. Then she wiggled her leg side to side.

Looking at her right now, Doc would have no idea that she was a world-famous socialite. She looked like she could be one of his sister's friends. Any moment now, Mama Luisa was going to open the door and tell them it was late and they needed to get some sleep.

But this wasn't Georgia. And she sure as hell wasn't someone his sister had ever brought home.

How long she sat there looking up at the stars, Doc wasn't sure. He didn't really care; he'd let her stay as long as she needed. But eventually she turned to look at him. Given the darkness, Doc didn't think she could see him all that well, since he'd propped himself against the wall on the other side of the room.

"Your friends said something that made me curious," Ember began.

Doc stiffened. Shit. There was no telling *what* they'd said. He loved his friends, but now that they were mostly all married, and deliriously happy, they'd gotten pretty obvious about wanting to set up both him and Grover. "Yeah?" he asked.

"Yeah. They said that we had a lot more in common than I might think. It seemed ridiculous at the time. Now I'm not so sure. I know you're uncomfortable around me, but I feel comfortable with *you*, and I don't know why. Normally I would never, ever go to a room with a man I'd just met. But there's something about you that makes me trust you. It's weird."

"It's not weird. I'd never hurt you or *any* woman."

"I know. *How* can I know that, though? I just met you."

Doc shrugged, even though she probably couldn't see him. "Maybe we should start over. Get rid of both our preconceived ideas of who the other is."

"That sounds good."

"Hi, my name is Craig Wagner. But everyone calls me Doc."

"I'm Ember Maxwell. Everyone calls me Ember," she said with a small smile. "Why Doc? Are you a doctor?"

"No, although Mama Luisa would've loved that. When I was in basic training, we were practicing hand-to-hand combat. One of the privates got a little too enthusiastic and hit his partner in the face. Knocked the guy right out. I was closest and kind of took over making sure the dude was all right until the ambulance arrived. I didn't really do much, but one of the drill sergeants started calling me Doc...and it stuck."

"I suppose you could have a worse nickname," Ember said.

"Very true."

"I have another question."

"Shoot."

"Mama Luisa?"

Doc nodded. "Yeah. My mom. She's not my biological mother, but I love her more than I could ever explain." Doc debated telling Ember his story, then decided to go for it. His friends had been right; they *did* have more in common than anyone would think at first glance.

"When I was five, my parents were killed in a house fire. I was spending the night at my friend Deiondre's house. He lived a block over, and his parents and mine were best friends. The fire was deemed accidental. The stove had a faulty switch or something. Anyway, I was devastated; of course I was. But Mama Luisa and her husband didn't even hesitate to apply to foster me. They went through hell to get the right to keep me, and five years later, after countless court dates and a ridiculous uphill battle, they were finally able to adopt me."

"I don't understand. Why was it such a big deal? If they were best friends with your parents, and you wanted to be with them, why was it so hard?"

In response, Doc took his wallet out of his back pocket and pulled out a picture. He smiled at it for a moment, remembering how Nichelle, his sister, had worked so hard to set it up. They all were wearing matching colors, and even though his dad and Deiondre had bitched about the entire thing, their smiles belied their words. Doc had a larger version of the picture back in Texas, framed on his wall.

Family meant everything to him. Jaime and Luisa didn't have to take him in. Their lives would've been easier in a lot of ways if they hadn't.

He pushed off the wall and walked toward Ember. He handed her the picture and said, "My family," before backing up once again.

Ember stared down at the picture in her hand for a long moment. Then she met his gaze and said, "They're Black."

"Yup."

"I take it that was an issue."

"Not to me, but to what seemed like everyone else, yes. On the surface, America seems like it has its shit together when it comes to racism, but that's often not the case. Mama Luisa and Jaime went through hell when I was little. I can't even remember the number of times the cops were called when we were out together, because people thought I'd been kidnapped. They couldn't wrap their minds around a white boy being raised by a Black couple. Hell, we were at Disney World once, minding our own business, enjoying our day, and we were *all* detained. I was separated from the people I loved and trusted most in the world and basically interrogated.

"I still remember how scared I was, thinking they were going to take them away and lock them up even though they hadn't done anything wrong. The security guards thought I'd been brainwashed, and I was a basket case by the time they finally let us go on our way. Needless to say, family vacations after that were things like camping and staying close to home."

"That's bullshit," Ember said softly.

"Yeah, it is. That sort of thing continued throughout my childhood. Whenever I hung out with Deiondre and Nichelle —my brother and sister—I was warned that they'd bring me down or get me arrested. One night, we were at a party that got busted. The yard was full of drunk high school students, and Deiondre and I were hanging back, trying to do the right thing and not run from the cops. This one man passed by at least a dozen other kids and instead zeroed in on my brother. He wasn't doing anything, literally was just standing in the yard, and this asshole flung him to the ground and screamed at him to stop resisting. Of course, I wasn't going to stand for that shit, and so I shoved the cop off Deiondre. You know what happened?"

"What?" Ember asked.

"*Deiondre* spent a night in jail, and I was sent home with a stern warning." Doc shook his head, outraged by the memory. He took a deep breath, knowing he was getting riled up just thinking about the racism his brother and sister, and his parents, still fought against today. "People who say they don't see color when they look at people are fooling themselves. It's human nature, it can't be helped. But what *can* be helped is how they react when they see that color. Do they cross the street in fear for their life when they see a Black man walking toward them? Do they pass over an Asian or Middle Eastern woman for a job because they think they're not as smart as a white person? It has to stop."

Ember looked down at the picture she still held and stared at it for a long moment. Then she said, "Once when I was a teenager, I went for a run in my neighborhood in Beverly Hills. I knew I should go to the gym, but I was mad at my parents and just needed some space. I hadn't been running for more than fifteen minutes when a cop car pulled up next to me and wanted to know what I was doing in that neighborhood. I didn't have an ID with me, and I could tell he didn't believe me when I said I *lived* there. He escorted me home, and it wasn't until he saw my parents that he finally left me alone. I learned my lesson. I know I was raised with so much more privilege than a lot of Black people have, but I'm still judged by the color of my skin."

"I looked at some of the comments on your IG account," Doc said. "You're very well loved in the world, and yet there are still those ignorant assholes who feel the need to make nasty and uneducated comments."

Ember nodded.

They stared at each other, and Doc could practically feel the connection between them growing. "The color of your skin doesn't matter to me in the least. I walked away at lunch because of your fame. That's my problem though, not yours," Doc said honestly.

"For what it's worth...I never wanted to be *the* Ember Maxwell. When my mom hired someone to take over my social media, I didn't care. I was too busy trying to please my coaches, do my schoolwork, and make my parents happy. I did what they told me to do, not wanting to rock the boat. I posed for pictures when they told me to, had my nails and hair done where and how they told me to. I smiled as directed. Didn't even stand up for myself or what I wanted when that damn contract for the reality show was signed. I've worked hard to be here today. I'm proud of myself for being an Olympian, but it was never *my* dream. It was my parents'. And my fans'.

"Don't get me wrong, I want to medal. I'm competitive, and I've worked damn hard over the last few years. It would be stupid to make the Olympics and not want to do well, for myself *and* my country. But if I had my way, I'd win a medal, then disappear from social media forever. No more photo ops. No more influencer endorsements. My parents have made me more money than I could ever spend in two lifetimes. I know it's silly, because with that kind of money, I could've quit long before now, but I think it was just easier to go with the flow. Do what they wanted me to because I wasn't sure what I wanted to do with my life."

"And you do now?" he asked, not harshly.

"I know I want to *live*. Not spend every second of my life training. I want to move someplace where no one knows me and live my life in peace. Maybe I'll become a professional puzzle putter-togetherer. Or a hermit who only leaves the house to yell at the kids who dare step foot in my yard."

Doc smiled. Christ, she was adorable. "Why don't you?"

"Why don't I what?" she asked with a tilt of her head.

"Disable your accounts. Move. Do what you want with your life."

She stared at him silently.

"You're an adult, Ember. I get that you don't want to disappoint your parents, but you also need to do what *you* want to do."

"I'm not sure it's that easy," she whispered.

"Oh, there will be tears and heartache," Doc agreed. "But nothing worth doing is ever easy."

"I *do* know my passwords to IG and Facebook," Ember mused.

Doc smiled.

"Holy shit. Am I really even considering that?" Ember asked quietly. "My mom would absolutely lose her shit. Not to mention the four social media managers she hired for me. My dad would probably understand...maybe. He knows how overbearing my mom can get."

"First things first, champ. You've got a couple intense days of competition ahead of you. Why don't you get through those before you make any huge life decisions?"

Ember stood then and walked toward him.

Doc tensed. For some crazy reason, he wanted to reach out and pull her close. Put his arms around her and see if they fit together as well as he imagined they would. She wasn't too much shorter than his six-one. And strong. He wouldn't have to be afraid he'd smother her.

He also had a feeling that, once she came into her own, she'd never let anyone dictate her life again.

He held his breath as she walked into his personal space. She didn't touch him, but was definitely standing closer than two people who'd just met hours ago normally would.

"You have a nice-looking family," she said as she held out the picture he'd shown her.

Doc took it from her. "Thanks."

"I'm sorry I make you uncomfortable."

"It's my issue, not yours."

"Still. Thanks for letting me use your window."

"Anytime. I mean that. If you want to come over and look at the stars tomorrow, it's not an issue."

"I won't be bothering you?" Ember asked.

"Nope."

"What time do you get off tomorrow?"

"Five."

"You want to meet up and eat dinner tomorrow? In the cafeteria," she clarified. "I'm not ready to unleash Ember Maxwell on South Korea. I'm told that I have quite a few followers over here, and I'd hate to disrupt things for the other athletes."

"I'm not sure other influencers would care about something like that. They'd probably be all about the free publicity."

Ember wrinkled her nose. "I think we've established that I'm not like them."

"True. In that case, I'd love to have dinner with you. I'll most likely need to shower beforehand, so why don't I knock on your door when I'm ready. That way you don't have to wait downstairs for me and risk getting yourself into uncomfortable situations with others who might recognize you."

She stared at him for a long moment.

"What?" he asked.

"For someone who isn't comfortable with my fame, you sure seem to know how to deal with it."

"I know jack shit," Doc admitted wryly. "But I *do* know how to fly under the radar."

She tilted her head. "You aren't a regular soldier, are you?"

"No," Doc said simply. It was too soon to get into more. Besides, they'd be going their separate ways in a week or two. She had no reason to know he was Delta.

"Right." She took a deep breath, then stepped away from him.

Doc couldn't help but feel a sense of disappointment. He

did his best to rein it in. "What's on your schedule for tomorrow?"

"Working out. I'm supposed to meet up with Leila, Nick, and Aiden to practice and to do a few interviews with the press. We've also got some photos we have to do. Samer—he's one of my social media managers—came over with us, and he has all sorts of things planned. He's super-excited about getting new pictures and some live videos for my accounts. In the afternoon, I think my mom's set up a few interviews too. And I'm sure there will be more pictures."

Doc winced.

Ember sighed. "Yeah. I think I'm supposed to do a live reading of some of the letters of encouragement I've received. And acknowledge some of the comments on my IG. Followers love that kind of thing."

Doc shrugged. "I wouldn't know."

"You don't have a Facebook or IG account?" Ember asked.

"Fuck no," Doc told her. "I've got no time, or use, for that shit. You met my friends, the people I care about, earlier at lunch. I see them just about every day, and we hang out at each other's places at least once a week. I don't give a fuck what someone I went to high school with is doing today. If they didn't bother to keep in touch with me after we gradu-ated—and believe me, no one has—then I don't care to see pictures of their happy families or vacations or whatever bull-shit they want others to know about them."

"Wow, don't beat around the bush, tell me what you really think," Ember said with a laugh.

Doc ran a hand through his hair. "Sorry."

"No, don't be. It's actually refreshing. Most people kiss my ass all the time and only tell me what they think I want to hear."

"I don't bullshit," Doc told her honestly. "Ever."

"Good to know."

Glancing at his watch, Doc was surprised at how long they'd been talking. "It's late. You need to get some sleep. I'll knock on your door around five-fifteen or so. That'll give me time to clean the stink of the day off myself before we head down to the cafeteria."

"Sounds good. See you tomorrow."

"Be safe out there."

"I will. You too."

Ember gave him one last long look before she headed for his door. Doc followed at a respectful distance and stood in his doorway, watching her walk down the hall toward her room. He waited until she was safely inside before shutting and locking his own door.

He stood there in the dark for several minutes. Thinking over their conversation.

He genuinely liked Ember. He hadn't wanted to. Had wanted to think she was just another annoying social media star. For that matter, he'd never expected this trip to be anything more than just another mission.

The fact that he couldn't get Ember off his mind for most of the night made him realize he might truly be in trouble here. He probably should have told her that he had to work and couldn't have dinner with her. Why start something when she lived in California and he was in Texas? There were way too many obstacles to any kind of relationship between them.

So why was he already looking forward to tomorrow? To finding out how her day went? And why was he itching to pull out his phone and make an IG account so he could follow her and see any live videos she was planning on doing?

Disgusted with himself, Doc shook his head. He pulled his wallet and phone out of his pockets and threw them on the desktop. Then he stripped down to his boxers and climbed under the sheet of the too narrow and short bed.

Closing his eyes, he tried to tell himself that he was only being nice to Ember because she really seemed like she could use a friend.

If Mama Luisa was here, she'd smack him upside the head and tell him to stop lying to himself. He was being nice to Ember because she fascinated him. Intrigued him. And because he desperately wanted to know more about her.

Shit. He was fucked.

He'd seen his friends fall hard and fast for their women. He recognized the signs. The difference was that he was setting himself up for heartbreak. Ember was a fucking icon. Recognized the world over, with more connections than probably even the infamous Tex had. She'd never in a million years want to hook up with a plain ol' Army soldier like him.

CHAPTER FOUR

Ember was more excited than she'd been in a very long time. Not about competing in the Olympics tomorrow...but because she was going to see Craig soon. She couldn't call him Doc; that was a bit too weird for her.

Her day had been long. She should be meditating or visualizing her fencing techniques for the round-robin competition in seventeen hours or so. Instead, she couldn't think about anything other than hanging out with Craig again.

Seeing if the spark she'd felt around him last night was still there.

Maybe she was attracted to him because she hadn't been on a date in...she couldn't remember when. Maybe it was hearing how he'd been raised by a Black family that had intrigued her enough to want to know more. Or maybe it was just because when she spoke, all of his attention was focused on her. Not on who else might be watching them. Not her boobs. He looked into her eyes, as if what she was saying was the most important thing he'd ever heard.

She instinctively knew he didn't want anything from her. Didn't want her to sell something for him. Didn't want to be featured on her IG account. In fact, she suspected he'd be horrified if his picture was posted there. With Craig, she could be herself. Just Ember.

Maybe that was the wrong reason to be infatuated with someone, but Ember wanted more of it. Wanted to soak in every second of time with him. Wrap up how he made her feel, as if she was a normal woman, so she could bring it out and bask in the memory of his comforting presence in the future.

Her practice today had gone well. She felt good. Really good. Leila had been happy to see her, and they'd laughed and chatted with a kind of nervous energy. They would be competing against each other, but they were both representing the United States and wanted to do the best they could. Nick and Aiden had been in good moods today as well. They'd all joked together as they posed for pictures for the press. The modern pentathlon wasn't exactly the most anticipated sport in the Olympics, but Ember being on the team had upped their popularity tenfold.

Even dealing with her parents today hadn't brought her down. Samer had taken a ton of pictures for her account and had talked happily about what he was planning to post in the near future. He'd picked some comments for her to read out loud, and though Ember had felt silly doing so, she didn't make a fuss. It felt as if the entire country had their eyes on her, and Ember was determined to do the absolute best she could. This may not have been her dream, but the closer she got to actually competing, the more excited she became.

Maybe it was because for the first time in her life, she could see the finish line.

Ember knew her parents wouldn't be happy with her decision to retire from the sport, but she'd decided she was done. Ready to move on with her life.

Talking with Craig had helped solidify her decision. She

was twenty-five. Not fourteen. She needed to move out of her parents' house and make her own way in the world. On one hand, she'd always be grateful to her mom and dad for pushing her, for putting enough money in her bank account so she could literally do anything...or nothing. But on the other hand, she'd started resenting them more than she was thankful for their pushiness. She needed to get out from under their control before their relationship was irreparable.

She was also ready to give up being Ember Maxwell, social media darling, and start using her platform for something worthwhile.

An idea had formed in her mind last night, after she'd gone back to her room. She'd thought about what the hell she wanted to do with the rest of her life. She didn't have a college education, but it wasn't too late to get her degree. And she'd thought about Craig and what had happened to him. How he'd lost his parents in a fire when he'd been so young. He had to have been confused and scared, though he'd been lucky that Mama Luisa and her husband had taken him in. It couldn't have been easy for any of them; interracial relationships of any kind weren't easy in this country.

It made her want to hug the child he'd been. Made her think about the other children who might be going through similar tough times. Sports had given her a sense of belonging when she'd been in grade school... Maybe she could work with children. Kids who would never dream of participating in an expensive sport like fencing. Or horse jumping. She could put together a mini-pentathlon kind of gym. Where the kids got to fence, swim, ride horses, run, and shoot. It would be more about fun and companionship than competition.

Her mind practically raced with the possibilities, and the more she thought about it, the more it appealed.

She had the money, and she could use her name to hopefully recruit employees and even participants. She envisioned it being free for those who were underprivileged, and having only a nominal fee for other children.

For the first time in her life, she was excited about her future—and Ember knew she had Craig to thank.

Hearing him talk about how much he hated the limelight made her realize that many men were probably the same way. And the ones who weren't, she didn't want to be with. If she ever wanted to have her own family, she needed to stand up to her parents, and do what *she* wanted to do for once.

The photo ops they'd arranged that afternoon had gone as expected. She'd smiled and posed as directed. Her parents seemed happy with the attention she'd gotten, and Ember knew the photos were probably already up on her social media accounts. For the first time in a long time, it didn't bother her.

Big changes were going to happen after the Olympics, and Ember couldn't wait.

Her excitement about the future seemed to reenergize her. Made her more excited to compete and hopefully kick some major butt. End her career on the highest note possible. She was actually looking forward to competing. To doing the best she could and maybe even taking home a medal.

And that same excitement extended to Craig. Being around him made her feel like a different person. Someone she actually liked.

A knock sounded, and Ember sprang up from the edge of the mattress and practically skipped over to the door to open it.

"Hi!" she said happily.

Craig blinked at her. Then he smiled—and Ember just about melted where she stood.

"Hey. You're very chipper this afternoon."

"I am. I had a good day, and I'm ready to get this competition started."

Craig tilted his head and studied her for a moment. "Something's different with you," he stated.

Ember beamed. She was ridiculously pleased he'd noticed. "Yeah. Our talk last night made me think about a lot of stuff."

"Hopefully that's a good thing."

"It is."

"You hungry?"

"Starving," she told him.

"Me too. Today was long."

It was Ember's turn to study the man in front of her. She'd been so caught up in her thoughts and excitement about the future, she hadn't noticed at first...but now she could see he looked a little harried. There were lines in his forehead, as if he'd been frowning all day. "Is everything all right?"

"Yeah. I'm just stressed."

"Anything I can do?"

"Yes. You can be extremely careful. Be aware of your surroundings at all times and don't go anywhere by yourself. If you can get Nick and Aiden to accompany you and Leila, that would be great."

Ember stared up at Craig. "What's going on?"

He ran a hand through his hair, looking down the hall, then took a step toward her, forcing Ember to back up. He shut her door behind him, but didn't move closer. Ember wasn't afraid of Craig, though he was looking very intense at the moment.

"You know I'm here to help with security."

Ember nodded.

"I'm Army Special Forces. Delta Force. My team and I had a tour of the venues today, then a long meeting about the security protocols in place, and honestly, we think they could be more strict. The Olympics are a perfect opportunity for any of the many terrorist groups around the world to strike."

"You really think someone is planning something?" Ember asked.

"Terrorist groups are *always* planning something," Craig said with a shrug.

"Like what?"

He sounded almost bored as he answered, "Car bombs. Pipe bombs. Coordinated attacks on athletes."

Ember's head was spinning. "Seriously?"

"Yeah."

"Are we in danger?"

Her question seemed to pierce through Craig's internal musings, because he took a step toward her and put a hand on her shoulder. "I hope not. Just stay alert when you aren't competing. Keep your eyes on those around you. If anyone looks out of place or is acting suspicious, get the hell away from them as fast as you can."

"Okay," Ember agreed immediately.

Craig squeezed her shoulder comfortingly, then dropped his hand. "I'm sorry I scared you. That wasn't my intention."

"It's okay. Everyone in my life talks *around* me. They make plans without telling me. They schedule appointments, photo shoots, and basically run my life without asking for my input. You not hiding that something could happen...it actually means a lot. Thank you."

"Just be aware of what's going on around you, Em," Craig said.

Ember blinked. Had anyone ever given her a nickname? A *nice* one? She couldn't remember it if they had. Her parents had always called her Ember, saying they'd picked it specifically because they liked the way it sounded, and shortening it was uncouth. "I will."

"Good. But for the record, my team and I have you

covered when you're with us. You shouldn't have to worry about anything else on top of competing."

"So your friends...they're all special forces too?"

Craig nodded.

Ember smiled.

"What?" Craig asked.

"Nothing. It's just...it's cool."

Craig's shoulders relaxed a fraction, and Ember felt good that she could do that for him. "It's just a job."

Ember snorted. "Yeah, right. And I'm the President of the United States."

They shared a smile.

"Come on, I'm just as hungry as you are."

"You sure it's safe?"

"You're with me. It's safe," he said simply.

Ember had no doubt that was true.

"You gonna carbo load tonight? Or do you like to load up on protein before you compete?" Craig asked.

Ember knew he was intentionally changing the subject, but that was okay. She planned to go online later and find out as much as she could about Delta Force. She knew enough to know they were pretty badass, but that was about it. "A little of both," she said as he opened the door for her. She walked out into the hall in front of him and watched as he made sure her door was secure before gesturing for her to precede him toward the elevator.

She noticed that his eyes were constantly in motion. Scanning the hallway, alert for anyone who might not belong or for anything out of the ordinary. Thinking about it now, she'd noticed his friends doing the same thing in the cafeteria. It was obvious being aware of their surroundings was as engrained in them as breathing.

He stood close to her in the elevator, and when it stopped on a lower floor, he moved in front of her, as if protecting her from whoever might get on. It was a little excessive, but Ember couldn't deny the sense of security it brought. She'd had bodyguards who weren't as alert and attentive as Craig.

As they walked into the cafeteria, he said, "I hope you don't mind, but Trigger and Lefty are joining us for dinner."

"That's fine."

"I mean, I wanted to have you to myself, but with everything going on, I figured it wouldn't hurt to have extra eyes while you were out and about."

She liked that. A lot. Not the extra eyes thing...but that he'd wanted her to himself. Goose bumps broke out on her arms. "It's okay."

Craig stopped her and put a hand on her elbow, turning her so she was facing him. "I'm serious, when you're out of this building, you need to be on alert. You're a high-value target, Em. Any terrorist organization would get a lot of publicity if they managed to hurt or kill Ember Maxwell at the Olympics."

She understood that. Probably more than he did. Hell, her eating a candy bar in public was huge news in some circles. Getting shot or killed? Shit, people would lose their minds. It wasn't an ego thing, it was just a fact. Her parents were very smart and both had a head for business. They'd made her into a household name, succeeding in that goal beyond any of their imaginations. It was a pain in her ass...and she knew there were people out there who didn't like her, who might see her as a target for their own agendas.

"Okay," she said softly.

Craig looked like he wanted to say more, but someone cleared their throat nearby.

His reaction was instantaneous. He moved so his body was between her and whoever had approached them.

"It's me," Trigger said.

Craig nodded and turned to Ember. "Come on. Trigger

will have your back while we go through the line."

Ember followed behind Craig as he led the way to the buffet. Luckily, it was relatively quiet. She could feel people's eyes on her, but with the way she was sandwiched between Craig and his teammate, no one felt brave enough to approach.

The feeling of safety she experienced, standing between the two men, was something she'd never really felt before. That was exactly why, over the last year or so, she'd become even more of a recluse. Whenever she went out, people stared or approached or took pictures. Being famous pretty much sucked, and it made Ember extremely uncomfortable. So she'd gotten used to going to work out, then straight back home. She'd lost touch with the few friends she'd made in middle school years ago. The only people she talked to regularly were the other athletes at the facility where she trained. And Bobby, Julio, Shawn, Lori, Megan, Marie, and Becci were all very used to having her around. She was just another athlete they trained with, not the famous Ember Maxwell. Other than the fans who sent her letters, she had little contact with the outside world.

Her dad didn't understand why she liked to read her fan mail, saying they had people to take care of that stuff, but even the rude or mean letters made her feel more human, not as much like a cartoon version of herself who only existed online. The pictures posted to her accounts were always filtered so she had no blemishes, makeup and hair perfect, and her teeth shone whiter than white.

"Em?"

She jerked and looked up at Craig. "Sorry, what?"

He smiled down at her. "Fucking adorable," he murmured under his breath. Then louder, he said, "I asked if you wanted a salad plate."

Ember flushed, thankful it would be harder to see with

her dark skin. "Yes, please."

They moved through the line fairly quickly, and Craig led the way to a table along the back wall of the room. She hadn't really noticed the day before, but she realized they'd been sitting at an out-of-the-way table then too. "Could we get any farther from the food?" she joked.

"No one can come up behind us here," Trigger said as he sat next to her. Craig was on her other side, all three of them facing the room, and Lefty was sitting at the end of the rectangular table.

Ember nodded. She was beginning to suspect everything they did was very deliberate and for safety-conscious reasons.

Talk was a bit stilted at first. Ember felt a little awkward, unsure what to say. Craig was fairly quiet, so Trigger and Lefty were forced to carry the conversation.

Lefty asked, "So have you had a chance to meet many of the other athletes?"

Ember shrugged. "Some. Most are kinda keeping to themselves and their teammates. I'm guessing after they compete, they'll open up a bit more and be a bit friendlier."

"Yeah, there's a weird tension in the air," Trigger agreed.

"Can you blame them? This is the Olympics. Probably the most important competition they'll have in their lifetime," Lefty said.

"Wow, thanks for trying to make me feel less nervous," Ember joked.

Both Lefty and Trigger stared at her with anxious expressions.

"Shit," Lefty swore.

"Dumbass," Trigger admonished.

Craig chuckled.

Ember glanced at him and shared a grin.

"Are you fucking with me?" Lefty asked.

Ember shrugged. "A little."

"Damn," Lefty said on a sigh. "I thought I'd really screwed up there."

"You aren't nervous?" Trigger asked.

"Oh, I am, but honestly, I feel so much less stressed about everything today than I did yesterday," Ember said.

"Why? What changed?" Lefty asked.

Ember's eyes involuntarily flicked to her left, and she saw Craig staring at her intently. She reached for her water glass to give herself a moment to think about what she wanted to say. After she swallowed, she said, "Being away from my parents helped, for one. They're pretty intense and always on me about thinking and breathing everything having to do with the pentathlon or social media. Don't get me wrong, I love them and am appreciative of everything they've done for me, but not having to be Ember Maxwell has really helped relax me over the last twenty-four hours."

"I can't imagine how difficult it would be to always have to be on," Trigger said.

"It's hard," Ember agreed.

"Hard. I'm guessing that's an understatement," Lefty commented.

"Yeah. Anyway, before yesterday, I felt as if I had the weight of the world on my shoulders. That if I didn't win, or at least medal, I'd be a complete failure and I'd let down every single one of my followers. But I'm starting to realize that I don't owe anyone *anything*. All I can do is my best, and if that means I come in dead last, so be it. No one can take the fact that I'm an Olympian away from me."

"Very true," Trigger agreed.

"What are your chances of medaling?" Lefty asked.

Trigger turned and smacked his friend on the back of his head. "Don't ask that, asshole! Didn't you hear her just say she didn't care about that?"

"I did, but I'm still curious," Lefty said.

Ember wasn't offended. She liked these guys. They were honest to a fault, which was a rare treat in her circle. So often someone would be friendly to her face, then turn around and bash her on social media. She got along with the athletes she trained with, but those were superficial relationships at best.

"It's okay. Honestly, I'd say I've got a fifty-fifty chance to medal. I'm an okay fencer, a little weak in horse jumping, but I'm damn good at running and shooting, if I do say so myself. If I can manage to get enough points to be in the middle of the pack before the run starts, I've got a shot."

"How do you feel about spectators?" Craig asked.

Ember turned to him. It was the first time he'd spoken since the conversation started. "What do you mean?"

He shrugged. "With everything going on, I managed to get reassigned to the security team for your venue tomorrow."

"You did?" she asked with raised brows.

"He did," Trigger agreed. "The rest of us will be at the stadium where the first basketball games will be held, but he switched places with someone on another team."

Ember couldn't take her gaze from Craig's. "I don't mind spectators. I usually block out everything except what I'm doing."

"Good. I'll already be at the venue when you get there tomorrow, but I arranged for you and the rest of your teammates to be escorted from the dorm in the morning."

"Is that necessary?" Ember asked.

"Yes," all three men said at the same time.

"Look," Trigger said. "We know Doc told you about our dissatisfaction with venue security. Better safe than sorry and all that."

Ember immediately nodded. "I agree. And I'll gladly accept the escort. Thank you."

"I'll be there to bring you back to the dorm at the end of the day," Craig told her.

"Again, thank you."

He nodded at her.

"So...any chance you know Shin-Soo Choo?" Lefty asked.

Ember's brows rose at the abrupt change of conversation. "The baseball player? As a matter of fact, yes. Why?"

All three men's eyes widened comically.

"You do? I was totally joking. That's awesome!" Lefty said.

"I met him a few years ago. We did a photo shoot for minority athletes. He came to Los Angeles, and I got to know him and his family. They're awesome," Ember said. "I was so happy for him when he made the Olympic trials. He's one of the oldest players on the team."

"We need his autograph," Trigger said. "Well, not *we*, but Logan does."

"Logan?" Ember asked, vaguely remembering the name from lunch yesterday.

"What these two jokers aren't explaining well is that Oz—our team member who isn't here because his wife is about to have a baby—his boy is infatuated with Choo. Has posters on his bedroom wall and just started in a baseball league himself. He idolizes the man, so we all kind of promised we'd track Choo down and get an autograph for Logan."

"Oh, okay. That should be easy enough. Even if we can't get to him here—because I heard that most of the basketball and baseball players aren't staying in the village—I can get in touch with him when I get back home, and I'm sure he'd be glad to send some stuff to Logan."

"Oh my God, that would be so awesome," Lefty said with a huge smile.

"We don't want you to go out of your way," Craig said.

"Shut up! Yes we do!" Trigger interjected with a laugh. "I can't wait to tell Lucky that he wasn't the lucky one *this* time. Ha!"

Ember watched in amusement as the men around her

turned into little boys, giddy with excitement over getting one over on their friend. She made a mental note to ask Shin-Soo to send a box of merch to the little boy. She had to admit that it felt good to *not* be the one asked to send stuff. She wanted that part of her life to be behind her sooner than later. And while she knew because of the internet and that damn reality show, she'd never be fully incognito, she guessed most people would forget about her fairly quickly.

As they all chatted, Ember was aware of people staring over at their table, though she had a feeling it was less because of *her* than the three handsome men she was sitting with. They continued to laugh and joke throughout the meal, and Ember felt even more relaxed by the time they stood up to take their trays to the bins. She hadn't thought about her competition the next day at all, which made her feel even less stressed about it.

Trigger said he had a meeting to attend, and she caught a few intense glances between him and his friends, but both Craig and Lefty merely nodded and said they'd catch up with him shortly. She was escorted back up to their floor by Lefty and Craig, and Lefty headed to his room after thanking her again for helping with Shin-Soo's autograph for Logan. She and Craig headed to the right, toward their rooms.

"You want to look at the stars again tonight?" Craig asked. Then, without waiting for her answer, continued, "You're more than welcome. I need to head out and chat with Trigger in a bit, so you'd have it to yourself. You can visualize or meditate or whatever you need to do to get ready for tomorrow."

"I'm about as ready as I'm gonna get," Ember admitted. "I'm in the best shape of my life. I've had a good meal and I'm feeling pretty damn mellow. But...if it's okay...I wouldn't mind using your room for a while. I mean, I'm not usually superstitious, but I'd rather not push my luck at this point. I just want to change first."

Craig smiled at her. They were standing by his door, and he reached out and unlocked it with the key card, which he then handed to her. Here you go. I'll be headed out in about fifteen minutes or so. If you need anything, Lucky and Grover are staying on the floor, watching over things. I'll let them know you're using my room and to keep an eye out for you."

"You really *are* close to your friends, aren't you?"

Craig nodded. "They're more than my friends. They're my lifeline when we're on missions. We can practically read each other's minds."

Ember felt a pang of jealousy but pushed it down. In a week, she'd hopefully be free to find her own tribe of friends. They wouldn't be special forces soldiers saving the world from terrorists and other dangers, but maybe, just maybe, she'd find some people she could form close bonds with.

"I love that for you," she told him.

"Thanks. Me too."

"I'll be fine here. Are you going out on patrol?"

"No. Just meeting up with some guys from another special forces team who're here. Comparing notes. Trying to identify any vulnerable spots in the security."

Ember felt safer knowing Craig and his friends were taking their jobs very seriously. "Okay. What should I do with your key?"

"Stay here until I get back," Craig said firmly.

"How long will you be gone?"

"I don't know."

Ember stared at him. He was suddenly being a little bossy. "What if I only want to stay for, like, twenty minutes?"

"I'm gonna be longer than that," Craig answered.

Ember huffed out a breath. "Right—and what if I only want to stay for twenty minutes?" she repeated.

Craig ran a hand through his hair...and Ember began to suspect he did that whenever he felt frustrated or unsure. "I'd like to see you when I get back," he admitted in a low voice. "I didn't get you to myself at dinner, so I thought maybe we could talk a bit. But yeah, that's stupid. You need to get some sleep so you can be ready for tomorrow. Just leave the key card on the desk, I'll get another before I come upstairs."

Ember's heart melted. He didn't want anything from her... well, nothing other than her company. She couldn't remember the last time that had happened. "I'll wait for you."

But Craig shook his head. "No. I was being silly."

Taking a chance, Ember put her hand on his arm. She realized for the first time how tan he was. Her skin was darker, of course, but the contrast wasn't startling. They seemed to blend together perfectly. "I'd like to hang out with you for a while. I like your friends, but I was looking forward to talking with you...*just* you...too."

Craig nodded. "Okay. I'll try not to be too late. But if you get tired, get some sleep. We can talk tomorrow, after you compete."

Ember nodded. They stared at each other for a long moment, until she realized she was still touching his arm. Reluctantly, she dropped her hand and stepped back.

When he didn't move, just continued to stare at her, Ember asked nervously, "Are you gonna watch me walk to my room...?"

"Yeah."

That was it. Just "yeah."

"I'm sure there won't be any terrorists jumping out and attempting to kill me while I change clothes," she joked.

"If there are, I'll deal with them," Craig told her, completely straight-faced. Then he sighed. "Humor me, Em. It's in my DNA to make sure you get inside your room safely."

Since she had his key, he couldn't leave his doorway without the door locking behind him, so she nodded and walked backward a few steps, holding eye contact with him, before spinning and heading for her own room. She fumbled with her key for a moment, then finally got it to work. She glanced back down the hall once more and saw Craig was still watching her. She gave him an awkward little wave and saw his lips quirk upward. He gave her a chin lift, and she sighed as she closed her door behind her.

Shit. She was falling for the guy. She'd known him for what...a day? It was crazy. Ridiculous.

But it felt so damn good.

Craig was a wonderful guy. Special forces, handsome, and his friends obviously cared about him a great deal. She could do a lot worse, that was for sure. Was he interested in more than talking? Long-distance relationships rarely worked out.

But hadn't she just decided that she was done letting her parents run her life? That she was going to stop being Ember Maxwell, social media influencer, and be her own woman?

She could live anywhere she wanted. She had plenty of money and was an adult. If she wanted to move to the ends of the earth, she could. But it would be crazy to decide to move to a different state just because of a guy, right?

Ember knew she shouldn't be thinking about this right now. This wasn't the time to be making impulsive decisions.

Pushing the thought of dating Craig out of her head—it was pretty ridiculous anyway—she decided to wait thirty minutes or so, then head down to Craig's room so she could watch the stars. When he got back, they'd talk for a bit, then she'd return to her room and get some sleep.

A shiver traversed her spine as it hit her that tomorrow, she'd be competing in the *Olympics*. She wanted to do well. Not for her parents. Or her fans. Or her coaches and everyone else who'd helped her. But for herself. She *wanted* a medal. She'd worked her ass off for years, she deserved it.

Suddenly, tomorrow couldn't come fast enough.

Smiling, Ember headed for the dresser where she'd put her comfiest clothes.

* * *

Alex paced the room excitedly. It was almost time. Ember would be competing soon. She was going to kick some serious ass and raise the profile of every modern pentathlon athlete around the world. The sport would finally get the attention it deserved.

And with the special connection they shared, Alex would be a shoo-in for the next Olympics.

Alex and Ember were like two halves of the same soul. They'd connected on a deep, deep level. Tomorrow was the next step to Alex's rise to glory.

Throughout the years, Alex had sent Ember lots of gifts to let her know how special she was, and was already planning the perfect gift to send after she brought home an Olympic medal. It didn't need to be gold...silver or bronze would be just as good.

Alex smiled and glanced at the television. Earlier there had been a special profile on Ember and her family, as well as some history on the modern pentathlon sport. Millions of people had probably watched it, and even now, Alex *knew* the popularity of the sport was rising.

It was late, almost three in the morning, but Alex was too excited to sleep. Soon, Ember would prove to the world that she was a great athlete...and in the process, change Alex's life for the better.

Life had been shit for way too long. Change was due.

And it would come...right after Ember brought home a medal for the United States!

CHAPTER FIVE

Doc swore under his breath. His meeting with the other Delta team had gone on for over four hours. Everyone had agreed that the security seemed too lax at the sports venues. There hadn't been any specific threats made, but the Delta teams knew better than most that any kind of huge world-wide event like the Olympics was bound to attract terrorists. The teams had mapped out the venues and identified the most vulnerable areas—agreeing there could also be more security at the entrance gates to the Olympic Village—then did their best to come up with plans to mitigate danger, should it arise. Trigger and the other team leader would be meeting with the other heads of security and police to see if they could ferret out any specific threats, as well as add to the security numbers.

Doc was uneasy for a reason he couldn't name, the hair on the back of his neck standing up, but there was nothing more they could do tonight.

Everyone agreed that the athletes were safe while inside the village. Everyone had to present credentials to get in, then show them again to get into the dorms. But when the athletes ventured out tomorrow to the various venues, they'd be fair game. As would be the workers, volunteers, spectators, and fans. A terrorist group could strike at any time, and they all needed to stay on their toes.

Doc looked at his watch and sighed. It was eleven-thirty, and Ember was probably sound asleep in her own room by now. He stopped by the reception desk and got another key to his room before heading upstairs. He'd been looking forward to talking with her some more. Getting to know her better. What he'd learned about her so far, he liked. A lot. The uneasiness he'd felt when he'd first seen her hadn't gone away, but it was now only a distant throbbing, instead of an uncomfortable beating in his head.

Nothing had changed...she was still famous. Still in the limelight. And if—no, *when* she won a medal in the next two days, she'd be even more in the spotlight. But even that thought couldn't keep his interest at bay. Though she'd been raised in Beverly Hills by wealthy parents who'd done every-thing in their power to make her into the woman she was today, he could see she was itching to break out of their control. He wanted to help her in any way he could.

But that was stupid. She didn't need his help. Who was *he*? No one. Just another admirer. She could literally have any man she wanted. Why would she want *him*?

Still, if he could help her by letting her use his window to look up at the sky, he would. He'd do what he could to keep her safe and relaxed so she could perform up to her potential. Then she'd forget about him as soon as she got home.

The dorm was quieter tonight than it had been other nights, which Doc was glad about. He wanted Ember, and her teammates, to have every advantage possible to be at the top of their game tomorrow for the first round of fencing.

He stuck his key card into the slot of his room, stepped inside—then froze for a second. He immediately realized he wasn't alone, but even as his hand went to his weapon in the hidden holster at the small of his back, he realized who was in the dark room with him.

Ember.

She was lying on his bed, fast asleep.

Doc laid his weapon on the desk without a sound and silently walked farther into the room. He was glad he hadn't flicked on the light, as that would've surely woken her up. She'd left the curtains open, and he noticed she'd pushed the bed closer to the window. He figured she could probably see the stars from where she'd lain her head.

The absolute last thing Doc wanted to do was disturb her. At rest, she fascinated him even more. He couldn't deny it. She looked completely relaxed, as if she didn't have a care in the world.

He'd done an internet search on Ember Maxwell earlier that day, and he'd seen picture after picture of her completely made up, smiling, laughing. Most of the pictures were obviously posed. And while she was beautiful in each and every one of them, Doc much preferred her like this. Her face scrubbed clean, her hair in disarray on his pillow. Wearing sweats and a T-shirt.

He recalled the few candid pictures he'd uncovered in his search. They'd all seemed incredibly intrusive. In one, she was sitting against the wall in a gym, probably where she worked out, her shoulders slumped as if she was tired or upset. The caption had said, "Ebony Princess Loses."

Some of the comments were mean, demeaning, or racist, but the majority were positive and encouraging. It was obvious most of Ember's fans loved her and didn't hesitate to stand up for her.

Another candid picture featured Ember wearing a beautiful green dress at some formal event. She'd been shot from a distance, standing off by herself while clusters of other pretty women were nearby, seemingly excluding her. He didn't remember the caption exactly, only that it was something petty and spiteful about Ember thinking she was too good for the crowd she was with.

He'd closed his browser after seeing a few more pictures with hateful captions and comments. Yes, she had her supporters, but it was obvious some people hated her as well.

Doc understood that kind of hate all too well. He'd lived amongst Black friends and family long enough to see the effects of discrimination up close and personal. It bothered him then, and it bothered him now. He never understood why skin color was a factor in deciding what kind of person someone was. He'd met assholes of *every* race. He'd learned from a young age to judge people by their actions and words, not the color of their skin.

But he was very aware plenty of people in his country—and around the world—still thought like should stick to like. Black people should date and marry Black people. White people should date and marry white people. Asian people should only be with people of Asian descent. It went on and on, no matter where someone lived, or what their culture and religion was, the belief that people should stick with those who looked and thought the same as them would remain. Discrimination was rampant *everywhere*, and was a major factor behind wars. Why teams like the Delta Force were necessary.

Reading some of the comments on Ember's Instagram account made him equal parts happy and pissed off. Happy that so many people supported her, pissed at the hate people spewed as they hid behind their keyboard.

Putting his back to the wall, Doc slid down silently, keeping his eyes on a sleeping Ember as he admitted to himself what he wasn't ready to say out loud.

He wanted her. It was that simple...and that complicated.

He knew she was out of his league, but that didn't make the want go away. He wanted to see her smile and make her happy. He wanted to give her everything she longed for...but what could he give her that she didn't already have or couldn't get for herself? She was smart, successful, and an amazing athlete. She had more money than he could even imagine. She was beautiful and popular and was an inspiration to a lot of people.

She deserved to live in the light. To shine bright and inspire as many people as possible. He was like a mole to her eagle. She soared high, and he lived in the underbelly of the world. Slinking around in the dead of night.

But Doc couldn't make himself stay away from her.

He'd soak up her light for as long as he could.

Ember stirred but didn't open her eyes. She rolled to her side, facing him, and Doc couldn't take his eyes from her. He should wake her up and get her back to her room. But she had to compete tomorrow, and if she was asleep now, he didn't want to risk her feeling awkward and not being able to go back to sleep in her own bed.

So he sat there. His back against the wall, watching over her as she slumbered.

His eyes eventually drooped, and Doc rested his head on the hard concrete behind him. It wasn't exactly comfortable, but he'd slept in worse places in his life. He wasn't in the mud and rain, and he was ninety-nine percent sure he wasn't going to be ambushed in the middle of the night. It was enough to let him doze off.

* * *

Ember rolled over onto her back and took a deep breath. She'd always been a morning person; it came with all those five a.m. swim practices she'd had growing up. Her room was still dark, but she'd left the bathroom light on and it gave the space a dim glow.

Peering at her watch, she saw it was almost time for her to get up. Today was competition day. The thought made her smile.

Turning her head, she froze.

She wasn't in her room at the Olympic Village dorm.

Craig was lying on the floor—the *floor*—across from her. There wasn't even a damn rug on the hard tile. He was on his back, with one hand under his head. He was fully dressed and sound asleep.

Ember remembered immediately what had happened. She'd been watching the stars and had gotten drowsy. Figuring he'd be back any minute, she pushed his bed closer to the window and had lain down, intending on taking a cat nap until Craig returned.

But she'd obviously been more tired than she thought and had fallen into a deep sleep. So deep, she hadn't even heard Craig enter his room. And he obviously didn't want to wake her.

She felt incredibly weird about the whole thing. So many emotions welled up inside her. Gratitude. Embarrassment. Concern for him. Affection.

Ember sighed. She was already falling for him...a man she barely knew...despite the fact it would be almost impossible for anything to happen between them.

Hoping to sneak out of his room so she didn't have to deal with her suddenly riotous emotions, Ember shifted until her feet were on the floor. She started to stand—and froze again as Craig's eyes popped open and he stared at her from across the room.

"What time is it?" he asked groggily.

"Early. I'm so sorry I fell asleep in your bed. I'm going to go back to my room, so you can get some decent sleep."

Craig yawned and sat up. He stretched, and Ember heard one of his bones crack. "Sleep okay?" he asked.

Surprised, Ember could only nod. "Yeah. Great, actually."

"Good."

"Why didn't you wake me up? I didn't mean to fall asleep."

"You were *out*. I figured you needed the sleep if you didn't hear me come in. You compete today, and I thought if I woke you up, you'd be embarrassed and it would take you forever to fall back asleep in *your* room, because you'd be thinking too much about how I felt, finding you asleep in my bed. So I decided to let you rest."

Ember opened her mouth to say something, but shut it again because she didn't know how to respond to that. He was right on the money. Hell, she was embarrassed *now*, but if she'd gone back to her room last night, she would've done just as he said. Overthought what had happened.

Craig shifted around until he was sitting and his back was against the wall. He lifted one leg and rested his arm on his knee. Even though he was all the way across the room, sitting in the dark with him felt intimate.

"You excited about today?" he asked.

"Yes and no," Ember said honestly. The darkness, and Craig himself, encouraged her honesty. She knew he wouldn't judge her. "Being an Olympian was always my parents' dream. They pushed me hard when I was a teenager, and even harder after I graduated from high school. They sacrificed a lot for me to have the best coaches and be in the best programs. But I feel as if I've missed so much in the last ten years. My entire existence has been about working out and putting on a show for the outside world. I'm ready to get this over with and move on with my life."

"You aren't going to keep competing for the next Olympics?" Craig asked.

Ember wrinkled her nose. "Lord, no. I know that's what everyone wants me to do, but it's not what I want."

"Then don't."

His response was succinct, but it felt so good to have someone on her side.

"On the other hand, it's finally sunk in that I'm at the Olympics. There are only thirty-five women in the *world* who're here in my sport. I've worked my ass off, even if it *was* with my mom and dad prodding and browbeating me to get here. I'm excited to see what I can do. Am I the best? I don't know. But I'm kinda pumped to find out."

"You're gonna kick ass," Craig said quietly.

"Thanks."

"What time do the bouts start this morning?" he asked.

"Ten. The projected end of the rounds is around four. Of course, there's time between matches for resting and refueling. Nobody fences for six hours straight. There's a lot of administrative stuff and moving people around that happens."

"When do you have your first match?"

"I think around twelve-thirty or so."

"You truly don't mind me watching?"

"Of course not. I'd...I'd like that."

"Great. I'll be there then."

"Craig?"

"Yeah, Em?"

She opened her mouth to speak, but closed it again. Not sure how to articulate what she was thinking.

Craig pushed himself off the floor and approached. He sat on the mattress next to her. He wasn't touching her, but he was damn close. His hair was mussed and sticking up in little bunches on his head and she could see the scruff of a beard on his face. He looked like he'd just rolled out of bed...and it was sexy as hell.

"You impress me," he said.

Ember blinked. "Why?" she blurted.

He smiled, and the white of his teeth seemed bright in the dim light from the bathroom in the otherwise dark room. "You've got an amazingly positive attitude. Other people might be bitter about being pressured into doing something they didn't really want to do. I can't pretend to know anything about your life growing up, but the woman sitting in front of me right now is someone I admire a hell of a lot."

"Thanks," Ember whispered. Most of the time she didn't feel as if she was someone anyone should look up to. She hadn't found a cure for cancer, hadn't done anything noteworthy. She was blessed with good genes and was pretty enough, was lucky enough to be born into a wealthy family so she didn't have to overcome poverty on top of everything else, and her parents had some connections in Hollywood who had helped launch her popularity. But hearing Craig say he was impressed with her felt really good.

"Come on, I'm sure you have stuff you need to do this morning. Stay relaxed, don't let anyone's death stare rattle you, and do what you've trained your entire life to do. Okay?"

"Okay," Ember agreed.

Craig stood and held out his hand. Ember took hold and he pulled her upright. Without conscious thought, Ember stepped into his personal space. She wrapped her arms around him and gave him a long, heartfelt hug. His arms immediately came around her and held her tightly.

They stood like that for a long moment. "I slept really good last night," she told him.

"I'm glad."

"The linens smelled like you." Ember winced as soon as the words were out of her mouth. God, she was an idiot. She felt more than heard him chuckle.

"And now they smell like you. I have a feeling I'm gonna like that a hell of a lot myself."

Ember pulled back, but didn't drop her arms from around him. They stared into each other's eyes. "What's happening here?" she whispered.

"Magic," Craig responded softly. Then he lifted a hand and ran the backs of his fingers down her cheek. He fingered one of her curls briefly, then smiled. "Come on, let's get you back to your room."

Ember nodded and let him take hold of her hand and pull her toward the door. She slipped on the flip-flops she'd taken off the night before by the entrance. Craig walked her all the way down the hall to her room and waited patiently as she put her key card in the slot and pushed the door open.

She heard people stirring in nearby rooms and looked up at Craig.

"Good luck today," he said softly.

"Thanks."

He stared at her for a beat, then quietly muttered, "Fuck it," and leaned down.

Ember was more than ready for this, and she went up on her tiptoes to meet him halfway. Their lips met, and she felt tingles all the way down to her toes.

Ember had been kissed before, but this was different. More intense.

Craig didn't mess around either. His tongue sought entrance to her mouth and she immediately acquiesced, letting him in. She wasn't thinking about morning breath, or that she hadn't tamed her hair, or the fact that she wasn't wearing a bra and was in sweats and a T-shirt. All she could think about was how cherished this man made her feel. He wasn't kissing her for the cameras or because she was famous. They were simply a man and woman who were testing out the sparks that had been flying between them since the moment they'd met.

He pulled back way before she was ready, and Ember

licked her lips, tasting him there. She held onto his biceps and stared up at him, suddenly nervous.

Craig leaned down once more and kissed her forehead before he took a step away from her. Ember shivered as she lost his body heat.

"Kick some ass today, Em. I have faith in you."

She nodded. "I will. Thanks. You be safe too. If any terrorists are around, don't run into a bullet, okay?"

He smirked. "I won't. I'll see you after you compete. Don't leave the dorm today until your escorts get here."

"I won't," she echoed.

"I think Trigger was supposed to tell Nick, Aiden, and Leila that you guys would all be taken over to the venue together, but if you see them, make sure they don't decide to take off on their own."

Ember was impressed that he seemed to be very worried about all their safety. Not just hers...or the athletes of the more popular sports. "Okay."

"It's gonna be fine. Your job is to concentrate on competing. Let me worry about your safety."

Ember nodded again. "Thanks again for letting me steal your bed."

"Anytime."

The word was innocent enough, but it was the look in his eyes that had Ember's heart rate increasing.

Craig took a step back. Then another. As if he couldn't bear to look away from her.

Ember felt giddy. Happy. Excited. And it wasn't because she'd be competing in the Olympic Games today. Not entirely.

"See you later," she said lamely.

Craig smiled. "Later." He gave her a small chin lift, then finally turned and headed for his room once more.

Ember shut her own door and leaned against it and closed

her eyes. Her lips were drawn up in a small smile and she reached up to touch them. She could still feel his lips on her own.

It was insane to start something with the handsome special forces soldier, especially when they lived in different states and had such different lives. But she couldn't deny they had a connection.

Smiling, she headed for the bathroom. She had a long day in front of her. Competing, more pictures to take for social media, a few interviews...but at the end of the day, she'd get to spend more time with Craig. It was surprising to admit she was looking forward to seeing him almost more than competing.

CHAPTER SIX

Doc was pretty lost when it came to understanding what was going on during the fencing round-robins, but it was fascinating all the same. Once he figured out which one of the competitors was Ember—they were all covered head to toe in the same kind of outfit, including a mask that protected the face and head—he couldn't take his eyes off her.

She was magnificent. And he wasn't just saying that because he was falling hard and fast for the woman. She was graceful and athletic. He learned that she liked to make the first move when facing her opponent, not waiting on them to try to score. Sometimes her aggressiveness paid off and other times it didn't, but to his untrained eye, she was more than holding her own.

There were long periods of time between matches and many of the spectators looked bored, but Doc took that time to examine everyone around him. He was constantly on the watch for anyone or anything that might want to disrupt the competition. He hadn't been happy with the security, or lack of it, for spectators. The workers barely glanced inside bags and purses people carried in with them, and he wasn't sure the metal detector was even working. He'd shown his credentials that gave him permission to carry his weapons. After a cursory glance, the security team waved him in without bothering to ask for more information about who he was and what he might be carrying.

It wasn't hard to spot Ember's entourage. Her parents were sitting in the front row and there were several people with them who were holding high-tech cameras. A man sat next to her mother and barely looked up at the action in front of him. His head was bent over his phone the entire time. Doc remembered Ember telling him about the full-time managers for her social media accounts, and he would bet this man was one of them. He was probably posting pictures of Ember competing and stirring up as much interest as he could.

After the competition was over, Ember had finished in tenth place. He had no idea if she was going to be happy with that or not, but he was damn proud of her. Doc had access to the behind-the-scenes areas of the arena because of his credentials, but he didn't want to interfere in anything Ember had going on. He'd told her he'd meet her by the athlete exit after she'd spoken to her parents and done whatever else needed to be done to get ready for the next day's competition.

He knew tomorrow was going to be even longer for her than today. And much more intense. She had another round of fencing, then horse jumping and swimming the two hundred meters. Then the culmination event in the afternoon of running and shooting.

It was two hours after the competition had ended when Doc finally saw Ember coming toward him. She looked exhausted, but she was smiling.

"Hey," he said when she got near.

"Hi. I'm so sorry I took so long," she said, her words

jumbled together as if she couldn't apologize fast enough. "My parents set up a digital interview with Oprah that I couldn't get out of. Then I had to pose for more pictures and they'd set up a mini meet-and-greet with some fans and supporters. Samer wanted more pictures and Sergei—that's my fencing coach—wanted me to review some of my bouts so I'd be ready for tomorrow."

"Em, take a breath. It's fine."

She closed her eyes for a second and let out a long breath. Then she looked up at him. "So? What'd you think?"

"I think you're amazing. Tenth place. That's good, right?"

She beamed. "Yeah. Really good. I won't have to participate in as many rounds tomorrow in fencing, which will help since the day will be so long. And the extra points will also help, as I'm not as strong in the horse jumping portion. I should hold my own in swimming. So if all goes well tomorrow, I'm hoping to start in the upper third of the pack for the run and shooting." Her voice lowered. "I might just have a chance to medal, Craig."

He couldn't help it, he loved the excitement and pride in her tone. He reached for her and hugged her tight. She returned the embrace and nothing felt better. "I'm proud of you, Em. You hungry?"

"Starving," she said, pulling back.

Doc reached for her bag and threw it over his shoulder.

"I can carry that."

"I know. But now you don't have to," he said easily.

Ember linked her arm in his and rested her head against his shoulder for a split second. Then she straightened and said, "Thanks for being here."

"I wouldn't have missed it. I saw your parents."

She wrinkled her nose.

"I can see where you got your good looks," Doc told her.

"Thanks."

"And that's quite the entourage with them. I understand why you wanted to stay in the dorm."

Ember chuckled. "Yeah. Between my three coaches, Samer and Alexis—who's another one of my social media managers, and who I didn't realize was coming—it's a lot. They all mean well, but the constant picture-taking and talking about what will make the biggest impact on social media gets to be a bit much."

"I bet. But it seems as if most of your twenty-five million followers are happy for how well you did today."

She looked up at him. "You have Instagram?"

"Well...I may or may not have created an account with a fake name so I could check you out."

She laughed. "Thank you? I think."

"Do you ever get worried about some of those crazy people who comment on your posts? Some of them seem...unbalanced."

"I'm sure they are. I don't worry too much about it. I mean, I can't. There are lots of people who hate me because of my looks. Others because they think I have a perfect life. Others because they don't like that I'm a good athlete. And still others because they don't like red, and I wore a red shirt once. I can't let myself get bogged down with that stuff. I rarely read the comments anymore. I used to all the time, but it got me in such a funk, I had to stop.

"I read some of the letters that people send. Someone who doesn't like me is a lot less inclined to go through the trouble of writing that hate on paper and sending it through the mail. But online? People are way too mean. They don't think twice about saying they wish I would die, or telling me how much they hate me...when they wouldn't dare say something like that to my face. It's difficult, because social media literally earned me enough money that I don't have to worry about anything for the rest of my life, but it also feels like such a scourge on society. To say I have mixed feelings about it is putting it lightly."

"How about if we don't think about it for the rest of the night. I need to get you back to the dorm so you can eat, then rest. You have a big day in front of you tomorrow," Doc told her.

They headed out a back door of the competition venue, thereby avoiding most of the crowds hanging around hoping for a glimpse of a famous athlete. There were shuttles taking athletes back and forth to the Olympic Village, but because of the interviews and pictures she'd done, they'd missed the last one.

It was late enough that the sun was no longer beating down, but not so late that it was dark outside. They had to walk about a half mile to reach the entrance to the Olympic Village, and from there they could catch a shuttle to the building where they were staying. Most of the shops in this part of the city were full of Olympic souvenirs and everyone they passed seemed to be in good spirits.

Doc was aware that they didn't exactly blend in. He was taller than most of the locals and Ember was...Ember. She was beautiful. The crowd around them was a mix of tourists and locals, giving the area a very international flair.

Feeling good about their safety, Doc was enjoying simply being with Ember, who was still basking in the glow of a successful competition, when his phone rang. Seeing it was Trigger, he immediately answered.

"What's up?"

"Where are you?" his team leader asked without preamble.

"About half a klick from the entrance to the village. Why?"

"Trouble's brewing outside the gates," Trigger told him.

"What kind?" Doc asked, taking hold of Ember's arm to stop her.

"You know those protestors who've been camped outside various venues since we arrived? Well, things are turning ugly. Now there's a big crowd outside the Olympic Village, and some protesters are trying to force their way inside. Everyone's being locked down as we speak, but there are still way too many athletes making their way back here after competing today."

"Shit. I hate when we're right. The security should definitely be tighter than it is. We'll step up the pace and after I get Ember safely in the dorm, I'll head back out to help."

"Be careful, Doc. If you can't get in safely, find somewhere to hole up."

"Will do. Keep in touch," Doc told Trigger.

"Of course. Let me know when you're in."

"Ten-four." Doc clicked off the phone and put it back in his pocket.

"What's wrong?"

"Hopefully nothing," Doc told her. "But it looks like our slow stroll back to the dorm has been changed to a power walk. You okay with that?"

"Of course. But what's wrong?" she asked again.

"Protestors outside the village are getting restless. Trigger's afraid things might turn violent. Stay by my side—*right* by my side."

Her eyes got big, and she nodded.

Doc hated to scare her, but he wasn't going to take any chances with her life. They could go around to the smaller west entrance to the village, but there was no guarantee the protestors hadn't gathered there too. And it would take twice as long to get there. He wanted to get Ember to the dorm and inside where she'd be safe. Then he'd find his team to see how they could help mitigate the situation.

They began to walk quickly toward the Olympic Village, but he knew before he could even see the large courtyard outside the entrance that they were too late. People were running past them in the opposite direction. Shop owners slammed and locked their doors.

"Fuck," Doc muttered. His phone rang, but he couldn't stop to answer it right now. He was more concerned about Ember's safety. He shifted her backpack so it was on both his shoulders, freeing up his hands. He grasped Ember's hand and felt her tighten her fingers. She didn't speak, clearly understanding the gravity of the situation.

Doc moved forward cautiously, not wanting to burst into the middle of a situation he didn't have all the facts about.

"Boot the oppressors!" someone shouted from nearby.

"Open the gates!" another voice yelled.

The volume got louder and louder as more people joined in the chanting. Then suddenly there were more people running *toward* the protest—and the gates leading into the Olympic Village—than there were running away.

Doc and Ember were swept up in the chaos and herded into the middle of the protest.

"Don't let go of me!" he yelled, raising his voice to be heard above the chanting.

Ember nodded, and he felt her fingers tighten around his hand yet again.

Doc couldn't risk pulling out his firearm in this crowd. So far the protesters weren't being violent, but he knew it could only be a matter of time before things changed. It looked as if there were more than a few people who were doing their best to incite the crowd, stirring it up and encouraging everyone to get more and more vocal.

"Communism equals oppression!"

"Free Hong Kong!"

"Absolute power corrupts!"

"Commies shouldn't be allowed to participate!"

Doc wasn't sure exactly what the people were protesting. It sounded like various things, including the fact that athletes from alleged communist countries were allowed to participate in the Olympics.

At the moment, however, it didn't really matter. The crowd was riled up and the peaceful protest had evolved into something more dangerous. He and Ember stood out in the crowd—Doc because he was tall and white, Ember because she was a celebrity of sorts. Most of the people around them were Asian. Doc had no idea if they were all locals, or if there were any terrorists mingling with the crowd.

Someone pushed him, and Doc did his best to keep his feet. Then they were being jostled by everyone around them.

Doc's entire objective was focused on getting him and Ember out of this mob. He desperately looked around, trying to find an escape route. He wouldn't hesitate to hurt anyone who dared put their hands on the woman by his side.

He wrapped his arm around Ember's waist, anchoring her close as the shoving continued from all sides. Things were getting uglier by the second, and he needed to get them out of there. Now.

Then, for a split second, Doc's gaze caught that of a man standing almost in the very middle of the crowd. He was holding a backpack in his arms...and he smiled. A cold, evil smile.

And just like that, Doc knew the protests had been a cover for what he and his team had feared all along. An organized terroristic attack.

"No!" Doc yelled—but it was too late.

The man detonated the bomb he'd been carrying in the backpack.

The explosion ripped through the people standing near the bomber, instantly killing at least a dozen men and women. Doc dropped to the ground, practically on top of Ember.

The shouts turned into screams as people realized what had happened.

Just as everyone began to run in the opposite direction from where the bomb had gone off, another explosion sounded on the outskirts of the crowd.

If Doc thought things were chaotic before, they were absolutely frenzied now. No one knew which way to run to safety as a third explosion blasted through the panicked crowd closer to the gates leading into the Olympic Village.

Doc wasn't about to wait for a fourth bomb to go off. He stood and grabbed hold of Ember's arm, hauling her up next to him without trying to be gentle. His only thought was to get them the hell away from the danger.

Weaving in and out of the stunned crowd, pushing past people still standing in place with signs and looks of horror on their faces, he towed Ember behind him, toward where the second bomb had exploded. Instinct told him if there were more terrorists with explosives, they'd set them off in areas that hadn't been bombed yet.

The carnage around them was immense, and Doc felt sick inside for all the people moaning and crying on the ground. It was going to take a very long time to get everyone who needed medical help to the hospital. Ember hadn't made a sound throughout the chaos, which Doc appreciated. He wouldn't have blamed her if she had, but his respect for her was rising with every second that passed. She was keeping her head and not freaking out.

A loud rumbling made Doc turn his head...

A white van was barreling down one of the roads that led into the courtyard. Two people were run over, and still the van didn't stop.

It looked like it was headed straight for the gate to the Olympic Village.

If it rammed it, and created an entrance point for terrorists to get inside, there was no telling how many more people would get injured or killed. If a terroristic organization wanted to start an international incident and get publicity for their cause, hurting and killing athletes from around the world was a good way to get it.

That wasn't happening. Not on Doc's watch. They'd already killed too many people; he wasn't going to let them get inside the gates to kill more.

The van wasn't slowing, and he knew it would reach the gates before extra security could arrive. He had to do something. *Now.*

Stopping in the middle of an open space, Doc went down on one knee and reached for his weapon. He wished he had his rifle right about now. The range was longer. But he'd use what he had.

"Do you have another?"

The question came from Ember. She was crouched next to him.

In any other circumstance, Doc would say no, that he didn't need help. That he didn't want to get a civilian involved. But this wasn't just any civilian. She was a pentathlete. Shooting was one of her best skills.

Without a word, he pulled his second pistol out of his ankle holster. She grabbed it expertly and flicked off the safety.

Nodding at her, Doc turned his attention back to the rapidly approaching van. He narrowed his focus on the driver. He could shoot the tires, but that wouldn't necessarily stop the vehicle. He had to take out the driver. Get him to take his foot off the gas. Stop him from getting to the gate.

He just had to wait until the van was a bit closer.

The driver caught and held his gaze. They were playing a game of chicken, and the terrorist thought he was going to win.

He was wrong.

Doc waited until the last second—then he unloaded his clip. One shot after another. Desperate to stop the van.

He vaguely heard shots above his head, and realized that Ember stood behind him and was shooting as well. He wanted to tell her to get the fuck down but didn't have time.

Seconds ticked by, every one seemingly in slow motion.

He knew he'd struck the driver. Or maybe Ember had. Either way, the man was most certainly dead. But the van hadn't stopped. The man's foot hadn't fallen off the gas pedal.

The vehicle was yards away, headed right for them. There wasn't enough time to get out of the way.

But Doc had to try.

He turned and wrapped his arms around Ember's thighs in the same moment he literally threw them to the side.

The vehicle passed so close to them that for a split second, Doc thought they'd been run over and just couldn't feel it yet. But by some miracle, he'd managed to get them out of the path of the van. By the time it hit the entrance gates to the Olympic Village, it had lost enough velocity that it didn't break through...barely.

Doc knew the danger wasn't over. If there were explosives inside the vehicle, all hell was about to break loose.

He forced himself up off the concrete and, once more, pulled Ember up with a strong grip on her arm. He had no idea where either of his pistols were, but at the moment, he was more concerned about getting them both the fuck out of there.

Doc practically carried Ember out of the carnage. He didn't know where he was going, just knew he needed to get away.

Movement caught his eye. A slight Korean woman was waving at him frantically from a shop at the edge of the plaza. Doc made a beeline for her and the second he cleared the door, she slammed it shut behind them.

"Kamsahamnida," he said, thanking her in Korean.

She said something back, but Doc was already turning toward Ember.

"Are you okay? Are you hurt? Shit, talk to me, Em!"

"I'm good," she said in a shaky voice.

"Fuck," Doc muttered. Then said it again. He was having a hard time wrapping his mind around what the hell had just happened.

His phone rang, and he only now realized it had been ringing nonstop since the shit hit the fan.

With a trembling hand, he pulled it out of his pocket and held it up to his ear.

"Yeah?"

"Holy fucking shit! Doc? Are you all right? Where are you? Is Ember all right?"

Taking a deep breath, Doc couldn't help but grin. The unflappable Trigger was definitely rattled. It didn't happen a lot.

"We're okay," Doc said, taking a second look at the woman standing next to him. Her eyes were wide in her face and he could see her pulse hammering in her neck. She was holding her left arm close to her side, supporting it with her right. He frowned.

"All right. We're stuck on this side of the gate," Trigger said. "We're holding steady here in case they get through so we can take them out and protect the athletes."

"We're okay where we are for now. A lady let us take refuge in her shop."

"Thank fuck. For the record, man...Ember is *badass*. We couldn't see everything that went down, but since you weren't answering your phone we figured you were in the middle of that shit. We saw that van coming toward the gate and knew that must've been their objective the entire time. Then suddenly through the smoke, we see you kneeling and aiming for the driver—and Ember fucking standing behind you, arm outstretched, firing that damn pistol as if she was in the middle of her pentathlon competition! Seriously, man. Damn! It was impressive."

Doc wasn't surprised. He had a feeling Ember could do anything she set her mind to. But at the moment, something was wrong with her arm, and he needed to find out what it was. "We're all right. We're going to keep our heads down for now. When it's clear, will you let me know?"

"Ten-four. Doc?"

"Yeah?"

"Glad you're all right."

"This might not be over yet. Those assholes might have more bombs or cars. Stay alert," Doc said.

"Will do. The South Koreans look like they're getting things under control. It'll take a while to help all the wounded. Just stay holed up and I'll be in touch."

"Later."

"Later."

The second Doc clicked off the phone, he reached for Ember. "What's wrong with your arm?"

She flinched as he touched her left biceps. "I'm okay."

"You aren't. What's wrong? Were you hit?" Doc hadn't even thought about that. He didn't see any blood on her arm, but that didn't mean there wasn't a wound under her shirt or something.

"No. You protected me when that bomb went off. I wasn't hit."

"But...?" Doc asked.

She sighed and her brown eyes met his. He could see pain there. "I think my shoulder's dislocated."

Doc stared at her blankly for a second. Then the ramifications of what he'd done hit him like a ten-pound brick. "Fuck," he swore. "I hurt you!"

"You didn't mean to," she said softly.

That didn't make him feel any better.

"I injured my shoulder falling off a horse when I was a teenager. It never really healed properly and has a tendency to pop out every now and then," she said quickly.

"It came out when I jerked you up, didn't it?" he asked.

Ember nodded, but then said, "It's not your fault, Craig. Seriously."

"The hell it's not," he said, distraught.

"It's my left arm. It's fine," she said. "Good thing I'm a right-handed shooter, isn't it?"

Shit. He hadn't even been thinking about her having to compete tomorrow. He'd been more upset that he'd hurt her at all—but knowing he might've fucked up her chance to medal? He felt like complete dog shit. He couldn't believe he'd jerked her off the ground so hard he'd actually pulled her arm out of socket.

"Craig," Ember said gently, putting her hand on his cheek. "It's okay. You saved my life. That's way more important than anything else."

Ember stood next to Craig with her hand on his cheek and did her best to comfort him. Her shoulder throbbed, but she had so much adrenaline coursing through her veins that she barely even felt it.

This man had saved her life. She knew that as well as she knew her name. Not only that, but he hadn't hesitated to give her a pistol. He'd trusted her enough to help him. In that moment, she wasn't a pampered social media influencer. She was his *partner*.

She'd been scared to death when the explosions started going off, and when that van had been barreling toward them, but she'd used everything she'd learned over the years to hold her hand steady and block out the chaos as she aimed at the driver.

She'd known the second Craig had dislocated her shoulder. It was when he'd jerked her up after that first explosion, to try to get them out of the line of fire.

He shook his head and closed his eyes. "I'm sorry, Em. I'm so fucking sorry."

She pressed her lips together in frustration, a trickle of anger seeping in. "Sorry for what? For getting me out of there? For protecting me? For trusting me to have your back? What exactly are you sorry for?"

His eyes opened, and he stared at her for a long moment. "You got hurt because of me," he finally said.

"I would've been dead *without* you," she said.

"You don't know that."

Ember shrugged one shoulder. "I know that I was a hell of a lot better off with you than without you. Are you going to help me put it back or what?" Craig blanched, and she couldn't help but chuckle. "I know you've seen and dealt with injuries a lot worse than a dislocated shoulder before."

"But they weren't you," Craig said softly.

"I need you. I can't do this by myself," she told him.

That seemed to do the trick. He stood straighter and nodded. The shop they'd taken refuge in was a deli of some sort. The tables around them would be perfect for what she needed. Craig seemed to know exactly how to help her. He moved the chairs away from one side of the nearest table and gestured for her to lie down.

Craig shrugged out of her backpack and headed for the kitchen. The older Korean woman didn't try to stop him. She was just watching them curiously.

Ember was glad Craig wasn't there to watch her get situated. She grimaced as pain shot through her shoulder when she let her left arm dangle off the side of the table. She did her best to relax her muscles, knowing this would be a lot easier if she wasn't tense.

Craig returned with a large bottle of oil.

Ember would've laughed if she didn't know how much the next few minutes were going to hurt.

Sitting down, Craig untied his boot and used the lace to tie the bottle to her arm. The weight of the oil and gravity would be just enough to reposition the ball of her arm bone toward the socket. It should just pop back in.

"You've done this before," she said quietly.

Craig nodded. "Ready?" he asked as he knelt by her side holding the bottle so it didn't put pressure on her arm until she was prepared.

Ember took a deep breath and closed her eyes. "Yeah. Do it."

Ever so slowly, Craig let go of the bottle and gently applied a steady downward pressure to her arm. His actions, along with the weight of the oil, achieved what they were supposed to. It didn't take more than half a minute for her shoulder to cooperate and pop back where it belonged.

Sighing in relief at the immediate release of pressure and the lessening of pain, Ember opened her eyes, only to find Craig's gaze boring into her own.

"Are you going to be able to compete tomorrow?" he asked. She could hear the agony and concern in his voice.

"Yes," she said without hesitation.

"You haven't even tried to move it to see how much it hurts."

"Craig, I'm a professional athlete. This isn't the first time my shoulder's been knocked out of its socket and it won't be the last. I'll take some painkillers and it'll be fine. Wait, do you think they'll continue on with the competitions after what happened?"

"Yeah. No one wants to let the terrorists know they got to them. I'm pretty sure things will go on as planned."

"I hope there weren't any athletes killed," Ember said softly. "I mean, I hate that *anyone* was hurt or killed, but the idea that someone who'd just wanted to compete for their country may have died makes me really sad."

"I know," Craig said.

She could see the sorrow in his own eyes. She had a feeling he was still thinking about her shoulder and the fact that he'd hurt her. She hadn't lied, she'd be able to compete tomorrow...but it was going to hurt like a bitch, especially the swim. Because she was right-handed, she'd be all right with the fencing and shooting. The horse jumping would be a crapshoot, but there was no getting away from the fact that she had to use her left arm to swim. And she couldn't take any hardcore pain meds because of the strict rules about that sort of thing and the drug test she was required to take after finishing competing.

Ember would internalize any and all pain just so this man didn't beat himself up anymore. She truly believed he'd saved her life, and she'd take a dislocated shoulder over death any day.

After ten minutes or so, Ember sat up and the Korean woman made a sling out of a couple fabric napkins. Both she and Craig thanked her once again, and she didn't miss it when Craig took out all the South Korean won he had in his wallet and left it under a book on the checkout counter.

They stayed hunkered down in the small café for twenty more minutes, until Trigger called and told them things had been secured and that it was safe for them to make their way to the gates of the Olympic Village. When they headed back outside, it almost felt as if they were in a different world. Craig grabbed a baseball hat that was lying forlornly on the ground and put it on her head, pulling it low over her brow. "The last thing we need is a picture of you with that sling on to show up on social media," he mumbled.

Ember wasn't sure a hat was going to make her incognito, but she didn't say anything. There were a few people standing around looking shellshocked, but for the most part the area had been cleared. It was dusk now, and it wouldn't be long before darkness fell.

Before Ember knew it, they'd made it past security and Lefty, Brain, and Trigger were meeting them in a golf cart. Each of the men gave her a long, careful hug, telling her how relieved they were that she was all right. Trigger also mentioned how impressed he was with her shooting and wouldn't stop calling her a badass.

Craig helped her into the back seat, and she was soon sandwiched between his large body and Trigger's. She was surrounded and felt completely safe as they headed to the dorm without speaking.

Upon arriving, as Brain drove off to who knows where, Trigger, Lefty, and Craig escorted her up to their floor. The men on the water polo team were gathered in the multipurpose room, talking about what had happened, but Craig hustled her past without stopping when the athletes spotted them and tried to ask questions. Trigger stayed behind to talk to them, to reassure them that the danger had passed.

Ember was relieved she didn't run into Leila, Nick, or Aiden. She didn't want their sympathy...or morbid curiosity over what had happened.

She wasn't surprised when Craig walked her to her room, then entered behind her.

"Do you need help in the shower?" he asked.

Ember's eyes snapped up to his in surprise. But he obviously wasn't trying to make a move on her, he was genuinely concerned for her health. "I'll be okay," she told him.

"Are you sure?"

"Yeah."

"Okay. I'll be out here when you're done. Do you have a tank top? That might be the easiest thing to put on for tonight."

Ember stared at him for a moment, then nodded. "Yeah, I've got one."

"Where is it? I'll get it for you."

Ember told him, then watched in bemusement as Craig went through the rest of her drawers and pulled out a pair of underwear and shorts, as well. She should've been angry about the way he was pawing through her personal stuff, but it felt kind of good to be looked after.

He went into the small bathroom and put the stack of clothes on the counter. Then he turned to her. "What else can I do?"

"Stay?" The request popped out before she could think better of it. As soon as the word left her mouth, Ember cringed. He'd already said he'd be there when she was done.

"Of course," he replied. "While you're showering, I'm going to go change myself. I'll be back in five minutes. If you need help, just hang tight and I'll be right back. Don't hurt yourself more."

It was obvious it was going to be a while before Craig forgave himself for what had happened. Ember stepped toward him until they were plastered together from head to toe. She rested her forehead against him and sighed in contentment when he wrapped his arms around her carefully.

They stood there for a few minutes, not talking, just existing in the same space.

"I'm okay, Craig. Promise. And if I'm being honest, I'm pretty damn proud of myself. I don't know whose bullet hit that driver, but doing my part to protect others is so much better than getting first place or winning a damn medal. Maybe I was put on this earth to be a pentathlete just so I could learn to shoot, so I'd be exactly where I was tonight. I don't know. But no matter what happens tomorrow, I don't regret meeting you, being with you, or anything that happened today." She looked up into his eyes. "Okay?"

"Put *that* way, how can I be anything but okay?" he asked.

"You can't," she said with a small smile. "Now, go change. And maybe shower too. I don't want to smell smoke for a very long time."

"Yes, ma'am. For the record? Trigger's right. You *are* badass." Craig kissed her softly, then headed for the door.

Ember stood where she was for several heartbeats, smiling, before heading for the small bathroom.

CHAPTER SEVEN

Doc sat next to Grover in the bleachers and studied Ember. He hadn't been able to watch her compete in her other events today, but there was no way he was going to miss the laser-run. It was the last event for the day...and his heart hurt for her. Looking at the starting lineup of the athletes for this event made it clear Ember hadn't had a good day. She was starting in twenty-ninth place. Sixth place from last.

He felt horrible. He knew, no matter how much she'd tried to downplay her injury, that he'd been the one to derail her Olympic dreams. He hadn't meant to haul her around as roughly as he obviously had, but at the time, he was more interested in getting her to safety than being gentle.

"I'm impressed she was even able to swim at all," Grover said quietly.

Doc nodded. He'd thought about that too. The horse jumping probably didn't feel great on her shoulder, same with the fencing, but she could've muddled through those events all right. But swimming? Yeah, that had to have hurt like hell. And it was obvious she'd struggled, if her current starting position was any indication.

"Trigger called me right before we met up and updated me about the shit that went down last night."

"Yeah?" Doc said distractedly.

"The Japanese Red Army has already claimed responsibility."

Doc sighed. The JRA had been highly active in the early seventies but was currently making a comeback. He knew they were a community militant group whose goal was to overthrow the Japanese government and the monarchy. They also wanted to start a world revolution, which made their attack on the Olympics make much more sense.

Grover went on. "A few weeks ago, a man with apparent ties to the Red Army was arrested in Japan, and he had documents on his computer detailing plans to disrupt the Olympics."

That got Doc's attention. "Are you shitting me? How come we weren't informed?"

"I guess the powers that be in Seoul either didn't take the threat seriously, or they didn't want to risk anyone pulling out of the Games or have their ticket sales tank."

Doc could only shake his head at the idiocy of that decision.

Grover went on. "Trigger also said that by some miracle, there were only two people killed in the explosions, not including the terrorists. But if that van had managed to break through the gate, the authorities think there may have been as many as two dozen Japanese Red Army sympathizers ready to storm through behind it and kill as many people as they could."

"How come they didn't start shooting when the bombs went off? Or try to take out me and Ember?" Doc asked.

Grover shrugged. "No clue. Maybe they were told to wait and conserve their ammunition until they were inside the gates so they could take out athletes, instead of wasting the bullets on civilians?"

Doc growled. "Fuckers. Where are these sympathizers now?" Doc asked, glancing at Grover.

"When they saw the van wasn't able to break the gate, we assume they bolted. They're probably back in whatever holes they'd crawled out of."

"So we should expect more trouble?"

"Trigger and the others don't think so. They think this was their big plan, something they'd spent months organizing. At least now the security will be much tighter. Better late than never I suppose. The South Korean police and military have shut down all traffic within half a mile of every venue and the Olympic Village itself. And no one is allowed into the athletic venues without going through two metal detectors. The last thing the government wants is an athlete being assassinated on their watch."

Doc nodded. All that was good and he was relieved. But he was still upset for Ember's sake. There was no doubt he'd been in the right place at the right time, but he hated that she'd gotten hurt in the process. She'd sacrificed so much over the years to be here, and because of him, she'd been in the thick of things last night.

"Trigger and the others are monitoring the internet for videos of what happened, and luckily most of them are from quite a distance. You aren't recognized at all."

"Good. What about Ember?"

"With the shitty videos, she should be in the clear too."

Doc breathed out a sigh of relief. He'd been worried about that.

"Also," Grover went on, his voice lowering, "you might be interested to know that the medical examiner finished his autopsy of the driver of the van. He was killed by a bullet to the head."

Doc nodded, not surprised.

"You gave Ember your backup pistol, right?" Grover asked. "The one without the hollow-point bullets?"

Doc nodded. "Yeah. Why?"

"It was *her* bullet that took him out," Grover said quietly. "He had plenty of your bullets in him too, but the one that stopped him—dead center of the forehead—wasn't yours."

Doc stared intently at his teammate. "No one tells her that. *Ever*. The last thing she needs on her conscience is the knowledge that she killed a man. Even if it was someone hell-bent on murdering innocent people. Understand?"

Grover nodded solemnly. "Trigger figured you'd feel that way. He's already taking care of the report on our side so it doesn't accidentally get out."

"He's changing the report?" Doc asked in surprise.

"Only about which gun had the hollow-point bullets," Grover said.

Doc was surprised. Their team leader was a stickler for the rules and sticking to the facts in his reports. Saying it was always better to be honest than to try to sweep anything under the rug. He owed him for this. Big time.

"With South Korea flooding the Olympic grounds with more of their military, we're also being sent home a bit early."

"How early?" Doc asked, not happy about that news at all.

"Just a couple days. We leave in four more days instead of six."

Doc nodded. He knew from talking with Ember that she'd be heading home the day after tomorrow anyway, so he wouldn't miss much time with her. The fact that she was his biggest concern said a lot.

"So...Devyn's been getting my mail while I've been gone," Grover said.

Confused about his friend's odd change of topic, Doc said, "Yeah?"

"Yeah. She said I got a letter. From Sierra."

"The contractor from Afghanistan? That's great! We thought she may've been kidnapped. If she wrote you, she's obviously okay."

"It was post-marked almost a year ago," Grover continued in a flat tone.

Doc wasn't sure what to say that. "Wow. That was around the time you last saw her, right?"

"Yeah. I didn't ask my sister to open it, but I can't stop thinking about it. We both know the mail from overseas isn't reliable, so it's possible it got lost in the system."

"For a year?" Doc asked skeptically.

"Yeah, I know, it seems unlikely. But for the sake of argument, let's just say it was lost in some overwhelmed or disorganized foreign mail service. Then someone found it and sent it along...I can't stop thinking about what she might've said. Maybe whatever's in that letter explains why no one has heard from her in so long."

Doc nodded. Grover had been increasingly concerned about the woman he'd met in the chow hall when they'd been in Afghanistan a year ago. Even with a somewhat rocky start, they'd agreed to keep in touch. Grover had emailed her but never heard back...and the entire team knew how much it had bothered their friend. Even more worrisome were the reports of contractors allegedly being kidnapped by Shahzada, the worst terrorist the area had seen in over a decade. He was ruthless and very vocal in his hatred for Westerners. He'd been gaining more and more power since their last mission in Afghanistan, and it was obvious he'd have to be dealt with sooner rather than later.

"We'll be home soon and you can read it and see what's up with her yourself," Doc said, trying to reassure his friend.

Grover nodded. "You know, a lot has changed for our team recently, and at first I was kinda upset about it. Afraid it would change the dynamic between us. But I couldn't be happier for the others. And you."

"Me?" Doc asked.

Grover chuckled. "Yeah, you. Look at us, man. We're sitting in a half-empty stadium watching the modern pentathlon instead of attending the basketball game. Before we got here, we hadn't even heard of this event."

Doc chuckled. His friend had a point.

"For the record, we all really like Ember. It's a given *you'd* be focused when that van was barreling toward you...but she was pretty fucking impressive, standing behind you, her legs apart, arm outstretched, completely focused on the van. I know you've mentioned wanting to find a woman who's happy to fade into the background with you. Someone content to hang out at home and live the quiet life. But that's not what you need. You need someone who will force you out of your comfort zone. Who will challenge you, make you laugh, and drive you crazy at the same time."

"And...what? You think Ember is that woman? Grover, she lives in Beverly Hills. Has more money than I could ever imagine having. She's practically internet royalty. Besides, we've only known each other for a few days."

"You know as well as I do that sometimes that's all it takes. You've seen it firsthand with our friends. When you click with someone, you click. And you and Ember have definitely clicked. I know I'm probably the worst one of our team to give you advice, since I'm still single, but don't let her slip out of your grasp, Doc. She needs you as much as you need her. Do you honestly think she's happy living in her gilded cage?"

Doc pressed his lips together and shook his head. He knew she wasn't. She'd said as much. But he still couldn't imagine Ember living in Killeen, Texas. She would stick out like a sore thumb. Not because of the color of her skin, but because once she got out from under her parents' control, she was going to shine brighter than she'd ever gotten the chance to before.

"I think about Sierra every damn day. I wonder where she is and if she's okay," Grover said. "I worry that she's been killed and I'll never get the chance to really get to know her. I have regrets, Doc, and I don't want you to experience that."

Doc really *looked* at his friend. The team had known Grover was interested in the contractor, but none of them had realized just *how* deep that interest ran. "Have you told Trigger about the letter you got from her?"

"No. But, depending on what it says, I'm planning on it. She's in trouble," Grover said in a low tone. "And more than other contractors disappearing and the unanswered emails, I feel it in my gut. But I can't just run off to Afghanistan and start looking under rocks. We need a reason to go over there. It's wrong, but...part of me can't help but hope Shahzada does something stupid, just so we get deployed and I can try to find her. Hell, maybe she married a local and is living a quiet life devoid of modern conveniences like the internet. But then again, maybe she's been a captive of Shahzada all this time. Or maybe she's dead. I need to know one way or another, Doc."

Doc reached up and clapped his friend on the back. He couldn't find the right words to comfort him, but he didn't need them. Grover knew he cared.

He turned and looked Doc in the eye. "If what you've told us about Ember's parents is true, about how intense and controlling they are, and how nasty some of her followers can be, she's gonna need all the support she can get," Grover said.

Doc nodded. "I peeked at her IG account after we sat down, and her damn social media manager posted a picture of her sitting on the side of the pool with her head down, looking miserable, with a caption that said, '*That* didn't go as

I'd planned.' Who *does* that? And of course that opened the floodgates for the nasty comments. God, I really hate people, Grover."

"I know," he agreed readily. "I'm sure Gillian, Kinley, Aspen, Riley, and Devyn would have her back though."

Doc couldn't help but chuckle. "Oh, *that* was subtle. Not."

"Just sayin', man. Ember could use some friends who'll stand by her no matter if she gets first place or last. Who like her because of who she is, not what she can do for them. And the women in our circle...that's who they are."

"She needs unconditional support more than anyone I've ever met," Doc said. "I don't know how she's gone this long without it."

An announcer came over the loudspeaker, introducing the beginning of the event, ending Doc and Grover's conversation.

Doc scanned the field before focusing back on Ember at the back of the pack. He remembered her explaining their placement for starting the run was determined by the points they'd earned in the other events. She was definitely starting with a significant handicap. He knew this was her best event, and luckily she shot right-handed, but her shoulder still had to hurt and it would have an effect on her run.

"Come on, Em, you can do this," he muttered.

Then the competitors were off.

Doc kept his eyes on Ember. She fidgeted as other women sprinted toward the shooting station. She had to wait until it was her turn, which had to be nerve-wracking.

When it was finally her turn, she took off for the shooting platform quickly. She looked good, strong. Doc narrowed his eyes as she lined up her first shots. She had to hit five targets, "reloading" after each shot. She'd shoot as many times as necessary to hit the targets, but obviously if she kept missing, it would take longer before she could continue.

It seemed to Doc that she hit her shots very quickly.

"That's it. Keep going," he said.

She looked strong on the first eight hundred meter run as she circled the course, making her way back to the shooting platform. He knew from talking to her that in this competition, whoever crossed the finish line first was the winner. Ember was pretty far back in the pack still, but they all had a ways to go.

It looked like she missed a few shots on the second round of shooting. "Steady, Em. Concentrate on your own target, block everyone else out."

She was passing people pretty regularly, but there were still quite a few competitors ahead of her. It was obvious she wasn't going to be able to catch up to the leaders, but Doc couldn't help but be proud of her regardless.

On the last round of shooting, Ember hit all five of her targets without missing once.

"Damn, she's good. No wonder she outshot you," Grover commented.

Doc didn't even mind the ribbing. Ember *was* an excellent shot.

The cheering in the stands rose to a roar when the first woman crossed the finish line. Then the second. And the third. Leila crossed the finish line in tenth place, and Ember wasn't too far behind her at fifteenth.

Doc was proud as could be. Yeah, it wasn't the finish he knew she wanted, but she'd literally passed ten people in this last event. Ten people who'd had head starts on her. He kept his eyes on her as she smiled and waved at the crowd. Then she headed for Leila and his heart almost burst with pride as she engulfed her teammate in a heartfelt hug. Her smile for her friend was big and it was obvious she was happy for her.

Doc lost sight of Ember as she disappeared into a crowd of participants and coaches along the side of the track.

"You gonna go down and meet her?" Grover asked.

Doc shook his head. "Not yet. After the medal ceremony."

"You think she'll stay for it?"

"Oh, yeah. She might be disappointed in where she finished, but she'll be genuinely happy for the others."

"Doesn't sound like a spoiled diva to me," Grover said.

"She's not," Doc told him.

"I was kidding," Grover said with a roll of his eyes. "I think that was made perfectly clear last night."

The medal ceremony was moving, and Doc couldn't shake the disappointment he felt on Ember's behalf. Every time he caught a glimpse of her, though, she was smiling and being supportive of the other athletes.

As things wound down and people began to leave the venue, Doc made his way toward where he'd last seen Ember. With his security credentials, he was allowed onto the field without any grief. He saw her standing with her parents ahead of him, and made his way over.

As he got close, he could hear her mother berating Ember—and so could everyone else who was standing close by.

"I don't know what the hell happened today, but that was disgraceful. Pathetic! You were almost last in swimming! If you hadn't been, you'd have started today in tenth place. And I added up the times in the run—you would've placed third if you hadn't fucked up so bad in the pool!"

"Seriously, Ember, you've disappointed *everyone*," her dad threw in with a shake of his head.

Doc had heard enough.

He walked up behind Ember and put his arms around her waist, pulling her back against him, careful not to jostle her left arm, which he knew had to be sore as hell. "You were amazing," he told her after kissing her temple gently.

"Excuse me!" her mom blustered. "You don't have the right to be touching my daughter!"

Ember turned in his arms, and he could see the pain in her eyes. But she smiled up at him. It was a fake smile, but Doc wasn't surprised she was hiding her feelings. There were too many people around.

"Hi. Thanks."

"You ready to go?" he asked.

"She's not going back to the dorm," her father said. "She's coming to the hotel with us so we can discuss how the hell we can salvage this entire fiasco. We need to figure out what to say on IG to spin this in our favor."

"Sorry, Dad," Ember said. "I'm going with Craig."

"No, you aren't," her mom insisted.

"*Yes*, Mom. I am. I love you, and I appreciate everything you've done for me, but I need to decompress tonight. I'm sorry I disappointed you. I'll come over to the hotel tomorrow and we can talk."

"Not good enough, young lady! Besides, I'm not sure what you need to decompress from. We need to figure out what went wrong so we can fix it for the next Olympics. We've got a lot of work ahead of us."

"Us?" Ember said. "I didn't see *you* out on that course tonight."

Both her parents stared at her for a moment, speechless, before her mom's eyes narrowed. "Wrong. We've given up our entire *lives* for you. For this moment. And you blew it!"

"I didn't ask you to do any of it," Ember told them. She spoke calmly, but Doc could feel her trembling in his embrace, and he tightened his arm around her in support.

She went on. "Again, I'm sorry I let you down. Both of you. And all my coaches. And those who helped me train. But I did the best I could, and the fact that you can't be happy that I'm even here, that I was competing in the freaking

Olympics, says more about you than me. I'll come by the hotel tomorrow and we can talk once we're all feeling less emotional."

"So you're going to celebrate your failure by having sex with *him*?" her mom spat out. "He's white!"

Doc stiffened.

"I'm twenty-five years old, Mom. Who I have sex with isn't your concern. More importantly, I can't believe you're pulling the race card. If I want to have sex with a white guy, a Black guy, or a purple two-headed alien, I will. I'm an adult—and it's about time you started treating me like one."

"When you start acting like one, we will," her dad interjected.

"We're done," Doc said. He wasn't going to stand there and listen to Ember's parents tear her apart any more. He was appalled at the way they were speaking to her. He knew it was because they were disappointed, but he needed to get her away from them before anyone said something that might permanently harm their relationship.

He turned with Ember in his embrace and kept his arm around her lower back as he led her away from her parents, who didn't say another word. For which Doc was grateful.

"People will probably take pictures," Ember said quietly.

Doc stopped and changed course. Instead of going out the main gate, he headed for the gate he'd entered through earlier, the one reserved for athletes and officials. He pulled his phone out and clicked on Grover's name.

"What's up? Everything all right?" Grover asked by way of greeting.

"How far away are you? Can you come back and pick up me and Ember?"

"Of course. Give me ten minutes?"

"We'll be by the athlete entrance. Things are probably too hot at the main gate."

"Ten-four. I'll bring the fancy golf cart with the tinted windows."

"Appreciate it."

"See you soon."

Doc clicked off the phone. The Korean officials had supplied dozens of the specialty golf carts for the Games, and he was grateful that Grover had thought to grab one.

He stopped a short distance from the exit, not wanting to leave until Grover was there, just in case fans were waiting outside. "You okay?" he asked Ember. "That was kind of intense."

"I'm fine," she said with another fake smile.

She wasn't fine. That was obvious. But he wasn't going to push her right now. "For the record...I think Grover wants to recruit you. No matter what he promises you, don't believe him."

Her smile gentled, and he could tell it was a bit more genuine now.

"But seriously, you shot amazingly well."

"It's funny. I've always struggled to concentrate on my own target. It's hard to block out the sounds from the other competitors, especially when you know they hit their five and get to move on. But today, I barely heard any of them. I knew I was out of medal contention, and that seemed to help. Also, I couldn't help but think of last night. That was life and death. Literally. This? Even though it was the Olympics...it didn't compare. It made it easier to not be tense and just do what I've trained to do."

"You only missed, what, three shots out of the twenty?"

"Something like that," she said modestly.

"I'd love to take you to a range," Doc mused. "You could be like a pool shark or something. We could sucker someone into a friendly competition. They'd think because you're so pretty that you couldn't hit the broad side of a barn. Then—wham! You'd hit every shot and wipe the floor with them."

Ember giggled. "That wouldn't be very nice."

"Don't care. It'd be worth it to see their expression when you outshot them." Doc was relieved to see she'd relaxed somewhat with their banter.

"I'd love to go shooting with you. Do you and your team work out every day?"

"We try to. It's important we stay in shape."

"I love running. It's one of my favorite things to do. I can lose myself in my head and block everything else out. Maybe it's the endorphins or runner's high or whatever, but I've always loved a nice long run."

"Are you a morning person?" Doc asked.

"Absolutely. I usually go to sleep around eight-thirty or nine, which I know is pretty ridiculous, but I get up around four-thirty to head to the gym. I swim first thing, before doing anything else," Ember said.

"Something else we have in common," Doc told her with a smile. "I don't need as much sleep as you, but I do like getting up and starting my day early. I'd love to go running with you. And swimming, for that matter. We're well matched."

Ember stared at him, and Doc stared back. There was so much he wanted to say, but this wasn't the time or place. He slowly reached up and palmed her cheek. "You were amazing today," he said gently.

Tears immediately filled her eyes, but she shook her head and refused to let them fall. "I can't do this right now. Please."

Doc nodded. "All right, Em, it's okay. I understand." And he did. She was holding on to her composure by the skin of her teeth and the last thing she wanted to do was lose it in public. Luckily, he saw Grover pull up in the golf cart outside the entrance. He once again put his hand on the small of Ember's back and led her to the door.

"Good job today!" one of the guards called to Ember.

"Thanks," she responded.

"Hope to see you back in four years! You'll crush everyone. I know it!"

Ember smiled and waved to him and let Doc guide her to the cart. He held up the tinted plastic window and she crawled into the back seat. He followed her, and the second he was sitting, Grover hit the gas.

They drove back toward the Olympic Village in silence. The main entrance was now closed so they headed for one of the others. Within ten minutes, they'd pulled up in front of the dorm and Doc hopped out with Ember on his heels.

Without thinking about it, he took her hand in his.

"We've got patrol in three hours," Grover reminded him.

Doc nodded. He'd traded shifts with another special forces members so he could watch Ember compete in the run and shooting event. It wasn't a full shift, as he'd worked a few hours that morning, but he wouldn't have missed her final event for anything. Grover had volunteered to accompany him. He had the best friends.

"Are you hungry?" Doc asked as they headed inside.

She shook her head.

Doc wasn't so sure about that, but he didn't push. Ember was practically vibrating next to him. She greeted other athletes they passed and thanked them when they congratulated her, but otherwise didn't say much.

Without discussing it, Doc led her to his room and unlocked the door. She stood in the middle of the room without moving, and Doc couldn't stop himself from going to her as if his life depended on it. He turned her around and saw the tears she'd desperately been keeping at bay, finally spilling over.

She choked on a sob, and his heart broke for her. He pulled her close and felt her legs give out from under her. He eased them both to the hard tile floor and held her as she cried as if her best friend had just died. Doc didn't tell her to hush, didn't promise everything would be all right. He just let her get it all out.

She'd worked her ass off for years, just for this one day, and it hadn't ended the way she'd hoped. He hated that her mom had to bring up the fact that she would've medaled if she hadn't done so poorly in the swim. That was like rubbing salt in an open wound. It was insensitive and hurtful, and Doc was livid that she'd had to deal with that.

She was probably well aware of where she would've placed if her shoulder hadn't been dislocated, which only made her finish all the more difficult to take.

"I'm sorry. I'm so sorry, Em," Doc murmured, rocking her back and forth as she soaked his shirt with her tears. "If I could go back and change yesterday, I would. I shouldn't have been so rough with you. This is my fault. God, I'm so fucking sorry."

She shook her head against him. "N-No—"

"It is," he insisted, interrupting her. "But I'm also so damn proud of you, I can't even put it into words. Do you know how many people I would've trusted to have my back like you did yesterday? Six. Trigger, Lefty, Brain, Lucky, Grover, and Oz...who you haven't met yet. That's it. Anyone else, I would be afraid they'd somehow shoot me instead of the bad guy. Or they'd bolt, leaving my six vulnerable. And before yesterday, I've never, *ever* given my spare weapon to a civilian. But I didn't think twice about handing it over to you. I fucked up your Olympic dream, and I'll spend the rest of my life kicking my own ass about that, but I've never been as impressed with anyone as I was with you last night."

His words seemed to make Ember cry harder, so Doc decided to shut up and just hold her. Giving her the support she should've gotten from her parents.

It took a while, but eventually her sobs changed to the occasional sniffle. Then she mumbled, "I think my ass is asleep."

Doc smiled and shifted, easily getting to his knees, then his feet, with Ember in his arms. She didn't panic, didn't act as if she was afraid he was going to drop her, simply wrapped her arms around his neck and held on as he moved them to his bed. He sat with her legs draped off to the side and lifted his hand to her face. He wiped the tears off one cheek, then the other.

"Feel better?"

She shrugged. "A little."

"Good. Want to talk about today?"

Ember sighed. "The fencing went okay. My balance was a little off, but I held my own. I lucked out and got a good horse in the jumping and compensated for my shoulder with my right arm, but I was sitting a little lopsided and it threw the horse off. By that time, my swim coach, Lonnie, and my parents figured something was up, but I didn't tell them what happened. They talked a little about the attack this morning, and I didn't tell them I was involved."

"Why?" Doc asked.

She met his gaze and said, "Because you're Delta Force. I know enough to know that what you do is top secret."

Doc closed his eyes and tried to control his emotions. This woman was fucking perfect—and he had no idea how to make things work between them. They were in an impossible situation.

She apparently didn't realize how much she'd just rocked his world, because she kept talking. "I knew the swim was going to suck. I could get by without using my left arm more in the other sports, but you need both arms in the freestyle. It hurt. A lot. But I powered through. Obviously my time suffered though."

"You're seriously impressive," Doc said softly.

"Right now, I pretty much just feel like a failure. I'm sure my followers are losing their shit at how bad I did."

"Fuck them!" Doc exclaimed.

Ember looked startled for a second, then her lips quirked.

"I mean it. It's easy to sit behind a keyboard and judge, but they weren't the ones who spent over a decade of their lives training. They weren't the ones swimming with a recently dislocated shoulder. They weren't the ones facing off against a terrorist—driving a van possibly filled with explosives—with nothing but a pistol."

"I know."

"Do you? Seriously, Em, you're so much more than a social profile. Assholes will always be assholes. Even if you had won gold, they probably would've said that you cheated somehow. Or that you were treated differently because of the color of your skin, or that you paid someone off to win. *You* know what you did. And *I* know it. And I don't have the words to express how proud I am of you."

"You're right."

"Of course I am," Doc teased.

She smiled, and this time it was a real smile. He relaxed a bit.

"Honestly, this made the decision about what to do with my life easier. If I'd have medaled, everyone would've wanted me to keep going. But now I can hopefully retire and fade off into the sunset."

Doc burst out laughing.

Ember smacked him on the arm. "What's so funny?"

"You. Thinking you'll just fade from people's memories. Em, you're so fucking beautiful, inside and out, people are drawn to you. How do you think you got so many followers?"

"Because my parents paid for them?" she asked dryly.

"No. Because you're a shining light. Even though you

aren't posting yourself. And even though most of the pictures posted are posed...your followers still see someone special. Someone they want to be close to. Someone they want to be friends with. I have no doubt whatever you decide to do with your life, you'll excel."

Her eyes filled with tears once more.

"Shit, I didn't mean to make you sad," Doc told her.

"I'm not sad. I'm...happy. Or grateful. Or thankful. Whatever."

"So...what's your plan now?" he couldn't help but ask.

"Tomorrow I'll go talk to my parents, tell them I want a break. From everything. Pentathlon, social media. All of it."

"And how do you think they'll take that?"

"They're gonna freak," Ember said honestly. "But I don't care."

"If things get too intense...you could always come to Texas," Doc said. He'd wanted to sound nonchalant, but he knew he'd failed.

Ember stared at him. "Yeah?"

"Yeah," he told her. "I could take you shooting and you could show up the team. You could meet Oz and his baby, which will probably be born any day now. And of course the other women. I know you'd like them, and they you. We could go for some runs...although Texas is hotter than you're used to, and there aren't any pretty beaches to run on. The sunsets can be pretty amazing though." Doc knew he was babbling, but he didn't want to stop talking and have her let him down easy by saying there was no way she was moving out of Beverly Hills.

"I think I'd like that," she said softly.

She hadn't agreed that she'd come, but she hadn't told him he was crazy either.

Doc couldn't stop his head from dipping to save his life. He needed to kiss this woman more than he needed anything else at that moment. He hadn't forgotten their first kiss. How perfect it had been.

She met him partway, tilting her chin up and tightening her hand on the back of his neck. Closing his eyes, Doc sighed in relief when their lips met. He wasn't in a hurry, wanted to show Em how much he treasured her.

They made out on his bed for several minutes. Doc was careful to keep his hands from straying, no matter how much he wanted to ease her onto the mattress and make love with her.

She did it for him. He liked everything about her. Her muscles, the way she leaned into him as they kissed, how she let him take control at first, but then insisted on taking over. He felt comfortable with Ember in a way he'd never felt with any other woman before.

One hand was on her head, supporting her, and the other clenched her thigh just above her knee. He couldn't help that his cock had hardened the second their lips met, but she didn't seem to be offended by his obvious arousal.

When they pulled apart, they were both breathing hard.

Her pupils were dilated now and there were no signs of tears. Her eyes were still a bit bloodshot from her crying jag, but now all he could feel from her was arousal.

Doc was about ready to suggest they check out the shower together when her stomach growled. Loudly.

Dipping her head and resting her forehead against his shoulder, Ember moaned. "Oh, God. How embarrassing."

"You burned a lot of calories today," Doc said with a smile, loving the feel of her in his arms. "How about you take a shower while I go down to the cafeteria and see what I can scrounge up for you?"

"Here?"

"Here what?" he asked.

"Can I shower in your room?"

"Fuck yes. You can pretty much do whatever you want."

She grinned, then got serious. "Craig?"

He loved the way his given name sounded on her lips. He never really understood why his friends liked their women calling them by their real names, but now he got it. It was something special just between them. "Yeah?"

"I don't know what the future holds for me, but I don't want to give you up."

"Then don't," he said simply. "But you need to know, I can't move to California. I have an obligation to my team, the Army, and my country. I'm at their mercy."

"I completely understand, and I respect that."

She didn't elaborate, and Doc didn't have the guts at the moment to ask what that meant for them. "If you get up, I'll go get you some food."

Ember didn't move, simply stared into his eyes for a long moment. Then she must've decided something, because she nodded to herself before slowly sliding off his lap. Her eyes flicked downward and she grinned. "You gonna be able to walk like that?"

Doc stood and grimaced. "It'll go down...maybe."

Ember stepped into his space and hugged him.

"This isn't helping," he told her honestly.

When Ember pulled back, Doc could see that she was well and truly relaxed for the first time since finishing her last event. "I know I said this already, but I'm gonna say it again, because I think it means more now. I don't regret what happened last night. I can't deny I was disappointed that I didn't do better today, but being there by your side, protecting others, was so much more important than a stupid medal."

"No one will know what you did," Doc told her solemnly.

"I'm okay with that. Honestly. I was sad, disappointed,

and upset. I cried. But I'm okay now. We saved people's lives."

"We did," Doc agreed.

"That's way more important in the grand scheme of things. I've always lamented the fact that I'm famous for doing absolutely nothing. There are so many other people doing amazing things out there. And I have all this money for doing nothing more than getting my picture taken with a certain cosmetic or for mentioning some business or another. Last night? I did something. *We* did something. Something good. It feels pretty damn wonderful."

Doc couldn't resist. He kissed her again. Holding her against him as he devoured her mouth for a moment. When he pulled back, he kissed her nose. Then her forehead. "It does feel good. *You* feel good. Now, go shower before your stomach tries to eat you from the inside out. I'll be back in twenty minutes or so. Is that enough time?"

"More than," Ember said.

Doc nodded, then reluctantly dropped his arms from around her. He spun and headed for the door, knowing if he didn't go now, he might not ever want to leave her.

* * *

Two and a half hours later, Ember stood in her own doorway with Craig in front of her. She'd showered, he'd brought up way too much food from the cafeteria, and they'd talked and laughed together until he'd said that he needed to get ready to head out for his shift.

Ember was dead on her feet. He'd made her take some more painkillers and with everything that had happened, she was ready to crash. He'd walked her to her room and placed her bag inside. Now they were saying their goodbyes. They'd only known each other a few days, but it seemed more like a lifetime. So much had happened, it had solidified their friend-ship…and relationship.

"Be careful tonight," she said.

"I will. You gonna be all right without your stars tonight?" he asked.

Ember smiled. "Yeah, I'm gonna be asleep before my head hits the pillow."

"Okay. And for the record, there are some pretty amazing views of the stars in Texas. Less light pollution and all that."

Ember grinned. He was adorable. She hadn't decided exactly what she was going to do with her life, but she couldn't deny she was excited about her future. She had some ideas in the back of her mind and was ready to put them in motion. She hoped she might be able to include Craig in those future plans as well, but she wasn't ready to commit to anything. She had to talk to her parents and get her life in order before she could make any promises or concrete plans.

"I'll keep that in mind," she told him with a smile.

"You do that. You've got my address, phone number, and email," he reminded her. "Use them."

"I will. And don't hesitate to contact me too."

"Oh, don't worry about that," he told her.

Ember loved how he wasn't coy in the least.

"Will you let me know how it goes with your parents tomorrow?"

"Yeah."

"Don't let them make you feel bad. You did a great job today," Craig told her.

"I'll try."

"Remember that I'm proud of you. And Trigger called you badass. And the other guys on the team are impressed as well. You're incredible, Em. Don't forget it."

Ember couldn't resist this man. There was something

about him that drew her. She went up on her tiptoes and kissed him. Hard. Tears threatened but she forced them back.

"This isn't goodbye," she said forcefully.

"No, it isn't," Craig agreed. "I'll talk to my commander about seeing if I can get some leave time and come out to California to see you."

"Really?"

"Yeah, really. I don't know how we'll make this work, but I want to try."

That was all Ember needed to hear. It made the plans in her head all the more clear. "Okay," she said simply.

"Okay." Craig's gaze roamed her face, as if he was trying to memorize it.

"Oh! I don't even have a picture of you. Will you take a selfie with me? I promise I won't put it on social media. It's just for me."

"Of course I will," Craig said. He turned her so she was at his side and Ember dug into her pocket for her phone. She swiped right and brought up the camera. She held the phone in front of her and for the first time in a very long time, she didn't have to worry if her makeup was perfect or the lighting was right. She just wanted a picture of her and Craig together.

She touched the button to take the picture and laughed at the short preview she caught a glimpse of. "You weren't even looking!" she exclaimed.

"Sorry, do it again," Craig told her.

She did, and this time was satisfied that she'd captured both of them looking at the lens.

"I'll talk to you soon," Craig said.

This was it. He had to go.

"Same."

Craig's arms dropped and he took a step away from her in the hallway. "I'm gonna miss you," he said softly.

Ember's heart melted. "Me too."

"Be strong, Em. You're an amazing woman."

"I will."

"No goodbyes," Craig reiterated.

"Later," Ember said.

"Later," Craig echoed. Then he spun and walked away.

Not able to watch him leave, Ember backed into her room and shut the door. She looked down at her phone still in her hand and clicked it on to look at the pictures she'd just taken.

The last one was cute. They both had goofy smiles on their faces and even though her hair was extra crazy and Craig's forehead was shiny from the overhead lights, she loved it. Then she swiped to the first picture she'd taken. The one where Craig hadn't been looking at the camera. She stilled...

Craig was looking at her with an expression so intimate, she knew she'd treasure this picture forever. She was grinning at the camera, and his eyes were glued on *her*. He had a small smile on his lips and the admiration in his gaze almost leapt off the screen.

God. Had anyone ever looked at her like that? If so, she couldn't recall.

She wanted this man. Full stop. Period. She had no idea why or how he was still single. Maybe he was a slob. Or had a drinking problem. Or was a complete asshole after he got to know a woman. But she didn't think so.

They'd been in the right place at the right time to meet, to save lives, and to connect.

Ember was ready to move on with her life, and Texas was looking more and more like the perfect place to put her plans into effect.

First she had to deal with her life in California. It wouldn't be easy, but she was determined to stop being Ember Maxwell, social media star, and start being simply...Em.

* * *

Alex scowled at the phone yet again in disbelief. Ember Maxwell had choked!

It was unfathomable.

She was supposed to be this amazing athlete, and yet when push came to shove, she'd completely folded. She was an embarrassment to the sport, and to all the athletes and coaches who'd trained with her and shown her support over the years.

Not only that—her failure was an end to Alex's dreams as well.

Ember's performance was a huge slap in the face after all the encouragement Alex had given her!

Alex was the first person to defend Ember when people talked shit about her online. Endured name-calling and threatening DMs over supportive comments posted for the gorgeous athlete. Hundreds of dollars in gifts had been sent to the woman Alex admired and looked up to.

Alex wanted to be just like her...successful and loved and famous...and over the years had been nothing but supportive.

And for *what*? For her to *choke*? It was despicable. Unbelievable!

Alex's rage exploded, thinking about all the years of supportive messages that had been wasted on the useless bitch. *Fifteenth place*? The other woman who'd made the US team wasn't half as good, and she'd placed eleventh!

Years of admiration turned to hate in the space of a breath.

Ember didn't *deserve* anyone's support. Didn't deserve all the nice things said about her. Didn't deserve Alex standing up for her against the internet trolls over the years.

Come to think of it...not *once* had Ember responded to those messages and posts.

She hadn't sent a thank you for any of the gifts.

She was nothing but a fucking *bitch*—and she was going to regret spurning Alex's friendship!

If Ember thought people were mean before, she hadn't seen anything yet. Her failure at the Olympics was a huge display of disrespect and betrayal—one that Alex wasn't going to let her get away with. *No. Way.*

Ember would feel Alex's wrath and would regret not trying harder. Not *winning*.

Second place was for losers...and fifteenth place?

That was a death sentence.

CHAPTER EIGHT

Doc stared through the window at his backyard and barely registered the rabbits hopping around. He'd bought the house when he'd first moved to Killeen. It was in an older, racially diverse neighborhood, and he loved it. But it needed a lot of work. Work he was doing himself. It kept his mind occupied when he wasn't on a mission and helped keep his demons at bay.

For the most part, Doc didn't have flashbacks or PTSD from the missions he'd participated in. But for the last week, he couldn't get what had happened in South Korea out of his mind.

He hated that he'd hurt Ember, but more than that, if they'd been two minutes earlier or later, the outcome of the JRA attack could've turned out so differently. Ember could've been killed.

It was a vision of her lying in the middle of the street, bleeding and dying, that haunted him.

He'd talked to her every day in the week since he'd arrived home. But it wasn't the same as being able to see her. For one, he had a feeling she was keeping a lot of what was happening back home from him. Rationally, he understood why. They'd only known each other a few days, even if they'd gotten very close in that small timeframe.

But even with FaceTiming, he couldn't read her expressions as well as he had in person. She said things were going well, but he could hear an undercurrent of...*something* in her tone. He wanted to be there for her, to support her, to encourage her.

She told him that she'd changed all her site passwords, and predictably, her parents and social media managers weren't happy. She'd hinted that other big changes were coming, and while Doc was thrilled she was taking control of her life, he still worried about her.

He wanted to fly out to California, but things were pretty busy here. Riley'd had her baby. A perfect, chubby little girl they'd named Amalia. Logan and Bria were over-the-moon excited about their new baby sister, and Oz was as proud as he could be—and relieved that everyone was healthy.

Then there was Grover. After receiving the long-lost letter from Sierra...he wasn't doing well. The team had a meeting just today to try to figure out what the hell their next steps were.

In the middle of his musings, Doc's phone rang. He pulled it out and smiled when he saw it was Ember.

"Hey, Em."

"Hi."

Doc could tell immediately that she sounded off. He turned away from the view and headed for his couch. He wanted to be able to concentrate one hundred percent on Ember. "What's wrong?"

She chuckled. "Why do you automatically think that something's wrong when I call? Can't I call just to say hi?"

"Of course you can, and I welcome being able to talk to

you as much as possible. But I know you. I can tell that something's up."

She sighed. "How is it that I've known you for such a short period of time and you know me better than the people I've been around my entire life?"

Doc didn't have an answer for that. At least not one that would sound rational. "Talk to me, Em."

"Today was...hard."

"Wait, where are you now?" Doc asked.

"In a hotel. I needed a break from my family and...from everything."

Doc's worry increased. "What can I do to help?" he asked.

"This. Talk to me. Listen."

"Of course. You were going to have a heart-to-heart with your parents today. I take it that didn't go well?"

"Honestly, it went much like I'd expected. They aren't happy that I'm done with competing. They told me that I was throwing away over a decade worth of hard work. That not medaling at the Olympics was a result of me being stubborn and stupid and wanting to stay in the village instead of with them in a hotel. They basically accused me of being selfish and acting like a kid. They wanted me to give it another four years. To atone for my 'failure,' as they called it. I refused. They yelled. My mom cried. My dad put on his disappointed face...

"But it was when I told them I was also done with Ember Maxwell, the social media influencer, that they *really* lost their minds."

"They're losing control of you, and they don't like that," Doc said.

"Yeah, but I think they're also worried too. They made me a lot of money. Money they put in accounts in my name. Yes, they're on the accounts too, but the money is mine—and they know it. I could really screw them, and I think they're scared of losing that income stream."

Doc nodded. He could understand that. "Did you tell them that you'd never leave them penniless?"

When Ember didn't immediately respond, Doc frowned. "Em?"

"Yeah, I'm here. How do you know I won't?"

"Leave with all the money? Because you're too kind to do something like that. Yes, your parents have pushed you hard. They've browbeat you and made you do things you didn't want to do. But you love them. I can tell. And you've said time and time again that you appreciated their pushing, even if you haven't liked every decision they've made on your behalf. You could no more leave your parents destitute than you could walk by someone hurting and not try to do something about it."

"See?" she whispered. "You know me better than my own parents! They truly thought I was going to leave them without a dime. It was *crazy*. I told them that I'd never do that. That they'd be taken care of for the rest of their lives, even if I disabled all my accounts and disappeared off the face of the Earth."

"Is that what you're planning on doing?" Doc couldn't help but ask. "Disabling your accounts."

"No. I thought about it. I thought about what a relief it would be, but then I decided that would be stupid. I have this huge platform, one my parents built from scratch. Twenty-five million people see what I post. It would be irresponsible to throw that away when I can use it for good. Instead of posting pictures of myself, I can try to bring social injustices to light. I want to make a difference in the world, Craig, and I think I can use my platform to do that."

"I think so too," Doc agreed. "You can do any damn thing you put your mind to. I know it. You're an amazing woman."

"Thanks," Ember said softly. "I also had a long talk with Alexis, Harris, Betty, and Samer. They're the people who've been managing my social media accounts. They were all pretty shocked when I'd changed my passwords and essentially locked them out. Alexis especially. He actually lost his shit, telling me I didn't know what I was doing and that I'd ruin years of his hard work."

"What are you going to do with them?" Doc asked.

"Probably give them a few months' severance pay and see if my parents can find them other jobs."

"How'd they take *that*?"

Ember sighed. "They weren't thrilled. I think working for me was a pretty easy job, all things considered. Alexis stormed out of the room, Harris and Betty called me a few choice names under their breath, but still left with a little less anger than Alexis."

"And Samer? He was one of the ones at the Olympics, right?"

"Yeah. He actually wished me well. Said that if anyone can do good things with their social media, it was me. He also told me if I had any questions, I shouldn't hesitate to contact him, which I appreciated."

"That sounds promising. Are the others going to cause problems for you?"

"I hope not," Ember said emphatically. "But we'll see. Anyway, after I talked to my parents and my social media team, I went to the gym to meet with my coaches and the men and women I've trained with for years. I apologized for my performance at the Olympics and—"

"That's bullshit," Doc told her. "You shouldn't apologize for doing the best you could."

"You didn't let me finish," Ember said with a small laugh. "They pretty much all said the same thing. I explained that I had dislocated my shoulder, but didn't tell them the specifics.

They were supportive, but I have a feeling behind my back, they'll be bitching about me leaving."

"Why?"

"Well...me being there brings attention to the sport and to the center. And money in the form of endorsements. My parents paid my coaches a pretty penny to make me the best, and now that I'm quitting, they won't get that money anymore. It all comes down to the almighty dollar," Ember said with a sigh.

"I'm sorry it's been a rough day for you," Doc said.

"Thanks. But you know what?"

"What?"

"I feel pretty good about everything."

"I'm glad."

"It's kind of scary to change everything I've done over the last decade, but I'm excited about it too."

"That's great to hear. I have no doubt you'll kick ass in whatever you decide to do."

She chuckled. "Thanks. So...how are things there?"

It was Doc's turn to sigh. "I told you about the woman Grover met in Afghanistan, right?"

"Yeah. Sierra."

"That's her. Well, Grover brought in the letter he'd received from her. It wasn't good, Em."

"Why? What'd she say?"

"It was postmarked almost a year ago. In it, she told Grover how much she was looking forward to getting to know him; that if it was all right with him, she'd like to exchange letters instead of emails. She liked the old-fashioned aspect. She knew it would make their correspondence slower, but she hoped it would make what they talked about more meaningful."

"She's not wrong," Ember said. "I think the art of writing letters has mostly been lost. One of my favorite things to do is read old letters from wartime. They're poignant and touching and not as...superficial? I don't know if that's the word I'm looking for."

"I know what you mean, and I agree."

"So...what? Grover's upset that he could have been writing her all this time but hasn't, thinking she wasn't interested?" Ember asked.

Doc hadn't previously talked much about this particular detail with Ember. It was personal for Grover, not to mention tied to top-secret Army business. But he trusted her enough to tell her what he could. "Well...sort of. But we also became aware that no one had seen her in months. And now it's been almost a year. She disappeared without a trace soon after she sent the letter."

Ember gasped. "Seriously?"

"Yeah. And you're right, Grover's definitely not happy because he just assumed she wasn't interested. Now it looks as if that wasn't the case, and if Grover had known then what he knows now, he would've pushed harder for someone to do something about her disappearance. She actually said in her letter that things had been 'weird' on the base, but she didn't explain what she meant."

"So where did she go? What happened to her?" Ember asked.

"Nobody knows. But there have been several incidences of contractors disappearing from the same area where she was working since she and Grover met," Doc said.

Ember sucked in a breath. "Holy shit. She was kidnapped?"

"Maybe. Possibly."

"And she's been gone for a *year*," Ember said. "That's horrible."

Doc didn't mention the fact that it was unlikely she was still alive. Shahzada wasn't known for being merciful. If she'd been taken—and what other explanation could there be for her disappearance?— she'd probably been tortured and killed. "Grover's beside himself," Doc said.

"Yeah, I can imagine. Maybe... I have followers from all over the world, Craig. Do you think it would help if I posted about her? Maybe put up her picture and ask if anyone knows anything about where she is, to contact the authorities?"

Doc loved Ember's huge heart. "I don't know that the people who follow you would be from the area where she disappeared," he said gently.

"You don't know that. Craig, she was on an American Army base. I bet the soldiers there have social media. They might be back in the States now, but maybe they saw or heard something and my post could trigger them to remember. Maybe she was moved. Taken across borders. Put into the sex industry. Maybe someone bragged about their American captive. You said it yourself, you don't know what happened to her or where she is. It couldn't hurt."

Doc nodded. "You're right. It's a great idea."

"And I could do the same for other missing people. The media seems to concentrate on kids and white women, but I could highlight more adults that have disappeared. People of color. Men as well as women. It's heartbreaking...and maybe I can help."

Once again, Doc's pride bloomed for this woman. Ember was one of the most tenderhearted people he'd ever met. "I think that's a great idea."

"Craig?"

"Yeah?"

"I miss you."

"I miss you too, Em. I sent you something yesterday, you should get it soon."

"You did? What is it?"

He chuckled. He'd learned Em both loved and hated

surprises. He would've let the package be a complete surprise, but he needed to explain it. "The third-highest personal decoration for valor in combat is the Silver Star. It's awarded to members of the US Armed Forces for gallantry in action against an enemy. I've received a few of them over my career, and my commander told me he'd be nominating me again for what I did in Seoul. I have no idea if it'll be approved or not, and even if it is, no one will know about it except for me and my team. But I got to thinking that it isn't fair I might be awarded such a high honor, and you aren't. It's not an Olympic medal, but...I dug out one of my Silver Stars from the shoebox under my bed, polished it up, and sent it to you."

"I...I don't know what to say," Ember whispered.

"You don't have to say anything. I know what happened out there, and without you by my side, things might not have gone so well. You saved a lot of people that day, Em, and I want you to know how much I respect and admire you."

"I'll treasure it," Ember told him.

"I'm sorry we can't tell the world that you're a hero," Doc said.

She snorted. "I'm no hero. If it was up to me, I would've run in the opposite direction."

"Wrong. A hero does what needs to be done even when their knees are shaking and they want to throw up."

"You feel like that?"

"All the time," Doc admitted.

"Thank you for what you do," Ember told him.

"You're welcome. Now...have you eaten? I know it's two hours earlier there, and even though you're holed up in a hotel, don't forget to eat."

She chuckled. "I won't. Promise. I've already scoped out the room service menu."

"Good."

"You know what else I'm looking forward to?" she asked.

"What?"

"Cooking for myself. It sounds stupid, but we've had a cook for so long, I don't even know how to make ramen noodles. I've never had a chance, or the time, to learn."

"Well, ramen is overrated, but I have a feeling you'll be an expert in no time. I'm happy to teach you what I know, although that's not a hell of a lot."

"Deal."

Doc realized what he'd said a bit too late. How could he teach her what he knew if they lived a thousand miles apart?

"I'm sure you have stuff you need to do," Ember said. "So I'll let you go."

Doc wanted to protest, tell her that there was nothing he'd rather do than talk to her. That he'd been staring at his yard absently when she called, but he pressed his lips together. He didn't want to look desperate, even though he felt that way.

"Take care of yourself," Doc said. "Be safe."

"I will."

"I'm proud of you for standing up for what you want to do with your life."

"Thanks. So am I. I'll talk to you soon."

"Later."

"Later."

Doc clicked off the phone. They'd continued their vow not to say goodbye to each other even on the phone.

Doc stared into space for a few minutes after he hung up. He could be doing several different things to continue to fix his house, but at the moment, all he could think of was Ember and how much he missed her. Talking to her was great, but it wasn't the same as being with her in person.

The shit thing was that he saw no way of being with her except by her moving to Texas. And he wouldn't ask that of her.

Her life was in California. He had no doubt she'd patch things up with her parents and her friends at the gym. They wouldn't be able to stay mad at her for long, she was too good a person.

But where did that leave them? Talking on the phone and making quick visits when they could fit them in? That wasn't the kind of relationship he wanted. He wanted what his teammates had. Someone to be there at the end of the day and when he came home from a mission. It wasn't fair to *any* woman; the danger of his job and how often they were deployed made for a hard life. He and his team had been lucky in that they hadn't had to change bases all that often, but that was another hardship on a military spouse and any children they might have...quitting a job, changing schools, and moving to a new city.

Sighing, Doc got up. He couldn't sit and mope on his couch for the rest of the night. He needed to do something. Keep his mind occupied. He ignored the fact that his house seemed quieter than he remembered it being in the past. Ember's laughter echoed in his head, and he couldn't help wishing that things were different.

* * *

Ember hung up the phone and flopped back on the bed. She'd checked into the hotel needing some space from her disapproving parents. But it was past time she took control of her own life. The attack in Seoul had changed her. It had been frightening, but also life-altering. She'd stood up for what was right and hadn't backed down. Facing that van barreling toward them had scared the crap out of her, but she'd held her ground and persevered.

She knew her bullet had been the one that killed the driver, even if Craig and his team hadn't admitted it. She'd stared right into the man's eyes and shot. She'd seen him keel over just before Craig had pulled her to safety.

She should feel remorse that she'd taken a life...but she didn't. The man would've killed others. By taking him out, she'd saved lives. She was proud of that.

She wanted to do more. More to help, not just be a pretty face on Instagram. And the first step toward that had been to change her passwords.

She hadn't exaggerated when she'd told Craig about her social media managers' reactions to what she'd done. She also knew Alexis had gone straight to her parents to complain. None of them understood what she was doing. Everyone wanted to keep things the same as they'd been for years. They thought she should continue to train and post filtered, fluffy pictures of herself with products people paid her to hawk.

She was done with all of it.

She wanted to do just what she'd told Craig, share pictures that would help in some way. Missing people. Highlighting injustices. But first she needed to make a statement about what was going on. About her intent.

She'd been silent for a week, not posting anything at all. The last posts that had gone up were about the Olympics.

Ember knew she'd lost followers already, but that didn't bother her. If the people who were only there to harass her or to see her fail left, all the better.

She looked through the pictures the photographer hired by her parents had sent after the Olympics. Many were hard to look at, because Ember knew how much pain she'd been in when he'd taken them. But the second she saw the picture taken at the end of the medal ceremony, she knew it was the one she wanted to post with her statement.

She'd gone over to congratulate some of her competitors. The photographer had captured the moment Ember had hugged Wang Wei, the Chinese athlete who'd gotten the bronze medal. They'd been joined by Chloe Esposito from Australia and Mariana Arceo from Mexico. They weren't rivals at that moment. They were simply women supporting women.

She clicked on the picture and uploaded it to her Instagram account. She'd had to do several internet searches to figure out how to use the platform, but she was fairly confident she had the hang of it. Taking her time, Ember posted a long, heartfelt note to her followers.

I know many of you may have wondered where I've disappeared to over the last week and what I've been doing. I've been reflecting on my life and things I've done.

To those of you who've been supportive of me over the years, thank you. I know my performance at the Olympics was disappointing; it was to me as well. But I learned a lot about myself. I learned that there's more to life than winning. Would I have liked to cross the finish line first, to have worn the gold medal around my neck? Of course. But coming in fifteenth place in the Olympics isn't exactly something to be ashamed of. What most of you don't know is that I dislocated my shoulder the night before the second day of competition. Is that an excuse? No. It simply explains why my swimming time was so off. But I didn't quit. I didn't throw a tantrum and say "life's unfair" and demand a do-over. I did the best I could at the time. And I'm proud of where I ended up.

I love the picture accompanying this post. It's beautiful. Four women who come from different backgrounds and different countries. Four women who speak three different languages coming together in solidarity. Four women supporting and loving each other. It's what I want for the world...to stop thinking about the color of someone's skin, or what country they're from, or how much money they have or don't have, or what God they believe in. None of that makes us more or less valuable as human beings.

With that in mind, I'll be making some changes in my life...and in this profile. You'll see fewer pictures of me. Less hawking of beauty products. I want to share more of what's important. I want to make a difference. Be someone who stands up for what's right and who doesn't sit back and say "there's nothing I can do about it" when shit happens. More standing up for those who can't stand up for themselves.

I've officially retired from competing in the modern pentathlon. But that doesn't mean I'm leaving it behind. I want to help others find the joy in pushing their body to its limits. Give kids who might never otherwise have a chance to fence, swim, ride horses, run, and shoot.

I hope you'll stay with me. Follow along in my new life as I do what I can to make this world a better place. Thank you all for your support. It's meant everything to me. Love, Ember Maxwell.

#makeaadifference #modernpentathlon #diversity #loveoneanother #differencemaker #embermaxwell #lovenothate #respect #blacklove #asianlove #womenlove #hispaniclove #pride #loveislove #findthemissing #newbeginnings

Ember sat back and stared at the post. Her heart was beating fast in her chest. She wasn't sure she'd explained herself very well. Samer, Harris, Alexis, or Betty could probably create a post that was much more eloquent, but what she'd written came from her heart. She also knew hashtags were important, but she had no idea if the ones she'd chosen were right.

She couldn't think any more about what she'd written. Before she chickened out, Ember hit the publish button. In an instant, her words and picture were posted on her Facebook account, Twitter, Tumblr, and Instagram, all at the same time.

Almost immediately, comments began appearing.

. . .

I love you, Ember
> *You've got a fan for life!*
> *I'll be here to help how I can*
> *Love this!*
> *You go girl!*

But along with the positive comments, there were negative ones.

You're a loser and trying to make excuses.
> *I don't want to hear about your do-gooding!*
> *White power!*
> *Fuck you!*

Closing her laptop, Ember put it aside and lay back on the bed and stared at the ceiling. She would never understand how people could be so...cruel. How did they get that way? She had no idea how they made it through life with so much rage inside them.

But from this point on, Ember was going to do her best to concentrate on the positives in *her* life. On those people who were kind and who genuinely wanted to do something good for others. She knew she'd stumble along the way, but her heart was in the right place.

Thinking about her heart made her thoughts turn to Craig.

Was she crazy for considering moving to Texas?

Probably...but she didn't care. Talking to him was the highlight of her day. He liked her exactly how she was. She wanted that. Needed it. Needed someone who didn't see Ember Maxwell, but saw *her*. Em.

She wasn't sure if she should tell him she was on her way. That she'd already started making arrangements. On one hand, if he didn't want her there, it would be better to find out before she'd driven all the way to Texas. But she was ninety-nine percent sure that he'd be surprised in a good way. If not...she'd eventually find somewhere else to settle. Nothing was going to stop her from making a new life for herself.

Even after everything that had happened earlier that day, Ember was happy. And excited about her future for the first time in a very long time. She had a lot of work to do. She needed to research missing people, see if she could make some connections... She'd met Ed Smart once. She'd reach out to him and see if he could help her. He'd been a tireless advocate for missing people after his daughter had been kidnapped and subsequently found alive.

She needed to find a place to live in Texas and to get her belongings packed and moved. She needed a real estate agent...should also talk to her attorney. She wanted to contact her financial advisor and make sure her parents were taken care of, their assets protected.

Smiling, she got up and headed to the desk in the hotel room and pulled the complimentary pad of paper and pen toward her. She uncapped the pen and began to make a list of everything she could think of that she needed to do. It got longer and longer, but with each item added, Ember's smile grew. As scary as this was, it was also exciting.

* * *

Alex glared at the phone, rereading Ember Maxwell's latest post.

Bitch!

She was turning her back on *everyone* who had made her who she was.

She wanted to be a *do-gooder*? Barf!

Ember had hinted that she was going to be leaving California—another slap in the face.

But Alex still had every intention of making the bitch pay for letting everyone down. There was nowhere Ember could hide.

Alex had fully planned to ride Ember's coattails. Victory had been so close this year! With Ember as a training partner, Alex knew the Olympics were just around the corner. The plan was to get even closer...to become Ember's best friend. Hoping some of her fame and fortune—not to mention her athletic ability—would rub off.

And now she'd ruined everything!

Helping *kids*? Fuck that!

Missing people? They didn't even matter! Were probably dead anyway.

And Alex didn't give two shits about race. It was more important to use whoever it took to get to the top, regardless of color. Anyone who could help was fair game, exploited until they were no longer any use.

And any advantages to getting closer to Ember were definitely over.

But Alex couldn't just forget about her and move on. There was no one to move on *to*. Not yet. Ember had been at the top. The ticket to a better life. Money and fame. And she'd thrown all of it away as if it meant nothing. As if *Alex* meant nothing.

Fuck that shit.

Ember would rue the day she'd turned her back on the world...and on Alex.

CHAPTER NINE

"Holy shit, man, you should've seen Logan's face when he opened that box," Oz told everyone several days later. They were once again at the base discussing world affairs. Grover was quieter than usual, and they all knew it was because he was frustrated that their commander hadn't immediately approved them heading off to Afghanistan to try to find the missing contractor, Sierra Clarkson.

"What'd he send?" Trigger asked.

"Well, first, there was the handwritten letter from Shin-Soo Choo, telling Logan how impressed he was with his dedication to the sport of baseball. He said that he himself got a late start, and that anything was possible with determination and hard work. I swear Logan has read that letter a hundred times already," Oz said.

"Wow, how'd he know so much about Logan?" Brain asked.

Oz looked at Doc. "I'm guessing Doc told Ember, who told Shin-Soo."

Doc smiled. His friend guessed right. In one of their first phone calls after they'd gotten back from South Korea, she'd asked for more information about Logan. She hadn't forgotten her promise to get in touch with Shin-Soo to see if he could send merch to Logan.

"Which reminds me, I need her address so Logan can send her a thank you card," Oz said.

"Of course," Doc told him.

"Get back to the box. What else was in it?" Lucky asked.

"What *wasn't* in it?" Oz countered. "Two signed baseballs, a signed baseball mitt, autographed pictures and trading cards from the entire team. A uniform—that was Logan's exact size, I might add. Not only that, but he also included a newborn outfit for Amalia and a shirt for Bria too. I've never seen Logan so excited and overwhelmed at the same time. He slept in his shirt last night and couldn't wait to get to practice this afternoon to brag about everything he'd received."

Doc was happy for his friend and Logan. The kid had been through hell, as had his sister, and they all deserved the best.

"I saw Ember's IG post," Brain said.

"You did? Since when are you on Instagram?" Lucky asked.

"I'm not. But when her words are plastered all over every entertainment network, it's hard to *not* see them," Brain said.

It was true. Doc couldn't imagine having everything he said be scrutinized and picked apart like Ember's words had been. But he was impressed as hell with her. What she'd posted had obviously come from the heart...and it showed.

Of course, there were those people who thought it was an angle, that she was trying to find new ways of getting attention, but they were dead wrong. She wanted the opposite. She wanted the attention on those who needed it most, not her.

He hadn't heard from her in two days...and truth be told, he was getting worried, though he didn't want to be that guy. The one who hovered and looked like a stalker. The last he'd heard, she'd met with her financial advisors and had gotten everything squared away. Her parents would be fine, money wise, for the rest of their lives...as would she.

She told him she'd cried when she received the Silver Star he'd sent, but all in all, she'd sounded great. Happy. And perversely, it made Doc kind of sad. He wanted to be there to see her blossom. To cheer her on. But all he could do was listen after the fact and tell her what a great job she was doing. It wasn't the same as being by her side as she was accomplishing everything she wanted to in her life.

So, after much thinking the previous evening...he'd realized that he couldn't do this. Couldn't be in a long-distance relationship with Ember. He thought he could, but it was too painful. His abrupt change of heart didn't say good things about him, but she deserved a man who could be there for her whenever she needed him, and that wasn't Doc. Not when he was all the way across the country.

Maybe taking the last two days off from talking to her had been a good thing. Would make it easier to start distancing himself. It was obvious she could stand on her own two feet. She didn't need him.

He'd slowly ease off their contact, until she barely remembered he existed. She was extremely busy. She'd be all right.

In contrast, ending contact would *kill* Doc. He treasured their conversations and missed her after only two days. She might be better off without him, but the reverse wasn't true. Though he'd do what was best for her, no matter how much it hurt.

Doc turned his attention back to the team. He'd live for his friends and their families. He'd do whatever it took to help Grover find out what happened to Sierra, even if they never got sent overseas to investigate themselves. Maybe he'd buy another house and flip it. He hadn't finished his own, but having another house to work on would keep him busy, and his mind off what Ember was doing.

The day passed slowly, and Doc couldn't help but check his phone during breaks to see if Ember had texted or called. She hadn't. He wanted to reach out and ask if she was all right. To check on her. Beg her to let him know she wasn't lying dead in a ditch somewhere.

Yeah. He would do a *great* job distancing himself.

When their meetings were over, it was looking more and more like they'd be headed to Afghanistan to investigate the missing contractors. There hadn't been any messages from Shahzada claiming responsibility for any kidnappings, but that was the most likely scenario. There was a Navy SEAL team in the area at the moment, attempting to track down hidey-holes and get more information. Once they reported back, the Deltas could be sent in to clear those hiding spots in the mountain caves. It would be a highly dangerous mission, but they were all one hundred percent on board.

If Shahzada was holding Americans—or *any* innocent human beings hostage—they wanted to find and free them. And they had an even bigger stake since one of those missing may be Sierra. It was obvious that she meant something to Grover. They'd teased their friend over the last year about her, but no one had suspected she was seriously in danger.

Perhaps there was a bit of guilt over not being more concerned about her silence. They'd just thought she wasn't interested in Grover. They should've known that wasn't the case. As for Grover...he wasn't the kind of man to fall fast for a woman, but it looked more and more like he'd done just that, and had kept his interest on the down low.

"Gillian wants to throw Oz and Riley a baby-warming party," Trigger said as they all headed for the parking lot.

"What the hell is that?" Lefty asked.

"You know, like a housewarming party, but with a baby instead."

"It's not necessary," Oz said, a huge grin on his face. "But I know our women never pass up a chance to hang out together."

"Gillian doesn't mind putting something together when she does it every day for a living?" Lucky asked.

"Nope. I asked her the same thing," Trigger said. "She told me that planning parties for her friends is way different than doing it for a business or strangers. For one, she knows whatever she plans won't be judged. Everyone will just be happy being together."

"It's true," Brain said. "I always hoped whoever I ended up with would get along with the women you guys chose, and the friendships Aspen has with everyone are rock solid. It makes me feel a lot better when we're deployed."

The others agreed.

As they exited the building into the hot Texas afternoon heat, Doc couldn't help but wonder what the other women would think about Ember. She was kind and charismatic. He didn't think she'd have an issue making friends, despite being too busy training to find any close confidants over the years. He had a feeling Ember would jump at the chance to have an "inner circle." Women who weren't competition. He knew without a doubt that Gillian, Kinley, Aspen, Riley, and Devyn would take to her. They might be intimidated by her fame at first, but after they got to know her, they'd realize how amazing she was.

He shook his head. It wasn't going to happen. Ember was in California and the women lived in Texas.

"This weekend. Saturday," Trigger said. "At Oz's house. Gillian feels bad that she's commandeering your house without checking with you first, but you can kick us out anytime you want. And she figured it would be easier for you guys. You won't have to haul Amalia's stuff all over the place. And Logan and Bria will probably be more comfortable in their own space."

"It's cool," Oz said. "We've got plenty of room. Tell Gillian to let us all know what to bring. And if she says nothing, there's gonna be trouble."

Trigger laughed. "Don't worry, she's learned her lesson. The last time she tried to provide everything herself, you guys went overboard bringing food and drinks we didn't need."

"Grover?" Lefty asked.

"Yeah?"

"You okay?"

Their friend sighed. "No. But I'm doing my best not to think about what Sierra might have gone through, or is still going through."

"You think she's still alive?" Lucky asked.

Doc winced. He knew Lucky hadn't meant to sound so surprised, but his disbelief was clear. Doc had only known Ember for a little longer than Grover had known Sierra, so he'd never tell his friend it was ridiculous for him to feel so much for the diminutive redhead after such a short period of time. He was proof that when you found the one meant for you...time made no difference.

"I don't know," Grover said. "Part of me hopes and prays she is. But another part knows that's selfish, and if she *is* alive, she's lived through absolute hell for the last year or so."

"Remember Kalee?" Doc asked.

Everyone turned to look at him.

"The woman who was taken by the rebels in Timor-Leste?" he continued. "She was with them for at least a year. And when her SEAL rescued her and brought her back to the States...she was okay. I mean, I don't know her whole story, but from everything I've heard, she and Phantom are doing great together. All I'm saying is, don't give up hope, Grover.

Women are tough. Look at Gillian and the others. We've got proof right in front of our faces how strong they are."

Grover's shoulders seemed to straighten a little. "You're right. Thanks."

Doc nodded.

"What's up with you and Ember?" Brain asked.

Doc was afraid someone was going to ask about her. He shrugged. "Nothing. She lives in California and I'm here. She's famous, and I'm in a profession where secrecy is everything."

"After the things she's posted on her IG account the last few days, she doesn't sound like the kind of woman who wants that famous lifestyle anymore," Lefty noted.

Doc shrugged. "There's still the matter of her life being in Los Angeles while mine is here."

"Don't write off a relationship," Trigger said. "You never know what can happen."

Doc nodded, though he'd pretty much already made the decision where he and Ember were concerned.

"See you guys tomorrow," Oz said. "I need to get home to my family."

"Same," Brain said with a smile.

"It feels good, doesn't it?" Lefty asked.

"To have someone to go home to? Yeah, damn good," Trigger added.

Doc caught Grover's eye and they shared wry grins. They wouldn't know about that, but were happy for their teammates.

"See ya tomorrow," Brain said as he headed for his car.

Everyone said their goodbyes, and despite everything going on in his teammates' lives, Doc was relieved their relationships hadn't changed. They made an effort to still get together outside of the job and no one seemed to mind that most of the time, those gatherings included all the wives.

Doc sighed as he started his Dodge Durango and headed toward the main gate of the post. It wasn't a long drive to get to his house, and halfway there, his phone rang. He answered via his Bluetooth, expecting to hear one of his teammates' voices.

"You got Doc," he said.

"Hey."

One word. That was all it took for a huge smile to break out on Doc's face. "Hey yourself. It's good to hear from you, Em."

"Yeah, sorry I haven't been in touch lately."

"It's okay. I'm sure you've been busy." Doc tried to tell himself to keep his voice a little aloof. That it would be easier to break things off with Ember if conversations were superficial between them. But he couldn't seem to do it. He was too damn happy to hear from her.

"I have. Things have been pretty insane, actually. Is this a good time to talk?"

"Of course. I'm headed home from work."

"Okay, good."

"What have you been up to?" Doc asked.

"I met with a lawyer, and we began the paperwork to start my new business venture. I have more papers to sign, but it's a step."

"Wow, you haven't wasted any time, have you?"

"Nope. I'm more excited about introducing kids to the modern pentathlon than I've been about almost anything I've done in the last decade. I want to make a difference, and I really think this is one way I can do that."

"I love it," Doc told her. "I can hear the excitement in your voice."

"I've also hired some people to help me."

"That's great."

"Yeah. I had long talks with some of the athletes I've

145

trained with. I told them what I wanted to do and asked if any would be willing to help. I offered a very competitive salary and agreed they could even keep training if they wanted."

"And did anyone take you up on your offer?"

"Yeah, Julio and Marie. They seemed pretty excited about it all. I can find other experts in the various events to help out too. I should be able to find someone to help coach the swimming part, and I'll need to team up with someone who has horses and wouldn't mind kids using them. The fencing won't be too hard, I can buy the equipment for that; same with the laser sights and guns. And of course, we can run anywhere."

Doc enjoyed hearing the excitement and energy in her voice. She'd obviously done a lot of thinking about what she wanted, and he wasn't surprised she was making it work. "I can't wait to hear more about it, and what the kids think when you start."

Damn. He was supposed to be distancing himself, but it was impossible. Her enthusiasm was infectious.

Doc pulled down his street and waved at a few of his neighbors who were sitting on their porches, enjoying the fresh air. It was still warm, but for this part of Texas, it wasn't too bad this time of evening.

When he saw a BMW he didn't recognize sitting at the curb in front of his house, he frowned.

"Craig?"

"Yeah?"

"You seem distracted," Ember said.

"Sorry. I'm about to pull into my driveway and there's a car I don't recognize here."

"Yeah?" she asked.

"Uh-huh. I'm gonna have to let you go and deal with—" Doc's words stopped abruptly as someone stood from the chair she'd been sitting in, on his front porch. "*Ember?*" he said incredulously.

"Surprise!" she said—sounding more than a little nervous. Doc could hear her voice shake on the word, even through the speakers in his car.

He didn't remember putting the vehicle in park or getting out.

He stalked toward his front door, his gaze taking in Ember from head to toe. She looked even better than the last time he'd seen her.

She wore a tank top that hugged her curves and showed off her muscular arms. Shorts emphasized her strong thighs and calves.

She clicked off her phone and put it in her back pocket. "Hey. I...um...I might have forgotten to mention that I'm planning on starting my new business venture here in Texas. If it's okay. I mean...I could really start it anywhere, but I figured since this was where *you* were, and I wanted to get to know you better, it would be as good a place as any to put down roots. But if this is creepy or something, I can leave."

She was babbling, but her last words finally got Doc's ass in gear. He practically leaped at her, snatching her up and holding her tightly to him as he spun her around in a circle and hugged her.

She laughed. The sound was carefree and happy, and Doc felt it all the way to his toes. "Don't leave," he managed to get out. When her feet were on the ground once more, he leaned down without thought. He was so glad to see her. So damn thrilled she was here...and was apparently planning on staying.

She eagerly opened under his lips, and Doc plunged his tongue into her mouth. Fuck, he'd missed this. He'd had erotic dreams every night since he'd left her in South Korea, and kissing her was even more satisfying than he remembered.

When she finally pulled back, they were both breathing hard.

"I was kind of afraid someone would call the cops on me," she admitted.

"Not in this neighborhood," Doc told her. "Part of the reason I picked it is because of the diversity. My neighbors on either side of me are Black. There's a Hispanic couple with three kids who live across the street. A few white families, a gay couple, a family from Israel, one from India, and even one from Pakistan. We're truly multicultural here—and our block parties are awesome."

"I love that."

"Me too. I can't believe you're here. You have to be exhausted. Did you drive all this way today? No, you couldn't have. Are you hungry? Come in, let me show you my house and get you something to eat and drink."

Ember chuckled. "You're cute when you're flustered. I'm a little hungry, but you know what I really need?"

"What? Anything."

"Anything? What if I asked for caviar and truffles?"

"Then I'd find a way to get them for you," Doc said, completely serious.

"I was kidding," she said softly.

"I wasn't," Doc told her. He still held her close and couldn't believe how good she felt in his arms.

"I need something green," Ember said with a small smile. "I ate a lot of crap on the road and a salad sounds like heaven."

"You're in luck, I went to the store yesterday and have all the stuff for a salad." Doc was moving before he'd finished talking. He unlocked his door and gestured for her to precede him inside. "It's still a work in progress," he told her a little self-consciously.

He dropped his arm as Ember wandered into his space, looking around curiously. After a long moment, she said, "It's wonderful, Craig."

Something inside him loosened. "It's not huge, but I've enjoyed fixing it up."

She ran a hand over the banister of the stairway as she turned to him. "You've done all of it?"

"Well, most of the woodwork, yeah. I'm not so good with plumbing or electrical stuff, so I've called in someone for that, but I've picked out all the fixtures, colors, flooring, that sort of thing. I handmade the cabinets in the kitchen because everything I saw looked cheap, or was way too expensive. And I made the banister slats and the railing myself too."

"It's amazing. Seriously. I'm impressed."

Doc shrugged. "Come on," he said, taking her hand in his. He loved touching her and had a feeling he'd take any opportunity to do it in the future. "Let's get you fed."

He led Ember to a stool at the bar extending from the island work space in the kitchen. She sat with a smile and watched as he got out the stuff he needed to make a salad for her.

"Do you need any help?"

"Nope, I got this. You relax." Then as nonchalantly as he could, Doc asked, "So...you have a place to stay tonight?"

She made a weird noise, and he looked up in alarm. She was smiling from ear to ear and trying very hard not to laugh.

"What?" he asked in confusion.

"Do you think I'd come all this way and *not* have a place to stay? Or that I'd just assume I could stay with you?"

"Well, um...I don't know."

"Craig, I'd never be so presumptuous. I like you. A lot. I wouldn't be here if I didn't want to see where things between us can go. But I'd never pull up to your house and inform you that I was moving in."

Doc didn't know whether to be relieved or disappointed.

"Besides, I'm looking forward to being on my own. I've lived with my parents literally my entire life. I can't wait to go to the grocery store and fill my fridge and pantry with whatever I want. To make my own meals. To decorate the way I want to. I've never been able to do any of that before. I know it's kind of pathetic, but I'm excited about it."

"It's not pathetic," Doc reassured her. "I think it's...adorable."

Ember rolled her eyes. "Just what I want to be. Anyway, to answer your question, I rented a hotel room for tonight, and tomorrow, I'm meeting with the landlord to move into my apartment."

"You already rented one? Where is it? Is it in a good part of town? Did you check out the reviews beforehand?" Doc fired the questions at her.

She chuckled. "Yes to most of your questions. It's not too far from the Army post. And if it doesn't work out, I'll find something else once I get to know the area. I wanted to be semi-close to the building I bought for my gym, and I was reassured by the landlord that the security was good."

"Wait, you already bought a building too?" Doc asked, his mind spinning.

"Yup," Ember said, looking extremely proud of herself.

"Damn," Doc muttered.

"Hey, when I put my mind to something, I don't fuck around," Ember said.

"I guess not."

"But, Craig...seriously, if you aren't happy to see me, and were just trying to get laid while you were at the Olympics...I don't have to stay. I can just as easily go down to the Austin area. As much as I want to see where things might go between the two of us...I really did come with my business in mind."

Doc was once more moving before his brain had time to understand what he was doing. He stood close, cradled her head in his hands, and said in a low, earnest tone, "I haven't had a serious relationship in a year. And that one was more serious on her side than mine. Leaving you in Korea sucked. I never thought I'd miss someone the way I've missed you. I hated not being with you when you went home. After you posted that letter on your social media, I wanted to hold you and tell you how proud I was of you. I wasn't looking for a one-night stand, and I'm still not.

"I'm so fucking happy and relieved that you're here. I can't believe it. And I want to get to know everything about you. All of it. I want to go running with you and take you shooting. I want you to get to know my friends and their wives, and spend my evenings and weekends either hanging out with you or working with you and your kids. A part of me is impressed as hell at everything you've done in such a short period of time, and another part is pouting because you obviously don't need me at all. You're incredible, Em, and I want to be a part of your life any way you'll let me."

Tears had filled her eyes by the time he was done speaking, and Doc couldn't resist leaning in and kissing her once more. He felt her hands slip under his shirt, and he shivered as her nails lightly scored the sensitive bare skin of his lower back.

"I've got connections for all the business stuff I want to do, but what I don't have is friends. I haven't been very lucky in that area in the past. People either want to be around me because of what I can do for them, or because they're hoping to get famous."

"Gillian and the others won't give a shit about that," Doc told her with confidence.

"I can't wait to meet them. You've told me so much, I feel as if I know them already."

"It's good you said that, because Saturday we're having a get-together at Oz's house to celebrate the birth of his daughter. And you'll get to meet Logan. And I'll warn you, you'll have a friend for life once he finds out you were the one who got Shin-Soo to send all that stuff."

"Maybe we should wait to see if things between us work out," she said, biting her lip in concern.

"We're going to work out," Doc said firmly.

"You don't know that," Ember said.

"I do. Wanna know how?"

"Yeah."

"Because I've never felt this way about anyone before. The last two days have been hell. I've missed talking to you so much, I actually made a decision to back off, to try to let you go, because I knew if I got any closer to you, I wouldn't be able to handle not physically being with you all the time. But you're here. You came to me. You made your decision...and I've made mine."

Her lips quirked up a bit. "You're kinda bossy."

Doc shrugged. "Comes with the territory. I'm a Delta Force operative, Em. I'm used to making life-or-death decisions at the drop of a hat."

"This isn't life-or-death," she noted.

"Wrong. Without you, I'm not sure I'd *have* much of a life." Doc had never been so blunt and honest with a woman before. Especially not this early in their relationship. But the rightness he felt when he'd pulled up to his house and saw her there wasn't something he could explain. He understood her wanting to live on her own, and respected it. But that didn't mean he wasn't going to be seeing her every day.

"Wow. I think that's the nicest thing anyone's ever said to me," Ember said quietly.

"I'm not an easy man to be with," Doc warned her. "I'm hardheaded and stubborn. I'm also very protective. But I understand needing to make it on your own. I'll stand by your side and support you however you need and want me to. I actually like that you're independent, because you'll *need* to be when I'm away. I won't be able to tell you where I'm going or how long I'll be gone when I get deployed. It's hard to be with a military man, and even harder to be with a special forces soldier. But I swear I won't cheat on you. The thought makes my stomach turn. Things won't be easy with me, but I know that I can make you happy if you'll let me."

"Shit, Craig, now I'm crying," Ember said, as she wiped away a tear.

Doc pushed her hand out of the way and brushed the wetness from her cheeks. "These had better be happy tears, because I can't stomach the thought of hurting you."

"They are," she reassured him. "I don't need or want a man to take over my life. I've had enough of people doing that to last a lifetime. I need you to support my dreams and aspirations. To be there if I need you. To laugh with me. To watch cheesy movies. To help me break out of this bubble I've lived in my entire life."

"You've got me," Doc said immediately.

She smiled. "What would you have said if I'd told you I didn't have a place to stay?"

Doc grinned back. "I would've informed you that I have three empty bedrooms, and that you were welcome to any of them."

"Seriously?"

"Yup."

"So we're on the same page then?"

"When it comes to you and me? Absolutely," Doc reassured her. "The guys are gonna be so jazzed to know you're here."

"They barely know me," Ember protested.

"They know all they need to know," Doc said.

"And what's that?"

"That you had my back. That you stood by me and didn't lose your shit when things got tough. That goes a long way with them." He paused. "And it helps that you're drop-dead gorgeous and famous to boot."

Ember laughed and shoved him a little. "Whatever. Finish my salad, Army man."

Doc loved seeing her look so happy. She seemed a hundred times more relaxed than she'd been in South Korea. This was the real Ember, and seeing her blossom was fucking beautiful. He was also glad to do as she ordered. Little did she know, she had him wrapped around her finger already.

He wasn't concerned at all that things were moving so fast between them. It felt right.

Moving back around to the salad he'd abandoned, he continued chopping the vegetables. Within ten minutes, he'd set a large bowl full to the top with "green stuff" in front of Ember. Then decided to nuke himself some leftovers from the night before.

Doc couldn't remember a better dinner.

* * *

Ember couldn't remember having a better evening. After she'd eaten the delicious salad Craig had made for her, and he'd given her the grand tour of his house, they'd sat on his couch and talked for hours.

She'd caught him up with everything that had happened after she'd gotten home from the Olympics. He already knew most of it, but he wanted to know the tiniest details. He'd scowled when she'd told him more about her parents' reactions to her retirement and changing her social media passwords. He'd laughed as she recounted how Samer had talked to her for two hours, trying to teach her all the dos and don'ts for her own accounts.

She'd told him about her meeting at the gym with the men and women she'd trained with for several years, and how mostly supportive they'd been. They talked about the crazy people online who had nothing better to do than spew hatred in the form of awful and mean comments. She'd even told him how relieved she was to have lost a million followers after posting her heartfelt letter on Instagram. If those people were only hanging out to see the perfect pictures and endorsements that she hawked on her account, good riddance. She'd much rather interact with people who were genuinely interested in making the world a better place.

After she yawned a few times, Craig had decided they were done and she needed to get to the hotel and get some sleep. She *was* tired, but she'd hated to leave. Though she hadn't said goodbye right then, since Craig had insisted on following her to the hotel and walking her inside. It was dark out, and he said he wasn't going to take any chances with her safety.

Now, he was pulling one of her suitcases behind him while she towed the other.

"Is this a part of you being protective?" she asked in the elevator as they headed up to her room.

"Yup."

"And if I tell you I'm fine and don't need you to follow me?"

"I'd say 'too bad.' This is who I am, Em. I'm not the kind of guy who lets his girl drive to a hotel in a city she just arrived in, in the middle of the night, by herself. I'm just not. If this is a deal breaker, you need to decide now."

Ember stepped up to him, right into his personal space,

and kissed the underside of his jaw. "I'm not complaining. Just making sure."

Craig relaxed against her. "There are a lot of things I'll step back and let you do by yourself. Kick business ass. Run your social media accounts. Hire employees and basically manage your life. But when it comes to your safety? I won't compromise."

"And I'm one hundred percent all right with that," she said before reaching up and putting her hand on the back of his head and pulling him down to her. They were still kissing when the elevator door opened.

When they stumbled out of the elevator with her bags, Ember rested her head on Craig's shoulder and kept her free arm around him as they headed down the hall. She opened her door and they wheeled her bags just inside. After turning around to face him, for a second she felt as if she was back in that dorm in South Korea.

"What are you smiling about?" Craig asked.

"Déjà vu," she told him. "Standing in front of my door, not wanting to say goodbye to you."

"Never say goodbye, remember?" Craig asked.

She nodded.

"You're meeting with the manager of the apartment complex in the morning?"

"Yeah. At eight. I usually work out first thing, but I'm looking forward to sleeping in tomorrow, so I'll be lazy. After that, I'll verify with the movers where to meet me the day after next. Then I'll tour the building I bought for my gym to see what I need to do to get it up to speed. I have a meeting with a lawyer to finalize the papers to make my business official here in Texas, then I have a few interviews with some potential coaches. I need to make sure the apartments I found for Marie and Julio are acceptable, since they'll be here Sunday.

"Oh, and I've set up a meeting with the director of the Boys and Girls Club here in Killeen, to talk about partnering with them. She can help me decide which kids would be best for the program. Eventually, I want to branch out and meet with principals of schools, and someone in Child Protective Services too."

"Jeez, Em, you don't have to do everything in one day," Craig said.

She smiled. "I know, but I'm just so excited to get started. I also need to order some equipment, hire cleaning crews, find a good place where we can run and shoot, set up security, meet with a few local ranchers about using their horses, then meet with the YMCA director about dedicated pool time. Oh, and I need to move my stuff in, go to the store to buy food, and lastly—decorate my place."

"I'm tired just listening to everything on your list. You gonna be done with a few things by dinnertime tomorrow?"

"Of course."

"I can pick you up here and bring you to my house, if you want."

"I can drive myself."

"I know. And I meant to tell you before that your BMW is sweet. But humor me and let me pick you up on my way home?"

Ember couldn't help but love that he was so eager to spend time with her. "Okay."

"I'll text to make sure you're done with all your appointments before I leave post. Anything you want to eat tomorrow?"

"Anything's fine. I don't want you to go out of your way for me."

"I have a feeling I'd go to the ends of the Earth for you, Em. What time is your stuff supposed to arrive on Friday?"

"I'm not sure. Probably in the morning sometime."

"I'll talk to Commander Robinson and see if he'll give us some time off to help you move in."

"Oh, that's okay. I hired the movers for a few hours and I don't have that much stuff."

"Em, there's no way in hell I'm *not* going to help you move your stuff in. And the guys will feel the same way. And if the girls aren't working, they'll be there to help too. Although their help is more standing around drinking wine and watching us do the work, but they're damn cute while they do it, so we tolerate it."

Ember chuckled—and a pang of something so visceral hit her hard. She wanted to be a part of this man's tribe. Wanted that more than she'd wanted to win an Olympic medal. "Okay. Thank you."

"No need for thanks. If Gillian shows up, you can ask her what we should bring to the party on Saturday. She usually tries to say she's got it all covered, but that's bullshit. We all like to contribute. Tell her if she won't tell you, then we'll hire a bunch of clowns to come over and entertain Logan and Bria."

"And that's a bad thing?"

"Babe...they're *clowns*. Yes, that's a bad thing."

She laughed. "Right. Noted. I'll ask." She liked that he'd used the pronoun "we." To ask Gillian what *we* should bring. Being linked to this man was heady.

"Okay, I'm going to leave while I still can."

The look of lust was easy to see in his eyes. Ember had never been all that sexual, had never felt the *need* to have sex. But with this man, she was barely holding herself back from peeling off his shirt and climbing him like a stripper pole.

"And if you don't stop looking at me like that, I'm never gonna be *able* to leave," he drawled.

"Like what?" she asked coyly, playing with the buttons on the front of the shirt he'd changed into when he'd gotten home. She liked seeing him in his camouflage uniform, but she liked him dressed more casually like this too. The white button-down shirt brought out his tanned skin and the blue in his eyes.

"Like you want to swallow me whole," he growled.

Ember licked her lips and saw his nostrils flare. God, she loved knowing she affected him as much as he did her. "How long do you think we can hold out?"

He didn't pretend to misunderstand her. "Before we end up in bed? Not very long, if you keep looking at me like that."

For a split second, Ember debated pulling him into her room. But a yawn came from out of nowhere, surprising her.

Craig chuckled. "There'll be plenty of time for us to explore this chemistry we've got later. You have a long day ahead of you, and I know you're tired from driving the last two days." He pulled her into him and kissed her forehead, keeping his lips against her skin for a long moment. Then he stepped back and put his hands in his pockets, as if to keep himself from reaching for her again. "Sleep well."

"You too."

"I'll talk to you and see you tomorrow."

"Okay."

"Good luck with all your meetings, although it sounds as if you have everything under control."

Ember grinned. "I do."

"Fuck, I love your confidence. Later, Em."

"Later."

She liked that he was still careful not to say goodbye to her. It was silly and stupid, but she couldn't make herself say the word either.

She waited until she'd closed the door before closing her eyes and putting a hand over her heart. She had a huge smile on her face, but couldn't have held it back if she tried. Things were looking up, and she had a good feeling about her future.

CHAPTER TEN

Friday morning, Doc had picked up Ember at the hotel and they'd gone on a long, leisurely run. She'd complained good-naturedly about the heat, even at six in the morning, and he'd given her shit for being a baby. Afterward, they'd made out in front of her door at the hotel, then agreed to meet at her new apartment again at eight-thirty. Commander Robinson had given the team the morning off, but they all had to be back in the office after lunch to continue discussing the situation in Afghanistan.

She'd picked a good complex. Doc had been ready to encourage her to move if he found out her apartment wasn't one of the safer ones in the area, but there'd been no need. She'd done her research well. There were security cameras in the parking lots and sprinkled around the complex. There was a pool, workout room, and a ton of lights.

He knew about the lights because he'd driven around the entire complex last night, after he'd dropped Ember off, just to check it out.

He couldn't help but feel a pang in his chest when he thought about her moving into the apartment, instead of his house. She'd probably paid both first and last month's rent in deposit, not to mention the monthly maintenance fee the complex added. It seemed...permanent. At least in the short term. After all, no one would pay that much money, then decide to move in with *him* a few months later.

And just thinking about her moving in with him was crazy. Wasn't it? If he asked Brain—or Oz, or Lucky, or *any* of the guys—they'd say absolutely not. But he knew pretty much everyone else would disagree.

It was just that he and Ember felt *so* right. He couldn't imagine living apart from her for months, let alone possibly years. The thought of dropping her off and leaving her behind every night, for months on end, wasn't a good one.

"Hey, Earth to Craig!" Ember teased as she walked toward him.

Doc realized that he'd been standing by his car looking up at the apartment for so long, she'd been able to sneak up on him without his noticing.

"Hey," he said, opening his arms as he stood up straight. It felt good when Ember walked right into his embrace without hesitation. Inhaling deeply, Doc said, "You smell good."

"Thanks. That happens when you shower," she quipped.

Doc leaned back and looked at the woman in his arms. She was wearing a purple tank top and a pair of khaki cargo shorts. She had on the same shoes she'd worn for their run. Her hair was pulled back in a low ponytail and a hat was hanging from one of her belt loops. She was ready to work— and a bolt of lust hit him out of the blue. He wanted her. Hard. Fast. Slow. Now.

Ember stared up at him with her huge brown eyes and visibly swallowed. It was as if she knew exactly what he was thinking. Doc licked his lips, and she mirrored the movement. Dragging out the anticipation, he slowly leaned toward her.

"The truck's not here yet?" a loud voice called out.

Doc froze, staring at Ember's lips in frustration and desire.

She grinned. "Cockblocked by your friends," she said softly.

"Fuck," Doc grumbled.

The giggle that came from Ember was carefree and happy, and Doc wanted to hear it every day for the rest of his life. With a sigh, he turned to greet Trigger.

"Hey," Doc said, giving his friend a chin lift.

"Hey. Good to see you again, Ember. Welcome to Texas."

"Thanks."

"Sorry Gillian couldn't come this morning. She's meeting a new client and couldn't postpone," Trigger said.

"It's okay. I'm looking forward to meeting her tomorrow."

"So is she. She's over-the-moon excited about the party, but beware—she and the other women are gonna give you the third degree. I heard her talking with Kinley on the phone, and they've got a list of famous people they want to know if you've met." Trigger winked at her and grinned.

Doc, however, stiffened...but when Ember merely chuckled, he relaxed.

"I'm afraid they're gonna be disappointed. I mean, I spent most of my time training, not going to Hollywood parties."

"They won't be disappointed," Trigger said. "Believe me, they're excited to meet you. And I hope you don't mind, but Doc told us a bit about what you've got planned for our little city, and I told Gillian. She's already all fired up about fundraisers and getting the word out to help you find kids who might be appropriate to participate."

"Wow! Thank her for me."

"You can thank her yourself tomorrow," Trigger said with a smile.

"Yo! Let's get this show on the road!" Lefty said as he

approached. He was accompanied by Brain and Aspen, the latter holding their son against her chest. Chance was fastened in by some complicated-looking device with straps going every which way around Aspen's body.

"Hi! I'm Aspen. It's so good to meet you!" She held out a hand toward Ember.

Doc let his arm drop from her waist and watched as the two women met.

"I've heard a lot about you," Ember said easily.

"Don't believe a word these guys say," Aspen returned with a smile. "They're all full of shit."

"Language, Aspen," Brain chided.

The woman rolled her eyes. "Chance is like two seconds old. I don't think he'll be mimicking my bad words anytime soon," she told her husband. Then she turned to Ember and leaned in, adding in a stage whisper, "My smarter-than-the-average-joe husband is afraid Chance is going to start talking at three months. I mean, I know he hopes he's passed on his language savant ability, but that's pushing it a bit."

Doc smiled. Brain *was* paranoid that his son's first word was going to be a swear word. But Doc figured it would be some obscure Russian term or something that he picked up from his dad.

"Am I late?" Lefty asked. "It's good to see you again, Ember."

"You're not late, we're waiting on the truck. And thank you," she told him.

"Kins is working this morning, so she couldn't come, but she said rabid stray hippos couldn't keep her away tomorrow," Lefty said.

Ember laughed.

Oz, Lucky, and Grover arrived then and joined the group huddle. Logan walked alongside his uncle, and Devyn was there as well.

"I hope no one minds that I brought Slugger along this morning. Riley, Bria, and Amalia are having a girls' morning. Not to mention, Riley wants to work on a new book she got last night to proofread," Oz said.

"More hands is always a good thing," Ember said. She crouched down on the balls of her feet and greeted Logan. "I hear you're quite the baseball player."

Logan blushed and looked down at his feet for a second. He seemed to find his courage, looked up at Ember for a split second—then practically threw himself at her.

Ember's eyes widened as she caught the little boy and hugged him back, grinning.

"Thank you so much for having Shin-Soo send that box! It was amazing! It made my day! All my friends are *so* jealous, and I can't believe I have a mitt that he actually *used*! It's too big for me right now, but Uncle Oz says my hands will grow into it. I can't wait! I've got the pictures and poster up on the walls in my room, and I'm gonna put one of the signed baseballs into one of those plastic box things so it'll never ever get messed up."

Ember smiled wider as Logan finally stepped away from her. "You're very welcome. I was happy to talk to my friend and ask him to send it to you."

"I'm gonna be famous one day, and I'm gonna send boxes like that to *my* fans. Because I know how much it meant to me, so I want to do that for someone else."

"Good for you. I love your confidence. You know that's the first step to becoming a champion, right? Believing in yourself?" Ember asked.

Logan nodded. "That's what Uncle Oz says."

"Your uncle is a very smart man," Ember agreed.

"Not as smart as Brain, but that's okay," Logan said with a completely straight face, and everyone laughed.

Ember stood and Devyn stepped forward. "Hi. I'm

Devyn. It's very good to meet you. Congrats on being in the Olympics. That's impressive!"

Ember smiled. "Thanks."

That was another thing Doc liked about Ember. She didn't shrug off Devyn's congratulations. Didn't hem and haw and say she didn't compete as well as she would've liked, or that she was "only" fifteenth. She'd made the team; that said a great deal about her abilities.

"Hi, Ember," Lucky said, reaching for her hand.

Ember shook his and Grover's hands. "Thanks for coming to help me," she told everyone. "I told Craig it wasn't a big deal, that I don't have all that much stuff, but he insisted."

"As well he should've. This is kind of our thing. Helping people move in, then helping them move all their shit out not too much later," Trigger joked.

Doc glared at his friend.

The others all grinned.

"I don't understand?" Ember said, throwing a questioning look at Doc.

"He's kidding," he told her.

"Actually, he's not," Aspen said with a smirk. "It seems like the second we help someone move into a new place, we're turning around and helping them move again. To their man's place, to a bigger house...something."

Doc groaned. "Can we change the subject, please?" he begged.

A large moving truck pulled into the parking lot just then, and Doc was relieved that this conversation could be over.

"A few things?" Grover asked, one brow raised. "That looks like more than a few things."

"It's not all mine," Ember reassured the group. "When someone can't fill a truck, they put several people's things in. It saves money and cross-country trips. I was shocked when the truck backed into my driveway in California, since I didn't have enough stuff to fill it. Then relieved when they explained my stuff would be at the back, and the first to be unloaded."

While everyone was preoccupied watching the truck driver maneuver to get as close to the entrance as possible, where they'd be bringing in Ember's belongings, Doc leaned down. "You good?"

"Of course. Why wouldn't I be?" she asked.

"Just checking," he told her.

"So...you think we'll be doing this again soon?" she asked with a small grin.

Doc groaned. "Ignore them."

"But now I'm curious. I take it moving fast in a relationship isn't uncommon among you and your friends?"

"You have to understand...we've seen a lot of bad shit in our line of work. We've had friends die and leave behind their families. We've seen soldiers cheat on their spouses and not even care who knew about it. Hell, we've seen spouses cheat on soldiers, especially in special forces. We've seen death and destruction on a level that would make what happened in South Korea look like a walk in the park, Em. So when we find someone who can put up with our jobs, our idiosyncrasies, and *still* want to be with us...we hold on to that with both hands.

"I'm not saying we're gonna get married and have a ton of babies, but as a rule, the team hasn't fucked around when it comes to living our lives, because we know how *fleeting* those lives can be. And if that means asking the women we love to move in with us faster than what's considered 'normal,' so we can spend as much time with them as possible, that's what we do." Doc held his breath as he waited for Ember's response.

She lifted a hand and placed it on his cheek. "I get it," she said softly.

"I know you're looking forward to being on your own, and

I admire you for it. I won't rush you into anything you aren't ready for, but I *do* hope you're ready for me to be around...a lot."

"I'm ready," she told him without hesitation. "I wouldn't be here in Texas if I didn't see us being together for the long haul. I've never done something like this before. I've never moved across the country and made plans to put down roots in a city I've never lived in. I'm excited about my own place, but that doesn't mean I don't want you in it."

"Thank fuck," Doc muttered.

Ember smiled.

"Hey, you two, you gonna come help us figure out where we're going and what goes where?" Lucky called out.

Doc looked over and saw that his team had already helped the driver and the movers Ember had hired to open the back of the truck. "Go on up with Devyn and Aspen," Doc told her.

"I can help," she protested.

"I know you can, but you've got the six of us, plus the guys you hired. We'll have this done in no time—and I know Devyn and Aspen are probably dying to talk to you."

"It's too early for wine, but I may or may not have the makings for mimosas upstairs," Ember told him.

"Perfect," Doc said with a smile. He leaned down and kissed her. It was a brief kiss, but he loved the way her lips clung to his as he pulled back. "When we're done with your stuff, you want to go to lunch with everyone?"

"Absolutely."

He turned to go, and Ember put her hand on his arm. "Craig?"

"Yeah?"

"Is Grover okay? He's been very quiet."

"He's worried about Sierra." Doc was concerned about his friend, Grover wasn't his usual self. It was obvious the entire situation with the missing contractor was weighing heavily on him.

"I was doing some research last night on how to tell where my followers are from, and as far as I can tell, I've got about forty thousand who live in the Middle East. I know it's a long shot, but I still want to post about Sierra. Is there a picture of her I can use?"

"I'll get you one," Doc said, reminded once again that Ember was as far from the spoiled, self-centered, rich bitch many accused her of being as she could get.

"Get a move on!" Lefty shouted in their direction.

Doc couldn't keep from kissing her temple before heading for the truck.

* * *

Three hours later, Ember found herself sitting in the middle of a long rectangular table at a barbeque restaurant. Logan had barbeque sauce smeared all over his face, hands, and halfway up his arms, but no one seemed to care.

More than that, she hadn't seen one person surreptitiously taking pictures or video of her. It was a relief to be incognito here. Ember knew once word about her business got out, she'd probably be more recognized, but for now it was heaven.

The morning had been busy and fun. She never would've thought moving *could* be fun, but it was. The guys were hilarious and gracious, and Ember adored how they encouraged Logan and made him feel like one of the gang.

And Devyn and Aspen were open and welcoming. Aspen had even let her hold her baby—and when Craig had walked in and seen her with little Chance in her arms, she swore her ovaries had almost burst at the look in his eyes. It was a combination of lust, need, and gentleness. He hadn't said anything, but she knew she'd never forget that look.

Now they were eating lunch before everyone had to get back to work. Ember had a few more papers she needed to sign with the lawyer she'd met with yesterday, and she had to double check the arrangements she made for Julio and Marie to fly out.

Then she wanted to pinch herself to make sure all this was really happening.

It hadn't been too long ago that she'd been depressed and wondering what to do with her life. And now, here she was in Texas, with her own apartment, a man she cared about a great deal, and about to start up her own business.

Making a mental note to look into taking college classes online so she could get her degree, Ember happened to look across the table at Craig.

She was sitting between Logan—who'd insisted on sitting next to her—and Devyn. Across from her was Craig, Trigger, and Lefty. Grover had passed on lunch, saying he was going back to base to see if any new reports had come in that morning.

Aspen and Brain were sitting at one end of the table, and Brain was holding their son against his chest as he ate with one hand. Everyone was smiling and laughing, and not worrying about how many calories they were consuming or who might be watching. It was as different as night and day from her old life in California, and Ember was happier than she'd been in a very long time.

"When are you gonna come watch me play, Em?" Logan asked.

"Logan, that's rude," Oz admonished mildly.

"It's fine," Ember said quickly. She loved how the little boy had picked up on Craig's nickname for her. She loved being Em, and not Ember Maxwell. "I definitely want to. When's your next game?"

Logan looked to his uncle.

Oz chuckled. "I think it's next weekend, Slugger, but I'm not the schedule pro. That's Ri."

"She keeps us all in line," Logan agreed with a nod. "From Amalia's feeding schedule and doctor appointments, to Bria's play dates and activities, to my baseball stuff. Without her we'd be late all the time and probably miss everything."

Oz laughed harder. "He's not wrong. Ri keeps us all organized. I don't know what I'd do without her." He turned to Logan. "But no matter what Em said, it's still rude to almost demand someone come watch you play. It's more polite to say you're having a good time playing baseball, and then invite someone to possibly come and watch a game sometime."

"That's what I did!" Logan insisted with a confused look on his face.

"Subtle, he's not," Devyn said quietly from next to her.

"Besides, wouldn't it be cool for Em to say she watched me play when I was little after I'm famous? I bet if she took a picture of me today, it would be worth millions after I grow up and make it big."

"Not lacking in confidence either," Devyn quipped.

Ember couldn't help but laugh. "I'd be honored to come and watch you play, Logan. And I'll take tons of pictures, so when I get old and gray, they can finance my retirement. Okay?"

"Okay!" Logan agreed happily. "And you'll show the pictures to me too? Maybe I can have one?"

"Absolutely."

As Logan turned to tell his uncle that Ember was going to take pictures of him, even though Oz was sitting right there and heard the entire conversation, Devyn leaned in once more. "He doesn't have any pictures from when he was growing up. Either his mom never took any, or she didn't keep them for him. With everyone taking so many pictures of his newborn sister, Riley thinks he's feeling left out."

Ember's heart broke for the little boy, and for his sister, Bria. "I'll take so many pictures, he'll be sick of me," she promised.

Devyn eyed her for a long moment before saying, "You know, I wasn't sure what to think about you at first. When we heard Doc was into you, I went and checked out your Instagram...you know, to make sure you were good enough for him."

Ember smirked a little, and Devyn continued.

"I admit that I was skeptical. There was a lot of what seemed to be superficial stuff on there...but then I realized that your profile was basically a way to monetize your name, which is pretty smart. Just because I don't like selfies or wearing a lot of makeup, doesn't make it a bad business decision. Then the more I read about the modern pentathlon and how hard it is, and how much training athletes have to do in order to be good in all five sports, the more impressed I got. Now that I've met you, I feel bad that I had any judgmental thoughts about you at all. I also cried when I read that letter on your profile. I realized *that* was the real you. Just be you— Em. She's much more likeable than the fake Ember Maxwell."

"Thanks. I like being Em," Ember said.

The two women smiled at each other.

"I do have a question though," Ember continued.

"Shoot," Devyn said.

"How long did it take *you* to move in with Lucky?"

Everyone burst out laughing. Lucky leaned his elbows on the table and smirked, letting Devyn handle the conversation.

"Longer than everyone else, but that was because I was his friend's bratty little sister. Actually, it seems that we take longer than everyone on *everything*."

"What do you mean?" Ember asked.

Devyn gestured to Oz and Chance. "Marriage. Babies. That sort of thing."

"Oh, you aren't married?" Ember asked. She'd just assumed they were.

"Nope. I love Lucky, and he loves me, and we're fully planning on spending the rest of our lives together. But a quick courthouse wedding, or going to Vegas, would never fly with my family. So since neither of us is ready for the huge shindig up in Missouri that I know my mom and dad want, we're just shacking up together for now."

Ember looked from Devyn to Lucky, then back to Devyn. "Um...then why, when the guys talk about all of their women, do they say 'wives' and not 'wives and girlfriend'?"

To Ember's surprise, Devyn blushed a bright red. "Um..." She looked at Lucky, as if hoping he'd save her.

"I'm sorry, that was rude," Ember said, mortified that she'd somehow upset her friend.

"It wasn't rude," Craig said with a small smile. He glanced at Lucky. "Told you keeping it a secret wouldn't work."

Lucky sighed. "Right. So...the truth is that Devyn and I *are* married. I wanted her to have the benefits I get from being in the Army and to have the support if anything ever happened. But we haven't told her family yet. Or really, anyone outside the team. We aren't in a rush to get the fancy party her parents want, so for now, we're pretending we're just living in sin."

Logan frowned and asked his uncle, "What's living in sin mean?"

"We'll talk about it later," Oz told him.

Ember turned to Devyn. "Wow. Well, I'm sorry I didn't just let it go..."

"It's okay. I told Lucky I was horrible at keeping secrets," Devyn said.

"So you two *aren't* taking longer than everyone else to do things," Ember said with a grin.

Everyone at the table laughed, and it was another surreal moment for Ember. She liked this. A lot.

"Fine. We aren't. But I promise I'm not pregnant yet. We *are* waiting for that."

Baby Chance chose that moment to let out an ear-splitting wail. Ember jumped and Devyn chuckled.

"That kid's got a set of lungs on him for sure," she said.

Not too long after that, everyone began to get ready to go. Ember was surprised when Devyn gave her a hug.

Aspen approached and gave her a distracted hug as well. It was obvious she wanted to get to the car and take care of whatever had Chance so upset. "It was nice meeting you. See you tomorrow at Riley and Oz's house!"

Logan also gave her a long hug and said, "Don't forget! You promised to come to my game and take lots of pictures! Gotta have those when I grow up for throwback slide shows and stuff."

Ember couldn't help but laugh. "Got it. I won't let you down."

Logan looked her right in the eye and said, "I know. Because you're Doc's girlfriend." Then he spun around and jogged toward the door, where Oz was waiting for him.

"He's right, you know," Craig said as he put his arm around her waist and led her toward the door.

Ember loved how he always seemed to want to be touching her when they were together. Holding her hand, putting his hand on her knee, touching her back...it didn't matter where they were or who was around, he always maintained contact in some way.

It dawned on her then how little human contact she'd had in the past. Her parents weren't the hugging type, and she certainly didn't have friends who hugged her like Aspen and

Devyn had, and even little Logan. It was another thing she liked a lot.

She said goodbye to the other guys and then it was just her and Craig in his Durango. He was taking her back to her apartment, where she'd knock out her list of errands for the day while he headed back to post.

"I apologize for not telling you about Devyn and Lucky."

"Why? If it's a secret that's being kept between them and the team, you had no reason to tell me."

"I still feel bad about it. But I love that you're smart enough to figure it out on your own. I *am* sorry if Devyn offended you though," Craig said as they drove.

"She didn't," Ember said immediately. "Everything about my account *was* superficial and fake. But I'm changing that now, and if I lose followers, so be it. It feels good to have control over that part of my life...and to use my platform for something meaningful."

Craig smiled.

"What?"

"I was kinda talking about her crack about you being good enough for me."

"Well, I think there's a good chance I'm not."

"Wrong," Craig said immediately in a low tone. He took a breath and continued. "Sorry. I just don't ever want you to think that about yourself. We're well matched. I think our differences help us mesh together better. Besides, we have a lot more in common than anyone might think just by looking at us."

"I agree," Ember said softly. She'd been one of those people who thought they were completely different when they'd first met, but *everyone* was more than their outward appearance.

They drove the rest of the way in comfortable silence, and

Ember couldn't help but feel disappointed when Craig pulled up near the entrance to her apartment building.

"I'm sorry Gillian wasn't there today so I could ask her what we should bring tomorrow," Ember said.

"It's okay. We'll figure it out."

"I like your friends. They're really nice."

"They are," Craig agreed. "And now they're *our* friends. When you get settled, they'll help with anything you need at your gym space too."

Ember nodded. Having people to rely on and share her passion would take some getting used to.

"Don't cook tonight," Craig told her. "I'm gonna stop and get us something on the way home ...if that's okay. I thought I'd come over and hang with you here tonight. It's your first night in your apartment, I figured we could celebrate."

"I'd like that," Ember told him, thinking of all the ways she could celebrate with Craig.

"And don't look at me like that," he said with a laugh. "I'll have you know, I'm not that kind of guy."

It was Ember's turn to burst out laughing. "I don't think I've ever laughed as much as I have since meeting you," she told him.

"Good." He leaned over and kissed her on the temple. "Go on. Get to work. I know you have a list at least two pages long to get through today."

"You know me so well," she said with a smile.

"I'm trying," he returned seriously. "Go on. Scoot. I'll text you when I leave post."

Ember nodded and climbed out of the car. She paused before shutting the door. "Craig?"

"Yeah, Em?"

"I'm happy."

The smile that crossed his face was so beautiful, it made Ember want to cry.

"I am too. Later."

"Later," Ember responded and shut the door. Craig gave her a chin lift before pulling away.

* * *

Ten hours later, Ember was sitting on her couch, in her very own apartment, with a belly full of delicious Mexican food Craig had brought with him. He'd also bought a double chocolate cake, her favorite. She hadn't allowed herself to indulge in something so decadent in a long time, and it tasted even more delicious as a result.

The cake had "Happy Birthday" written on it, and Craig had blushed and said it was the only thing they had left. It didn't matter what it said, or that the icing was smeared on one side where it had gotten smushed against the side of the box. All that mattered was that Craig had wanted to make her first night in her apartment special.

He'd also brought over a six-pack of Ziegenbock beer. Apparently it was brewed in Houston and only sold in Texas. She wasn't much of a beer person, but she had to admit that it tasted delicious after a busy, tiring day.

Ember had thought long and hard about what to post on social media earlier, knowing she needed to be careful and not post anything that would indicate where she'd moved. She was enjoying the anonymity at the moment. She'd settled for taking an artsy picture of the parking lot at the new gym she'd bought. There were weeds coming up between the cracks in the concrete and it looked pretty sad. But she knew very soon, the weeds would be gone and the lot would hopefully be full of cars. The caption she wrote was, *There's beauty in everything...especially knowing you're about to make a difference.*

"There's a chance we'll be deployed in the next few weeks," Craig said out of the blue.

Ember looked over at him. He was sitting next to her on the couch, there were boxes all around them, and she hadn't had time to hook up her TV yet. The place was a mess, but she felt no guilt about it. She'd had a productive day and she'd much prefer to sit here with Craig than try to get her place put away.

"That's...good, isn't it?"

"Good?" Craig asked with a raised eyebrow.

"Right. I know you can't tell me where you'll be going or what you'll be doing, but you've left enough hints lately about Sierra and how worried everyone is about the situation over in Afghanistan with missing contractors. I might not have a college degree, but I'm smart enough to put two and two together. Which reminds me, thanks for sending her picture to me, by the way. I'll get that posted tomorrow before the thing at Riley and Oz's place."

"I'm sorry, I'm just so used to deflecting any and all questions about what the team is doing. And you're right. The tension in our meetings is palpable, and Grover is holding on to his patience by his fingernails. None of us blame him. We're just worried about him doing something rash."

"Like what?"

"I have no clue. But I'll tell you this..." Craig's eyes were locked on her own, and Ember couldn't look away. "If I knew *you* were in trouble, I'd do whatever it took to help you. Even if that put me in danger."

"Craig," Ember whispered.

"I can't explain how I know you're it for me," he went on. "People don't believe love at first sight exists, but from the second I saw you, something clicked inside me."

Ember swallowed hard.

"Do I love you? I don't know. That sounds lame, but it's true. I'd thought I was in love before, but nothing about what I feel for you is like what I've felt for anyone else. So maybe *this* is love, and what I felt before was nothing more than great affection. All I know is that I think about you all the time. I'm proud of you and want to tell everyone I meet how great you are. I can't wait to talk to you, and even getting a text from you makes me smile like a deranged psychopath. I can't stop thinking about all the things I want to do with you. Take you dancing, even though I can't dance at all. Take you to the range. Go to the movies. Even running this morning seemed easier with you by my side. And every day that goes by, I feel closer to you. It's scary as hell, if you really want the truth."

Ember gave him a wobbly smile. "I know," she agreed.

"I'm okay taking things one day at a time, but know that there isn't a day that goes by that I don't think about you. Where I'm not hoping I don't fuck things up by saying or doing the wrong thing. I was ready to distance myself from you before you showed up. I knew it would kill me to be just friends. To only talk on the phone and see you every now and then. And the thought of you meeting someone else? It almost destroyed me. Which is crazy, I realize, since we *were* nothing but friends."

"I don't think we've ever been just friends," Ember said quietly.

"You feel it too." It wasn't a question.

But she confirmed it all the same. "I feel it too. It's why I moved here. I didn't want a long-distance relationship with you either. I felt compelled to come here. To be near you. I think it was more than luck that the gym was available. And this apartment. And that Julio and Marie agreed to come help me. Things have fallen in place for a reason, Craig. I truly believe that."

"Me too."

"Right, so...how does it work when you get deployed?

Will you just up and be gone one day, or do you get advance notice?"

"I'll never up and disappear on you," Craig said seriously. "Sometimes we only get a few hours' notice, but we're always given time to come home and make sure our families are situated before we head out. Other times we have a few days to a week's notice. I'm hoping this time we'll have at least a day or two to get our shit together before we head out."

Ember nodded. "Okay. Can we talk while you're gone? Like, will you be able to get email and things like that?"

"Usually, no."

"That sucks, but I get it."

"It won't be easy being with me," Craig reminded her.

"Well, it won't be easy being with me either," Ember retorted. "Wait until we go somewhere and I'm recognized. It gets kinda crazy sometimes. And I'm gonna be spending a lot of time at my gym. I need it to be successful, and the best way to make sure that happens is to be there in person overseeing things. And helping and coaching the kids. I'm looking forward to that more than anything. So yeah, it'll suck when you're gone, but there will be plenty of nights where I'm too busy to do this...sit around on the couch and talk. Can you handle that?"

"Yes," Craig agreed immediately. "I—"

When he cut himself off and didn't continue, Ember asked, "You what?"

"I'm just overwhelmed. I don't know how we got here. Don't get me wrong, I'm happy we are, I just sometimes get afraid it's all an illusion and will disappear in a puff of smoke."

"Same here," Ember agreed on a sigh. She was glad it wasn't just her feeling that way.

Craig looked at his watch and winced. "It's ten-thirty. I'm sure you have a ton of things planned for tomorrow before I come pick you up to head over to Oz's."

Ember nodded. "Yeah. I was going to go for a swim. Then double check to make sure Julio and Marie's apartments will be ready next week, as promised, and pay the deposits. Then I have a meeting with a guy who said he has some fencing equipment I could buy. And I need to stop at the store after we figure out what to bring to the party tomorrow."

"I'll go with you to meet that guy, it's not safe to go by yourself. And I can go to the store, so you can cross that off your list. I'd invite myself to go swim with you, but that might be pushing my luck." Craig smiled.

"One of these days, I'll get brave enough to invite you to spend the night," Ember blurted.

"When you do, I'll accept," Craig said with a tender smile. "Even if that invitation is to sleep here on the couch while you're in your bed. Make no mistake, I want you, Em. But my desire for you doesn't overwhelm my need to simply be with you. Near you. Next to you. Does that make sense?"

It did. "Yeah."

"Good." Craig stood and held out his hand. Ember took it and he pulled her to her feet. He held her hand as they walked to her door. "I'll help you replace these locks soon," he said, eyeing the flimsy chain on the door. "We'll add a deadbolt too. It won't keep someone out if they're really intent on getting in, but it'll slow them down."

Ember didn't argue. It was a little discomfiting to go from her parents' house, which had a state-of-the-art security system, to this apartment with only a doorknob lock and chain. She'd bought one of those wedge things that went under the door and let out a loud, obnoxious noise if someone tried to enter, but she'd feel better with stronger locks.

Craig turned to her and without a word, Ember went up on her toes. She kissed him hard and deep. Her hands roamed, and when he finally pulled back with a groan, she realized she was gripping his ass as if she never wanted to let go.

"Happy first night in your own place," Craig said softly.

"Thanks."

"Call if you need anything."

"I will."

"Let me know when you're meeting with that guy tomorrow. I'll come and pick you up and we'll go together. All right?"

"It's supposed to be at nine-thirty. I looked up the address and it's not too far from here."

"Okay. How long will it take? Will we have time to come home and change before we head to Oz's house?"

There was that we pronoun again. She freaking loved it. "I think so."

"Good. I'll see you in the morning then. Sleep well," Craig said and squeezed her hand.

"You too."

"Not a chance," he said with a grin, before opening her door.

Ember grinned back as he headed down the hallway. She wasn't going to sleep well either, and it was going to be all his fault. She wanted Craig. Desperately. But it was obvious he understood that she needed to have this first night in her place by herself. Needed to truly appreciate being on her own for the first time ever.

But tomorrow? She was ready to move this already-moving-at-light-speed relationship forward. She wanted to see the long hard cock she'd felt against her belly minutes earlier, up close and personal. She wanted to feel his calloused hands against her skin. She wanted to spend the night in his bed, or have him in hers. She didn't care which. All she knew was that if she didn't make love with Craig soon, she was going to explode.

Smiling, Ember locked her door and set up the wedge security alarm at the bottom. She turned off the lights and headed for her bedroom. Devyn and Aspen had helped her make the bed earlier so it would be ready for when she went to sleep. She still needed to go shopping for things like a rug for the bathroom and a shower curtain. That was partly why she'd decided to swim in the morning; she could shower at the Y. She was looking forward to putting her apartment together, but she couldn't help but think about Craig's house. It also needed a lot of finishing touches. Rugs, pictures for the walls, pillows.

Ember changed her clothes and climbed under the sheet and comforter. Grabbing her phone, she checked her IG account. Now that she was posting her own pictures, she had more of a need to see what her followers thought. The posts were more personal, more meaningful to her, and she wanted others to see the beauty that was her new world.

Most of the comments were positive, wishing her luck and saying how much they loved the imagery behind the empty parking lot picture she'd posted. But there were, of course, the angry, hateful comments as well. Those that said they hoped she crashed and burned, hoped that her new beloved gym burned down.

You're gonna fail, bitch. And we'll laugh when you do.

Could you have chosen a worse building?

You've stepped on everyone around you to get where you are. You don't deserve to be happy.

Seeing you flaunt your wealth is sickening.

The only good nigger is a dead nigger.

. . .

Seeing the n-word still made her breath catch in surprise and fear. It was hard to believe in this day and age, people still hated someone because of the color of their skin. But then again, it wasn't all *that* long ago that Black people had no rights and were actually considered property.

Trying to put the hateful word out of her mind, Ember continued to read the comments, searching out the positive ones and trying to ignore the mean ones.

I love what you're doing.
 You're truly making a difference in the world.
 Can't wait to see everything when it's done.
 A truly beautiful picture.
 I love getting to know the real *you.*

Ember smiled at that last comment. She liked getting to know the real Ember too. So far she liked what she'd learned. Clicking off her phone, she put it on the small table next to the bed. She wanted to focus on the good in the world instead of the hate. It was harder to do when scrolling through social media, that was for sure.

Making a mental note not to look at comments on her account right before she went to sleep ever again, Ember did her best to think about the new friends she'd made that day and look forward to the ones she'd make tomorrow.

And tomorrow night...well, hopefully she wouldn't have to say goodbye to Craig at her door. He'd either stay, or he'd invite her to stay at his place. The last thing she thought about before falling asleep was to make sure to pack an overnight bag, just in case.

* * *

Alex scowled at the new picture on Ember's account. And she wasn't responding to anyone's comments either. Which just proved how stuck on herself she was. Bitch was pretending to care, when in reality she was just using this new gym venture as another photo opp.

Oh, it was obvious she was going through with it. Buying a building, hiring people to work for her. But the motivation behind Ember's sudden need to help the disadvantaged seemed disingenuous at best.

She was a huge failure at the Olympics, and all this charity out of nowhere was just her way of making everyone forget how much of a loser she *really* was.

Not only that, but how fucking wrong was it that she could get her new business up and running so quickly? All she had to do was flash money around and *boom*! Everyone did her bidding. It was sickening—and just another reason to hate her.

Alex would make sure she didn't exploit anyone ever again. Not like she'd done with so many in LA. Everyone who ever worked for her was just a stepping stone to get whatever she wanted. The coaches, hairdressers, makeup people, photographers, the athletes she trained with, her social media staff...even her parents. She just took and took, giving nothing in return, then dumped anyone she no longer needed.

It made Alex sick!

Ember Maxwell's a user—and she can't just move away, leaving destruction in her wake.

She can't leave people behind without a second glance. That just isn't cool.

It isn't fair!

Frowning, Alex took several deep breaths, trying to make all the voices shut up. They were getting worse, speaking all at once, deliberately being confusing.

Taking one last deep breath, Alex focused on the plan for Ember.

It was time to deal with the bitch.

She wouldn't know what was coming. There would be no warnings. No reason for her to get suspicious or hire extra security. No. Alex was coming for her—and within a week, she'd be nothing more than a memory.

No more big plans to exploit little kids. No more using everyone around her to make herself look good. No more flaunting her privilege.

Alex would do what needed to be done.

Then everyone would forget all about Ember Maxwell, because she was nothing more than a fake, greedy, money-grubbing, fame-seeking bitch.

Smiling, Alex relaxed. Soon. Within a week, all would be well. Ember would be dead, and all would be right with the world again.

CHAPTER ELEVEN

Ember was nervous but excited for the party. She'd woken up early, as usual, and had gone for her swim. Her shoulder had healed up nicely and she only felt a twinge now and then. The lifeguards had been friendly and the few other people she'd seen hadn't really seemed to look twice at her, which was a nice change of pace.

Then she'd had a bit of time to kill, so she'd made blueberry muffins. They were from a box, but she wanted to bring something to the get-together with Craig's friends. She was anxious. She wanted the other women to like her, though she suspected she'd have to overcome whatever preconceptions they had about Ember Maxwell coming into their inner circle. She'd be equally wary if the roles had been reversed.

Craig had shown up at nine-fifteen and they'd gone to meet the man who had some secondhand fencing equipment. It turned out what he had would be perfect, at least for now. Ember knew she'd need to get some smaller uniforms and more épées, the weapon used in the modern pentathlon, but this would be a good start. The man used to own a fencing studio, but had retired and was happy to sell her what he had.

Then Craig had stopped by his house and changed and grabbed what seemed like way too much food. When he said he'd take care of getting stuff to bring over, Ember had no idea he'd buy out half the store. Her two dozen muffins sitting in the back of his Durango seemed somewhat pathetic now.

"What's wrong?" he asked as they were finally on their way to Riley and Oz's house.

"Nothing."

"Em, talk to me," he said firmly.

"I just didn't realize how much you were going to get. I wouldn't have bothered to make muffins if I had. They're kinda pathetic-looking. Lopsided, not all the same size. I'm sure some are probably raw inside. I'll just leave them in the car and throw them out when I get home."

"Look at me."

Ember sighed and looked over at Craig. He looked so damn handsome today, as usual. He'd put on a pair of knee-length tan cargo shorts, a dark blue T-shirt that brought out the color of his eyes, and had a pair of flip-flops on his feet. It seemed strange and somehow intimate to see his bare feet. She'd gotten used to seeing him in combat boots, pants, and long-sleeve shirts. He seemed impervious to the Texas heat. But seeing him dressed so casually was...nice. As if he'd let down his guard to show her the real Craig.

"While you weren't looking, I snuck one of your muffins. It was delicious, and I'm not just saying that. Do you think the first time you meet the people I hope you'll make lifelong relationships with, that I'd let you be embarrassed? The answer to that is no. So while it's probably not cool for me to have done it, I stole one of your muffins because one, I was hungry and they looked so good, and two, because I wanted to make sure they tasted all right—but only because you said you hadn't had a chance to learn to cook. Are you mad?"

"No." The answer was immediate and heartfelt. She'd eaten one of the muffins herself, for exactly the same reason he had. If she'd messed up when adding the ingredients, the last thing she wanted was for someone to spit out her food after tasting it. She'd be mortified. So no, she wasn't upset that Craig had been looking out for her. Had wanted to spare her embarrassment. "Thank you for telling me."

"No secrets," he said. Then wrinkled his nose. "That sounds silly to say with my job, but no secrets when it comes to you and me. If you don't want to do something I suggest, speak up. That goes for anything outside the house, as well as in it. Watching TV, sexual positions, volunteer opportunities, activities on the post...all of it."

Ember couldn't help but smirk. "Sexual positions?"

Craig returned her smile. "Yeah, well, you never know, we might have very different ideas of what we like in the bedroom."

That sobered Ember a little. "What if we aren't compatible?"

"We are," Craig said without hesitation.

"You don't know that," Ember insisted, not knowing why she was arguing about this.

"Em, no matter what it is you want to do or not do, I'm on board."

She furrowed her brow. "So if I told you that I'm a Domme and want to take complete control in the bedroom, you'd let me? What if I wanted to tie you up and flog you?"

Craig chuckled. "You aren't and you don't."

"But you don't know that," she repeated.

"Em, I do. And I'm not talking about doing anything that would hurt either of us. If you want to experiment with some light bondage and spanking, I'd be fine with that. With you tying me up, as well as me tying *you* up. If you want to watch sexy movies or porn together, again, I have no problem with that. Experimenting sexually is exciting. It can be embarrassing and awkward too. I'm willing to endure that because I know, whatever happens, we'll be in it together."

"I can't believe we're talking about this before we've seen each other naked," Ember muttered. She looked over at Craig and saw he was smiling. "What?"

"I just like this," he said, meeting her gaze for a second before turning his attention back to the road. "Being open and honest. I've never had a relationship like this. It's always been a guessing game to try to read my girlfriends' minds as to what they want, what they're thinking. With you...you never leave me guessing. And I'm not afraid to say what *I'm* thinking or what I want either."

It was Ember's turn to smile. She knew exactly what he meant. She'd spent so much of her life hiding behind a fake smile and never daring to speak her true feelings, being with him was refreshing and so...easy.

"And to bring this conversation full circle...your muffins are fucking delicious. I would've snuck more than one but you would've noticed. The people we're hanging out with today won't give a shit about a lopsided muffin or even if they're a little underdone, which they aren't. Hell, the girls would probably like them more if there was gooey batter in the middle. They're good people, Em, and I know you're gonna fit right in."

"I hope so."

"I know so," Craig said firmly.

Ember made a decision right then and there to relax and be herself. She'd spent so much of her life trying to be someone she wasn't, and she didn't want to start out her friendships with these women being anything less than genuine.

They pulled into a driveway behind a Jeep Grand Cherokee and a Chevy Blazer. Craig grabbed most of the bags with the food he'd bought and Ember got her plate of muffins. They walked up to the door and before they could knock, it opened.

"Hi!" Logan exclaimed. "Did you bring your camera, Em? Because I thought maybe you could take some pictures of me in my backyard."

"Logan," Oz chided, coming up behind his nephew. "That's rude."

The little boy looked up at his uncle. "Sorry."

"Don't apologize to me, apologize to Ember."

"Sorry," Logan said, dutifully looking up at Ember.

"It's okay. And for the record, the camera on my phone is pretty darn good. I'd love to take a few pictures of you in the shirt Shin-Soo mailed, so I can send them to him."

Logan's eyes got huge in his face. "Seriously? Yes! I need to go change!" Then he pushed past Oz and ran back into the house.

Ember chuckled.

"Sorry about that, he's a little...enthusiastic when it comes to anything baseball," Oz said.

"It's fine. I'm happy to do it, and I know Shin-Soo will get a kick out of the pictures."

"Don't just stand there in the doorway," a woman said from behind Oz, who smiled and moved so he could put his arm around her.

"This is Riley...and Amalia."

The baby was adorable, as most babies were. "It's nice to meet you," Ember said with a smile.

"Same here. I've heard a lot about you, and I have to say... you're even prettier in person," Riley said.

Then a little girl with red hair and huge hazel eyes came up beside Riley and stared at Ember. She looked to be around seven or eight.

"Hi," Ember said softly.

Instead of answering, Bria tugged on Riley's shirt.

The other woman leaned down. "Yeah, sweetie?"

"She looks like Princess Tiana."

Riley straightened and smiled. "She does, doesn't she?" she asked the little girl. "Bria, this is Ember, Doc's friend. Ember, this is Bria. She's Oz's niece, my daughter, and now Amalia's sister."

Ember had heard the story of how Bria and Logan came to live with Riley and Oz, and she couldn't help but love the little girl on sight. The fact that she thought Ember was a Disney Princess just endeared her even more.

Oz reached for the plate Ember was holding and she gave it up without a fuss. "We're still waiting for everyone to get here, but, Bria, maybe you can give Ember a tour of the house?"

"Wanna see my room?" the little girl asked shyly.

"I'd love that," Ember told her.

She was shocked when Bria moved away from Riley and came toward her to take her hand. The surprised looks on Riley's and Oz's faces confirmed this wasn't something the girl usually did.

"I've got a ton of Barbies, maybe we can play."

"Not now, Bria. Maybe later," Riley told her gently. "Ember's here to play with the adults. Carrie's coming over soon, you can play Barbies with her."

Bria pouted, and trying to appease the girl, Ember quickly said, "I'd love to see your Barbies before your friend gets here."

Smiling, Bria pulled Ember from the doorway into the house. She let herself be led up the stairs to her room. She spent ten minutes admiring Bria's Barbie doll collection and being shown all of her favorite things. The room was large and airy, and Ember guessed that was intentional, that Riley and Oz had made sure the little girl never felt hemmed in.

After everything Bria had been through, they'd done a wonderful job of making her room a safe space for the little girl.

Eventually, they left her room and Bria briefly showed her the other rooms upstairs. The house was huge, with six bedrooms. Craig had told Ember that Riley and Oz really wanted a big family, and he wouldn't be surprised if Riley turned up pregnant again sooner rather than later.

Bria abandoned Ember after she got bored playing tour guide, so she made her way back down the stairs by herself. As soon as Craig saw her, he headed her way.

"You good?" he asked.

"Of course. Bria is adorable. And this house is huge."

"Yup. Told you. Come on, everyone is here now and Gillian already has the margarita machine fired up."

"A margarita machine?" Ember asked. "Isn't that like, a blender?"

"Shhh," Craig said with a smile. "Trigger is responsible for keeping the drinks flowing...she calls *him* the margarita machine."

Ember couldn't help but laugh at that.

Craig leaned forward and kissed her temple, then interlaced his fingers with hers and headed for the kitchen. The space was huge, with top-of-the-line appliances and granite countertops, but with all the people standing around, there wasn't an inch of space to spare.

He led her to a woman about her height, with blonde hair and green eyes. "Gillian, this is Ember. Ember, Gillian."

"Hi!" Gillian said happily. "I'm so glad to meet you. Do you want a drink?"

"Um...sure," Ember said.

"Awesome. Walker?"

Trigger chuckled, handing over a glass with a straw in it.

Gillian took it from him, leaned up to kiss him on the

lips, then handed the drink to Ember. "I hope you like 'em strong."

Ember couldn't help it, she looked at Craig and squeezed his biceps before taking the drink. "The stronger the better."

Gillian threw her head back and laughed, then nudged Craig out of the way. "You and the rest of the guys need to head out. Your girl's in good hands."

"That's what I'm afraid of," Craig muttered.

Then he leaned down and, to Ember's surprise, kissed her on the lips. And it wasn't a quick, chaste kiss either. He used tongue and put his hand behind her neck, holding her to him as he kissed her deeply. When he pulled back, he stared down at her for a long moment before giving her a small grin. "Have fun."

Ember licked her lips and watched as Craig and the rest of the guys headed into the other room. She had no idea if they were going to go grill something, have a shooting contest out in the yard, or engage in a few arm wrestling contests. With the testosterone she could practically feel vibrating in the room, she wouldn't be surprised with anything that happened.

One of the women she hadn't met yet fanned her cheeks with her hand. "Lord, that was hot."

"Right? I told you," Aspen said with a grin.

"Told them what?" Ember asked.

"That the two of you were combustible. Just being around you two yesterday was enough for me to see that, even without the kissing."

Ember had a feeling she was blushing, and was glad they probably wouldn't notice.

"I'm Kinley," said a black-haired woman a few inches shorter than Ember, holding out her hand.

Ember shifted her drink and shook her hand. "It's good to meet you." In the pause that followed, she took a sip of the margarita ...and nearly choked. It was more tequila than anything else.

"Told you it was strong," Gillian said with a smile. "As far as I know, none of us are pregnant, and our men are gonna be heading out soon, so we need to let loose. Brain's got Chance, Oz is in charge of Amalia...so there's no excuse for us not to have a little fun."

The women all agreed, and Ember found herself relaxing. She wasn't a big drinker. Her training schedule had never really given her time to go out to bars and trying to work out with a hangover wasn't her idea of fun. Besides, she'd never had a group of friends to go out with. She'd been looking forward to today. To relaxing and having some fun. But she made a mental note to take it easy on the margaritas. She'd be passed out on the floor if she drank too many of the potent drinks too quickly.

An hour later, Ember was sitting on the huge back deck with the women. There was a plate of snacks on the table in front of them and everyone had a drink in their hand. Lucky and Grover were playing catch with Logan, and Trigger and Craig were watching Bria and her friend play on the swing set in the corner of the yard. Lefty and Brain were at the grill, cooking up hamburgers, hotdogs for the kids, and shish kebabs.

"Do you guys know much about Sierra?" Devyn asked quietly.

"No," Gillian said.

"I've just heard her name in passing," Riley said.

The others all shook their heads.

"I talked to my brother about her the other day, and he's *really* worried about her," Devyn said.

"Your brother?" Ember asked.

"Yeah. Grover."

"You and Grover are siblings?" Ember asked in surprise.

Devyn smiled. "Yeah. I moved to Killeen because he was here, and we've always been close. Blah blah blah...now I'm married to Lucky and couldn't be happier."

"Devyn!" Gillian exclaimed.

"What?"

"I thought that was a secret," Gillian said.

"It was. It is. But Ember kind of figured it out. Actually, I guess it was the guys who tipped her off, because they kept saying 'wives' instead of 'women' or calling me a girlfriend." Devyn shrugged. "Whatever. It's fine."

Gillian just rolled her eyes and shook her head.

"I think it's great," Ember said with a smile.

"Thanks. But anyway, back to Sierra," Devyn said. "Fred told me that he assumed she'd just blown him off. He was upset about it. Apparently, something about her really struck a chord in him. You know how the guys are...once they find a woman who intrigues them, that's it."

Yeah, Ember knew that, and was more than thankful for it. She couldn't help but look over at Craig. He was pushing Bria on a swing, and she loved how gentle and patient he was with her.

"Anyway, he was worried about her with all those disap-pearances going on over in Afghanistan—which look like kidnappings now—but there wasn't anything he could do about it. Then he got that letter from her. It really shook him."

"I can't believe it was lost in the mail for a year," Kinley said with a shake of her head. "Talk about bad luck."

"Yeah."

"That reminds me," Ember said, pulling out her phone. "I've been so busy, I haven't had time to post her picture yet."

"Post her picture?" Riley asked.

"Yeah, on my IG account. I have no idea if it'll do any

good, but maybe publicizing the fact that she's missing can help in some way," Ember said.

Aspen leaned forward. "I checked out your account."

Ember did her best to stay relaxed. She was kind of getting used to people telling her that. And, besides, she would've done the same thing if she'd been in any of these women's shoes. "Yeah?"

"Yeah. I have to say...I think I like you better like this." Aspen nodded to Ember's outfit.

She'd decided to go casual, since today was a relaxed get-together with Craig's friends. She didn't want to look like she was trying too hard, and she'd gotten comfortable in her more laid-back clothes. It was too hot to deck herself out anyway. She had on a pair of jean shorts, a tank top, and cute flip-flops with huge flowers on them. She'd seen them in Walmart when she'd been shopping the other day and couldn't resist. Her mom would die if she saw them. She'd always harped on Ember about wearing designer clothes whenever she left the house in case someone took her picture.

"Me too," she told Aspen honestly.

A few minutes passed as Ember typed out a post. The other women talked amongst themselves as she concentrated on her phone.

"What are you going to say?" Devyn asked after a while.

"How's this sound?" Ember asked.

I hope you're all having a great weekend. I'm hanging out with some new friends, sweating in the heat, listening to children laughing, and about to eat some fattening but oh-so-good food. But not everyone is as lucky as I am. They're hungry. Or scared. Or being abused. I wanted to take a moment today to highlight a friend of a friend, who may or may not be in trouble. Her name is Sierra, and she was last seen working on an Army base in Afghanistan as a contract worker.

You might be wondering why I'm sharing this, when I'm here in Texas. And you might be in California. Or New York. Or Paris. Or South Africa. Nowhere near Afghanistan. The reason is because it's been a long time since anyone has heard from Sierra. She could literally be anywhere.

Have you seen her? Have you heard anything about a red-haired, green-eyed petite woman being held against her will? Above is a picture of Sierra. If you know anything about her whereabouts, please post below or call your local investigators. Sierra's life could be saved by just one phone call.

The women around her were all silent when Ember finished reading back what she'd typed. "Too much?"

"No!" Riley said emphatically.

"Not at all," Devyn said with a sniff.

"I think you using your platform to help others is amazing," Kinley told her.

Ember shook her head. "Sometimes it feels like too little, too late. You've all seen the superficial shit that was posted on there for years. I feel disconnected from most people because I was raised in Beverly Hills, with all the money I could ever want or need, and I existed in my own little bubble. Not everyone has been so lucky. It's time I got my hands dirty, so to speak. Use my privilege for good instead of selfish gains. That's what my gym, The Modern Kid, is about."

"Is that the name? I love it," Aspen said.

"Yeah. It's a play on the modern pentathlon. I wanted it to be kid-centered but cute at the same time," Ember said shyly.

"It works. And...even if the chance is low that someone in

the Middle East will see Sierra's picture and remember her, I think it's better than nothing," Devyn said.

"Me too," Ember agreed as she hit the button to publish the post. She put her phone back down on the table and took a large sip of her drink.

"Speaking of your social media accounts...why are so many people such douchebags?" Riley asked.

"Right? Like if someone posts something happy, why do there have to be so many downers?" Gillian asked.

"And if someone says something on their own account, why do people feel as if they have the right to go on there and disagree, most of the time in a shitty way?" Kinley threw in.

"Yes! And why so many stupid dick pics?" Devyn asked.

Ember almost choked on the sip of drink she'd just taken.

"I bet you get a ton of those," Aspen said with a smile.

Ember nodded. "You know, I never saw them before because my parents hired people to manage my accounts. But once I took over, I was shocked by how many guys think nothing of taking pictures of their junk and sending them."

"I bet they're not theirs though," Riley said. "They probably watch porn, take a screen shot, and send that."

"True," Gillian said. "Most likely because their dicks are tiny."

Everyone laughed.

Ember relaxed in her chair, a huge smile on her face. She loved this. Laughing and joking with people and not having to watch every little thing she said for fear it would be misconstrued or all over the internet the next day.

"Aren't you worried about the obviously crazy people who post on your account, Ember?" Riley asked quietly. "I mean, I've worked with some authors who have had some pretty weird stuff sent to them. I've heard about one woman who had a guy show up at her house with a huge bouquet of flowers for her. It freaked her and her husband out so much, they moved out of state and pretty much stopped posting anything on social media."

Ember took another sip of her drink. She was tipsy, but not drunk. Yet. Her inhibitions were down just enough to be honest with these women. "Sometimes? Yeah, it scares me. Before, like I said, others managed my accounts, so I was in the dark about it. But every now and then I'd get something in the mail that was super creepy and security would be stepped up a bit. But I can't live my life in fear. I won't."

"Walker would lose his mind if I was ever threatened online or by mail," Gillian said.

"Right? Gage would lock me in the house and never let me leave until he was sure the threat was over. Especially after everything that happened to me. Even when I *was* on alert, evil still managed to find me," Kinley said.

"And you had to go into deep hiding to escape it," Aspen agreed. "Witness protection had to have been awful."

"It wasn't fun," Kinley agreed. "I missed Gage so much."

"I've arranged for security for the gym," Ember said. "Not for me, but for the kids. I know having a child-centered business makes those kids vulnerable to predators. I'm more worried about them than me."

"But I've read some of the messages on your posts," Devyn insisted. "Those kids aren't in danger; it feels like *you* are." She pulled out her phone and clicked on a few things before saying, "Like this. On that post you just put up on Sierra. Most people are saying how horrible it is that she's missing. But there are a few comments that seem to be direct attacks at *you*. Like this one...*Maybe someone will come and kidnap your ass so we don't have to see your posts anymore.* Or this one...*No one cares, bitch.* Oh, and this one by this Alex guy is pretty rude...*Why even pretend you care about others? We all know you're self-centered, narcissistic, and don't care about anyone other than yourself.* I'm not sure I'd be able to deal with that kind of hate directed at me. What does Doc say about it?"

Ember shrugged. "It comes with the territory. I know not everyone is going to like me, there's nothing I can do about that. And I refuse to let them freak me out. Or live in a bubble. I did that for years, and I like it on the outside too much to go back."

"But such outward hate? I wouldn't be able to do it," Kinley said.

Ember put down her drink and slowly met the gazes of the women around her. "I'm Black," she said bluntly. "People hate me because of the color of my skin. I'm also rich, and pretty. So they hate me because of those things too. They don't have to know me to hate me. To think that I don't deserve the same rights they have. It's ridiculous and crazy. Do I care about people saying they hope I die? Of course. But if I let everyone's opinions of me dictate how I live, I wouldn't be living at all. I'm sure there are many people who don't think Craig and I should have a relationship. They don't agree or approve of interracial marriages. Does that mean I should break up with him?"

"No."

"Absolutely not."

"Love is love."

Ember appreciated the other women's support. "Exactly. I can't live my life in fear. Does that mean I'm going to skip out the door without a care in the world? No. I'm gonna watch my back and do what I can to protect myself and those I love. Let those keyboard cowards hide behind their fake accounts and mean words online. The people who matter to me are the kids I can hopefully make a difference for. My neighbors. My friends. My family. Craig and his Army family."

"Damn," Riley said as she wiped a tear from her eye. "Stupid post-pregnancy hormones."

Everyone laughed, breaking the tension in the air.

"I love that you're so courageous, but that doesn't mean I'm not still worried about the hate," Devyn insisted. "And again, does Doc know that people are threatening to kidnap you on social media? Or that they're calling you names and hoping you die?"

Ember opened her mouth to answer, when a deep voice spoke from behind her.

"Someone threatened to kidnap you?"

Shit. Ember turned to see Craig standing with Trigger. "It's the same old stuff they always say," Ember answered, trying to defuse the situation.

"She just made a post about Sierra," Kinley said, less than helpfully. "And someone posted that they hoped *she* disappears too."

"And someone named Alex has posted several times, even since the last time I looked," Devyn said, still reading her phone. "He agreed with the other guy and hopes someone wipes you off the face of the Earth. And," she tapped her phone a few more times, "look...here on Facebook...this Alex jerk has posted several gifs of guns against people's heads on one of your posts over there too."

"We need to talk," Craig said, reaching for Ember's arm.

She let him help her up and followed him into the house without a word. She really didn't want to get into this now, but it didn't look like she had a choice. She wasn't mad at the girls. They were just trying to look out for her well-being, which honestly felt really good.

Trigger followed behind her, and the other guys were already inside the house. Somehow in the midst of her conversation with the girls, she'd missed them going inside.

"What's wrong?" Lefty asked as they entered.

Craig led Ember over to the couch and once she sat, he

paced the floor in front of her. "Ember's getting death threats."

"What?"

"Holy shit!"

"From who?"

The concern and horror from the other men was immediate and heartfelt.

"It's not like that," Ember said, trying to calm everyone down. But Craig had his phone out and was already scrolling. Shit. That wasn't good.

"She posted that picture of Sierra," Craig told his friends.

"Thank you," Grover said, the gratitude easy to hear in his tone.

Ember nodded at him.

"It seems as if every post she puts up that isn't superficial, or showing off some worthless product, gets more and more nasty comments," Craig said.

"Maybe you should take a break from posting for a while," Trigger suggested.

"No," Ember said emphatically. "Look, I know you guys are worried about this, but honestly, this isn't anything new. Go back to the older posts from before the Olympics. From when I had that stupid reality show. People have always hated me. *Will* always hate me. They'll make up something if they have to, just so they can hate me even more."

It was as if she hadn't spoken.

"Maybe we can analyze the comments and see who's repeatedly posting threats," Lefty suggested.

"Yeah, we can see if they've escalated or stayed the same," Brain added.

"We could trace the IP addresses," Oz threw in.

"I wouldn't be surprised if the people posting mean shit were using their real names too," Lucky said.

"Damn, she said she was in Texas...not where, but we'll have to stay on our toes," Trigger said.

"What about fan mail and gifts? Have you received hate mail through the postal service?" Grover asked.

"Yeah, that would make it an actual crime," Craig agreed. "We could turn that shit in and see if we couldn't bring up charges."

"I wonder if we could match gifts to the posts online?" Brain asked.

Ember stood and held up both hands. "Stop!" she ordered.

All seven men stared at her in surprise.

"I get that you want to help. That you're worried. But as I told the others outside, I can't and *won't* live in fear. Like it or not, I'm famous. It's not something I necessarily wanted, but I can't go back and change what's already happened. I'm convinced that the people who don't like me will eventually unfriend and unfollow me online. They'll move on to hate someone else. If I freaked every time someone said they didn't like me, I wouldn't be able to function."

"Saying they hope you die and that they want to kidnap you is *more* than not liking you," Craig said.

"I know. And as much as I hate it, they'll turn their vitriol on you too, once they know we're dating. But I don't care about them. I care about *you*," Ember said, her gaze fixed on Craig.

"And I care about *you*, which is why I can't just ignore this."

They stared at each other for a long moment.

Then Trigger spoke. "How about this? You let us investigate a bit. See what we can find out. If the people spewing hatred at you are also doing the same to other people, it lessens the threat somewhat. We'll get in touch with your former social media managers and see what they say about any patterns they might've noticed. We'll also talk to your parents about the fan mail you've received. If someone has sent over-the-top presents or hate mail, we can look into them, turn that shit over to the FBI. Let us help keep you safe, Ember."

She looked around the room at the men. She'd just met these guys. They didn't really know her. Why were they so concerned? "Why?" she asked softly.

"Because you're with Doc," Trigger said.

"And you're badass," Lefty added.

"And you don't deserve this. No one does," Brain argued.

"You're one of us now," Oz added.

"And *no one* messes with our family," Lucky agreed.

"You have a huge heart," Grover said. "Not many people would care about a stranger who disappeared halfway around the world."

Ember wanted to cry. Had she ever been this accepted before?

The answer was easy. No.

"Okay," she whispered. "But start with Samer. He was the most supportive of my social media managers when I said I wanted to take over my own accounts. Alexis was the most pissed, so contacting him probably wouldn't be the best idea."

"Alexis?" Trigger asked with interest. "He could be going by Alex and posting because he's pissed about being out of a job. We'll look into it." Then he turned to his friends, giving them assignments to find out more information about the people who'd been so cruel online.

Craig pulled her into his arms and held her close. Neither said anything, and Ember soaked in his affection.

It was Grover who picked up her drink and handed it to her. "I highly suggest you partake in a few more of these," he said with a small smile. "It'll make us taking over your safety and security much easier to bear."

Ember chuckled lightly and took the glass from him.

"Thanks. And I have a feeling you guys will make my parents seem like amateurs."

"Damn straight," Grover said with a wink.

"Are you guys done taking over Ember's life?" Devyn asked as she stuck her head inside the room.

"For now," Lucky agreed with a laugh.

"Good, because we're hungry, Logan's bored, Bria wants to eat dessert first, Riley and Aspen need to nurse, and we're out of margaritas."

Everyone burst out laughing.

"Well, by all means, come in!" Oz told her.

Seconds later, Ember was surrounded by her new friends. Each of the women gave her a big hug and told her to trust the guys and that everything would be all right. Logan had asked her for the millionth time if she'd take some pictures after they ate, and Bria handed her a dandelion she'd picked from the yard.

The online threats were nothing new, and Ember was determined not to let everyone's concern over them freak her out. She was going to enjoy this party, and her new friends, no matter what.

Tipping her glass up and finishing the rest of her drink, she grimaced at the strong taste of the tequila, then grinned as Craig kissed her temple and took the glass from her hand.

Yeah, it was safe to say she was happier than she'd ever been in her life.

Ember watched as Craig headed toward the kitchen, probably to get her a refill once Gillian's "margarita machine" —aka her husband—made a fresh batch of drinks. His ass flexed as he moved, and she couldn't help but feel a fresh wave of lust move over her.

She wanted Craig. And later tonight when he brought her home, she'd invite him in and seduce him. She didn't know how, but she'd figure it out. Craig Wagner was meant to be hers, and she was going to grab hold of her deepest desire with both hands and never let go.

"You go girl," Gillian murmured from next to her, obviously seeing her ogle Craig.

Ember merely smiled. "I will," she told her.

Gillian wrapped her arm around Ember's and laughed. "For the record, you're exactly what Doc needs, and I'm happy for you both."

"We aren't running off and getting married tonight," Ember told the other woman. "So don't get your hopes up."

Gillian snorted. "Right, you say that now. If the way you're looking at his ass is any indication, after a few more drinks, you'll be dragging that ass down to the courthouse faster than we can blink."

"The courthouse? No. The bedroom? Yes," Ember said.

Gillian burst out laughing. "Sounds like a good plan to me."

"Me too," Ember agreed.

"I like you, Ember Maxwell," Gillian said.

"I like you too, Gillian Nelson," Ember told her

They shared a heartfelt look.

"Come on, let's go get drunk so we can fuck our men properly later," Gillian said with a grin.

Ember was totally on board with that.

She planned on rocking Craig's world tonight when he brought her home.

CHAPTER TWELVE

Doc looked over at Ember and knew he had the goofiest smile on his face. He'd already thought she was hardworking, passionate, determined, beautiful, smart, and strong as fuck. But now he could add adorable to that list.

She was drunk.

Smashed.

Hammered.

The women had decided that they wanted to go out after they'd finished all the tequila at Oz's house. Brain and Oz had stayed at the house to watch the kids, Grover had headed home, and Trigger, Lefty, Lucky, and Doc had accompanied the six women to a bar and kept watch over them as they got to know Ember and had a rip-roaring good time.

Now Doc couldn't stop smiling. He'd been pressing water on her for the last hour, in the hopes it would combat the hangover she was sure to have when she woke up, but she was still as drunk as a skunk.

At first the women had made the guys sit at a separate table, but as the alcohol flowed, Gillian, Kinley, Devyn, and Ember had invited their men to join them. Aspen and Riley were the first to bail, probably not liking that their men weren't there and because they missed their kids. Trigger and Gillian had driven them back to Oz's house.

Lefty and Kinley had left next.

Then Lucky and Devyn had called it a night, leaving Ember and Doc to fend for themselves at the bar. When Ember sat on his lap and inched her hand under his shirt, Doc was done. As much as he loved her hands on him, that wasn't the time or place. He'd had to practically carry her to his SUV, but so far he was glad to see she didn't seem to be in danger of puking all over his car.

"Craig?" she asked with a small smile.

"Yeah, Em?"

"I really *really* like your friends."

"I'm glad."

"No, seriously. They're *so* nice."

Doc chuckled. "They are."

"When that guy took my picture...Aspen marched right over to him and demanded he give her his phone. And he thought she was hitting on him! But instead, she deleted the picture he'd taken. *Then* she wagged her finger in his face and told him how rude he was, and that if he ever wanted a girl to look at him twice, he needed to stop that shit." Ember giggled. "That was *awesome!*"

Doc let her babble. He'd been there. He'd seen what Aspen had done—and he and Lucky had been standing behind her, making sure the guy knew better than to do anything stupid. He hadn't, and Aspen had walked back to the other women smiling like a Cheshire cat.

They'd all danced, laughed, and if he didn't know better, Doc would've thought the women had been friends forever.

"Glad you had a good time, sweetheart," Doc told her.

"I did. I really did. And no one even shot up the place."

Doc frowned in confusion. "What? Why would you say that?"

"Because we're in Texas. *Everyone* has a gun. I expected there to be a shootout."

Doc chuckled. "I'm guessing there are more guns per capita than in a lot of the States, but we don't have shootouts in public bars."

She pouted. "Doesn't seem fair. I bet I could outshoot everyone."

"You probably could," Doc agreed. He'd seen her shooting ability firsthand in Korea. "But it's probably not a good idea to encourage drunk people to pull out their weapons in a crowded bar."

"True," she agreed. "Craig?"

Doc's grin widened. "Still right here, Em."

"Do you think your family will like me? Will they be surprised that you're dating a Black woman?"

"They're gonna love you. How could they not? And honestly, Mama Luisa is just going to be excited that I'm dating *anyone*. I think they despaired of me ever settling down."

"Are you settling down?" Ember asked.

"Oh, yeah."

"With me?"

Doc laughed. "Yeah, babe. With you."

"Good. Because I'm not leaving. Are you gonna be sad if my parents aren't as happy that I'm dating you?"

"Because I'm white?" Doc asked, genuinely curious.

Ember shook her head. "I think it's more that they're snobs. They've lived in Beverly Hills too long. They wanted me to marry someone rich. From their country club."

"You're always gonna have more money than me," Doc said. "Does that bother you?"

Ember waved her hand in the air drunkenly. "*Pbsshaw*. No.

I'd rather live in a rundown house in a crappy part of town and be with someone who loves me, and I love back, than be trapped in a huge mansion with a fancy car and a million bucks in the bank with someone who's only with me because of what I can give him."

"You already have a fancy car and a million bucks in the bank," Doc couldn't help but point out.

"Yeah, but I don't have the love part," Ember pouted.

Doc pulled into his driveway and waited for the garage door to rise. He pulled in and shut off the engine. He wasn't sure Ember even realized that he hadn't brought her back to her apartment. There was no way he was going to leave her alone when she was as drunk as she was. It wasn't exactly how he'd envisioned the night ending, but he was still with Ember, so he couldn't complain.

He reached out and palmed the side of her neck. Ember immediately tilted her head and gave him the weight of her head. "You have the love part," he said quietly.

She looked confused for a moment, then her eyes closed and her lips quirked up in a small smile.

"Come on, let's get you inside before you pass out in my car." Doc ran his thumb along the underside of her jaw, then said, "Stay put. I'll come around."

"'Kay. Your car is spinning too fast for me to stand up anyway," Ember mumbled with her eyes still shut.

Doc hopped out and hurried around to her side. He opened the door and laughed out loud when Ember jerked in surprise. "Come on, sleeping beauty, let's get you inside. Can you walk?"

"Of course I can walk!" she said indignantly, then promptly tripped over her feet. She would've sprawled to the floor of the garage if Doc hadn't been there to catch her. This time he didn't bother letting her try to walk; he put one arm under her knees and the other around her back and lifted her.

Ember immediately wrapped her arms around his neck. "I like this," she said.

"Me too," Doc admitted. He had a little trouble opening the door to the house, but eventually managed to turn the knob and get them inside without dropping her.

He'd made it to the bottom of the stairs when he felt Ember's lips close around his earlobe. Doc shivered.

Fuck...his ears were so sensitive! He hadn't realized that about himself, as no other woman had taken the time to kiss him there, but Ember was sucking on his ear as if it was his cock. Using her teeth to nip it, then sucking on the small piece of flesh almost aggressively.

"Em?" he asked.

"*Hmmm?*" she mumbled.

"You need to stop." His cock was as hard as steel and throbbed in his pants. He'd gone from slightly aroused—he was always that way around her—to being ready to fuck in two-point-three seconds. All it took was her mouth on him and he was a goner.

"No," she said, then licked the side of his neck before latching onto his earlobe once more.

Doc groaned and tightened his hold on Ember as he headed up the stairs. One of her arms stayed around his neck and the other moved down to knead his chest. Fuck, he loved her touching him.

He practically ran into his bedroom and leaned over his bed, dumping Ember onto her back on his sheets. But she didn't even miss a beat, sitting up quickly, her hands under his shirt before he could stop her. Her fingernails lightly scored his stomach, making his cock twitch in impatience.

Then she surprised him again by rising to her knees and whipping her shirt over her head. Her hair was mussed and even curlier than he'd seen before. She'd worn it down tonight, and he loved how full it was. The white bra she wore contrasted beautifully with her dark copper skin. And even though she was in better shape than the majority of women, she still had the tiniest pooch of a belly. Her arms were muscular and firm...but Doc had a hard time taking his eyes off her stomach. His hands itched to touch her there. To see how soft and silky her skin was. To nuzzle his way down to her pussy, see if she tasted as good as he'd imagined in his dreams.

"Fuck me," she said softly.

Doc's hands had moved to the waistband of his pants as soon as she'd uttered the second word.

But when she swayed and almost fell over, he froze.

Ember tried to push his hands out of the way and take over undoing his pants, but he resisted. As much as he wanted this woman, craved her, he wouldn't make love to her for the first time when she was three sheets to the wind. He wasn't that kind of guy. As painful as it was, he swallowed hard and turned away from her.

Walking over to his drawers, Doc took deep breaths, trying to tamp down his libido a couple notches. He pulled out one of his workout Army T-shirts and turned to Ember once more. She'd managed to push her pants down and was doing her best to undo her bra. But she was uncoordinated and clumsy, the alcohol wrecking her fine motor ability.

Fuck, she was so damn beautiful.

Doing his best to ignore all that creamy skin, he walked back over to her.

"I can't reach it," Ember said with a pout. "Help me?" she asked coyly.

Doc knew he should put his shirt over her head, then undo her bra...but he couldn't resist getting a glimpse of her perky tits, teasing him from behind the cups of her bra. He was doing his best to be a gentleman, but that was too tempting even for *him* to pass up. He wanted to be good, but he'd reached his limit.

Putting his arms around her to reach the clasp of her bra, Doc jerked in surprise when Ember latched onto his neck, sucking hard.

"Fuck, are you giving me a hickey?" he muttered, putting a hand on the back of her head and holding her to him, instead of jerking away.

She hummed but didn't lift her head. One hand palmed his cock and the other dug into his ass, making Doc freeze in place. He'd never been as turned on as he was right now. He wanted to push Ember back on his bed and fuck her. Hard.

She tilted her head and smiled up at him, as if proud of the mark she'd put on his neck. Her hands hadn't moved off his body; she continued to knead his cock, even as she swayed in front of him.

It was the sway that finally got Doc's brain working again. He could smell the tequila from her drinks, which also helped bring him back to the present. He wasn't going to take advantage of Ember. No way. When they had sex for the first time, she was going to be stone-cold sober and completely sure this was what she wanted. Because once he took her, that would be it. She'd ruin him for any other woman. He knew it as well as he knew his name.

Trying to ignore the way she was holding his cock, Doc reached behind her and quickly unhooked her bra. She had to drop her hands to get the straps off, and Doc could only stare at her tits. Damn. She was absolutely perfect. Her areolas were darker than her skin, the shade of a starless night. Her nipples were the same dark color—and they were pointing straight at him.

Doc's mouth watered. He wanted to lean down and taste. But he knew if he started, it would be almost impossible to stop. Especially since Ember wasn't exactly pushing him away.

She arched her back and put her hands behind her, smiling as she preened for him. "Like what you see?"

"Fucking love it," Doc said, as he reached for the T-shirt. "Sit up, Em."

She did, and he quickly put his shirt over her head.

"Arm," he ordered.

Em frowned and seemed extremely confused as he dressed her in his shirt. Doc ignored her questioning look and reached over and pulled back the covers. "Scoot in."

"But...I thought we were going to have sex?"

Doc got her settled under his covers, and the sight of her in his bed was almost as arousing as seeing her naked. Almost.

"We are," he told her. "But not tonight."

"Why?" she asked. "I thought... Oh, shit...you don't want me?"

"I want you," Doc was quick to reassure her. "But the first time we make love isn't going to be when you're drunk. I want you to remember every single second of our time together. We'll only get one first time, Em, and I want you to be completely sober. I want your head to spin because of the orgasms I give you, not because of the alcohol running through your veins."

"Orgasms? Plural?" she asked breathlessly.

Doc chuckled. "Yeah, sweetheart. You think one is gonna be enough?"

"Um...yes?"

"No fucking way. I want to see you get off with my mouth on you. I want to watch you get yourself off in front of me, so I can learn what you like. Then I'm going to fuck you so hard and deep, you aren't going to be able to think of any other man being inside you ever again. And I want to feel you come on my cock, pushing me over the edge."

"Yes. Please," she said, the longing easy to see in her eyes.

Doc shook his head. She was so damn adorable. And she was his. All his.

"I should go home," she sighed.

Doc's heart almost stopped beating for a second. She wanted to leave? But then he saw how her eyelids drooped and she seemed to melt even farther into the sheets.

She didn't want to leave; she was trying to be considerate.

"It's late," he told her softly. "And you're already in bed. Stay." He'd take her home if she really wanted to go.

"'Kay."

"I'm going to go get you a glass of water and some painkillers. I have a feeling you're gonna be hurting in the morning. You gonna stay put?"

She nodded.

"Good."

"Craig?"

"Yeah?"

"Most other guys would've taken what I was offering."

Doc figured she was right. "Probably."

"Are you sure you don't want to have sex? I don't mind. And I really do want you."

"I want you too. But it wouldn't feel right to take you when you're this drunk."

"I didn't mean to. I got nervous about tonight and figured I'd have a few drinks to loosen up."

"I know. It's okay. You're allowed to have fun, Em."

"But I really wanted to see your penis."

Doc burst out laughing. "Penis? Lord, woman. Don't call it that. It brings back too many memories of health class in middle school when we were showed diagrams of penises and vaginas."

Ember grinned. "Sorry. Your dick. Cock. That big, huge monster in your pants."

He loved her teasing. "That's better."

She sighed again, then whispered, "Don't hurt me, Craig. Please."

"I won't. How could I hurt the best thing that's ever happened to me?"

She smiled, then turned onto her side and curled into a ball.

Doc knew if he didn't get the water and pills in her soon, he'd lose his chance. Leaning down, he kissed her temple gently. "I'll be right back."

"I'll be here," she mumbled.

It took two and a half minutes for Doc to return with the water, and he was able to rouse Ember enough to sit up and drink half the glass. She swallowed the pills, then immediately lay back down and closed her eyes.

Doc sat next to her for twenty minutes, watching her sleep. It was sappy, and probably a little creepy, but he couldn't take his eyes off her. The day had been good. She'd clicked with the women in their circle and everyone had loved her. He hadn't doubted they would, but it was a relief to know he hadn't been blinded by all that was Ember Maxwell.

He wanted to stay. Wanted to slip under the covers and curl up behind her. Feel her bare legs tangle with his own. But he knew it would be safer to sleep elsewhere.

Leaning down, Doc kissed her temple once more. She sighed in her sleep and smiled.

"Sleep well, love," he whispered, before standing and heading for the en suite bathroom. He'd change and spend the night in the room across the hall. He'd be close enough to hear Ember if she happened to get sick or if she otherwise needed him, but far enough to give her some privacy...and to hopefully get his libido under control.

* * *

Ember woke up the next morning and groaned. Her head was pounding and she felt like shit. Some things were a little fuzzy from last night—but she remembered everything that happened when she got back to Craig's house.

She'd thrown herself at him, practically stripped naked, and he'd been a complete gentleman and had gotten her situated in bed—*his* bed—and hadn't taken advantage of her.

She also remembered what he'd said he wanted to do to her, and it made her clench her thighs together and squirm under the sheet.

She wanted that. All of it. She'd never touched herself in front of anyone before, but for Craig, she had a feeling she'd do whatever he asked.

Looking at the clock, she saw it was seven-thirty. It had been a long time since she'd slept in this late. Ember wasn't sure what time they'd gotten back to the house, but it had to have been a couple hours after midnight.

Stretching, she sat up and contemplated what to do next. She had her overnight bag in the back of his car, but she hadn't brought it inside last night. Looking around Craig's room, she blinked in surprise when she saw her bag sitting next to the bathroom door. At some point, Craig must've gone out to get it and brought it upstairs.

God. He was amazing. Thoughtful, observant, and kind, all at the same time. And he had a hell of a body to boot. Ember remembered the feel of his hard cock under her hand last night. Thinking back to how appalled he'd been when she'd called it a penis made her smile.

Ember couldn't deny she was a little embarrassed at how everything had gone down last night, but knowing Craig wasn't the kind of man to take advantage of her when she wasn't thinking straight was pretty awesome. Living in Hollywood had made her jaded, that was for sure.

Ember climbed out of bed and headed for the bathroom.

She grabbed her bag on the way and decided that Craig had made a mistake, giving her his shirt to sleep in. He wasn't getting it back. It was old and soft, and it was obviously well worn. And now it was hers.

Twenty minutes later, Ember was dressed in a pair of jeans and a pale green scoop-neck shirt. With her head still pounding, she made her way down the stairs. Craig had told her he was a morning person, and he hadn't lied. He was sitting at his kitchen table with a cup of coffee next to him and an empty plate.

The second he saw her, he stood and came toward her. He put his hands on either side of her head, tilted it up, and studied her closely. "How do you feel?" he asked quietly.

Ember shrugged as she reached up and took hold of his wrists. "I'm okay. I have a headache and feel slightly queasy, but based on how much I drank, I think I got off easy."

"I'm sorry I already ate, but I figured it would be better to cook before you got up, just in case you were nauseous. Can you eat anything? How about some dry toast to start?"

Some women might've gotten irritated with their men for not waiting to eat with them, but the reasoning behind his decision was thoughtful and caring. "Dry toast sounds great. And I'd love some coffee too."

"Sit. I'll bring it to you." Then he kissed her briefly on the lips before escorting her to the chair he'd just vacated. While Ember waited for him to toast some bread, Craig brought her a glass of water and some more painkillers. "Best to stay hydrated today, it'll help you feel better faster. If you can, drink that first, then the coffee. Okay?"

Ember had been waited on her entire life. Her parents had a live-in cook who brought her meals three times a day. But she'd never felt as cared for as when Craig brought her two plain pieces of toast and a cup of coffee.

She nibbled on her bland breakfast, happy it seemed to be settling well.

"I'm sorry about last night," she said after a moment.

"For what?"

"Um...well...for getting trashed. I hadn't planned on that."

"I know, you told me."

"Right. Well, I'm sorry you had to take care of me. I'm sure I'd have been fine if you had dropped me off at my apartment so you wouldn't need to babysit me."

"Em, there's no way I would've left you alone in the shape you were in. You could've thrown up in your sleep and choked. Or stopped breathing."

"Thank you then, for looking after me. I'm also sorry for being so...aggressive. Sexually."

Craig grinned. "I'm not." He tilted his head and brought a hand up to finger a dark spot on his neck. "I can't remember the last time I had a hickey. The guys are going to give me all sorts of shit."

Ember dropped her forehead into her hand. "Crap. I'm so sorry."

"Don't be. Thinking about how you sucked on me...it's hot as hell, Em. And just saying...turnabout's fair play. I thought about all the places I want to mark you when I saw my neck this morning."

Ember wasn't sure what to say about that. Some people thought hickeys wouldn't show on Black people's skin, but they were wrong. Maybe they weren't as noticeable, but they'd definitely show up.

And now she couldn't stop thinking about where Craig might want to suck on her.

"Then thank you for being so...honorable last night. I was kind of obnoxious."

"Do you remember what I said about what I wanted to do to you our first time?"

Ember's cheeks heated. "Yes."

Craig nodded. "Good. I was worried that might've been lost in your alcohol haze. The hardest thing I've ever done in my life was leave you half naked in my bed, Em. But hear me loud and clear, I'll *never* take advantage of you. Not your wealth. Not your fame. Not when you're drunk or not feeling yourself. I'll protect you from everyone—even from myself and my libido, if necessary. When you're with me, you're safe. Period."

Ember wanted to cry, but she controlled herself. "Thanks."

"And for the record? Your tits? Damn, woman. You almost pushed me over the edge with that arching-your-back move."

Ember giggled. "Um...sorry?"

"No, don't be sorry. I dreamed about them last night. And it was a damn good dream." Craig smiled at her.

"I wish I didn't have to pick up Julio and Marie at the airport today," she said. "Now that I'm sober, I want to go right back upstairs to your bed and have you do all those things you told me we'd do last night."

"What time does their flight arrive again?"

"Noon, in Austin. I've paid the deposits on their apartments, but their stuff isn't supposed to get here until later this week. I was going to take them to lunch, give them a tour of Killeen and the gym, then bring them to their hotel."

"You must be pretty close with them," Craig said.

Ember did her best to get her mind off sex so she could have a normal conversation with Craig. "Yes and no. I mean, I've known Julio for a few years. He started training at the same gym where I did back in California about four years ago. He's the resident expert at fencing and helped me improve a lot. He's in his late twenties and..."

"And what?" Craig asked.

Ember shrugged. "That's just it...I don't know a lot about

him. I mean, I saw him at least twice a week for four years, and all I know is how old he is. And I only know *that* because in some competitions, the participations are grouped by age."

"You want me to run a background check on him?" Craig asked.

"Can you do that?"

"Well, not me, but I know people who can," he said mysteriously.

Ember shook her head. "No, I'm sure he's good. I'm assuming he's single, because I don't think he would've agreed to come to Texas and help me if he wasn't. I think he was born and raised in California, so I'm not sure what made him agree. I was just so thrilled that I'd have help, I didn't stop to find out his motivation."

"Maybe you should do that," Craig suggested.

"I will."

"And Marie?"

"I've only known her for two years, but when I mentioned moving out here to Texas after I got back from the Olympics, and what I wanted to do, she was the one who actually asked if I needed any help. I hadn't thought that far ahead, but it made sense. Bringing in people I know seemed a lot better than trying to find people who knew what the pentathlon was all about. At least to start with."

"And neither seem resentful of your success, wealth, or fame?" Craig asked.

"No, of course not."

"*Hmmm.*"

"What does that *hmmm* mean?" Ember asked.

"Just that it seems a little weird to me that they were both so willing to give up everything to move out here with you, to a place they've never been. I'm just wondering what their agenda is."

"Do they have to have an agenda? Can't they just want a

change of pace and scenery...and maybe to do some good in the world?" Ember asked, a little frustrated.

"Of course they can. I didn't mean to upset you. But my job is to have your back. To make sure no one takes advantage of you or does anything that will come back and bite you in the ass. That makes me suspicious of *everyone*, but I won't apologize for it. My background has made me understand that even the most innocent-looking person can secretly be planning your demise."

Ember stared at Craig for a long moment. She couldn't deny that his questions made her feel a little stupid. She probably should've asked more questions before spontaneously hiring Julio and Marie. Her parents had called her naïve before she'd moved out, and they were probably right. But she could admit she also liked the fact that Craig was trying to have her back. She hadn't really had anyone put her welfare before everything else before.

"I'm sorry you've had to learn that the hard way," Ember said at last. "And as uncomfortable as what you said made me feel, you still made some good points. But I know Julio and Marie. I've sweated and worked out with them, side by side, for years. They were both disappointed not to make the Olympic team, but I think they knew it was a long shot. With only two places for each gender on the team, it's very hard to make the cut. And they both have their weaknesses. Julio's is the swim, and Marie's is the shooting. I think they jumped at the chance to help me because four years until the next Olympics is a long time. And they're both getting older, as am I. So maybe it's also that we all need to move on with our lives and figure out what comes next."

Craig nodded. "That makes sense. But, with your permission, I'd still like to have a background check done on both of them. See who they hung out with back in California, if they have police records, see what their finances are, that sort of thing. I know you want to be just another businesswoman, but the fact remains that you're Ember Maxwell. You're famous, rich, and beautiful, and there will always be those who want to take advantage of that. Of you."

"I don't like the thought of prying into their lives," Ember hedged.

"If they have nothing to hide, then they won't even know," Craig retorted.

"*I'll* know," Ember said softly. Then she sighed. "But I get it. I do want to be normal. But I've been privileged to grow up the way I have, and I need to deal with it. Fine. Do your background check. But if you find anything, I want to know right away."

"Deal," Craig said immediately. "So you'll get back here around five or so?"

It took Ember a moment to bring her mind back around to the original conversation. "Yeah, that sounds about right."

"And what's your schedule on Monday?"

"More of the same. Working out, meetings, getting Julio and Marie situated, and chatting with a woman who owns some land outside Killeen. I think it'll be great for setting up a running course. If that conversation goes well, I'll set up a time later this week to go check it out with Julio and Marie. See what they think. Depending on how the meeting goes with the local Boys and Girls Club on Tuesday, I could possibly have my first class as early as Wednesday."

"Wednesday? Seriously? That soon?"

Ember shrugged a little sheepishly. "What good is having money if you don't use it, right? I'm paying out the nose to get things moving as fast as possible. And the building was in pretty good shape to begin with. Not *everything* will be done, but enough that the space will be useable."

"It's all falling into place for you, isn't it?" Craig asked with a smile.

"Amazingly, yes. I never dreamed everything could happen this fast."

"Well, when you have a motivated and enthusiastic CEO, it can."

That was true. Ember knew she'd been a little crazy about her schedule and getting things up and running, but this was important to her. She couldn't wait to share her love of the modern pentathlon sport with those kids who might never otherwise have a chance to experience it.

"How about if I make us dinner tonight then?"

"You don't have to constantly wait on me, Craig," Ember said with a frown. "I'm not going to starve if I'm left to my own devices."

"I know, but I want to. I want you back here tonight. I want you to spend the night again, so I can show you how amazing you are. So I can do all those things I promised you last night."

Ember swallowed. "Are you making a date for us to have sex?"

He grinned. "If you want to put it that way, yes. I have a feeling between your schedule and mine, we'll need to pencil in time to make love more than we'd like."

That was true. "So...I'm going to have to think about you making me come three times all day?" she asked with a grin.

"Yup. And I'm gonna have to think about how good your pussy's gonna feel around my cock. And how hard I can get those nipples you showed me last night."

"Damn," Ember said softly. "That wasn't fair."

Craig moved so quickly, she didn't have a chance to evade his grasp. He hauled her out of her chair and across his lap and had his mouth on hers before she could say another word.

He tasted like coffee and bacon, and Ember moaned as he devoured her mouth. Unlike the other times he'd kissed her, his hands roamed. One arm held her tightly against him so she didn't fall off his lap, and his other hand snuck under her shirt and palmed one of her breasts.

Ember squirmed on his lap, feeling his hard cock under her ass. It felt good knowing she could turn him on so much, and so quickly, because it felt as if she'd gone from zero to one hundred in a millisecond herself.

"Craig," she moaned when she lifted her head to take a breath.

He didn't respond, just pulled the front of her scoop neck down and latched his mouth onto the fleshy part of her upper breast. She felt him suck her skin into his mouth, and she couldn't help but moan again.

He lifted his head a minute later and gave her a grin as he met her gaze.

"Did you just give me a hickey?" she asked.

"Yup," he said without apology. "But it's in a place only I can see. I don't want anyone looking at you and thinking about sex. Well, any more than they already do because of how damn gorgeous you are. And tonight, I'm gonna find a lot more places to mark."

"You're lethal, you know that?" Ember asked.

"I've never felt this desperate to make love to someone before," Craig said seriously. "But I swear if I don't get inside you sooner rather than later, I'm gonna literally die."

Ember couldn't help but smile. "That was a little dramatic, don't you think?"

"No."

"Do I need to stop and get condoms?" Ember asked a little shyly. She knew adults talked about this kind of thing, but it was harder than she'd thought.

Craig gave her a tender smile. "No. I'll take care of that today."

"Thanks."

He shook his head. "You don't have to thank me for taking care of you. It's my pleasure."

"What are you going to do today while I'm busy with Julio and Marie?"

"Going to the grocery store, checking in with the guys to make sure everyone got home all right and all is well, making sure Grover hasn't decided to head to Afghanistan by himself, buy some condoms, and wash my sheets."

Ember's head spun. "Wash the sheets?" she asked.

"Yeah. I want our first time to be perfect. And I can't think of anything better than taking you on fresh, clean sheets."

"Right." Ember liked that he'd thought about that small detail.

No—she loved it.

"Is there a chance Grover will go overseas without you guys?"

Craig sighed. "I'd like to say no, but I've never seen him so worked up about a mission before."

"I'll check my account today and see if anyone mentioned seeing Sierra."

"I know you were glad to take over your own accounts, but maybe you should think about hiring someone again."

Ember opened her mouth to disagree, but Craig kept talking before she could speak.

"I'm not saying someone who would take over. But they could respond to posts and keep you updated on whether there's anything you should be concerned or informed about. You aren't going to have time to keep it up once the gym gets going. You can tell the person what to post and stuff, and you wouldn't have to read all those horrible, mean comments."

Ember thought about his suggestion for a moment. It was actually a good one. She didn't love all the crap that came along with her accounts. She thought she would, but once she took it over, she realized what a time suck it could be. And Samer had been extremely helpful about answering any questions, even after she'd basically fired him. Maybe seeing if he'd consider working for her—and not her parents—would be a good idea. "I'll think about it," she told him.

"Good," Craig said. Then he kissed her hard and fast on the lips and stood, taking her with him.

Ember's feet hit the floor and he steadied her. "We've got some time to kill before you need to head to Austin. Do you want to go to the store to get stuff for your apartment? I could come, then help you unpack and put things away...if you wanted."

"I'd love that," Ember told him with a huge smile. She hadn't had time to pick up some of the things she needed, like rugs for the bathroom, pillows, and other odds and ends. And having Craig by her side would make it even more fun. She also appreciated that, even though it was obvious she'd be spending the night at his house tonight, he wasn't pressuring her to give up her apartment already.

It was silly, but even if she spent a lot of her free time with Craig at his place, she still liked the idea of having her own apartment. Of being independent. She could have a boyfriend and still be independent. Was looking forward to it, actually. Craig would be deployed, probably sooner rather than later, and there would also be days when she wanted some time to herself. She wasn't assuming that she'd have her apartment forever, and she certainly wanted things to continue to progress with Craig...but for now, she needed her own space. Didn't want to trade one form of dependency— living with her parents—for another by moving in with a man.

"Why don't you go pack your stuff. Leave anything you want to use Monday. You can grab what you need for tonight after we shop and set up your place. I'll do the dishes and then we can head out."

"You do dishes?" Ember teased.

"Yup. And vacuum, mop, and do the laundry too."

"Be still my heart." Ember was kidding, but kinda not.

"Adorable," Craig muttered, then gave her a small shove toward the stairs. "Go now, before I decide I don't want to wait for tonight."

Ember paused and put her hand on her chin, as if deep in thought.

Craig laughed. "Go. Have pity on me."

So she went. But she did so smiling.

CHAPTER THIRTEEN

The day had seemed to last forever. Doc kept looking at his watch, hoping time had moved faster than it seemed. He'd been getting update texts from Ember that made him smile.

Holy crap, this airport is tiny compared to LAX!

I found a spot right near the stairwell! It's a miracle.

Got Julio and Marie, headed back to Killeen now.

They love the gym! I'm so relieved.

Thanks for recommending the Mexican restaurant. It was delicious!

I talked a little to them about why they wanted to move to Texas, will tell you about it later.

The apartments were fine, move-in day is scheduled for Friday.

Is this day moving really slowly, or is it just me? :)

I just dropped J and M off at the hotel. J's gonna rent a car. His and M's cars are being brought over from CA.

Do we need anything from the store? I can stop if we do.

I'm more than ready for this, Craig. See you soon.

. . .

He was thrilled she was anticipating their night together as much as he was. He'd remade the bed, cleaned the bathrooms, vacuumed, had three boxes of condoms stashed around the house...which was overkill, but he didn't want to have to stop and go hunt down a box if things progressed somewhere other than the bedroom.

He'd decided on stuffed green peppers for dinner; they were easy to make and already in the oven. They'd be ready when Ember arrived. If he could keep himself from attacking her the second she walked in, they'd be good.

Grinning, Doc couldn't help but wonder if *Ember* would be doing the attacking. He loved that she wasn't shy to tell him what she wanted. That she was independent. That she was working as hard as she could to make her dream a reality. He'd once thought that he wanted a woman who wouldn't mind staying at home more often than not...but he'd been an idiot.

Ember was perfect. Ambitious and not content to let him make all the decisions. She liked to call the shots, at least when it came to her life, and he was more than all right with that. He'd gladly let her take control in the bedroom as well—but not tonight. Tonight, *he* was in charge. He was going to show her how much she meant to him and how much he adored her.

"Honey! I'm home!" she quipped as she walked into his house.

Doc had unlocked his front door after he'd received the last text, telling her to just come on in when she got there. His heart yearned to hear those words for real, for this to *be* her home, but he'd take things one day at a time. A woman like Ember wouldn't want to be rushed into making any kind of decision. She relished making her own choices about her life for the first time ever. He'd make it clear she was welcome here anytime, but when she knew down to her very bones that this was where she was meant to be, she'd make that decision.

It didn't mean Doc wouldn't try to convince her. He'd already planned on giving her a key.

Smiling, he walked toward Ember with his arms open. To his surprise, she jumped at him when he got close.

Laughing, he caught her and spun her in a circle. "Have a good day?" he asked.

"Yeah. Although it was loooong. The next time you want to tease me with a night of debauchery...don't."

"It was long and *hard* for me too," Doc teased.

Ember rolled her eyes. "Oh, man, that was bad."

"You hungry?" he asked, wanting nothing more than to strip her shirt over her head and go down on her right then and there.

"For food? Not really. But it smells delicious in here, and I'd hate to have your dinner go to waste."

Doc seriously contemplated heading into the kitchen, turning off the oven, and carrying her up the stairs as he'd done last night, but then he forced himself to drop his arms from around her. As much as he wanted Ember, he wanted to give her a perfect night that she'd hopefully remember the rest of her life.

"I feel like the traditional roles are reversed," he said as he took hold of her hand and led her into the kitchen. "You're the bread winner coming home from a long day of work and I'm the spouse slaving over the housework all day. Making sure a hot dinner is ready for you when you walk in the door."

Ember put her hand on his arm. "You don't expect me to be that kind of woman, do you?"

"Hell no!" Doc said. "I want you to be exactly who you are. If that means I do all the cooking and cleaning, so be it. I just want you to be happy, Em."

"I am. I know everything in my life has been turned

upside down lately, and my parents—and probably much of the world—think I've rushed into this thing, but I've wanted to do something like this for so long. I've wanted to give back, to be more than a pretty face on the computer. I suck at housecleaning, and I'll probably work really long hours and you'll have to force me to take time off. But I'll do my best to do my part."

Doc kissed her. "That's all I can ask for. I made stuffed peppers tonight. If you like them, I can teach you how to make them later."

"Awesome."

"You want to help me make a salad?"

"Sure. Just tell me what to do."

"Why don't we start with the lettuce. I'll chop, you tear."

"Yes, sir!" Ember teased.

They worked side by side, and Doc loved every second of it. She told him more details about her day and how Julio and Marie seemed happy to be in Texas.

"I asked them why they'd accepted my job offer, and Julio told me that his sister had gotten mixed up in a gang and had been killed. I didn't know that at all. I thought he had a normal middle-class upbringing. Anyway, he said he was really excited about doing something to help kids stay out of that kind of lifestyle. He had a teacher when he was in elementary school who'd gotten him interested in fencing, and that morphed into getting involved with the pentathlon. He said it literally saved his life."

"That's great," Doc said. And it was. But...he still couldn't help but wonder if there was more to it. He needed to talk to Trigger and see if he would contact their old friend, Tex, to do a background check. If he wasn't available, there was a woman down in San Antonio who Ghost and his team of Deltas were close with, who sometimes worked with Tex. She could probably get it done just as easily. Doc would call in favors if necessary in order to protect Ember. "What about Marie?"

Ember shrugged. "She didn't have any kind of story like Julio. She just said that she wouldn't mind getting out of California and seeing more of the world. She apparently doesn't get along well with her family. I think she's just restless and a little lost after the Olympics. She hasn't seemed like herself ever since I got back from South Korea, and I think it's because it hit her that her chances of making the team are pretty slim. I think it's good for her to break out of the rut she was in back in California. Out of the two of them, I think Julio will probably stay with me longer, but that's okay. I don't expect either of them to work for me forever."

"That's a good attitude to have," Doc agreed. "Although you paying their rent is pretty big."

"I'm not paying their rent. I just found the apartments and put down the deposits. They know they're responsible for everything after they move in."

"Good. I guess I misunderstood," Doc said.

"I thought about it, but it felt too much like buying their loyalty. I want them to stay because they believe in what they're doing and have a passion for it. I don't want to be a free ride for them."

"That's smart," Doc said.

"For someone without a college degree," she said self-deprecatingly.

"No, it's smart for a businesswoman," Doc corrected. "I've known plenty of officers with college degrees who are dumber than a box of rocks. And I've known a ton of enlisted guys who are fucking geniuses, and they have nothing more than a GED or a high school diploma. Don't sell yourself short, Em. You're going to make this idea of yours work, and the kids in this area are going to be better off because of it."

"Thanks," she said softly.

"You're welcome. Now, do you want me to cut off the seeds on the cucumbers or leave them on?"

"On. Do you have croutons?"

"Is a salad a salad without them?" Doc asked.

She laughed. "I think having you as my chef is going to spoil me."

"Good," Doc said, leaning in to kiss her briefly. Anything more and he wouldn't be able to control himself. His cock was half hard, had been that way all day, anticipating what tonight would bring.

"I've also been thinking of your suggestion, and I'm considering asking Samer if he'll come back and work for me. I didn't realize how much time social media takes up. That, and I really don't like reading the comments. I figure if I can convince him to do all that for me, it'll free me up to do a lot of other things. What do you think?"

"I think it's a great idea," Doc said honestly. "As long as you make sure he understands that he isn't to post anything you don't approve ahead of time. You don't want him posting pictures of you again, do you?"

"Oh, hell no. And I don't think he will. Alexis, on the other hand...he'd probably go right back to what he'd been doing before."

Doc made a mental note to have Tex look into this Alexis person too. The name thing was too much of a coincidence to overlook. If the Alex who was posting such hateful comments on Ember's social media accounts was actually Alexis...Tex would get to the bottom of it, and make sure the man stopped his harassment.

Dinner was relaxed, despite the palpable air of anticipation around them, which Doc loved. After eating, they got the dishes put into the dishwasher and cleaned up the kitchen. It was too early to go to bed, but Doc couldn't think about anything else.

He turned to Ember to suggest doing something that would hopefully kill some time until he could take her upstairs, but let out an *oof* when he literally ran into her because she was standing right next to him.

"Shit, sorry," he told her.

Ember put her arms around his neck and pressed herself against him from chest to knees. "You've fed me, Craig. I can't wait any longer. It might make me a whore, but I can't think about anything but having you inside me."

And just like that, Doc lost the battle with the erection he'd been fighting all evening. "You aren't a whore," he said firmly. "I've thought about having you all day." Keeping her close, he began to maneuver them toward his stairs. He couldn't bear to let go. He lowered his head and kissed her. They ran into the wall, a chair, and he almost tripped over the first step, but he refused to take his mouth from hers. As they climbed, their kiss got more and more desperate. When Ember's hands fumbled with his shirt, Doc paused only long enough to rip it over his head.

Ember's hands were on his chest immediately, kneading and caressing his muscles. He groaned low in his throat when she teased his nipples. Fuck, he hadn't realized how sensitive he was there. Probably because no one had really bothered to find out before.

Their teeth clicked together as they kissed, neither one caring about finesse. Doc's hands went to Ember's jeans and she almost fell when he shoved them off her hips. They'd made it to the middle of the hall leading to his room, but it barely registered. All of Doc's attention was focused on the wet spot on her panties, between her legs. His mouth watered.

Ember got her shirt off by herself, then her hands went to the fastening of his pants. Doc knew the second she touched his cock, he'd lose all control...what little he still had.

Careful not to hurt her, he quickly leaned over and put his shoulder to her belly, hefting Ember up and over his shoulder.

She giggled, and he could feel her hands on his back, holding herself up. He knew this couldn't be all that comfortable for her, but it was mere seconds before he'd gotten to the edge of his bed. He bent and dropped her on the mattress, hearing another giggle as she bounced.

Doc was frantic to get his mouth on her. He kneeled on the floor by his bed and roughly grabbed her hips, pulling her to the very edge of the mattress. He pushed her legs apart and leaned in, inhaling her aroused scent.

"Damn, Em, you are so fucking irresistible."

"Craig—"

That was all she got out before Doc pulled the gusset of her panties to the side and dove in. He ran his tongue up her slit, loving her tangy taste, before latching his mouth over her clit.

He couldn't go slow. He needed her to be as desperate for him as he was for her. And the last thing he wanted to do was hurt her when he entered her body. He wanted her to be dripping. When he got his pants off, he wasn't going to be able to wait.

"Holy shit, Craig," Ember muttered.

He felt her hands caressing his head, but all his attention was between her legs. He used a finger on one hand to tease her folds and entrance, but kept his mouth over her clit. She squirmed under him, and it took everything he had to keep his lips on the small bundle of nerves.

Her thighs tightened around his head, but he used his free hand to press against one, keeping her open for him. He had one goal in mind—to make her come. He needed to do that for her. To give her the ultimate pleasure.

Doc wished he'd had the patience to take her panties off before he'd gone down on her, but it was too late to do anything about it now. Way too late. He wasn't lifting his mouth from his prize. No fucking way.

The wet sound of his finger moving in and out of her body was getting louder, which pleased Doc to no end. He'd never been this desperate for a woman. His cock was weeping precome in his pants and it was obvious he wo gonna explode the second he got inside Ember's body.

Doc glanced up as he ate her out. Her adorable little stomach quivered with every inhale, and her tits shook as she writhed against him. He hadn't managed to remove her bra before he'd attacked her, but he couldn't be upset. She was sexy as hell like this. Lost in the pleasure of what he was doing to her, her underwear still on, holding on to him as if she'd never let go.

"Right there. More! Shit, Craig, yes!"

Closing his eyes, Craig lost himself in the taste, smell, and feel of the woman under him. Her hips were thrusting against his finger and his tongue, trying to get herself over the edge.

"Please, Craig!"

That was it. He was done. No way would his woman ever have to beg him for *anything*.

Using his tongue like a piston, he concentrated on her clit, flicking it over and over. He turned his hand and eased another finger inside her. She jerked against him and froze as he touched that special spongy spot deep inside. Smiling, he curled his fingers and rubbed against it as he continued his assault on her clit.

Within seconds, she was shrieking and bucking uncontrollably against him. He couldn't keep his mouth on her with the way she was writhing, so he moved his other hand between her legs and thumbed her clit as he continued to manipulate her G-spot.

Ember lost in orgasm was the sexiest damn thing he'd ever seen in his life. Her back arched, she clutched his shoulders as if she'd fly into pieces if she didn't, and the image of her excitement leaking from her body and coating his fingers was something he'd never forget as long as he lived.

As her orgasm waned, Doc stood. He ripped her underwear over her hips and down her legs. "Sit up," he ordered gruffly.

Ember didn't move, and Craig couldn't stop the satisfied grin from crossing his face. He helped her into a sitting position and undid her bra before helping her move to the center of the bed. He couldn't help but stand there and admire her for a moment.

Then she blew his control to smithereens when she slowly parted her legs and moved one hand between them, lightly fingering herself.

That was it. She'd pushed him over the edge.

* * *

Ember could barely move or think. Craig had literally blown her mind. She'd had plenty of orgasms before. Had even had what she'd thought was fairly good sex. But what Craig had just done? No, that was new.

He'd gone down on her as if he was a starving man and she was a Thanksgiving feast. He hadn't been shy about it either. She loved his confidence, and he definitely knew how to please a woman. She'd never had a G-spot orgasm before, and she felt wrung out and completely boneless as a result.

But seeing Craig standing by the side of the bed, staring down at her as if she were his Christmas and birthday present all in one? She was ready for more.

There was no embarrassment or hesitation as she spread her legs to tease him. She saw the second his control snapped. One second he was a lover admiring his woman, and the next he was a predator on the prowl. She watched as he shoved his jeans and boxers off at the same time.

She only got a glimpse of his long, thick cock before he was straddling her. Ember couldn't hold back a moan. This man wanted *her*. His Em. Not because of what she could give him or do for his career. But because of the connection they'd made.

"I can't be gentle," he rasped.

"I don't want you to be."

He leaned over and fumbled with the drawer in the nightstand next to the bed. Ember sat up just enough to latch her mouth onto the fleshy skin next to his nipple. She sucked. Hard. It wasn't her fault; when he'd leaned over, his chest was right there, in her face. She couldn't resist. She felt one of his hands cradling the back of her head, holding her against him as she did her best to mark her man.

He scooted them back into the middle of the bed, but she still didn't take her mouth off him. Ember couldn't get enough.

When she finally let go and lay back down, she saw she'd definitely done what she'd set out to do. He was going to have a hell of a bruise on his chest, and she didn't feel the least bit bad about it.

"Happy?" he drawled.

Ember lifted her gaze to meet his and smiled. "Yeah."

He looked down at his chest, then back at her. "That's gonna take a while to disappear."

"Yup. And every time you see it, you'll remember this. *Me*."

"Fuck yeah, I will," Craig said roughly. Then he grabbed her hips once more and pulled her closer. Ember loved how he manhandled her. He wasn't hurting her, not even close. She didn't want to be treated like a piece of china. She wanted all of Craig. His passion and enthusiasm and impatience.

She widened her legs even more in invitation. Looking down, she saw Craig take hold of his cock. He'd put a condom on already, probably when she was giving him the hickey. He smacked her pussy lips with his dick, and she gasped. Then he ran his length up and down her weeping slit.

"Stop teasing and fuck me already," she complained.

"I was gonna have you masturbate for me. Show me what you like, but I don't think I can handle that right now. I need you too badly."

"Fine by me," she said with a smile.

"This is it," Craig told her seriously. "When I get inside that hot, wet pussy, you're mine. Got it?"

"Yes!" Ember exclaimed. "And you're mine. No other women, Craig. I mean it. If I even think you're fucking someone else, I'll probably lose it."

"Why the fuck would I want anyone else when I have this?" he asked, running a hand down her body. He gripped one of her breasts tightly, then tweaked the nipple before continuing downward. He palmed her belly and smiled. "I love this pooch."

Ember rolled her eyes and panted, "You aren't supposed to talk about a woman's flaws in the middle of sex."

"Flaws? Good God, woman, this isn't a flaw. It's sexy as hell. You've got muscles on top of muscles, could probably flip me on this bed easily, but this? It's soft and sexy. It reminds me that you're all woman...and I can't help but imagine a little Ember nestled inside, growing and being nurtured by your body."

Ember moaned. Fuck. The man was talking about kids. She'd never thought too much about them, being too busy with her athletic career. But now? The thought of having

Craig's babies filled her with a sudden and overwhelming need.

And that was insane. She wasn't ready to be a mother. No way, she had too much to do with her life. But someday? Yeah...she wanted that.

"Fuck me," she ordered.

"Yes, ma'am," Craig said with a smile. But it quickly disappeared as he stared between her legs. As aggressive as he'd been, Ember was surprised when he gently placed the head of his cock against her dripping pussy and pushed in the barest of inches.

"Craig!" she said in exasperation.

"Give me a second," he begged between clenched teeth as he dropped down over her. His hands were resting on the mattress by her shoulders and his head was bowed. Just the tip of his dick was inside her, and Ember needed more. Needed all of him.

She squirmed and lifted her hips, successfully getting more of his cock.

"Fuck," he swore, before plunging his entire length inside her with one fast and hard thrust.

Ember closed her eyes and cried out.

"Shit, did I hurt you?" Craig asked, sounding as if he was on the verge of panicking.

"No," she reassured him. "It's been a while for me so it's a little uncomfortable, but you feel so damn good."

Craig stayed completely still as she acclimated to having him inside her. When the slight pain faded, she opened her eyes and looked up. Craig's jaw was clenched as he stared down at her with concern and lust. Bringing a hand to his face, Ember caressed his cheek briefly.

"I'm okay," she whispered.

"Are you sure?"

"Very."

"I'm not gonna last," Craig informed her. "I almost came the second I bottomed out inside you. Once I start moving, it's gonna be over for me pretty quickly."

"It's okay," Ember said with a satisfied smile.

"You like that," he said.

"What's not to like? My man is so overwhelmed with pleasure that he can't hold back. That's the best compliment ever."

"I thought women liked it when men lasted a long time."

"Not me," Ember said, not feeling weird in the least that they were having a conversation while he was deep inside her body. She felt connected to him in a way she'd never experienced with anyone else before. "Thrusting in and out for thirty minutes? That shit's uncomfortable. I would much rather have a hard and fast fuck, and have both of us get off quickly, than have you down there pumping away for an hour."

"Noted," Craig said with a chuckle. "And it's a good thing. Because I have a feeling I'm always gonna bust a nut fast when I'm inside you. I'll always make it good for you though, Em. Before and after."

"You *did* claim that you could give me three orgasms...I might have miscounted, but I think I'm only at one right now," she teased.

"One? I'm guessing you had at least two earlier, one right after another," he boasted.

He may be right...but Ember wasn't going to admit it.

She was startled to realize that this was *fun*. Sex had never been fun before. Intense, satisfying, boring, unfulfilling? Yes. But not fun.

"You ready?" he asked.

Ember nodded.

"Hold on."

"To what?" she asked.

"To me," Craig said without missing a beat.

Ember reached up and gripped his biceps tightly. Then he moved. Pulling back slowly before slamming back inside her. His pubic bone pressed against her clit when he bottomed out, and she moaned.

Suddenly he was thrusting fast and hard, like he'd warned. Ember tried to help, to lift her hips to meet his thrusts, but he was bucking too aggressively. She couldn't do anything but lie under him and take it. And she *loved* it.

Like he'd predicted, it wasn't long before he was on the verge of coming. Fascinated, Ember watched as the veins in his forehead and neck stood out. He thrust a few more times, then shoved a hand under her ass and pulled her butt cheeks apart. That gave him room to get inside her another fraction of an inch, and she moaned. He groaned a second later, and Ember swore she could feel him twitch inside her as he came.

It took quite a few seconds before his body slowly began to relax. But then he surprised the hell out of her by sitting up, keeping his cock deep inside her body. He pulled her ass up onto his thighs until her back was arching and she was resting on her shoulder blades.

He didn't ask permission. Didn't ask if she was ready. He simply brought his hand down and began to roughly flick her already swollen and sensitive clit.

"Craig!" she exclaimed.

He didn't stop; not that she actually wanted him to. Her inner muscles clenched against his softening cock, but he didn't pull out. It felt good to have something inside her as she ramped up toward another orgasm.

"That's it, Em. I can feel you on my cock...it's so amazing."

She wanted to respond, but could barely breathe much less talk.

He increased the pressure on her clit and Ember flew over

the edge. This orgasm wasn't as intense as the first he'd given her, but it was no less satisfying.

She felt Craig's hands running over her chest and belly as he soothed her.

Ember opened her eyes and looked up at the man she knew had changed her life. "Wow."

He smiled and the lines around his eyes deepened. "Yeah, wow."

She felt his cock finally slip out of her body and wrinkled her nose.

He laughed. "Think how I feel. It's cold out here."

Ember stared at him for a beat, then couldn't hold back her giggles. He simply smiled at her as she tried to get herself under control. She felt lighter than she had in ages.

Craig moved then, repositioning her, but not pulling up the sheet and blanket. When she reached for it, he shook his head. "Leave it," he ordered.

Raising an eyebrow at him, Ember just nodded.

"I need to take care of his," he said, nodding to his cock. Ember couldn't help but look. He wasn't hard any more, but even soft and covered in a used condom, he was impressive. "Stay right there and don't move."

"Okay," Ember agreed.

Their gazes met for a second, and apparently Craig saw whatever he was looking for because he nodded and headed for the bathroom. Ember admired the view from behind as he went. He had an ass to die for. She knew firsthand how hard it was to get muscles and an ass like that. The hours of working out, the dedication to eating right and taking care of your body. Craig was as much an elite athlete as she was...and she freaking loved that.

It wasn't long before he was returning with a washcloth in hand. Unconsciously, she spread her legs a little as he approached, anticipating him using that cloth between her legs—but he surprised her by running the warm towel over her chest.

"I'm not washing away your wonderful scent and juices yet," he informed her. "I'm not done with you."

Ember stared at him in surprise. "You aren't?"

"I said three, and I don't go back on my word."

"Um...it's a little soon for me," Ember admitted. She liked orgasms as much as the next woman, but it had been a while since she'd been with a man. She was a little sore as a result. Thinking about making love again so soon was a tad daunting.

"It's still early," Craig said. "I was too primed to pay you the proper attention. Like these nipples," he said almost nonchalantly as he ran the cloth over her hardening buds. "They're begging for me to touch, lick, and suck them. I could probably do that for an hour. Then I want to explore your pussy some more. Again, I was in too much of a hurry to pay you proper homage. Then a back and neck rub probably wouldn't be amiss. Once I've examined every inch of your beautiful body, *then* I'll see if that first orgasm was a fluke, or if I can find that G-spot again."

"Craig," Ember protested.

"Yeah?" he answered, still lazily running the cloth over her chest.

If someone had told her a month ago she'd be lying in the most amazing man's bed being worshiped like this, she would've laughed her ass off.

"After you come again for me, I'll warm this washcloth once more and clean your pussy for you. After that, we'll lie down and get some sleep. You want to run with me and the guys in the morning?"

It should've been weird to talk about their schedule for tomorrow when he was sitting butt-ass naked next to her, caressing her tits with a washcloth and looking like he wanted nothing more than to devour her. "Um...sure."

"Great. Just don't antagonize Trigger. He loves to add weight to our packs if someone says anything, like how it'll be an easy run or something."

Ember smiled. Trigger sounded like some of the coaches she'd had in the past.

Thoughts of Craig's friends and tomorrow's schedule flew out of her head when he leaned down and licked her nipple. It immediately hardened.

He smiled. "Fuck, that's beautiful." Then he lowered his head again...

An hour and a half later, Ember lay in a boneless heap in Craig's bed. She literally was too satisfied and exhausted to move. Craig had done exactly what he'd promised. He'd cherished every inch of her body and had done things to her that she'd never even dreamed about. He hadn't taken her again, but he'd given her a third—and fourth—orgasm. She'd reciprocated by giving him a hand job until he'd exploded all over their hands, which had both been jacking him off. She'd wanted to go down on him, but he'd told her tonight was all about her.

He'd cleaned them both up and finally covered them with the sheet and blanket, taking her into his arms. It was still fairly early, but Ember didn't mind. She was exhausted...and happy.

She and Craig were naked. The feel of his body against her back was comforting; being surrounded by him made her feel loved. Looking down, she couldn't take her eyes off their hands. His fingers were intertwined with hers, and the light against dark made her smile.

At first glance, they didn't seem to have anything in common. Hell, she'd been convinced of that herself. But now, she couldn't imagine being with anyone else. Ever.

"Craig?" she whispered.

"Yeah, love?"

Ember shivered at hearing the term of endearment. "I'm so happy."

He kissed the back of her neck before saying, "Me too."

"I'm also scared," she added.

"Of what?"

"That this won't last. That you'll get shit for being with me. That when you see how crazy my life can get when people recognize me, you'll bail. That my gym will fail. That I'll let people down. That—"

"*Shhhh*," Craig interrupted, tightening his hold around her. "This is gonna last. If anything, you'll be the one getting shit for being with a white guy like me. I'm not gonna bail, no matter what. Your gym is gonna be *the* gym people want their kids to go to, rich, poor, white, Black, purple, or green. You aren't going to let anyone down. You're going to make a difference in this world, and I'm thrilled to stand by your side and watch it happen."

"How do you always know the right thing to say?" Ember asked quietly.

"I don't. I'll fuck up in the future. Say the wrong thing. Piss you off. Piss others off. You'll want to kick my ass out and tell me to go to hell. You'll probably throw shit at my head because you're so passionate. But I hope you never forget how much you mean to me. How I'd literally go through hell to keep you safe from anyone who wants to do you harm. Not that you need me as a protector, you're badass all on your own."

"Okay, stop talking."

Craig chuckled from behind her. "Right, see? I'm already pissing you off."

"You aren't," she insisted. "But I can only take so much sweet at one time. And you've reached your quota."

"Okay, baby. I'll shut up. After I say one more thing."

It was a good thing Ember braced, because his next words tilted her world on its axis.

"I love you. I know it's early and people would say it's lust, not love. But they're wrong. I see *you*, Em. The woman you keep wrapped up and locked away from the world to protect yourself. But you don't have to keep her from me, because I see her. Being with me won't be easy. I'll be honest with you, my job is tough. It tends to chew relationships up and spit them out. But I've seen it work with other special forces teams and with my own friends. I want this. I want *you*, Em. And I'll do everything in my power to make you love me back."

Ember swallowed hard. She turned in Craig's arms, staring at the hickey she'd given him earlier. He'd returned the favor, but on her inner thigh so no one would see it and she wouldn't be embarrassed. Everything he'd done since she'd met him had been with her well-being in mind. She felt...treasured by him. "I can handle you *and* your job," she told him quietly. "I can handle all of it. Because I love you too."

Craig tightened his arms around her for a moment, and she felt him kiss the top of her head.

"This is gonna work," he said quietly.

Ember sighed in contentment. Yeah, this was gonna work. She'd do whatever it took to make sure of it.

CHAPTER FOURTEEN

The following day was as busy as any Ember had ever had back in California while training for the Olympics. Monday morning, she'd gone running with Craig and his team and enjoyed it so much, she'd made plans to go to PT with him on Tuesday and Wednesday as well. She shouldn't have been surprised at how hard the Deltas worked out, but she still was. Their workout kicked her butt, but she felt energized afterward, and working out for fun instead of because it was expected or required was exhilarating.

Monday night, after Ember's busy day of appointments, Craig had come over to her apartment and taught her how to make chicken parmigiana. They'd laughed and talked about their days. Ember had set up a meeting with the woman who owned the land she was eyeing for running and shooting training. They'd agreed to meet on Thursday afternoon, after Julio and Marie moved into their new apartments. They weren't supposed to be able to get in until Friday, but the apartments would be ready a day early. She wanted her colleagues' opinions on the land, so they'd go with her to the meeting after getting their apartment keys.

She'd also met with the Boys and Girls Club director and had arranged for her first class to meet on Wednesday. She was both excited and nervous as hell, but definitely ready to get things up and running. There were only four boys and two girls coming on Wednesday, but that was fine. It was a start. And if those kids had fun, Ember hoped it would get the ball rolling and word would get out about how awesome The Modern Kid was.

Craig stayed over at her apartment on Monday night. They'd made slow and sweet love, which had been as different from their first time as night and day. Ember couldn't decide which she liked better. Both were equally delicious.

Tuesday morning, she got up early and once again went with Craig to PT. They started with lifting weights, then did short sprints until Ember thought her heart was going to beat out of her chest. She attempted to do a sprint with one of their packs on her back and quickly realized it was too much. Her respect rose for the men even more. She was proud to know them.

After the workout, while they were sitting around talking about nothing in particular, Trigger brought up the topic of the threatening messages she'd received on her social media posts.

"I talked to your parents yesterday," Trigger said.

Ember's eyes widened, and she knew she probably looked like one of those cartoon characters whose eyes bugged out comically. "What?"

"I talked to your parents yesterday," he repeated calmly.

"Wow. Okay. How did that go?"

"They were leery at first. Your mom sounded kind of bitter. But when I explained that we were investigating some pretty serious threats made toward you on social media, she calmed down and said she'd do whatever she could to help. They love you, Ember. I know things have been tense between you guys, but the second they heard you might be in danger, they bent over backward trying to get us the information we wanted."

"I know. I love them too. I think things will get better in time. They need to come to terms with the fact that the pentathlon isn't my dream anymore. Did you find anything out?" she asked.

"I found out I never want to be fucking famous," Trigger muttered in disgust. Then went on, "I asked them if there had ever been a pattern of you receiving gifts or threats from the same person. Neither knew off the tops of their heads, because they'd hired someone to deal with your mail."

"I sometimes sifted through it," Ember told him.

"That's what your mom said. Did anything ever stick out?" Trigger asked.

Ember felt Craig shift a little closer. His thigh touched hers as they sat on the weight-lifting bench. She liked having his support. Liked that he didn't butt in and try to take over the conversation.

"Well, I got letters all the time from one person in particular. I think the guy's name is Pat, and he was always sending me nice stuff. I mean, I think it was a guy. I suppose Pat could be short for Patricia...but anyway, he or she was always writing and being supportive."

"Anyone else?" Brain asked.

Ember closed her eyes and tried to think back to the last few months. "I got a few gifts just before the Olympics. Some person sent homemade cards, an embroidered blanket, and a US Flag cross-stitched with my name under it. It was all very sweet stuff. I get those kinds of things fairly often."

"Do you write your fans back?" Oz asked.

Ember shook her head. "No. They get pre-signed pictures and things, but they're never personalized."

"That might've angered a fan. If they were seeking some

sort of recognition for their gifts and didn't get it," Lucky said.

"What about the nasty letters?" Grover asked. "I'm assuming you get those too."

"Yeah," Ember agreed. "But I didn't pay much attention to those. When I start reading and realize they're mean, I stop and put them aside."

"Her mom said they had stacks of mail that were piling up from after the Olympics. Said she'd go through them and see if there were a lot from the same person, or any that stuck out as being particularly threatening," Trigger said.

"Should we see if we can get one of the California SEAL teams to look into it?" Craig asked. "We all know Rocco and his crew—or Wolf and his—would be glad to drive up to Beverly Hills and take a day to look through the mail."

Ember glanced at Craig. She didn't know the people he was talking about, but she had no doubt if he trusted them, then they'd be able to ferret out anyone who was a real threat.

"I think we should wait for Ember's mom to see what she can come up with. She knows this is serious, especially after she looked at some of the comments on social media herself," Trigger said.

"Ember, do you remember the name of the person who sent those most recent gifts?" Brain asked.

"Um...now that you mention...I think his name was Alex," Ember said softly.

"The same name as the person leaving the threatening comments on your Insta," Brain said as he looked down at his phone.

"Alex is a common name," Oz noted. "Might not be the same person."

"Or maybe it is, and he's pissed that Ember didn't acknowledge his gifts," Brain countered.

"We need to find out the postmark, and if there was a

return address or last name associated with the gifts," Lucky said.

"I'm on it," Trigger said. "I'm supposed to talk to Deborah this afternoon."

"You're on a first-name basis with my mom?" Ember asked, honestly shocked. She usually preferred to be called Mrs. Maxwell by people she didn't know.

Trigger grinned. "Yup. And with Cedric too."

"Holy shit. Dad let you call him by *his* first name as well? I'm living in a parallel universe," Ember said with a shake of her head.

"I have to admit, I wasn't very impressed with them after the Olympics," Trigger said. "But now that they understand we have your best interests and safety at heart, they've changed their tune."

Ember looked around the room at the men surrounding her. "Why *are* you guys taking this to heart as much as you are? I've always had people who hate me, and always will. It kind of comes with the territory of being a social media influencer. I'm not saying I like it, but I take it with a grain of salt. Why are you so worked up over a few comments? Especially when the number of people named Alex in this world has to be astronomical."

"Calling you offensive names and saying they wished you were dead isn't normal. It's fucking crazy," Lucky said.

"And that guy saying he hoped someone kidnapped and tortured you? That's a direct threat," Brain agreed.

Lefty leaned forward. "No one threatens someone we love. *No one.* We know firsthand how shitty life can be and if we can keep that from touching those around us, we will."

Ember swallowed hard as emotion threatened to overwhelm her. She knew what Lefty's wife, Kinley, had been through. She nodded.

"After all that's happened to our loved ones, we aren't

going to let this spiral out of control. If we can nip it in the bud now, that's what we're gonna do," Craig said.

"Well, I appreciate it. But I can't live my life always looking over my shoulder. It would make me paranoid, and I'd probably hole up in my apartment and never come out," she told them honestly.

"That's what we're for," Grover reassured her. "To have your back, so you don't *have* to constantly look over your shoulder."

"Thank you. Seriously. I mean that," Ember told them.

"You're welcome. In the meantime, be smart," Brain told her. "Tell Doc where you're going and when you think you'll be done. If you go anywhere by yourself, it's probably best to wear a hat and try to be as inconspicuous as possible. I'm not saying someone won't recognize you, but there's no sense in flaunting the fact that Ember Maxwell's in the house...if you know what I mean."

Ember nodded. "I do. And I'd already decided not to post any more selfies of me on my IG. There's no need. It's narcissistic anyway. I'd much rather be artsy, or share pictures of others than myself."

The men all nodded. "Good. And you hired security for the gym?" Oz asked.

"Yes. They're starting tomorrow. I want to make sure it's a safe space for the kids."

"And for you," Craig added.

Ember shrugged. "Yeah. That too."

"The security guys you hired know who you are?" Lefty asked.

"Yeah, they do."

"Good. Maybe I'll stop over tomorrow and have a chat with whoever's working," Craig said.

Ember wanted to roll her eyes at his overprotectiveness, but secretly she kind of liked it.

"What are your plans for today?" Brain asked.

Craig groaned, and Ember chuckled.

"She's gonna be busy from the second she gets back to her place until I force her to sit and take a breath later tonight," Craig told his friends.

"Not one to sit still, huh?" Trigger asked.

"Not at all," Craig answered for her.

"Any chance you can find time to stop over and see Riley?" Oz asked.

"Why, is she okay?" Ember asked in concern. She'd just met the other woman, but she liked her immensely.

"Yeah, but I think she's overwhelmed with being a new mom, and with Logan and Bria being home for the summer," Oz said. "We've got meetings all day, so I'm not going to be able to get home to give her a break today."

"Of course," Ember said immediately. She would move some of her meetings around so she could visit Riley.

"Why didn't you say something earlier?" Brain asked. "I can have Aspen go over with Chance too."

"Gillian's got a big meeting with a potential new client today, but I'm sure she could stop by later."

"I appreciate it, guys," Oz said. "And I know the other women would drop everything and go over there, but Riley doesn't like to impose."

"It's not an imposition," Lefty said with a shake of his head. "Those women are closer than ever. I'll talk to Kinley. I'm sure she'd be happy to figure out a rotating schedule for them to visit and help out...and they'll make it seem spontaneous, just in case Riley gets it in her head to be stubborn about it."

Ember was so thankful she'd somehow fallen into this group of friends, she couldn't even describe how good it made her feel. "I'll swing by after the fencing épées and outfits arrive. The guy I bought them from was nice enough to offer to drop them off. I can have Julio oversee the contractor who's visiting today, to start work on the locker rooms I want her to remodel, and Marie can meet with the landscaper. That'll give me an hour and a half to visit with Riley. Is that okay?"

"It's awesome, thank you," Oz said, the relief easy to hear in his voice.

Craig leaned over and kissed her temple before standing. "As fun as this all is, Ember's got a meeting in an hour and she needs to get home and shower before heading over to The Modern Kid to get to work."

Everyone stood and headed out of the weight room. Ember made sure to thank each of them on their way out, then she and Craig made their way to his Durango. He held the door open for her and closed it once she was settled. He drove her back to her apartment and walked her to her door.

"Are you coming in?" she asked.

"I want to," he admitted softly. "I want to lick your pussy until you come on my tongue, then fuck you hard and fast."

Ember felt herself get wet immediately at his words.

"But you have less than an hour to get to work, and I know if I come in we'll *both* be late."

It sucked, but he was right.

Craig slowly brought a hand to her nape and pulled her toward him. Ember went eagerly. He kissed her long and slow, until she thought she was going to combust.

He finally pulled back, keeping her close. "I don't know if anything will come out of our looking into those creeps commenting on your posts, but be extra vigilant, okay?"

"I will."

"Because we don't know who these assholes are, or even *where* they are, I'd appreciate it if you can avoid going anywhere by yourself for a while."

"I'll do my best."

"I'm not trying to be a controlling asshole boyfriend here," he told her. "I love you and can't stand the thought of anyone threatening you. And make no mistake, those comments on your posts are threats."

"I know. I hate thinking about someone out there wanting to seriously hurt me. But if it continues or gets worse, I'm not opposed to deleting my accounts altogether. Yes, I want to do good things for the world and share things like Sierra's picture to try to help, but if people hate me so much that they literally want to see me dead...it's not worth it."

Craig took a deep breath and closed his eyes for a moment, as if her words had touched him in some way.

"Craig?"

"That makes me feel better," he told her. "But I don't think we need to go to that extreme yet. Let your mom look through the mail you've received on her end, and Trigger will continue looking into the comments on this end. Beth, a woman Brain contacted, will get back with him about IP addresses and locations, and we'll see if we have anything to worry about. If we do, we'll deal with it. Go to the cops and maybe the FBI, since they're threats on the internet. If it turns out to be a bunch of prepubescent boys thinking they're the shit, or jealous women, we'll figure out how to deal with that too."

"Thank you."

"No need to thank me. Just stay aware."

"I will."

"Okay, I'm really leaving now. If I don't, I won't be able to."

"Love you," Ember said shyly. The words felt right, but still a little weird so early in their relationship.

"I love you too. I'll see you tonight when you get home. You coming to my place or am I coming here?"

Ember loved that it wasn't even a question of whether

they'd see each other, only which home they'd be at. "I'll come to you."

"Sounds good. Later."

"Later."

Ember watched until Craig was out of sight, then closed her door with a sigh. Craig had helped her put on a deadbolt, and after she'd locked herself in safely, she headed to the shower. It was going to be another long day, but she was excited to get started. The minor gym renovations would continue, she'd discuss with Julio and Marie what they wanted to do with the first group of kids tomorrow, and she'd get to see Riley. Making time for both friends and hard work...it seemed like such a little thing, but Ember was happier than she'd ever been in her life.

* * *

Alex glowered, watching Ember Maxwell as she flitted around the gym. It was infuriating, seeing her so carefree and happy. How could she even show her face in public after failing so spectacularly at the Olympics? She was a disgrace! And thinking she should start a gym to train kids in the pentathlon? What a joke!

Ember was the *last* person who should be coaching others. She'd had her chance, and she'd blown it. This fucking farce couldn't continue.

It was up to Alex to end it once and for all.

To wipe that simpering smile off Ember's smug face.

She should've paid more attention. Should've acknowledged all those gifts she'd received. Should've thanked those around her who'd gotten her to the top. Instead, she'd used her looks and her money and had taken advantage of everyone. And for what? To be a big fat *loser*.

It was time. Time to stop her from conning people into

thinking she was something special. And Alex knew just how to do it. Ending Ember couldn't happen today—but it *would* happen. She'd learn how it felt to be helpless. To be discarded as if she meant nothing. To be at someone else's mercy.

Then, and only then, would Alex feel vindicated.

Alex had been careful not to leave clues or give Ember any warning of what was coming. Doing so would be colossally stupid. It would make Ember's new boyfriend even more watchful...

That was another thing that pissed off Alex; it wasn't fair that Ember was so damn content. She should be worried about this ridiculous business venture, but instead here she was, smiling and looking happier than ever, with some asshole treating her like a frickin' princess! The last thing Alex needed was more eyes looking after the precious Ember Maxwell. Her boyfriend could ruin *everything*.

No—the plan would work. Alex just needed to be patient. A couple more days and Ember would be no more.

A genuine smile blossomed across Alex's face. Ember's fate was sealed. Soon she'd be dead, no longer able to take advantage of others. Alex couldn't wait.

CHAPTER FIFTEEN

Doc ran a hand through his hair in frustration. As great as things were going with Ember, things at work weren't nearly as good. The SEAL team who'd been checking out the caves near the base in Afghanistan hadn't found anything, so they'd been sent to another locale on a different mission. And getting information from the base general was like pulling teeth. Trigger and the team didn't know if he was afraid of getting in trouble if he shared too much information about the contractors who'd gone missing, or if he actually didn't care since they weren't soldiers.

Grover wasn't happy. Trigger wasn't happy. Commander Robinson wasn't happy. The situation was impossible, and without good intel, their hands were tied. They couldn't exactly go over to Afghanistan if no one admitted there was an issue. But ever since Grover had received that letter from Sierra, he was more convinced than ever she'd been taken captive.

Doc couldn't disagree. Neither could the rest of the team. But they still had to sit tight until they had more concrete evidence that Shahzada was behind the disappearances.

Things with Ember, however, were going amazingly well. Being with her felt right. Natural. Making love had never been as satisfying as it was with her, and he literally craved the woman. Doc knew it would suck sleeping away from her and was somewhat dreading being deployed for that reason alone. He'd gotten used to having her in his arms, and he couldn't deny feeling a huge satisfaction every time she marked him. The guys gave him shit when he'd taken his shirt off that morning and they'd seen the hickeys she'd given him, but he didn't care. She'd been right when she'd said he'd think about how he'd gotten them every time he caught a glimpse.

He was planning a special night for her later. He'd bought cupcakes that spelled out "Congratulations" and had arranged to get dinner catered in. This was opening day for The Modern Kid, and he was excited to celebrate it with her tonight. He hated that he couldn't be there, but she'd reassured him it was fine. After all the renovations were done, and she had a bigger clientele, she'd throw a huge open house party to officially kick off the opening of the gym. For now, she was happy to have her first day be low-key with the small number of kids she'd signed up.

It was three o'clock and the team had been over the latest information from overseas four times, looking for anything that would give them the opening they needed to be sent over to hunt Shahzada. They were tired and grumpy, and worried about every single one of the contractors who were over there serving their country in their own way.

Doc was more than ready to change the subject. "Did you have a chance to talk to Ember's parents today?" he asked Trigger.

"I did. And I don't like what I heard."

Doc tensed. "What?"

"Her mom told me there had been several bags of mail that hadn't been looked through because of the Olympics, and everything that happened with Ember leaving when she got back," Trigger said. "She said nothing seemed odd at first. There were a lot of congratulatory letters and gifts from fans, as well as the usual negative letters. But when she and Cedric organized them, they realized there were several letters from the same person. Someone named Alex. The postmark was Los Angeles."

"Shit. Alex again. What'd they say?" Brain asked.

"The first one, mailed before the Olympics, was overly enthusiastic. Gushing about how amazing Ember was and how proud he was of her. Afterward, the tone changed. They were more critical. Angry. The last one Alex sent was five pages long and full of rambling, accusatory shit about how she hadn't tried hard enough. How she'd let down all her fans and..." Trigger's voice trailed off.

"And what?" Doc asked.

"He threatened her. Said he knew she'd left LA and there was nowhere she could hide. That karma would catch up to her."

"Why does this guy even care? Did Ember's mom mention if she'd had a bad breakup with anyone? Maybe Alex is an ex-boyfriend?" Lucky asked.

Trigger shook his head. "No. She hasn't had a boyfriend in a couple years."

"So all this hate is because someone decided they know her from her social media posts and they have a connection?" Brain asked.

"You forget that this guy's been sending her gifts for months. So if he thought they had a connection, Ember not doing as well as he'd hoped in the Olympics, then moving and changing the entire direction of her social media, could've pushed him over the edge."

"But it sounds as if the trigger was her performance in South Korea," Doc said.

"What did Beth have to say about the background checks or the searches on the assholes who left nasty comments on her recent posts?" Lefty asked Brain.

"I talked to her last night, and again on our last break, and was going to tell you about everything we discussed when we had a second," Brain said. "She hasn't done the background checks on Julio or Marie yet. Since we prioritized tracking down the IP addresses, she spent the last couple days doing that. And after Ember posted about opening her gym, she had a new slew of hateful comments, which increased Beth's workload. She's looked at the most hateful of the messages and done her best to track the addresses, especially that Alex character." Brain shook his head. "I'll never understand why some people have to be so horrible. Why can't they let others be happy? Anyway, Beth said last night that the IP addresses came back to cities all over the country. Seattle, New York, Birmingham, Dallas...but also a few here in Killeen."

Doc sat up straighter. "Should we be concerned about those?"

"Absolutely," Brain said. "I'd asked Beth to further narrow down the Killeen threats. Find actual locations and real names, if possible, so those people can be investigated. But that doesn't mitigate the threats that came from outside Texas. We all know if someone is seriously pissed off, they can find their way here and hurt Ember, no matter where they live."

Doc sighed. He understood what his friend was saying. The fact that there were people right here in Killeen who felt the need to take out their anger through their keyboard wasn't surprising. But the target of the nastiness wasn't just anyone. It was Ember. The woman he loved. "Do we have any addresses of the people in town who said any nasty shit?" he asked.

"A couple, yes. She has a few more to go. Names are

harder though, since it could literally be anyone in the house leaving the comments, and not necessarily the person renting the internet service."

"Any of them named Alex?" Oz asked.

"No. That was the first thing she checked," Brain said.

"What about any Alexes from LA?" Doc asked.

"Beth hasn't gotten there yet. She said just getting what she has so far took most of the night. She did say that was next on her list of things to do...along with the background checks of not only Julio and Marie, and her former social media managers—especially this Alexis guy—but the other people who worked for the Maxwells back in California, as well."

Doc pressed his lips together. He knew Ember wouldn't like hearing that. He'd wait until he found out what Beth came up with before breaking the news to her. Hopefully he'd be able to tell her everyone was in the clear.

"Do you want my opinion?" Lefty asked.

Doc immediately nodded. "Of course."

"Keep in mind this is coming from someone whose woman was taken and almost killed...I would hire extra security for Ember. She lived in Beverly Hills behind the walls of her parents' mansion, so I think she's still somewhat naïve. I know she wants her independence, but I don't think she fully understands what to look for in regard to someone who might want to do her harm."

Doc nodded. "She's not going to like it."

Lefty shrugged and kept his intense gaze on Doc's. "Maybe not, but trust me, the alternative isn't acceptable."

"I'll talk to her. Today was opening day, and while she didn't have that many kids there, I know she was both excited and nervous. I've gotten a few texts from her, and she said it's going well."

"No problems?" Grover asked.

Doc was glad to see his friend participating in the conversation. He'd been quiet most of the day, except when it came to expressing his frustration with what was happening in Afghanistan.

"I guess Julio was in a piss-poor mood this morning. Ember had to reprimand him and tell him to get his head out of his ass."

"How'd he react to that?" Lucky asked.

"He wasn't happy."

"I'll make sure Beth gets that background check done this evening," Trigger said.

"'Preciate it," Doc said. "But I got a text from her during the last break, and she said he was better, that working with the kids seemed to make whatever he'd been upset about fade." Doc looked at his watch. "She's got another hour before the kids should be picked up by their parents. She wanted to talk with Julio and Marie to get their thoughts on how things went, then she'll be heading home."

"The security she hired will stay until she's gone, right?" Lucky asked.

"Yes. I also know putting in a security system is on her agenda too. She had it scheduled, but they had to postpone the installation for some reason."

"Security is especially tricky because most of the sports, other than the fencing, will have to be done off-site, right?" Brain asked.

"Yeah. She'll have fencing and strength-training equipment in the gym. She's trying to work with the city and YMCA to get pool time. She does want to eventually buy horses the kids can train with, and of course they can run anywhere, but she's heading out with Julio and Marie tomorrow to look at some land where they want to make a cross-country course and laser-shooting stations."

"It's good that she's not going alone," Lefty observed.

"I asked that she not go anywhere by herself until we had a handle on the online threats," Doc told his friends.

"If you need help with anything, all you have to do is let us know," Trigger said.

"I know, and I appreciate it."

"And I'm sure Ghost and his team would help as well."

Doc nodded. "I'm planning on talking to him soon."

"No offense, but is having a girlfriend who's so damn famous worth it?" Grover asked.

Doc didn't even have to think about his answer. "Definitely. I admit, at first I couldn't imagine how in the world it would work. She's instantly recognized, and I'm in a profession where we do our best to fly under the radar at all times. But honestly, when we're out in public, no one even looks twice at me. And Ember isn't hung up about her fame in the least, or her looks. I've barely seen her wear makeup since she's been here. She's been one hundred percent focused on opening her gym."

"For what it's worth...she's the coolest famous person I know," Brain said with a grin.

"You don't know any other famous people," Oz told him with an eye roll.

"Right, so that still makes her the coolest famous person I know," Brain insisted.

"She gonna continue to work out with us?" Lucky asked.

"I hope so," Doc said. "She said she enjoys it. That it's nice to work out and know she doesn't have to impress a coach or worry about a fellow athlete looking for weaknesses to exploit."

"That's true," Lefty said with a nod.

"Will you thank her for me for going to visit Riley yesterday?" Oz asked.

"Of course. But I think it was good for Ember too," Doc told his friend. "She told me that they had a great time visiting and chatting about nothing in particular. They've already made a date to get together again in a few days."

"Bria told me last night that she wants to learn how to be a pentathlete," Oz said with a grin. "Logan's too busy and infatuated with baseball, but I think Ember has already converted Bria."

"Good," Doc said with a smile.

Trigger looked at his watch. "I don't know about you guys, but I'm beat. I'm ready to call it done and go see what my wife's been up to today."

Everyone agreed, though Grover stopped Doc before he left the room. After saying goodbye to the others, he turned to his friend. "What's up?"

"I just wanted you to know that if you need help watching over Ember, all you have to do is ask. I need to stay busy right now, and since the others are all occupied with their wives and families, I'm happy to volunteer."

Doc put a hand on his friend's shoulder. "Thanks, Grover, that means the world to me."

"I just don't want her to disappear like Sierra. I know it's weird that I'm as concerned about this woman as I am, but I can't help it. There was something between us when we met, and the not knowing is torture."

"You don't have to convince me you have a connection," Doc said honestly. "I'm the last person to judge you for being attracted to someone you only saw a few times. Outside our circle, people probably wouldn't understand how I can go from being single to wanting to spend every free moment with Ember in a span of days. They'd probably think I'm using her for some asinine reason. But that's not it at all. She's different from anyone I've ever met, and I can't imagine her disappearing without a trace."

Grover nodded. "I know I've been moody lately, but for the record, I like Ember. She's good for you."

"I hope I'm good for her too," Doc said with a chuckle.

"You are."

"Thanks. And I'll definitely take you up on your offer if I need to."

"Good."

"Grover?"

"Yeah?"

Doc paused, thinking hard about what he wanted to ask his friend...and ultimately felt he needed to. "Do you really think she's still alive?"

"Yes. And I know that's crazy, because she's been missing for so long, but something deep down inside tells me she's out there. Waiting for someone to find her. And that's what hurts the most. Here," Grover said, putting his hand over his heart. "I can't stop thinking about what she may have endured over the last year. It literally makes me sick."

"We're going to do everything we can to find her," Doc told his friend. "And you're right, most people probably think she's dead and buried in a cave somewhere in the mountains of Afghanistan, but we've all seen some pretty miraculous things in our time. If you think she's out there, then she's out there. I'll support you however I can, and I'll talk to Trigger and see if he can't pressure the commander a bit to let us do more than we're already doing...which is a lot of sitting around and waiting for information to trickle down from over there."

"I want to go to Afghanistan and look into things myself," Grover admitted quietly.

Doc didn't let his surprise show on his face. "I thought that's what Trigger was pushing for."

"He's trying to get the commander to agree to send all of us. I want to go by myself," Grover clarified.

"I'm not sure that's the best idea," Doc said quietly. "We work as a team."

"I know, but the seven of us don't exactly go unnoticed when we head into a situation. Once we're on the hunt, we can fade into the background, but when we first arrive? Everyone has a pretty good idea who we are and why we're there. If I go over alone, I can talk to the soldiers on the base and get their impressions of what's going on. I'd be able to talk to the contractors—those who are still there—and get their take on things. See what info I can get on Shahzada and if he's even involved, like we think he is. I might even be able to talk one-on-one with the base general, see if I can read him better in person than we can from those damn reports and emails. I *need* to do this, Doc."

"How long are you thinking?"

"Maybe a week. Not forever. I'll see what intel I can find out, and if I think it's worth having more boots on the ground to shake Shahzada out of whatever tree's he's hiding in, you guys could join me."

Doc had to agree that Grover's plan had merit. "Have you talked to Trigger?"

"I'm going to, but I was hoping maybe you could have some words with him too...let him know you support the idea."

"I can do that," Doc told him.

"I'd appreciate it. And, Doc? I'm truly happy for you and Ember."

"Thanks."

Grover gave him a chin lift in return and the two of them headed out of the conference room and down the hall. Doc pulled out his phone and shot off a quick text to Ember, checking on how things were going. He needed to stop and pick up their dinner, then hopefully he'd have time to get everything set up at his house before she arrived.

. . .

Ember: Today was amazing! There's one more parent we're waiting on, then I should be on my way home. Are you done for the day?

Doc: I'm about to head out now.

Ember: Great. Need me to stop and pick up anything?

Doc: Nope. Shoot me a text when you leave, and make sure security walks you to your car.

Ember: You find out something that I should be concerned about today?

Doc: Not specifically. We'll talk later.

Ember: Okay.

Doc: Be safe. Love you.

Ember: I will. Love you too. Later.

Doc: Later.

Doc put his phone in his pocket and tried to ignore the way the back of his neck itched. He sometimes got the same feeling when they were on a mission and something didn't seem right. It usually happened right before the shit hit the fan.

But Ember was fine. He was good. As far as he knew, everyone on his team was okay as well. He was probably just overly sensitive right now because of the threats on Ember's posts. The words he'd seen directed at her were hateful, poisonous, and hard to get out of his head. He'd just found Ember; he couldn't lose her.

Shaking off his uneasiness, Doc did his best to concentrate on the mini-celebration he'd planned for tonight. He was proud of how much she'd accomplished in such a short period of time. She'd worked her ass off, and he had no doubt her gym was not only going to be successful, but it would be a positive change for their community as well. Giving kids who'd never otherwise have a chance to ride a horse, learn to swim, fence, or even shoot was ambitious and generous, particularly when she was footing most of the bill for the participants. Doc hadn't sat down and discussed money with Ember, but he knew she had more than enough to cover any business expenses that might pop up for a long time to come.

Feeling lighter as he climbed into his vehicle, Doc knew it was because he would see Ember soon. He loved his job and the men he worked with, but there was something incredibly soothing about having a partner, someone you could talk to and share your hopes and fears with and not be judged for them. Not that his team judged him, not even close, but he knew Ember would always support him without reservation. Just as he'd do for her.

* * *

Ember couldn't stop smiling. Not only had opening day gone well, but Craig had surprised her with an amazing dinner—and cake too! Okay, cupcakes, but they were really just pieces of cake portioned in bite-sized pieces.

Now she was sitting on his couch, wrapped in his arms, and she'd just finished telling him about the amazing girls and boys who had been at her gym today, and how everything had gone.

"You know you're going to have a hard time leaving the teaching to your employees, don't you?" Craig teased.

Ember laughed. "I know. Julio and Marie were great today, but I couldn't help joining in."

"What do you think Julio's issue was today?"

Ember sighed. "Honestly? I think he's a little homesick."

Craig snorted. "Homesick?"

"Yeah. This is his first time out of California, and you have to admit Texas is very different from anywhere else in this country. Everyone saying 'howdy' and 'y'all.' All the friendliness is a little weird for those of us raised in California, where most people are assholes."

She felt Craig's chuckle reverberate through her body. His arms were wrapped around her chest and she was using him as a backrest. They hadn't bothered turning on the TV as she was too excited to tell him about every second of her day.

"Texans are pretty friendly for the most part," Craig agreed. "Do you think Julio has any resentment at all?"

Ember turned and looked up at Craig. "What are you really asking?"

She saw him sigh before he said, "The woman who was looking into the IP addresses of some of the nasty comments said a few came from Killeen. Julio hasn't been here long, but there were several threats posted on that last picture you put up, and he was here when that happened."

"You think *Julio* might be behind some of the nasty letters and stuff I've received?"

Craig met her gaze, which Ember appreciated. "I don't know who might be behind them. It's easy to make a fake account on social media and make up a fake name. Which in turn makes it easier to be threatening. It makes people feel as if they'll never be found out."

"It's not Julio," Ember said firmly. "We've trained together for quite a while now, and I think I'd have sensed some sort of resentment in him if he had it out for me."

"And full disclosure and all that...Beth is also going to be doing background checks on the people you hired to provide security around the gym, as well as Alexis, Samer, and others your parents hired."

Ember sat back against Craig, appreciating his transparency. "Do you really think it's all necessary?" she asked.

"Yes."

Ember had a feeling that was what he'd say.

"I know you want to live a normal life, but you *aren't*

normal. You're Ember Maxwell. The fact that you've been able to do as much as you have around here without the press descending is a minor miracle. I love that you want to do some good in the world, but it's naïve to think that no one will be hoping you fail. That there aren't people who resent you because you're pretty and rich."

"And Black," Ember added.

"Yeah. That too. Being with me probably isn't helping you any."

She turned in Craig's arms again. "What are you saying?"

"Just that we both know there are those who don't believe in interracial relationships. They think white people should stick with white people, Black with Black, Asian with Asian. It's fucked up, but some can't get their heads around the fact that we're all still human. It's all about what's on the outside rather than the inside for those types."

"Well, those people can fuck right off," Ember said with a huff as she settled against him again. She hugged his arms around her tighter. "I know I was raised in a privileged household, in the white-washed world of Beverly Hills, but I'm well aware of racism. And discrimination. I've experienced it first-hand. But that doesn't mean I can't see the goodness in people as well. I can. I think there are more people who are good and kind and truly believe the phrase 'love is love,' than those who refuse to believe people different from them have just as much value.

"Do I think there are problems in our society? Yes. But I also believe there are more good cops than bad. That there are more people who embrace their gay, lesbian, and trans-gendered children than those who shun them. That there are more people willing to stand up to injustice than those who are willing to turn their heads and pretend it doesn't exist. I know there are people who want me to fall on my face. Who loved that I didn't medal in the Olympics. Who are saying it's because I'm Black, and that I got what I deserved and I shouldn't even have tried to compete in a 'white sport.' But screw them!"

Aware she was ranting, but not able to stop, Ember shifted so she was straddling Craig's lap. "And if they want to come after me because of who I love, let them. I'll stand on the top of the White House steps and scream to the world that I love you before I'll let someone tell me it's unnatural. Or that I'm spitting in the face of my heritage. I love being Black. I'm proud of it. I wouldn't want to be white."

She took Craig's head in her hands and leaned in close. "I know you don't think I'm taking the comments and threats seriously, but honestly, it's not because I'm not concerned; I've just become somewhat numb to them. There will always be people who hate me for one reason or another. I can't let their issues take over my life. I have to live and act in a way that makes me able to sleep at night with a clear conscience. And helping disadvantaged kids is what's driving me. Okay. I'm done," she said as she blew out a breath.

Craig smiled and took each of her hands in his and kissed the palms.

Then she said, "No, actually I'm not done. One more thing. If you want to look into the backgrounds of everyone I hire, I'm okay with that. Not because I think they're secretly trying to sabotage me, but because I'd be stupid to completely dismiss that possibility. You're right, I *am* Ember Maxwell. I may not have wanted to be a household name or famous, but I am, and I can't change that now. I'm okay with you doing those checks because it means you care about me. Because it means you have my back...and it feels damn good."

"I've definitely got your back," Craig agreed. "But do your best to watch out for yourself at the same time. Pay attention to your surroundings. You're right, there are people out there who would love to see you fail, or who might want to become famous in their own right...by killing *the* Ember Maxwell."

Ember nodded soberly. "I will."

"That's all I can ask."

"Can I see the info this Beth person digs up on my employees?"

"Yes," Craig said without hesitation. "It's not my goal to keep anything from you. I happen to believe that knowledge is power. And if they have nothing to hide, then it'll all be okay."

"Craig?"

"Yeah?"

"Thanks for my mini-celebration."

He grinned. "You're welcome."

"I can't remember the last time someone went out of their way to do what you did for me tonight."

"You can expect a lot more of that kind of thing. I love seeing you lit up and happy."

Ember fingered the top button of the shirt he'd changed into when he'd gotten home from work. She popped it open, and saw him swallow hard in response. Smirking, she leaned forward and licked the hollow in his throat she'd just exposed. "Is my celebration over? Or do you have more surprises in store for me?" she asked coyly.

Without a word, Craig abruptly stood, making Ember cry out in surprise as she tumbled back to the couch. Then she laughed as he hefted her into his arms and started for the stairs.

"Maybe later, like ten years from now, I'll be able to withstand your teasing...but I can't right now," he said.

Ember wrapped her arms around his neck and leaned in, taking his earlobe between her teeth. She knew what that did to him and was hoping she could push him over the edge. She wanted him to take her hard and fast. Then later, maybe she'd get a chance to give him a blow job. He claimed he couldn't handle her mouth on him because he'd blow too soon, but perhaps after he'd had his first orgasm, he'd let her play. It was her celebration, after all.

"Should I be scared to know what you're thinking?" Craig asked as he carried her into his room.

"Oh, no," she said with a grin. "You should be excited."

"Lord help me," Craig said as he lowered her legs so she was standing by the mattress. "Strip, woman."

And she did.

Hours later, as Ember closed her eyes in contentment, she couldn't help but feel bad for all the bigoted people in the world who might have missed out on their perfect match because they couldn't look beyond outward appearances. "Love you," she whispered against Craig's bare chest.

"Love you too. Sleep."

Grinning at his bossiness, but loving him all the more for it because he had her best interests in mind, she did as he ordered. She slept. Deeply and with the knowledge that she was loved.

CHAPTER SIXTEEN

"Hey, you guys! How'd moving into your apartments go?" Ember asked Julio and Marie when they arrived after lunch the next day. They'd both had the morning off to get situated into their new places. Their furniture and belongings weren't supposed to arrive until tomorrow, but this morning was the first official day they could move in.

"Good. I went to the store bright and early and got a lot of little stuff I know I'll need. Like cleaning supplies, toilet paper, paper towels, a shower curtain, things like that," Julio said.

"Awesome. If you need decorating ideas...don't ask me," Ember teased.

"But I thought you were tight with all those kinds of people? Didn't you post some decorator's shit on your IG account?" he asked.

Ember laughed. "First, I didn't post it, my people did. And second, you know as well as I do most of the crap on my IG was basically paid advertising."

Julio shook his head, but the smile stayed on his face. "It

still blows my mind how different you are than what was posted on your social media all these years."

"Yeah. It's all crap. You have to get to know someone personally before you judge them. But anyway, I'm glad things seem all right with your apartment. You staying there tonight or in the hotel?"

"Hotel. I want to enjoy one more morning with breakfast being cooked *for* me before I have to fend for myself."

Ember laughed. She knew Julio wasn't a good cook. Hated it, in fact. She had a feeling a lot of pizza would be in his future. At least until he found a girlfriend. He claimed he wasn't ready to settle down, but he also hadn't made any secret of the fact that he loved the ladies...or that he relied on them to do the cooking.

"What about you, Marie?" Ember asked her other employee.

"I'm great!" she chirped.

Ember blinked in surprise. Not that she was surprised Marie was in such a good mood; it was more that she'd yet to see her so...enthusiastic. "Glad to hear it," Ember said.

"Yup. I woke up in a really good mood this morning for some reason," Marie said with another dazzling smile.

"That's great."

"I have a feeling the rest of the day is gonna be amazing."

"I hope so," Ember said, grinning. Her good mood was contagious, and she was glad she seemed to be happy. "Everything all right with your apartment?"

"Of course. Why wouldn't it be? You vetted them for Julio and me, so we knew they'd be great."

"You gonna stay there tonight?" Ember asked.

"Absolutely. I can't wait to have my own space."

"Do you have something to sleep on?" Ember asked, worried that Marie would be sleeping on the floor.

"Don't worry about me. I'm good."

"Okay, but if you need anything, don't hesitate to let me know."

"Ember Maxwell to the rescue," Marie said with a wide grin.

Ember wasn't sure how to take that, but because her friend seemed to be in such a good mood, she didn't want to question it. "Yup. That's me. All right, here's the plan for today. I've got an appointment in half an hour with the principal of one of the local elementary schools. Then I'll come back here and pick you guys up, and we can go check out that land for the running course. Okay?"

"Sounds good," Julio said. "What do you want us to do here?"

"Do you think you can work on painting?" Ember asked with a wrinkle of her nose. "I know it's not the most exciting thing, but once we get the base coat on that huge wall over there, I can get the artist I hired to come in and paint our logo."

"No problem," Julio said.

"Awesome-sauce," Marie echoed.

"I appreciate it so much. And if you get tired of that, no problem, you can work on testing all the fencing equipment. We need to make sure it all works as it should and that it's safe for the kids."

"Don't worry about us," Marie said with a smile. "We've got things covered here. Go to your meeting and we'll see you soon."

"Thanks. I should be gone about two hours. I'll text if I'm gonna be late."

Julio and Marie nodded then turned to get to work. Ember left the gym, relieved that she had such enthusiastic and happy people at her side. They still had a lot of hard work to do, but it would all pay off in the end. She just knew it.

The meeting with the principal went exceedingly well. The woman was excited about the opportunity for the kids to get involved in some unique sports in the fall. Especially since Ember told her it wouldn't cost anyone a dime. She explained how she planned on partnering with local businesses—putting their names on the equipment and other free publicity in return for their generosity. She'd learned a lot from her parents and from being an influencer. If she could use her name and fame to get people to donate money and other necessities to her gym, all the trouble her parents went through would be worth it.

By the time she went back by the gym to pick up Julio and Marie, it was past three. There would be times in the future that they'd all need to work late, but for now, before they had kids in the gym every day, she wanted to try to send everyone home by five. The land they were going to look at was only ten minutes outside the city limits of Killeen, which was ideal. She didn't want to have to drive a long distance with the kids.

Ember had hopes the land would be perfect for a running course and a shooting station. But more than that, she was thinking about where she'd house horses if she decided not to use a farm that was already established. She'd need room for a barn and a jumping ring. She couldn't wait to see if this plot of land might be appropriate for all of it.

"Hey, Ember, do you mind if I back out today?" Julio asked.

"Why? Is something wrong?"

"No, not at all. I got a call that the truck with my furniture is arriving early. They wanted to know if they can deliver it before five. Since I don't have a ton of stuff, they think they can get it all moved in pretty quickly."

"Oh my gosh, that's great. Of course. Go!"

"Thanks. I'm still staying at the hotel tonight, if that's okay."

"Why wouldn't it be?" Ember asked in confusion.

"Well, you're paying for it, and now that I have my stuff I could technically stay in my apartment," Julio said.

"It's not a problem. It's too late in the day to cancel the room anyway. And I'd hate to have you starve to death without breakfast tomorrow."

He laughed. "I appreciate it."

"What about your stuff?" Ember asked Marie. "Did it come too?"

"Not that I know of," she said with a smile and a shrug. "But it's fine. I'm sure it'll be here tomorrow."

Ember nodded. "Okay, go on, Julio. I'll see you tomorrow. The kids will be back, and we have two new ones joining us."

"Cool," he said. "Can we start the intro to fencing tomorrow?"

Laughing, Ember said, "Sure. I know you've been dying to get those épées in the kids' hands."

"I'm gonna show them a clip from *The Princess Bride* to get them excited, then we'll start with the basics," Julio said enthusiastically. "I'm out of here. See you both tomorrow!"

"Bye!" Marie called as she waved.

Ember walked by Marie's side toward her BMW. She climbed into the car and, after entering the address into her phone, asked, "How'd it go today?"

"Great. We didn't finish the painting because Julio got too excited about fencing," Marie said with a grin.

"Why am I not surprised he wouldn't be able to resist the épées?" she asked with a shake of her head.

Marie laughed almost hysterically at that...and Ember couldn't help but wonder what in the world had gotten into the other woman. She seemed almost hyper for some reason.

But at least she wasn't in a bad mood like Julio had been the day before.

Finding the turn-in to the property they'd be looking at was a bit tricky. It took two U-turns before Ember finally saw the dirt track along the side of the back road they were on. Even though they were only ten minutes from Killeen, it seemed as if they were in the middle of nowhere.

Ember's mind whirled with things that she'd like to do to make this piece of land work. She'd have to widen the entrance, put up some sort of sign, probably some fencing, but as she continued down the dirt track toward the center of the property, she had a feeling it would be perfect.

There were a few rolling hills, but nothing too extreme. Plenty of trees, but not enough that she'd have to chop any down for the cross-country course. She could design it around them. Ember stopped her BMW and cut the engine, climbing out quickly in her excitement to look around.

She could hear birds chirping, and it felt as if she was the only person in the world at that moment. Closing her eyes, Ember let the peace and quiet of the countryside sink into her soul. As someone who'd lived her entire life in a crowded city, having the opportunity to purchase this piece of land seemed almost unbelievable. She opened her eyes and began to walk forward.

"There," she told Marie, who'd finally gotten out of the car. "That's where we can build a small clubhouse kind of thing, where the kids can get out of the sun and wait for their turn to run and shoot." She turned and pointed to the right. "I think we could start the course there. It can go between those two large trees, swing around to the left, through that copse of trees in the distance, then snake back around to here. We can put the shooting range near the clubhouse, so we don't have to haul the targets very far when we set them up. What do you think?"

Ember looked over at her friend—and her brow furrowed in surprise. A second ago, Marie had been happy. Now she looked serious and somber and...almost angry. "What? What's wrong?"

"I'm not sure this is the best place for the shooting area. I think it might work better over there, closer to that hillside. We could use it as the background where we set up the laser targets."

Ember eyed the hill Marie had pointed out. "I don't know," she said diplomatically. "I was thinking that could be where we set up the barn and jumping area for the horses."

"We could try it out," Marie suggested. "You've got some targets in the car, I saw them in the back. Why don't we set them up and give it a try?" Marie asked.

Ember shrugged. "Okay, sure. Why not?" It wasn't a bad idea. Marie followed her back to the car and stood off to the side as Ember gathered two targets. She was a little irritated that Marie just stood and watched, instead of volunteering to help, but shrugged it off.

The other woman did lean in and pick up two of the laser pistols, then they headed toward the area Marie had indicated. Ember walked quickly, jumping over a few scraggly weeds, which she thought might actually be tumbleweeds. She'd never seen any in person; it wasn't as if they were rolling down the streets of Beverly Hills, that was for sure.

Ember was lost in her internal amusement over living somewhere that had genuine tumbleweeds when she realized Marie wasn't walking next to her anymore.

She turned to see where the other woman had gone, and blinked in surprise.

She'd managed to get a ways ahead, and Marie was now standing over ten meters behind her—pointing one of the laser pistols directly at Ember.

"Marie?" Ember asked in confusion. Throughout their

training, coaches had said over and over again that the weapons were never to be pointed at someone. The lasers weren't like bullets, but if someone looked right at the light when the trigger was pulled, it could be blinding. Every coach she'd ever had reiterated gun safety, as if the laser pistols were actual deadly weapons.

And since Marie had gotten the same training the last couple years, Ember was confused as to what in the world she was doing.

The sound of the pistol being fired was loud and obscene in the tranquil countryside.

Pain immediately blossomed in Ember's cheek and she dropped the targets as her body was propelled backward. She landed on her ass on the hard-packed dirt amidst the wild grasses, hitting her head on the ground in the process.

A second shot exploded, just as loud and startling as the first. A puff of dirt kicked up right next to her. Ember's head spun as she tried to figure out what the hell was happening.

Marie hadn't said a word. Had just calmly *shot* her.

As the searing pain in her face registered, Ember realized the gun wasn't one of the laser pistols they used. It was smaller—and obviously held real bullets.

Marie had deliberately tried to kill her. Could *still* kill her. Ember had no idea how many bullets were in the gun, but surely it was more than two.

As footsteps approached, Ember closed her eyes and did her best to slow her breathing. Instinctively she knew if Marie thought she was still alive, she'd shoot again.

Hell, she might do it anyway to make sure she was dead.

She could feel blood running down her face. She desperately tried to keep her body limp and her eyes closed. It went against every instinct she had. Ember wanted to jump up and fight, but Marie had the upper hand.

The footsteps stopped right next to her, and Ember held

her breath, trying not to let her chest move up and down and alert Marie to the fact that she was breathing.

"Bitch!" she heard Marie mutter before she kicked Ember in the side. Hard.

It took everything Ember had not to react. Sharp pain radiated from her side where Marie had kicked her...but her lack of reaction did just what Ember hoped. It convinced the other woman that her bullets had done what she'd intended.

Ember kept her eyes closed and stayed motionless as Marie's footsteps receded. After several tense seconds, she heard her car start up and drive away from the area.

Not only had Marie shot her, but she'd stolen her car and left her for dead.

Ember was in big trouble. She needed to get up. See if she could get some help. But her face hurt. Bad. And her side was throbbing. Not only that—she was having a hard time wrapping her mind around the fact that *Marie* had just tried to kill her.

They'd been worried about a nameless, faceless person on social media, when the danger had been right beside her all along.

Ember struggled to open her eyes, the pain in her cheek nearly unbearable. *I'll lie still for just a moment...gather my strength.*

It was Ember's last thought before losing consciousness.

* * *

Doc and the rest of the team had just finished sitting through a mandatory training session on harassment in the workplace when his phone vibrated with an incoming call. Not recognizing the number, but seeing it was coming from San Antonio, he answered.

"Doc here."

"Doc, this is Beth, Tex's friend."

"Hey," he said.

She didn't bother with any more niceties. "I got the background checks done on those people you wanted me to look into."

Doc didn't like her tone. "And?"

"The security guards she hired are clean. There's nothing concerning in their backgrounds. Samer is good to go as well. I'm still working on finding more information on that Alexis guy you seemed so concerned about, but honestly, he's just looking like a run-of-the-mill jerk to me. Julio McMillian is also fairly clean. He had one incident when he was fifteen, breaking and entering, but it seems that scared him straight and other than a few speeding tickets, he hasn't had any other dealings with the law. He has a few social media accounts, but there's nothing alarming on any of them. I dug into his messages and they all seem normal for someone his age. I also went further and checked his email accounts and hacked into his laptop, and other than some porn sites and some interesting Google searches, I'm satisfied that he's harmless."

Doc blinked. "Holy shit, you did all that since Brain last talked to you?" He felt a little uncomfortable at the depths Beth had gone to while investigating Ember's friend and employee, but he couldn't deny he was relieved to hear the results.

"Yeah," she said, brushing off his incredulity. "But that's not why I'm calling. It's about Marie Riggs."

"What is it? Put it on speaker," Trigger insisted, seeing Doc's sudden distress. The seven men were standing in the hallway outside the room where they'd attended training. Everyone else had left the area and it was just them.

Doc took the phone from his ear and clicked on the speaker button. "We're all listening," he told Beth. "What did you find out about Marie?"

"First of all, did you know her name isn't Marie? Well, not her first name. It's Alexandria Marie Riggs. She was born in Los Angeles and had a hell of a childhood. I won't go into all the details now, as it's not important, but she definitely had a hard start to life. She bounced around between relatives, no one seemed to want her to live with them for more than two or three years."

"Why?" Oz asked.

"According to the notes from various psychologists and doctors, she has a whole host of issues. Dissociative identity disorder—which used to be known as multiple personalities —schizoaffective disorder, and borderline personality disorder, among others."

"Holy shit," Trigger muttered.

"Yeah," Beth agreed. "The bottom line is that she was hard to live with, even at ten years old. So she kept getting shuttled to different family members. They'd welcome her with open arms, then after a few years of dealing with her outbursts, and trying and failing to discipline her, she'd be sent to someone else. By the time she was eighteen, she had nowhere to go and one of her swim coaches took her in. He introduced her to the modern pentathlon and she really took to it. Did you guys know she's thirty-two years old?"

"Seriously? I thought she was in her mid-twenties, like Ember," Doc said.

"She's not. It looks like she had a handle on her mental illnesses for a few years, and actually was doing pretty good. But after a while, her borderline personality disorder got worse. Or maybe she stopped taking her meds. Who knows? Her moods got more and more unstable and she began to act impulsively. She got evicted from her apartment and had to move into a low-end trailer park."

"How did Ember not know any of this?" Doc asked.

"I'm guessing Marie was pretty adept at hiding that side

of herself," Beth said. "But here's the part that's alarming. The zip code you gave me...the one on the presents and letters that Ember received back in California? It's the same as the trailer park where she was living. Now, that doesn't mean she was the sender, but when I checked the IP address of the Alex who was leaving the nasty messages on Ember's posts? It matches the hotel where Marie's staying.

"I didn't look into the hotel earlier because I didn't know where she was staying; you guys never told me and I didn't think to ask. But while checking the Killeen IPs again, I hacked into their database to access the guest registry, and discovered that's where Marie and Julio were staying. That, combined with everything else we know about Marie, makes me nervous."

Doc shook his head. No, Marie couldn't be the one behind all the hateful letters and comments...could she?

"I could give you a whole lot more evidence I uncovered that would make you extremely wary of the woman—but it was the comment she left about an hour and a half ago on one of Ember's posts that made me pick up the phone and call as soon as I saw it."

Doc braced as Beth continued speaking.

"It was kinda buried amongst all the other comments that had been left in the last few days, but she said, and I quote, 'After today, we won't have to read Ember's stupid posts anymore...because I'm gonna kill her.'"

The men were speechless for a second before Doc said, "Send what you found to Trigger. I need to find Ember."

"I will. I'll be praying," Beth said, then disconnected.

Doc immediately clicked on Ember's name on his phone and waited with his heart in his throat for her to answer. The call went straight to voice mail.

"Fuck," he muttered, then turned and stalked down the hall.

His entire team stayed with him.

"Where is she supposed to be right now?" Lucky asked.

"I don't know exactly, but she was going to take Julio and Marie out to that piece of land she was eyeing to turn into a running and shooting facility."

"Call Julio," Grover ordered.

As he walked, Doc did just that. The phone rang twice before Julio answered. Doc didn't waste any time with pleasantries. "Where's Ember?"

"I'm sorry, who is this?" Julio asked.

"Doc. Where is she? Are you guys together?"

"No. The movers arrived early and she let me head out to get moved into my apartment. Why? What's wrong?"

"Is Marie with her?"

"Yeah, they went out to look at that land."

"How long ago?" Doc asked.

"Maybe a little over an hour? Why? What the hell is going on?"

"Have you heard from either of them?" Doc couldn't take the time to explain how Ember could be in danger.

"No."

"Shit. Okay. If you do, will you call me back immediately and let me know?"

"Yes. Are they in trouble? What can I do to help?"

Doc liked Julio. He didn't really know the man, but he appreciated his concern and immediate offer to help. "I'm headed out to the property they were going to be looking at. I'll be in touch."

"Do you want me to go out there too?" Julio asked.

Doc didn't have time to discuss what was going on, but he also didn't want to leave Julio vulnerable, just in case Marie was a threat to him as well. "No, sit tight. And if Marie happens to stop by, do *not* open the door. Call me immediately."

Julio obviously wasn't stupid. Doc's warning was enough for him to figure out that Marie was involved in whatever was going on. "Oh, crap. Okay. If there's anything I can do though, please let me know."

"I will." He clicked off the phone without another word.

"I'm driving," Trigger told Doc.

He didn't complain. It wasn't a good idea for him to get behind the wheel of a car right now anyway. As they walked toward Trigger's car in the parking lot, Doc tried to call Ember again. It went to voice mail once more.

"Fuck," he muttered as he climbed into the passenger seat of Trigger's Blazer. Lefty and Brain got in the back seat and the others all headed for Oz's Expedition. There was no discussion about Doc overreacting or even if they all needed to go. It was just a given that they'd all band together when one of their own was in danger.

Please be all right, Doc thought to himself as Trigger raced toward the vacant property.

* * *

Ember regained consciousness, and the memories of what Marie had done flooded back instantly. She couldn't lie in the dirt, just hoping someone would happen to come by. She also didn't want to risk Marie returning to make sure she'd actually killed her. She was very lucky the woman hadn't shot her point blank as she'd stood over her.

Her side still throbbed, and her face hurt like hell, but Ember forced herself to sit up. The world spun around her as she tried to get her bearings. Using her shoulder, Ember did her best to wipe away the blood that was dripping off her chin. She didn't dare touch her cheek where the bullet struck. She had no idea if the bullet was inside her face or if it had just grazed her. At the moment, that was the least of her worries.

Rolling to her knees in preparation for standing, Ember knew immediately that was a bad idea. She was far too dizzy to safely walk anywhere. Glancing more than a dozen yards away, to the spot where her car had been parked, almost made her lie back down on the ground in despair.

How in the hell was she going to get to the main road when she couldn't even walk?

Then Craig's face flashed across her mind.

She wasn't ready to quit. Not when she had someone so amazing in her life.

Ember had *never* been a quitter, and she wasn't about to start now. She pictured the various coaches she'd had over the years, yelling at her, telling her to keep going, to stop being a baby. To pick up the pace. To get this shit done.

All the miles of running, the back and forth laps in the pool, the pushups and sit-ups... All of it was in preparation for this moment. Not the Olympics, but to get herself up out of the dirt and to find help.

Inch by inch, Ember crawled away from where Marie had shot her and headed for the dirt track. Once there, she knew she'd have to go at least a mile before reaching the paved road...but she'd do it, even if it took all damn night.

As she crawled slowly, Ember got mad. She had no idea what the fuck Marie's problem was, but she'd make sure the woman paid for trying to kill her, even if it was the last thing she ever did.

At one point on her way to the dirt road, Ember came across her cell phone, smashed to pieces. Marie must've done that before leaving. Wanting to cry, she continued, ignoring the way her knees and hands were getting scraped by the rocks she crawled over.

Then Ember heard something that didn't fit with the calm and serene atmosphere around her.

It was the sound of a car. And it was coming toward her. Fast.

Panicking, thinking Marie had decided to return after all, Ember looked around for a place to hide. The other woman would make sure she succeeded in killing her this time. Unfortunately, the scrub brush in this part of Texas didn't lend itself to concealing a person. The best Ember could do was try to cover herself with tumbleweeds and pray Marie would be so panicked to find her missing, she wouldn't search the area too hard before leaving again.

Ember crawled as far as she could into the scrub brush, doing her best to pull the sharp tumbleweeds over her body.

She didn't close her eyes this time. If Marie found her, Ember was prepared to fight. Even if she got shot again, she'd make sure Marie didn't escape unscathed. If she could scratch her face, her hands, injure her in some obvious way, the cops would have to be suspicious. After all, she was the last person who'd seen her. They'd figure it out. They had to.

Holding her breath, Ember listened as a vehicle drove onto the property at an extremely unsafe speed. She heard tires skid against the dirt, then car doors shutting as whoever was in the car exited.

Wait, car *doors*? More than one? Had Marie brought reinforcements with her?

Was this really her last few seconds on Earth? It was so damn unfair! There was so much Ember wanted to do!

"Ember?" a deep male voice called out.

"Ember? Are you here?" another said.

It took a second for Ember to understand what she was hearing, and when she did, tears leaked from her eyes without her even realizing it.

Craig had come for her, just as he'd told her he would.

And he'd brought his team.

For just a second, she let the relief that she'd been saved wash over her—then fresh panic set in.

What if they left before she could get their attention? She had to move! *Now!*

* * *

"Em!" Doc called out again. His gaze swept over the land and his heart fell as he didn't see anything but the tall grass blowing in the slight breeze.

"Tire tracks," Brain said, gesturing to the dirt with his head. "They were here."

"Look...I think it's a phone," Lefty said as he headed toward what looked like bits of plastic on the ground.

"What's that?" Grover asked, pointing ahead of them. They all ran forward about thirty meters and saw laser targets, the ones pentathletes used. There were two of them, lying discarded on the ground—but that wasn't what made Doc's heart stutter in his chest.

It was the small pool of blood next to them.

"Shit," Lucky whispered.

Doc could barely swallow. All he could do was shake his head in denial.

"There's no way Marie could've lifted Ember by herself," Trigger said. "And there's no drag marks. But...there's a trail." He pointed at scuffs in the dirt that led away from the blood.

Doc looked in the direction of the marks and immediately began to follow. He'd only taken five steps before he heard something. His attention had been on the ground, but he looked up to see what had made the noise.

"Ember," he whispered, his body frozen for half a second. Then he was running.

The woman he loved was on her hands and knees on the

ground. Her hair had sticks in it and her face was a mangled mess. But her beautiful brown eyes were alert and focused on him.

"Craig," she whispered as he got close.

He checked his speed right before he reached her. He could hear someone behind him on the phone, asking for an ambulance and relaying their location. Thankful once again that his team had his back, enabling him to concentrate one hundred percent on the woman he loved, Doc went to his knees in front of her.

"Em!" he said, the anguish easy to hear in his tone.

"It was Marie," she said without hesitation. "She always *was* a shit shot. That's why she'll never make the National team or the Olympics."

"*Shhhhh*, don't talk. We know. Beth called with the background check information," Doc told her. He wrapped his arms around her and sat on the ground. Rocks dug into his ass, but he didn't even feel them. He situated Ember in his lap and turned her head to face him. "Oh, Em," he couldn't help but say.

The flesh on her cheek was torn and blood was still oozing from the wound, dripping down her face, off her chin, and onto her shirt.

"I'm okay," she mumbled. "'Tis but a flesh wound."

A bark of laughter sounded from next to them.

"The woman's been shot and she's quoting Monty Python. If I wasn't madly in love with Kinley, I might propose right this second," Lefty quipped.

Trigger knelt beside them and lifted a hand, gently tilting Ember's head to examine the wound. "It looks gnarly, but I think it just grazed you."

"Are you hurt anywhere else?" Doc asked urgently.

"No," Ember whispered. "Not really. She kicked me in the side, but I think the second shot missed me."

Doc's anger threatened to overwhelm him. He wanted to find Marie and kill her with his bare hands. Literally. He could snap her neck and wouldn't feel the least amount of remorse for doing it.

As if Ember could tell what he was thinking, she put her hand on his arm, squeezing lightly.

Looking down at the thin smears of blood she'd left on his skin, Doc had an even harder time reining in his anger. Her palm was shredded from crawling along the ground. But before he could lose it, he felt Ember sag against him, giving him more of her weight.

"Em?" he asked urgently.

"I'm okay," she mumbled as she closed her eyes. "I'm just tired. And dizzy. I'm just gonna close my eyes."

Doc glanced at Trigger in alarm. Before he could demand she stay awake and keep talking, she went completely limp.

Brain and Oz helped him get to his feet with Ember still in his arms. They walked next to him, steadying him, as they all headed for their vehicles.

"Ambulance is on the way," Grover said.

"We aren't waiting," Trigger said. "We'll meet them on the road."

No one disagreed. As Doc slipped into the back seat of Trigger's SUV with Ember, he couldn't take his eyes from her. He wanted to know exactly what happened out here, but more than that, he needed Ember to be all right. They'd eventually know all the details, and Marie would pay for what she'd tried to do, but for now, all his concentration was on the woman in his arms.

"I love you," he whispered into her ear as Trigger backed out the way he came.

Ember didn't respond. She lay limp in his arms, and Doc prayed harder than he had in his life as they headed toward civilization and the help Ember needed.

CHAPTER SEVENTEEN

Two days later, Ember was ready to scream. But if she did, it would hurt her cheek, so she had to be content with glaring at the man she loved.

Craig had been amazing the last two days, but he was still driving her crazy. She wanted out of this hospital—now—but he'd talked the doctor into making her stay another night.

"I'm *fine*," she told him. "I want to go home. I hate it here. It's loud and I can't sleep worth shit. The food sucks too."

"You're staying," Craig said, not seeming to be upset at all by her whining.

"I have things I need to be doing," Ember argued.

"No, what you need to do is lie there and heal," Craig told her. Then he leaned forward and his forehead nearly touched hers. "One more day, Em. Then I'll take you home and make you whatever food you want. Besides, the plastic surgeon is going to come back to check on you today."

Ember sighed. How could she continue to argue when it was obvious how stressed Craig was? When she'd woken up, she could see the panic in his face. And he'd refused to leave her side for the last two days. Even when her parents had arrived, he hadn't left. When various members of his team came to talk to him, he didn't leave her side.

That meant she heard everything that was happening as far as the hunt for Marie went.

She appreciated that more than she could say. She needed to know what was happening and where the other woman was.

Marie had actually posted a picture of Ember lying in the dirt, bleeding from what looked like a fatal shot to the head.

The press had gone ape shit, of course, and Craig had dealt with *that* as well, for the first twenty-four hours after the shooting. One of his friends, someone named Tex, was dealing with the press now. And when Ember had snuck a peek at Craig's phone while he'd been sleeping, she'd learned Tex had somehow managed to publish a post on her social media accounts, saying she was fine and the picture looked far worse than the situation really was.

He'd even called Samer, who'd done an impressive job of keeping everyone calm on her social media accounts. She was thankful she hadn't had to deal with that on top of everything else.

Ember knew she'd probably have to make an official statement sooner or later, but for now, she was happy to leave the entire situation to the more-than-capable Tex.

"Okay," she told Craig.

He closed his eyes and sighed. "Thank you. I know you hate being here, but I just want to make completely sure you're all right."

"I am," Ember promised. "My ribs weren't even broken from that kick Marie gave me, I just have a huge bruise, and my cheek will heal. I don't care if I have a scar or not. The part of my life where I post photoshopped pictures of myself is over. I just want to be me. And if being me includes having a scar that proves I'm stronger than the evil that tried to take me out...so be it."

"You're much more forgiving than I am," Craig said.

"I'm not forgiving at all. I want Marie found and I want her to pay for what she did," Ember told him firmly.

Just then, the door opened and Trigger, Oz, and Lucky entered. Surprisingly, Julio was at their heels too.

Craig stood but stayed by the side of her bed.

"Hey," she said.

The three Deltas didn't even smile.

"What's wrong?" Ember asked.

"Marie's been found," Trigger informed them.

Ember inhaled sharply. "She has?"

"Yeah. She's dead," Trigger said bluntly. "She was found in a motel room south of Fort Worth. Your car was in the parking lot. She overdosed on a shit ton of pills."

"She left a note," Oz added.

Ember didn't know whether to be happy the woman who'd tried to kill her was dead, or disappointed she wouldn't get to ask her why. Why had Marie tried to kill her, after everything Ember had done for her?

"Beth's been dissecting the letters and gifts she sent, along with all the comments she posted, and those, along with the note, leave a clear picture that Marie's personality disorder had finally gotten the best of her," Lucky said.

"I want to read the note," Ember said as firmly as she could.

"No," Craig protested.

"Yes," Ember countered.

"It's not a good idea," Trigger said gently. "It's ten pages of ranting about stuff that makes no sense."

"I need to," Ember insisted. "I need to know if there was something I did to make this happen."

"You didn't," Trigger, Craig, and Oz all said at the same time.

Ember shook her head stubbornly. "I appreciate that, but you guys just met me recently. Marie knew me for *two years*. I worked out with her. We went through a lot together at the hands of our coaches. If there was something I said or did that made her go from allegedly worshiping me to hating me, I need to know what it was so I don't do it again."

"She had mental issues," Craig insisted. "Nothing you did or said was bad enough to make her want to kill you."

"You don't know that," Ember argued in frustration.

"I'll read it," Julio blurted from behind the other men.

Everyone turned to stare at him.

"I know you too, Ember. I've worked alongside you for years as well. Even longer than Marie. I can read her letter and tell you if there's anything in there that has a smidgeon of truth to it. That way, you won't have to read her hateful words."

Ember wanted to protest further. Wanted to keep insisting she had to read the letter herself. But the truth of the matter was, deep down, she *didn't* want to read the hateful words Marie had likely spewed in her suicide note.

"Are you sure?" Craig asked, taking the words right out of her mouth.

"I'm sure," Julio promised them.

"She never arranged for any furniture, her car, or anything else to be shipped here," Trigger said. "I think when Julio's stuff arrived, she knew her time was running out, that you'd find out her belongings hadn't been shipped. I'm pretty sure if Julio had gone with you guys to look at that property, he would've been shot too. She needed help, Ember. Help she never got from her family. And she'd gotten pretty good at hiding how off-kilter she was from everyone. She had no friends, and when she wasn't working out, she spent most of her time on the computer...or writing you letters."

Oz handed Julio his phone. "Here. Read it so you can set Ember's mind at ease," he said.

She couldn't participate in the small talk going on around her. All she could do was watch Julio's face as he read Marie's suicide note. It took him ten minutes, but finally he lowered Oz's phone and met her gaze.

"She's full of shit," he growled. "Nothing she ranted about was true. *None* of it. I've known you for years, and I've never *once* thought or seen anything she complained about. You've always been supportive and generous, and when you made the Olympics, you went out of your way to thank each and every one of us who worked out with you."

Julio walked closer to the bed and took her hand in his. "She really *did* need help, Ember," he said softly. "I think you just happened to be a convenient target for her to take her frustrations out on. Marie and I talked quite a bit about our goals and dreams over the years. Making the Olympics, being famous and revered, was what she wanted most in the world. She was so happy to be able to train with you. But I think when you didn't medal at the Olympics, Marie kind of lost it. If *you* couldn't medal, then the chances *she* would were slim to none. When you quit the sport altogether and moved, I'm guessing it kind of pushed her over the edge. But again, that's all on *her*, not you."

Ember's lip trembled. "Thank you."

"You're welcome."

They stared at each other for a moment as Ember did her best to get her emotions under control. Taking a deep breath, she said, "Talk to me about the gym. How are the renovations going? Did the painting get done? What about the mural? Did the people I called about painting our logo on the wall ever stop by to give an estimate? Were you okay this morning with the kids by yourself? I'll find someone to hire to help out soon."

"Nope," Craig said, interrupting Julio before he could answer. "Your gym is fine. Julio is doing a great job managing things in your absence. You'll be back there supervising everything sooner rather than later. For now, your only job is to lie there and heal."

The other guys all laughed, and Ember couldn't help smiling herself. "Fine. But if you need anything, Julio, don't hesitate to let Craig know. He can deal with it until he takes me off my leash," Ember said snarkily.

"Actually, your parents have been a huge help," Julio told her.

"Really?" Ember asked skeptically.

"Yup. They were there this morning with the kids, and they had a blast."

It was hard for Ember to imagine her parents playing with kids, but then again, they certainly knew the ins and outs of the modern pentathlon.

"I'm gonna head back to the gym. Make sure all's well before I go home," Julio said.

"Thanks," Ember told him.

"Anytime. I mean that. I appreciate you hiring me to help with the gym. It's a beautiful thing, and I'm proud to be a part of it," Julio told her. "I'm sorry about Marie. Not because she's dead, but because she couldn't see what an amazing person you are, inside and out."

Then without another word, Julio left the room.

"On that note, we're also going to head out," Trigger said. "Grover wants to have a word with the team."

"He wants to head over to Afghanistan by himself," Craig said.

"Yeah. I take it he talked to you about it?" Trigger asked.

"He mentioned it briefly. I was gonna bring it up with you, but didn't have a chance."

"What do you think?" Oz asked.

Craig sighed, and once again, Ember was touched they were talking freely in front of her. It made her truly feel as if she was a part of the group. Not that Gillian, Kinley, Aspen, Riley, and Devyn visiting over the last two days hadn't. They'd shown up as soon as she'd been allowed visitors and had been rotating their visits. It had made the two days she'd been here go by much faster, and she knew they were already planning on coming over to Craig's house at regular intervals to keep her entertained until she was back on her feet.

"I think it's not a bad idea," Craig told his teammates. "The only thing I'm worried about is him doing something crazy if he gets any indication of where Sierra might be or what happened to her."

"That's my concern too," Trigger agreed. "But we aren't getting the information we need on Shahzada and we can't track him down from all the way over here. Any info is delayed and practically useless by the time it crosses our desks. Having Grover talk to people one-on-one and get back to us immediately could really make a difference."

"He knows we have his back," Craig told his team leader. "If the shit hits the fan, we'll be there to support him...and Sierra and any of the other missing contractors."

"Agreed. Okay, I'll let you know how things shake out when we're done talking with him and Commander Robinson."

"Ember should be released in the morning," Craig told his friends. "We'll be at my house if you need me."

"Sounds good. Glad you're doing so well, Ember," Trigger said.

The other two nodded in agreement, then it was just her and Craig once more.

"Why don't you go home and get some real sleep?" she told him.

"You think I can sleep without you in my arms? No fucking way," Craig said with a shake of his head. He pulled the chair back up to the side of her bed and took her hand in his once more. "It'll be a while before I can get the picture of that pool of blood on the ground out of my head."

"I'm sorry," Ember whispered.

"Nothing for you to be sorry for," Craig told her. "I just realized at that moment how much I truly loved you. I mean, I said the words, but it hit me then just how much I might've lost. You're it for me, Ember. No matter what, I'll never love another woman the way I love you."

"I felt the same way. There was so much I hadn't done yet," she told him. "Including being married, having a family, and experiencing life with you by my side."

"You've got me," he said, kissing the back of her hand reverently.

Ember closed her eyes in contentment. She didn't know where her life would go from here, but she knew she'd have Craig at her side. What else could she ask for?

EPILOGUE

"Harder," Ember moaned as Doc gently made love to her.

"No," he said between clenched teeth. He knew it was probably too soon to be doing this, but he couldn't resist Ember when she pleaded with him. She'd said she wasn't in any pain, and when she'd begun to finger herself, he'd given in. But he was going to do this his way. Slow and gentle. Even if it killed him.

Looking down at Ember, he internally flinched at the mark on her cheek. The plastic surgeon had done a good job of sewing it up, but she still had a few months before the scar would fade. It would probably never disappear, but to Ember's credit, she didn't seem to care one whit about it.

She'd told him a week ago when she'd been released from the hospital that she looked at it as a badge of honor. She'd met evil face-to-face and survived. She wasn't going to let a scar on her cheek get her down when she was alive to see another day.

Doc had been able to keep her home for twenty-four hours before she'd put her foot down and insisted on going to her gym. She was as determined as ever to make The Modern Kid a success. The security guards she'd hired were keeping the press at a distance, and even now, another scandal in Hollywood was going viral, taking the attention away from what had happened to Ember. But the media frenzy did have one benefit—she'd already doubled the amount of kids who'd signed up at her gym. Now she was finalizing the purchase of the land she'd been shot on. Doc hadn't liked the idea of her ever going back there, but he'd been overruled by Ember's practical side.

Her parents had just left the day before, and she'd been surprised and pleased by their encouragement of what she was doing. They hadn't been that supportive of her moving and opening the gym in the first place, but after seeing what she'd done in such a short period of time, and visiting with the children who were participating in her program, they'd changed their minds.

His parents, Mama Luisa and Jaime, were planning a trip to Texas to meet her soon. Ember was nervous about meeting them, but Doc had no doubt they'd love her...just as most people did.

Having Samer take over her social media accounts had been one of the best decisions she'd made. She didn't have to worry about reading the hate people posted there, and Samer had no trouble passing along any threats to Doc. He'd been just as appalled by what had happened to her as everyone else, and he promised to do all he could to help keep her safe.

Doc had talked to Ember's security team as well. He wasn't going to take her safety for granted again. He'd learned his lesson.

"Craig, if you don't let me come anytime soon, I'm gonna have to hurt you."

Doc chuckled and brought his focus back to the woman

under him. He loved that she was demanding in bed. That she had no shame when it came to wanting to get off. Moving his hand between them, he began to thumb her clit just how she liked it. Hard and fast.

He knew he was on the verge of coming himself, and he'd be damned if he came before her. "That's it, Em, slow and easy. Don't hurt yourself."

But she ignored him, thrusting her hips up as best she could, despite him holding her down. When she finally went over the edge, Doc couldn't help but follow her. She was so damn beautiful, and she was all his. Before he could control himself, he'd exploded. Filling the condom—and already looking forward to the day when he could fill her with his come and they could make babies.

"Oh my God, Craig, yes!" she moaned.

He couldn't speak as his passion overwhelmed him.

When he was done, Doc eased out of her body and headed for the bathroom. He wanted to eat her out, to make her come again, but he needed to take it easy. It wasn't that long ago that she'd been shot and had almost died. He wet a washcloth with warm water and brought it into the other room to clean her up. Then he eased under the covers next to her and held her in his arms.

"Love you," he said quietly.

"Love you too," she returned. "I feel as if I've known you forever, but if I look at the calendar, I'm shocked at how little time has passed since the Olympics."

"I've never been as happy as I am now. I don't care if it's been a day or fifty years. I'll always love you. One day—not today, but one day soon—I'm gonna ask you to marry me."

"And I'll say yes," she returned immediately. "But I'm happy with the way things are for now. I think if the world hears that Ember Maxwell is engaged, two seconds after learning that I was shot, they'll never recover."

Doc chuckled. "That's probably true."

"I'm sure people are gonna want wedding details," she warned him.

"They can see a picture of your ring, and one picture of you on our wedding day, but that's it," Doc told her.

"I want everyone to see how handsome the man I love is," Ember pouted.

"I can't," Doc said a little sadly.

"I know. But I still want to show you off."

"How about we take a picture of when I see you in your dress for the first time?" Doc compromised. "You can be the focus of the shot, and it can be taken from behind me. So I'll be in the picture, but no one will see my face." He'd do whatever it took to make this woman happy. Including letting her post his picture on social media. Sort of.

"Deal." She chuckled. "Is it weird that we're talking about our wedding when neither of us are ready for that yet?"

"Nope. Because we'll get there. We both know it. You don't need to marry me for the benefits. You've got enough money to take care of yourself. And if, knock on wood, something happens to me, my team'll make sure you're taken care of. So there's no need to run off and get married. But...again... I *am* gonna ask you one of these days."

"And again...I'm gonna say yes," Ember told him.

Doc tightened his arms around her. He was more satisfied and content than he'd ever been in his life.

They lay there satiated and replete, reveling in the feeling of love between them for several minutes, when Doc's phone vibrated on the nightstand.

Because it was so late, he didn't hesitate to reach for it.

"Doc here."

"It's Trigger. We're going wheels up in the morning. O-six hundred. You need to be here at five."

"What's up?" Doc asked, alarm filling him at Trigger's tone.

"It's Grover. The damn fool's only been in the country a few days and he's been taken. There's video evidence from Shahzada's followers showing him being beaten. The Army's officially labeled him a POW. We need to go find him and bring him home."

"Fuck. All right. I'll be there. Keep me updated if you get any new info before tomorrow morning."

"Will do. See you soon."

"Later."

Doc hung up, and Ember asked, "What's going on?"

"It's Grover. He's missing."

"Missing? But...that doesn't make sense!"

"I know," Doc agreed. Grover was a damn good Delta. If he was a POW, there was a good chance he'd *let* himself be captured...because Doc couldn't think of any other way the man would be taken prisoner.

"When do you leave?"

"In the morning."

Instead of getting upset, Ember immediately nodded. "What do we need to do tonight to get you ready to go?"

Her reaction was just one more reason Doc knew he'd lucked out in finding her. Reluctantly, he threw the covers back. He needed to make sure he had what he needed and was all packed. Ember followed a little more slowly.

"I hate to leave you," he told her.

Ember merely shrugged. "Grover needs you more than I do right now. Besides, I have a feeling this was all part of his plan."

"What plan?"

"The plan to go overseas, find out where Sierra is, and get himself taken so you guys could then go and find them both."

Doc stopped in his tracks and stared at the woman he loved. He wasn't surprised she was on the same page he was.

"But don't you guys get taken too, all right? Because I'll fly over to Afghanistan and drag *all* your asses out of there if I have to."

Doc couldn't help but chuckle. "You would, wouldn't you?"

She walked around the bed naked as the day she was born, and Doc couldn't help but admire her. She was muscular and curvy at the same time, and he felt his cock twitch.

She hugged him, then looked up and met his gaze. "I'd do whatever it took to bring you home. You *and* your team. And their women. This is our tribe, and I'll spend every cent in my bank account to protect it if I have to."

"God, I love you."

"And I love you. Now, let's get you packed so you can get some sleep before you have to leave."

Yup. She was perfect. Practical and caring.

Doc kissed her once more, long and deep, showing her without words how much he loved her. When he lifted his head, he whispered, "Nothing will keep me from coming home to you."

"Good," she said softly. "Find Grover, and his woman, and come home soon."

"We will." It was a promise he had no problem making.

Sierra sat at the back of the cave she'd been thrown into a month ago...or was it two? She couldn't seem to keep track of the days anymore.

Her captors had dug out quite the complex in the side of the mountain. Even carved small niches in the walls and managed to attach bars in front of each one. At times, the four niches each held prisoners, but until this morning, it had been just Sierra for a while. She preferred it that way. The guards mostly ignored her when she was there by herself. It was only when they'd captured someone new that they seemed to remember how much fun it was to mess with her.

And by the sound of the beating going on in the small alcove next to hers, they were having a grand ol' time perfecting their torture techniques. They'd dragged a new prisoner in earlier, but she didn't get a good look at him. His head was hanging forward, and there had been too many men surrounding him.

Sierra dreaded them turning their attention to her after they were done with the new prisoner. But then again, considering how long they'd been going at this new guy, she thought maybe she'd escape their notice after all.

Staying very quiet to avoid bringing attention to herself, she was extremely relieved when the three men—along with Shahzada himself, the asshole—had left the cave. She heard Shahzada giving orders to one of his men to make sure the video they'd taken was sent to as many news stations as possible.

She felt bad for whoever had been captured. She didn't think it was a contractor because in the past, they hadn't been important enough to be videoed during a beating.

Sierra was still wondering who the poor bastard was when she heard the man groaning from the cell next to hers.

She crawled toward the front of her cage and listened quietly. She couldn't see whoever it was, but if she lay down on her side and put her arm through the bars, and the person in the niche next to hers did the same, they could actually touch hands.

She'd done that with another captive once. She'd held hands with the man, trying to comfort him as he lay dying.

He'd been a construction contractor with diabetes. And since he didn't have his medications, and because of the beating he'd received, he knew he was dying.

Sierra had felt horrible at the relief when he'd finally passed. But at least his suffering was done.

But hers continued.

"Is anyone there?" the man next to her asked quietly.

"Yes," Sierra responded. Her voice cracked, as it had been so long since she'd spoken.

"Do you know a woman named Sierra Clarkson? She's been missing for over a year."

Sierra blinked in surprise. The man's voice was slightly garbled, as if his face and mouth were swollen. He'd most likely been hit in the face over and over. Shahzada's men loved to punch people in the face.

"Hello? Are you still there? My name is Fred Groves, and I'm looking for Sierra Clarkson. Have you seen any other women being held captive?"

"*Grover*?!" she gasped.

"Sierra?" the man next to her said, sounding just as shocked as she was.

Sierra could only nod. Her throat had closed up and it was impossible to speak.

"I knew you were alive! I *knew* it!" Grover said. "My team'll be here to get us out soon. Just hold on."

Sierra had a million questions, but for now, all she could say was, "Okay."

* * *

Grover found Sierra, but can they both get out in one piece? And if they get out, will Sierra be able to resume a normal life? Pick up *Shielding Sierra* to find out how it all goes down!

Want to talk to other Susan Stoker fans? Join my reader group, Susan Stoker's Stalkers, on Facebook!

Also, sign up for my newsletter to keep up with all the new releases and Stoker info!
https://www.stokeraces.com/contact-1.html

Also by Susan Stoker

Delta Team Two Series
Shielding Gillian
Shielding Kinley
Shielding Aspen
Shielding Jayme
Shielding Riley
Shielding Devyn
Shielding Ember
Shielding Sierra (Jan 2022)

SEAL Team Hawaii Series
Finding Elodie
Finding Lexie
Finding Kenna (Oct 2021)
Finding Monica (May 2022)
Finding Carly (TBA)
Finding Ashlyn (TBA)
Finding Jodelle (TBA)

Silverstone Series
Trusting Skylar
Trusting Taylor
Trusting Molly
Trusting Cassidy (Nov 2021)

Eagle Point Search & Rescue
Searching for Lilly (Mar 2022)
Searching for Bristol (Jun 2022)
Searching for Elsie (Nov 2022)
Searching for Caryn (TBA)
Searching for Finley (TBA)

Searching for Heather (TBA)
Searching for Khloe (TBA)

SEAL of Protection Series
Protecting Caroline
Protecting Alabama
Protecting Fiona
Marrying Caroline (novella)
Protecting Summer
Protecting Cheyenne
Protecting Jessyka
Protecting Julie (novella)
Protecting Melody
Protecting the Future
Protecting Kiera (novella)
Protecting Alabama's Kids (novella)
Protecting Dakota

SEAL of Protection: Legacy Series
Securing Caite
Securing Brenae (novella)
Securing Sidney
Securing Piper
Securing Zoey
Securing Avery
Securing Kalee
Securing Jane

Delta Force Heroes Series
Rescuing Rayne
Rescuing Aimee (novella)
Rescuing Emily
Rescuing Harley
Marrying Emily (novella)

Rescuing Kassie
Rescuing Bryn
Rescuing Casey
Rescuing Sadie (novella)
Rescuing Wendy
Rescuing Mary
Rescuing Macie (novella)
Rescuing Annie (Feb 2022)

Badge of Honor: Texas Heroes Series

Justice for Mackenzie
Justice for Mickie
Justice for Corrie
Justice for Laine (novella)
Shelter for Elizabeth
Justice for Boone
Shelter for Adeline
Shelter for Sophie
Justice for Erin
Justice for Milena
Shelter for Blythe
Justice for Hope
Shelter for Quinn
Shelter for Koren
Shelter for Penelope

Ace Security Series

Claiming Grace
Claiming Alexis
Claiming Bailey
Claiming Felicity
Claiming Sarah

Mountain Mercenaries Series

Defending Allye
Defending Chloe
Defending Morgan
Defending Harlow
Defending Everly
Defending Zara
Defending Raven

Stand Alone
Falling for the Delta
The Guardian Mist
Nature's Rift
A Princess for Cale
A Moment in Time- A Collection of Short Stories
Another Moment in Time- A Collection of Short Stories
Lambert's Lady

Special Operations Fan Fiction
http://www.AcesPress.com

Beyond Reality Series
Outback Hearts
Flaming Hearts
Frozen Hearts

Writing as Annie George:
Stepbrother Virgin (erotic novella)

ABOUT THE AUTHOR

New York Times, *USA Today* and *Wall Street Journal* Bestselling Author Susan Stoker has a heart as big as the state of Tennessee where she lives, but this all American girl has also spent the last fourteen years living in Missouri, California, Colorado, Indiana, and Texas. She's married to a retired Army man who now gets to follow *her* around the country.

She debuted her first series in 2014 and quickly followed that up with the SEAL of Protection Series, which solidified her love of writing and creating stories readers can get lost in.

If you enjoyed this book, or any book, please consider leaving a review. It's appreciated by authors more than you'll know.

www.stokeraces.com
www.AcesPress.com
susan@stokeraces.com

facebook.com/authorsusanstoker
twitter.com/Susan_Stoker
instagram.com/authorsusanstoker
goodreads.com/SusanStoker
bookbub.com/authors/susan-stoker
amazon.com/author/susanstoker

CPSIA information can be obtained
at www.ICGtesting.com
Printed in the USA
BVHW041931070921
616242BV00006B/71